TRAPPED IN THE TUNNEL

Lungs bursting, the blood pounding in his head, he flung himself through, clutching with desperate strength at the hand rail as his feet slipped from under him on the slimy steps. Behind, he heard a tremendous boom of thunder and a single piercing scream of animal terror, before the water burst from the tunnel mouth like an erupting geyser. Clouds of spray vomited forth, half blinding him . . . Dimly, in the now almost total darkness, he saw the figures of his companions flung down the maelstrom that seethed around the iron gates . . . He made a last desperate attempt to clutch at the ladder, his fingers touching its rungs, then with a dull clang that rang through the chamber, the giant doors slid open and the whirling current swept him through the gates.

Bantam Books by Richard Doyle

DELUGE
IMPERIAL 109

DELUGE

Richard Doyle

BANTAM BOOKS · TORONTO · NEW YORK · LONDON

DELUGE

*A Bantam Book / published by arrangement with
Arlington Books (Publishers) Ltd.*

PRINTING HISTORY
Arlington Books edition published 1976
Bantam edition / September 1978

*Bantam Books are published by Bantam Books, Inc. Its trade-
mark, consisting of the words "Bantam Books" and the por-
trayal of a bantam, is registered in the United States Patent
Office and in other countries. Marca Registrada. Bantam
Books, Inc., 666 Fifth Avenue, New York, New York 10019.*

PRINTED IN THE UNITED STATES OF AMERICA

This is the B.B.C. Here is a gale warning issued at 2300 hours by the Meteorological Office for tomorrow Friday, February 4th, 1977.

Attention all shipping areas, especially Viking, Fair Isle, Faroes and Rockall.

Viking—Winds northwest, veering westerly, gale force eight increasing storm force nine or severe storm ten. Imminent.

Fair Isle—Winds northwest by west, gale force eight increasing storm force nine or severe storm ten. Imminent.

Faroes—Winds northwest, veering westerly, storm force nine increasing severe storm ten. Imminent.

Rockall—Winds northwest, veering westerly, storm force nine, increasing severe storm ten or locally force eleven. Imminent.

Chapter One

All day the weather had worsened. The wind, which had started at a comparatively normal thirty knots, had increased to force ten by six o'clock. Now, at midnight, it had reached hurricane strength. Howling gusts swept over the sea at speeds in excess of one hundred miles an hour, driving sheets of freezing spray from the giant waves. The trawler had long ago abandoned any attempt to reach port; nose to the wind, the one thought of captain and crew was to try and ride out the worst storm to hit the North Sea for over two hundred and fifty years.

Somewhere out in the darkness, to the southwest, lay the coast of Scotland, but at the moment all that could be seen was a succession of monstrous waves, enormous even by the standards of the North Sea. Again and again their crests rose high above the ship, great walls of foaming water that rushed down upon the tiny vessel with a terrifying speed. Time and time again it seemed as though she would be broken and capsized by the sheer volume of sea that crashed down upon her.

Miraculously each time she managed to lift her head,
shaking her bows free, the spray bursting clean over
the deck and superstructure, only to plunge once more
down into the trough of another wave, whose mountainous head already curved threateningly above her.

Inside the vessel the noise was unimaginable as many
tons of icy water repeatedly thundered down on to the
decks, smashing steel fittings like pieces of tin, the deep
shocks echoing ominously through the hull. The sound
of breaking equipment smashed by the waves could be
heard even above the wind, and at times the helpless
churning of the screws was audible as the plunging vessel bared them as she clawed her way desperately
through the towering seas. Every sinew of her hull
screeched and creaked under the terrible stresses as the
ship strained and twisted with the savage action of the
water.

The crew had known storms before, but never one
such as this, driving down out of the north, an arctic
hurricane of nerve-shattering power and intensity. Exhausted by hours of continuous efforts to repair damage
and handle the ship; numbed by the cold that froze
spray even as it fell; they reeled about their tasks like
automatons. On the bridge the captain and mate
watched in stunned disbelief as wave after wave flung
itself down on them, the thunder of their impact shaking the vessel from stem to stern.

"It's no use," the captain shouted to the mate, "we'll
have to send out a signal, she's taking on water faster
than we can pump it out. For a little while she'll be
down by the head and then one of those big ones will
take her and drag her under."

The mate nodded back across the bridge. He was
younger than the skipper, about thirty-five years old,
with gray eyes and thick black hair. In his face the
lines of strain and exhaustion were deeply etched. The
ship pitched sharply and another mass of water crashed

down on to the foredeck. Both men grabbed out to keep their balance.

"I suppose it might do some good, but who will be able to help in this sea. They'd never find us, and even if by some miracle they did, they wouldn't be able to get near. We can't launch a boat into this storm."

"We'll have to hope Scotland pick it up. Maybe they'll come looking for us at daybreak," the skipper shouted back as he wrestled with the wheel. "It's all we can do."

The radio man had been expecting the order, and moments later the call was going out over the air.

"Mayday, Mayday, Mayday, British trawler *Ross* taking water in very heavy seas. Request urgent assistance. Position approximately ninety miles east of Wick."

The storm had been born two days ago, on Tuesday evening, when a small current of warm air broke away from a large depression over the Atlantic midway between Iceland and the Azores. A wedge of cold air cut in behind and the weather charts the next morning showed a new center of low pressure traveling northeast and deepening rapidly. Twenty-four hours later it was off the northwest coast of Scotland; the wind over the North Sea was a gentle southwesterly. Behind the depression a long ridge of high pressure, extending from northern Greenland to the coast of Africa, was also moving east. In between these two pressure systems strong northwesterly winds were beginning to blow straight from the Arctic, uninterrupted by any land, driving the water of the Atlantic before them into the North Sea.

The polar winds reached an intensity never before known in the British Isles. By the time the trawler *Ross* radioed for assistance gusts of a hundred and twenty miles an hour were being recorded, with reports of widespread damage on sea and land. In the great pine forests of Scotland thousands upon thousands of trees were felled; whole valleys stripped bare by the wind. Roads already choked by snowdrifts were now completely blocked, with collapsed power lines, telegraph poles and other obstructions. Broken communications and electricity cables added to the confusion. In the ports hundreds of vessels sheltered from the storm, huddled together, battered and tossed by the angry waves.

While the vain attempt was being made to summon assistance to the *Ross,* the situation in the North Sea was being watched with mounting concern at the meteorological headquarters at Bracknell on the Berkshire Downs. As the pattern of cyclonic development had become clear they had issued storm warnings; but now the direction and strength of the geostrophic winds was blowing a billion tons of water into the narrow confines of the North Sea and the tide gauges at Wick, on the northeastern tip of Scotland, showed a rise of two and a half feet in the normal level of the sea.

The scientists examined the data from the coastal weather stations anxiously and by 1:00 a.m. on Friday, February 4th it was apparent that the freak conditions had combined to produce a highly dangerous phenomenon: an enormous mass of water piled up by the depressed storm center and driven by the hurricane force of the winds had begun to move down the east coast of the country; a storm surge was heading for London.

Nearly six hundred miles away in London, Derek Thompson switched off the lights downstairs in his Wandsworth home and walked slowly up to the bedroom. He was a powerfully built, dark-haired New Zealander of medium height with an attractive, mobile face. He was forty-two and chief engineer to the Greater London Council.

The sound of a radio became audible as he approached the top of the stairs; entering the room he saw

Georgina spread-eagled across the bed, her long ash-blonde hair falling over her face as she wrote in her diary. Going over to his wife he took a handful of her hair and let it slide gently through his fingers, the softness of it still fascinated him even after twelve years of marriage.

Georgina looked up and smiled, her green eyes regarded him thoughtfully; she had a small delicate face with high cheekbones.

"So," she said slowly, "is it to be wealth or duty; a life of sinful luxury in the sun or years of honorable service to the community?"

"Looking forward to a year round suntan are you?" Derek grinned back. "I can just see you, lying on the beach all day with servants bringing you iced drinks." He sat down on the bed and Georgina turned over on to her back, her long slender legs appearing out of her dressing gown. For the past four days they had been joking back and forth over the new job Derek had been offered.

"Do you think I would hate South Africa?" She was suddenly serious. "I'm sure I would get to like it after a bit, I'm very adaptable you know? At least the weather wouldn't always be so terrible." Derek laughed and ruffled her hair affectionately.

"If we went there you'd wind up in prison within a week. You know what you're like."

"What am I like?" In the background the radio had finished the news and was moving on to the shipping forecasts.

"Subversive, an enemy of the people," he replied.

"Subversive! I'll give you subversive." Derek laughed as she grabbed at him, sliding forward on top of her he seized her arms, feeling her body struggling underneath him. "Definitely very subversive," he said as he let one hand drop down feeling for the tie of her dressing gown, "altogether a most evil influence." He pressed his mouth down on to hers, beneath him her body moved to meet his, their limbs entwining as they fumbled with each other's garments.

They made love slowly and with passion, in the background the voice of the radio rose and fell.

"Forties: wind north-northwest. Storm force eleven rising force twelve. Imminent. Pressure nine hundred and eighty-two and falling. Visibility bad . . ."

At 12:45 a.m., while the storm was still hammering Wick, the duty officer in the Ministry of Agriculture was consulting his manual of standing orders. The night office was a small white-painted room, its walls were thick with lists of names, departments and extension numbers. In the center of the room stood two desks pushed together to face one another, on which stood several telephones, dirty ashtrays and half empty coffee cups. The duty officer was consulting the standing orders in force when a provisional flood warning was in operation. He knew that the warning had not been cancelled, as it would automatically be announced at this stage over the teleprinter from Bracknell, in the event of a change in the weather conditions. It was now thirteen hours before the predicted high tide at London Bridge and under the orders, with the alert still in force, it was his duty to call the flood room officer on standby from his bed to maintain a close watch on the situation. As he checked the time his assistant handed him a slip of paper with the name and telephone number of the engineer on flood duty.

"This is the one," he said, "Collins, lives in Hammersmith by the look of the number." The duty officer did not reply. Laying down the order book he took the paper and slowly dialed the number. It rang for a long time and he waited in silence as he lit a cigarette. At length there came a reply.

"Mr. Collins?" He spoke precisely and carefully. "This is the duty officer at the Ministry." He paused to allow the listener to digest this, then he went on: "The time is 12:48 a.m., sir, we have a preliminary flood alert of force condition yellow, and in accordance with standing instructions I must ask you to come into the flood room at once."

In the darkness of his flat in Hammersmith, Peter Collins cursed sleepily under his breath. "Are you sure it hasn't been cancelled?" he demanded. "What's the latest report on the tape from Bracknell? They bring that down to you, don't they?"

He listened while the duty officer read out the message. Five hundred miles away force nine winds were driving billions of tons of water into the North Sea; by morning its mean level would have been raised by over three feet. The storm surge was beginning its run down the coast.

"O.K.," Peter said wearily, "I'll come in now. Expect me in about forty-five minutes."

In the Ministry the duty officer put down the telephone. "Log the call," he instructed his assistant, "and call the main door security to let him in." It was exactly 12:53 a.m.

* * *

Despite the absence of traffic on the roads at night, it took Peter Collins longer than he expected to reach the Ministry. His car, parked all night in the cold air, had started with reluctance after some minutes and had stalled and spluttered in the little streets around the grimy pre-war houses of Hammersmith. It was not until he reached Kensington High Street that he managed to get moving. The night was very cold, made more so by the biting wind that whistled between the buildings. Traces of snow from the past few days' fall still remained in the gutter and under the bare trees.

In the entrance hall of the Ministry, Peter signed the night journal, handed to him by a sour-faced security night watchman, and went up to the flood warning room on the fourth floor. He noticed that the lights were on in most of the corridors and in one or two of the offices as well. This was the first time he had been called out at night, though he knew the procedure well enough. In point of fact his presence was not strictly necessary; the instruments would watch the behavior of the weather and the progress of the tide; they would also record what had happened and take the appropriate warning action if the situation should alter. A member of the staff was only present in case of emergency.

The office was small and had the peculiar makeshift appearance so common in government buildings. The only incongruous feature was a camp bed that stood made up in one corner. The walls were faced with fiber board painted sometimes white and sometimes pale blue. To the left of the door, panes of frosted glass admitted light from the corridor, while opposite a small window gave a view on to the inner yard of the block. It was an unprepossessing room. One entire side was given up to a series of maps. The largest of these was a scale map of inner London with areas along the river picked out in different shades of gray, indicating the parts of the city that were low lying and thus in danger of flooding, should the river top its banks. Next to this was a smaller map of the east coast of England, divided into sections and marked with prominent towns and ports. This was the divisional map of the storm tide warning service, which enabled the progress of the surge to be charted down the coast. It began at the Scottish border, the first division, coastal division one, running as far as Yorkshire. An arrow pointed to the port of North Shields. This was the designated reference port where the tide gauges were sighted. Division two, marked in the same way, was larger and reached as far as Norfolk; its reference port was Immingham on the Humber. Beyond this division three comprised Norfolk and Suffolk using the fishing port of Lowestoft as a tidal measuring point. Division four ran from Suffolk across the Thames estuary to Kent, using Walton-on-the Naze, the estuary itself being a separate division with its own reference port of Southend.

Beside this another chart gave the approximate length of time between high tide at these various ports and high tide at London Bridge. Peter knew, without referring to these, that the surge, which must now be running, would still be in its early stages and would not yet have reached Aberdeen. The instruments that kept watch were directly opposite the maps. First a tele-printer clicked constantly to itself in the corner. This machine digested and printed out information from the meteorological headquarters at Bracknell and gave an up-to-the-minute picture of climatic conditions in the area concerned, together with details of local weather conditions along the east coast, which had been routed through Bracknell as well. Next to this stood the wood-en and glass boxes that housed the tide gauge repeaters for points along the river itself, beginning with South-end and ending at Tower Pier, giving a picture of the river level as a whole.

Making a quick check that all the instruments were functioning correctly, Peter started the subsidiary tape transmitter that sent a copy of the information received in the room on to the flood control unit at New Scot-land Yard. From now on the police would be kept up to date automatically on the progress of the surge. Beside this stood the direct telephone link to the headquarters of London Transport Underground Rail Service, above Westminster station. Fully conscious of the risk to the scores of thousands of people who use the tubes each day, London Transport had installed this link to be sure of obtaining sufficient early warning of a flood coming up the river.

Peter yawned. There was virtually nothing for him to do. He recorded his arrival in the record book kept for the purpose, noted down carefully the figures on the four tide gauges and began to run checks on the transmission lines that fed information from the instruments strung out along the coast, maintaining their ceaseless watch on the sea. The cables that linked these to the flood room were specifically designed to resist attack by salt water, but as an extra precaution it was possible to obtain the information automatically via Bracknell. The tide gauges at Southend and on the river could also be operated by radio control direct from the flood room itself, if necessary. This safeguard had been incorporated into the system after the disastrous floods a quarter of a century earlier, in 1953, when many of the gauges had been swamped and their electric cables put out of action, leaving the authorities in London blind and helpless.

A sudden noise from the teleprinter startled him. Tape was rushing out of the box covered with closely set print: ABERDEEN—ABERDEEN 04.12 FRIDAY 4 FEBRUARY HIGH WATER 12 FEET WIND SPEED 86 KNOTS. "Christ," thought Peter to himself, and went to the desk by the window to check the tidal ranges for the port. It was, he realized, a spring tide. Even so, the figure on the tape was six feet above the figure in the book. Aberdeen's waterfront had become part of the sea.

The machine chattered again, as he expected. It was the weather center at Bracknell, this time with a summary of conditions on the east coast. The storm was only a little below hurricane strength and was moving steadily southwards, rolling the surge wave in front of it. The situation was ominous; the surge was six feet high now and by the time it reached Southend it would be considerably higher; ten or even twelve feet. Then when it came down the estuary the reduction in the width would squeeze the level higher still. Surges of thirteen feet had been known in the past. Today there could possibly be a freak surge of over fifteen feet and that on top of a spring tide of twenty-five feet.

Behind the bare statistics there lay a reality of hurricane winds, pounding waves and broken sea walls as the storm vented its fury on the towns and fishing villages of east Scotland. Peter imagined the flooded streets and damaged houses; winds of one hundred miles an hour tearing off roofs and shutters and snapping electricity pylons like matchsticks.

There had been similar storms in the past, Peter remembered, and on numerous occasions a surge had been seen to start ominously, only to die out as it rode south. It was very seldom over the British Isles that the winds continued at such a peak for any length of time, and probably by morning the danger would have passed. Even so it was an uncomfortable feeling sitting alone in the flood room, alone in the entire building except for the night duty officers and the security patrols, watching the instruments and powerless to help, as five hundred miles to the north a colossal threat to the safety of the capital moved inexorably nearer. All at once he felt very tired; stretching himself out on the camp bed he dozed fitfully.

Twice he was woken by the alarm buzzer, reminding him that fresh data was coming through from points further down the coast. At 4:30 a.m., North Shields on the far bank of the Tyne reported savage weather conditions and a tide eight feet above the predicted level. The report went on to describe "localized flooding in the port area, water three to four feet deep in some parts." The wind was still averaging ninety knots. After the North Shields message Peter dozed off again on the camp bed; he felt exhausted but slept with difficulty.

*   *   *

Against a background of darkness the white stone of Greenwich Palace gleamed palely in the moonlight. Its beauty seemed oddly out of place on this stretch of the Thames where the shore on both sides was lined with docks and warehouses, grimy commercial buildings and decaying wharves.

Stumbling through the dingy patch of public garden
that tipped the Isle of Dogs, Reg did not even give a
thought to the Palace on the opposite bank. It was simply a feature of the landscape, like the other buildings,
as far as he was concerned. Although he occasionally
used the foot tunnel that ran beneath the river to a
point beside the white walls, he had never thought to
look inside. Besides, tonight he was cold and late getting back, since he had walked from Bethnal Green.

Reg had once had another name, but it was a long
time since anyone, even he himself, had used it, and
now it was forgotten. To such friends as he had he was
Reg. The same was true of the police, who sometimes
moved him out of people's way, and the workers at the
soup kitchen, which sometimes fed him. Reg was a dosser, a down-and-out, a tramp, a man who had slipped
through the wide mesh of the welfare state and landed
in the gutter.

Usually, or at least for the past three weeks, he spent
the night in a large derelict building on a site behind
the waterfront, which was in the process of being
cleared by a demolition group. Half of it had already
been torn down. The portion that remained had solid
walls three storeys high and at the back, on the ground
floor, there was a room that was warm and dry. Here
Reg made a fire, slept and hid any objects of value to
him in a space underneath the floorboards.

Reg scrambled over the gate at the entrance to the
gardens and set off down the road. Slush and mud, all
that remained of two days' heavy snow, lay on the
pavement. His shoes were already soaked, but he did
not notice that, his thoughts were on the half-bottle of
gin which he clutched inside the pocket of his dirty
black coat. That bottle had given him much trouble;
bought in partnership with a friend, another dosser,
with money given to the two of them by a generous
passerby. It had been the cause of a violent argument
that night which had ended with Reg dodging his friend

through the streets of the East End. He had only dared to make his way back to his haunt by a circuitous route, which had taken time. Now he hurried on, keeping an eye open for pursuers and also signs of the police, who had yesterday warned him off the place because of the dangerous state of the building. He saw no one. It was nearly midnight and the streets were empty.

Turning to his right Reg entered the cleared area of the half-demolished site and began picking his way through the rubble. The ground contained several half-filled pits, formed by old cellars, and he skirted carefully round these past a section of the old river bank. Patches of melting snow still remained and the ground was soaked and heavy with water. There was moisture oozing down the near slope of the bank, he noticed, as it did in places when the tide was high. He hurried on, anxious to reach the shelter of his room. The outline of the building was visible now. It lay about thirty yards back from the river bank. One end was a half collapsed pile of masonry and girders and the remaining portion looked highly unsafe, even in the dim light. Reg was not perturbed, he had spent many nights in worse places. He hurried across the open ground and entered through a window.

Ten minutes later he was warming his hands before a fire and had made substantial inroads into the gin bottle. There was a pile of blankets and old clothes in a corner. Reg draped these round himself and settled down to finish his bottle before falling asleep. His thoughts were on the police; it was ridiculous to say that the building was unsafe, even if part of it had been knocked down. Why, any fool could see the iron beams holding up the roof!

Outside the river continued to rise; high tide was due at half past midnight, a spring tide which would produce one of the highest levels of the year. On the bank, above Reg's building, the increased pressure was sending more water trickling down the back slope in rivulets, adding its burden to the already soaked ground behind. The bank was composed of packed earth, reinforced on the riverward side with brickwork. It was old, dating back to the time of the first building on the site, and it was in a dangerous condition.

During their work on the site the contractor had used heavy vehicles to break up the buildings and carry off the rubble. In the process they had damaged an underground culvert that drained the area, causing the ground behind the bank to become waterlogged and unstable.

As the river rose to its maximum height the top of the bank began to lose its hold and slide forward. The movement was slow, imperceptible at first, but the effect was cumulative.

Suddenly a noise of rolling thunder shook the ground and brought nearby residents from their beds in time to see a foaming torrent of water pouring through the gap into Cubitt Town.

*   *   *

Derek woke, after what seemed about five minutes of sleep, to find the telephone warbling quietly, but insistently, in his ear. It never ceased to astonish him that such an insignificant sound could arouse him.

He lifted the receiver and growled sleepily. "Derek? It's Johnny Easton here, sorry to wake you, but we've had a bank failure. I thought you'd want to know."

"Hell," Derek cursed, "where is it and how bad?" Johnny was one of the junior engineers in the department and, as it happened, the best of them. Tonight he was on standby for emergency duty.

"Isle of Dogs, at the tip. About thirty feet of bank went at high tide and took out the bottom floor of a housing estate. It happened an hour ago. I've just got here."

Derek looked at his watch. It was nearly two o'clock.

"I'd better come and take a look," he said resignedly, "is the water still coming through?"

"Yes, but it'll stop pretty soon, I reckon, then we can start sandbagging. The local borough are getting hold of some men and I've put out a call for our people. As soon as we can we'll start work."

"O.K., Johnny, I'll come over right away. Where are you operating from?"

"The police station in Cubitt Town. See you later."

Putting down the telephone Derek switched on the light and slid carefully out of bed, in the faint hope that his wife would remain undisturbed. The room was bitterly cold since, in deference to Derek's country up-bringing, they slept with one of the windows open. He crossed the carpet and closed it hastily as a sudden gust of wind blew the curtains billowing into the room. It had started to rain and the drops were spattering against the glass.

Behind him he heard a groan of protest as Georgina turned over. Pulling on a shirt he leant across, "Georgie," he said softly, "there's been a bank failure on the Isle of Dogs. I've got to go out and take a look. I'll be back in a couple of hours, I hope."

"Oh God!" Georgina moaned. She buried her blonde head deeply into the bedclothes. "What time is it?" she asked in a muffled voice.

"It's two o'clock." Derek felt like adding that it was a filthy night, raining and freezing cold, but Georgina said nothing more and her breathing indicated that she had gone back to sleep.

Putting on a thick jersey, he grabbed his boots and a heavy anorak. From bitter experience he knew that flooding of any kind meant getting cold, very wet and probably covered in mud.

Thirty minutes later he had reached the scene of the disaster.

"It's one hell of a mess," Johnny was saying to him,

"and I think that it could be worse than it looks." They were standing ankle deep in mud, by the edge of the site. In front of them lay the breach, an ugly gash in the bank, in which the water still lapped, even though the river level had dropped considerably. Beyond the sea of mud and glistening water, lay the derelict site, marking the path of the torrent, where puddles of black water gleamed under the arc-lights that had been erected; but the main bulk of the flood still remained trapped among the flats and houses of the estate on the other side of the road.

"The water's at least four feet deep down there," Johnny went on, indicating the area beyond the circle of lights. He was a tall, very strong man, a little over thirty and had thick curly brown hair.

"It'll take a bloody week to get it out by the looks of it. I reckon the drains are all shot to hell." His face was broad, with a large hooked nose. In the past Derek had found him impetuous, but immensely capable. The two of them got on well together.

"You're right," he said, "the rest of this bank could go at any time, and it certainly will as soon as any weight is put on it. It will have to be completely rebuilt right along its length and properly drained."

"In the meantime, however . . ."

"In the meantime we'll just have to patch it up with sandbags and piles and hope it doesn't slip any further." Derek moved a couple of paces toward the edge of the breach and prodded the ground with his heel. A quantity of earth gave way and subsided noiselessly into the water beneath.

"When's the next high water?"

"Twelve-thirty," the young engineer told him. "Should be three inches lower than tonight's, for what that's worth."

Derek looked carefully round the scene again, trying to decide upon the best method of repairing the damage. It had to be quick so as to prevent more water coming in at the next tide, and strong enough not to give way beneath the pressure. Normally they would have laid sandbags at the bottom of the gap, supported by stakes, when the water was low, forming a temporary wall. But with the next tide due shortly after midday and no chance of heavy equipment being available immediately, it was doubtful whether they would have more than four hours of working time in which to do it. Moreover, if the job were badly done, it would probably cause further slipping.

"At the very least, we must block off this flow," he said, pointing to the muddy channel made by the river's inrush. "We'll lay a light wall at the head of the breach, which will give protection while we construct a second line of defense further back, where the ground is firmer and we can count on it supporting the weight. That way they can begin pumping out the houses, which will keep the local authority off our backs."

Together they walked back towards the road, following the path made by the flood.

"Go carefully," Johnny warned, as they squelched through the mud. "Some of the puddles are deep. One of the lighting crew went in up to his neck."

It became apparent that the flood had spread outwards on meeting the flat ground of the road. They came to a huge expanse of rubble, wrecked masonry and crazily shattered walls, which used to be a warehouse.

"Luckily, it was in the process of being torn down anyway," Johnny remarked. "The water must have undermined what was left and brought it down. Good thing it was empty. I'll try and use some of the remains on the breach."

Crossing the road they entered the flooded area. The greater part of the Isle of Dogs was much lower than the banks, and once water had got in, it remained trapped, until laboriously pumped out again. In front of them there stretched a black, evil-smelling lake, its surface ruffled by the wind. Patches of floating debris clustered round the walls of a shopping center, which fronted a housing estate. The flats were quite modern, Derek thought, set with trim blue panels below the windows. This was part of the new development which was intended to brighten up dockland. Now the ground floors were deep in stinking mud and heavy water. He had seen enough flooded houses to know what the interiors would be like. Ruined carpets and furniture, peeling wallpaper, electric wiring, televisions, fridges, washing machines and the lift useless; the possessions of a family entirely destroyed. When the water had gone, they would still be left with inches of mud and filth to clear up. Even then the smell would still linger.

"Some of those flats have got basements in them," said Johnny, hunching his shoulders inside his anorak, as a gust of icy wind whistled down the street. "God knows, they must have been aware of the danger, but they still built them."

"They need the space," Derek replied quietly. "None of these East End boroughs can afford too many safety measures. They've all got housing queues for years ahead. Where else can they put the people?"

In his own mind he knew part of the trouble was that the local boroughs were relying on the great flood barrier, under construction further downstream, to protect them against a major inundation.

"What's the full extent of the flooded area?" he asked.

"Two streets under water completely, and further south various areas submerged," Johnny told him. "Approximately thirty homes flooded, also," he consulted a list from his pocket, "a secondary school, eleven shops and a packaging company."

"What about services?"

"Electricity's gone, of course. The sub-station behind the estate's got water in it, but the telephones haven't been as badly hit as one would expect."

A few people were wandering about in the street, wading cautiously and with difficulty, some of them carrying pathetic bundles. Here and there a light flickered in a window. Evidently some of the residents had had recourse to candles and torches. In an adjacent street, Derek saw a squad of policemen methodically checking every house and flat. It was a miracle, he thought, that as yet no deaths had been recorded, especially considering the number of basements that had been flooded. Several times they passed men trying, in vain, to start their cars. It was a sad fact, he knew, that no ordinary vehicle could survive in a flood; even a fire engine was helpless in more than eighteen inches of water.

"Right," he said, when they had finished their brief examination of the flood zone, "we'll start at once. You take some men down to the breach and start them chaining in the sandbags. I'll begin organizing the equipment for the second wall. Once we've got that in place the town will be properly protected, which is the most important factor."

Johnny grinned, "I thought I'd be the one playing around in the mud with the heavies, while you sat in a nice warm office," he said cheerfully, running a hand through his shock of hair.

"Perhaps you would rather try and explain to the local authorities how this fiasco isn't our fault?" Derek smiled back.

"No, thanks, I'll take my chance in the mud. There's one thing I forgot to tell you though. There's a storm tide alert on, or, at least, there was when I came down. It may have been cancelled by now. They usually are."

"Great!" Derek heaved a sigh, "that's all we need."

* * *

Reg had been in such a deep drunken sleep that even the roar made by the collapsing river bank had failed to disturb him. The water raced down upon the building, in which he had sought refuge, rushing in torrents through the heaps of rubble that surrounded it. The half-demolished state of the building was, in fact, all that prevented Reg from being drowned where he lay, for he certainly would have lacked the strength to fight his way out, and, besides, the room which he had chosen was a semi-basement. However, the flood was initially prevented from entering his room by the heaps of fallen brickwork and other debris that blocked the doors and passageways inside.

This was only temporary, however, swirling past the walls the flood swiftly undermined one of the more precarious outer walls, which swayed at first and finally collapsed outwards, bringing down the remaining parts of the building which, until then, still stood erect. This time the noise and shock woke Reg.

He woke with a start at the first terrifying rumble of the collapsing wall. The room about him shook, showering him with plaster. Outside in the passageway, a section of the ceiling fell with a crash and clouds of dust billowed into the room. The noise grew louder as the shaking of the building became more intense. Above him he could hear the upper floor breaking up. It was impossible to see in the dark and dusty atmosphere, but Reg was conscious that the doorway was now blocked with fallen stonework. There was another terrific, ear-splitting crash and the ceiling of the room fell in, hurling him against the far wall. He heard more rumbling and the noise of debris falling from the rooms above.

In the pause that followed, Reg fought for breath, choking on the acrid dust, as he tried to pick himself up. There was another roar and falling rubble and bricks showered down on top of him. He felt a sharp, agonizing pain on the back of his head and fell back unconscious.

On recovering his senses, he could feel that the dust had cleared somewhat enabling him to breathe more freely. His head ached and he was aware of a painful throbbing in various parts of his body. Feeling cautiously about him he found he was lying, half-buried, amongst bricks and pieces of broken concrete. He struggled for a while to pull himself clear, but one of his legs seemed to be caught. He sat up, and struck his head on something jutting out in the darkness, causing a small avalanche of stones.

Reg's brain was still muzzy with the alcohol he had drunk, which shielded him from fully appreciating his situation. Instead of giving way to panic and fear, as he would surely have done had he been sober, he remembered that he had some matches in his pocket and began hunting for them.

The sight around him, lit up by the blaze of the match, however, was enough to terrify even a brave man, which Reg was not. He was lying in what was left of the corner of the room; a space about four feet wide and not as high. His back leant against the rear wall. Above his head a massive iron beam sloped downwards, resting on the pile of bricks which had trapped his legs. He tried pushing it, but succeeded only in dislodging more rubble.

As the match burned to his fingers and the darkness closed in again, Reg was finally seized with panic. He screamed out loudly and frantically struck match after match. His voice resounded hollowly in the cavity and, with a sinking feeling, he realized it was unlikely that he would be heard. He lay still for a moment and listened. All was quiet, except for the odd movement of a brick or piece of concrete settling. His trapped leg had grown numb from the cold and pain, which frightened him. He wondered how long it would be before the demolition men returned.

* * *

Peter Collins had woken at 6:30 a.m., some time before the next report was due. Dawn was breaking to the east, revealing a sky that was overcast and shot with angry red. Now and then the wind rattled the window. A light rain fell.

From the streets below came the sound of traffic; the city was gradually coming to life. His night's vigil was nearly over. Peter examined the map on the wall. The next town from which a report would come was Lowestoft, on the Suffolk coast, and it would be a critical one. On the basis of the situation there, a decision would have to be made as to whether to issue the first London warning. This would mean alerting hundreds of officials to man the flood control room.

Judging by the data that had been coming over the tape machine during the hour he had been asleep, the surge was moving down the coast faster than he had expected. High tide at London Bridge was predicted for 12:35 that afternoon, but now it looked as though it would take place some time earlier.

As if on cue, a telephone rang. It was one of the forecasters at Bracknell. "Our calculations indicate that high water will now occur at 11:00 a.m.," he said, "and we consider it essential to pass this information on to the authorities concerned."

"That's just what I was thinking," agreed Peter. "Do you have any calculations as to the height of the surge, as well?"

" 'Fraid not," the forecaster chuckled at the other end of the line, "but my private guess is that you've got trouble on your hands, unless the wind shifts in the next two to three hours. Lowestoft's having a rough time."

With a sinking heart, Peter set about telephoning the news through to those bodies that required it. The first person he contacted was Derek on the Isle of Dogs.

"Damn," Derek said reflectively, when he heard what Peter had to say. "I didn't realize it was as bad as that."

"It may not be," Peter pointed out, "there's still very

little to go on. These alerts are hardly ever confirmed."

"I know that, for God's sake," Derek replied with some asperity. "All the same, I don't like it. If those gales are as strong as you say, they are capable of running a king-sized wave up the river, in any case, putting high water an hour and a half early isn't a great help down here. I want you to let me know the moment you have any more information, and in the meantime, you'd better see if you can send me a few more men to help on this breach."

Peter had barely finished these tasks when the data machine came through with the report from Lowestoft. He scanned it with dismay. Somehow, he had been able to dismiss the earlier messages with their descriptions of havoc and flood damage in the north, without undue alarm, but the inexorable progress of the storm, moving into towns and districts less than a hundred miles away, without losing any of its devastating strength, frightened him.

He had once been to Lowestoft and he pictured it now; the storm center directly overhead, with lashing rain and one hundred mile an hour winds, waves beating furiously against the pier and crashing over the seafront, and wrecked fishing boats, driven aground by tremendous gusts of wind sweeping in from the sea. A lifeboat had been launched in that sea, in an attempt to rescue a twenty-thousand-ton grain carrier, which was drifting five miles offshore with her engines flooded.

All this was of relatively minor importance, however, compared with the one vital piece of data, upon which the whole warning system depended. The automatic tide gauge had recorded a level nearly five and a half feet above the predicted high, and it was still rising. The surge was less than four hours from the capital, coming in on the high tide, a high spring tide, as the forecaster at Bracknell had said, unless the wind altered during that time.

Abruptly Peter turned away. There was no time to

waste. A flood emergency had developed and it was his duty to start the procedure, which would call up the city's defenses and alert its citizens.

He reached for the telephone and began to dial.

* * *

When the news of the four-hour warning reached Derek, he was down at the breach again, watching the progress of work. After a quick succession of telephone calls, using his car radio, and by a combination of pleas and threats, he succeeded in collecting a fair number of men and even a few useful pieces of equipment, including an excavator. Under Johnny's energetic direction, several hundred sandbags had been filled and laid in the mouth of the breach, providing a temporary barrier. It had been dirty, tiring work, with the men standing waist deep in mud and water, in order to place the bags in position making a solid wall, which now rose to almost the height of the old bank. Another hour's labor would see it completed.

"Will you be using the excavator to fill in behind the wall, Mr. Thompson?" the gang foreman, a short, stocky man with powerful shoulders and a barrel-like chest standing near the edge of the site, asked Derek as he returned thoughtfully from the car. "I can put some of the men on to the second wall if you like?" he offered, scraping the mud off his hands, as he spoke.

Derek shook his head. "Can't do that I'm afraid, Jack," he replied. "If we pack any earth in behind these sandbags, there's a risk it will shift again, just as it did before. The soil is so unstable there that there's no cohesion at all. Once the wall is finished, I want every man back working on the second line of defense." He looked back as he spoke, to where the excavator was tearing at the ground, scooping up mounds of earth and dumping it in a long line that would cure across the site, round the breach, sealing it off. As yet it did not cover a third of the distance. Also, near the edge of the site, there was still much to be done.

Leaving the foreman in charge of the wall, he went over to join Johnny, under whose direction a squad of some fifteen men were putting the final touches to the earth bank.

The earth dropped by the excavator formed a series of irregular heaps about four feet high, but were being leveled out to form a continuous line. The earth was not as saturated as he had feared. Quantities of rubble had been mixed with it to obtain a more solid consistency.

Johnny was standing astride the mound. He grinned down as Derek approached. "Welcome to Hadrian's Wall," he shouted. "This'll hold an army by the time it's finished."

"It may have to," Derek replied quietly, as the younger man scrambled down to join him. "I've just heard from Peter Collins again. A four hour alert has been called and the picture isn't good." Johnny's face became instantly serious.

"What does the forecaster say?" he asked.

"There was a surge at Lowestoft of at least six feet, and it may be even higher. So far the wind is still north-westerly and storm force."

"Well, it's happened before often enough. We were called out twice last year, I seem to remember. They'll stand us down after an hour, I'll bet."

"Maybe you're right," Derek agreed. "All the same, I want this bank made fully secure by ten o'clock. We can't afford to take chances."

"I can put another couple of feet on top, if you like?" Johnny suggested. "The bulldozer will be here in half an hour, which will speed things up."

"No," Derek told him, "it's high enough; even allowing for the slope in the ground, the crest should be two feet higher than the top of the river wall when you've finished. If the tide comes up that high, it wouldn't stand the strain anyway, and so would be a waste of time. Just concentrate on making it really solid, so it will stand up if the breach fails again."

"I've got you. Don't you worry, we'll get it ready in time."

"I'll keep in touch over the radio and let you know as soon as there's any change. If you need anything, call the office," Derek told him and then returned to the car. Johnny watched him go. In the gray light the riverfront looked dismal and depressing; a wilderness of deserted buildings and half-cleared huts. A bitter gust of wind made him shiver, as he turned back to the bank with an uneasy heart.

* * *

Reg had lain quietly, still imprisoned, for several hours. The liquor he had drunk and the injuries to his head and leg had caused him to drift off into periods of semiconsciousness, during which he was hardly aware of his surroundings. When at length his senses returned, he was filled with renewed panic. The matches had all gone. He screamed desperately, hammering on the iron beam that pinned him down, with pieces of stone and brick. Outside it was light, but Reg had lost track of the time and had no idea how long he had been trapped. At moments he thought it was only a few minutes, but at others he was seized with a dreadful suspicion that he had been there for many hours already.

Suddenly he could hear noises. The sound of an excavator removing part of the fallen rubble for use on the earth bank faintly reached him through the thick walls. A surge of hope rose in him. There were rescuers at hand, soon they would work their way down to him. He began to shout and bang with renewed energy.

It was whilst he was fumbling for another piece of brick with which to hammer on the beam that he first felt the water. Scrabbling in the darkness, by his knees, his fingers came away cold and wet. Shocked, he drew back, and then began to search again with his hands. Again, he encountered water. This time it was a definite pool which had formed on the floor, amongst the dirt. Straining his ears, he could hear, through the rumblings outside, a faint, faraway tinkle of water trickling down into the cavity where he lay.

* * *

Derek had not been long gone when Johnny first saw the girl. He was supervising the laying of more sandbags on the sloping face of the bank, so as to hold the earth behind in place, should the water break through. At first he paid no attention to the figure picking its way carefully among the pools of water that lay everywhere on the site. It was only when the men with him began to look up and mutter with appreciation that he realized what she was.

She skipped across a scattered pile of stakes and came unhesitatingly up to the bank. Johnny and the men looked at her with interest. He guessed that she was about twenty-five, slimly built and about five feet six inches. Dark curls of hair stuck out from beneath a red woolen hat. She was wearing a Fairisle sweater underneath a corduroy tank top. Her jeans were tucked neatly into gumboots.

Amid a chorus of applause from the men, Johnny went over to talk to her.

"You're obviously looking for someone," he said, "will I do?" The girl looked up at him. Her face was small and delicate, but there was a firmness about the chin and jaw that indicated determination and character.

"Have you seen an old tramp around here, this morning?" she asked. Her voice was educated, but without the nasal twang of the upper class. "He used to sleep over there." She pointed to the remains of the warehouse. "Nobody's seen him around and I'm worried about him. He wears a black coat and he's called Reg."

" 'Fraid not," Johnny answered. "I'll ask the others, though." He turned back to the men, who were leaning on their shovels, eyeing the girl suggestively, and repeated the question. They returned a chorus of denials, interspersed with calls of endearments.

"Ain't seen no one, 'cept you, my love."

"Come on then, darlin', you an' me'll go look for 'im."

"Lost yer boyfriend 'ave yer?"

"Looks like you're out of luck," Johnny said. "Are you sure he was here last night. We haven't heard of anyone being hurt, apart from an old woman in one of the houses."

"I know about her," the girl said quickly, with a trace of irritation. She shivered and her face was pinched with cold. "No, it's Reg I'm looking for." Johnny felt suddenly sorry for her.

"Why don't you go and ask some of the people who live in Wharf Street," he suggested, pointing to a lane at one end of the site, which ran into Marshes Road. "Most of them woke up as soon as the wall burst. They may well have seen if your man was here then."

The girl smiled at him. "That's a good idea," she said. "Thanks, I will." Johnny watched her leave the site as she walked back towards the direction he had indicated.

Less than twenty minutes later she was back again, her eyes big with worry.

"I found a woman who says she saw a fire burning inside the warehouse at midnight," she said anxiously. "I think he may still be in there."

"He probably got out when the water started coming in," Johnny said reasonably. "There's very little chance he'd still be inside, I would think. Have you talked to the police, maybe they've seen him?"

"I saw them first of all. They say they checked the building at eleven o'clock last night and he wasn't there then, but that only means he wasn't there at eleven. He could easily have gone in later. In fact, he would deliberately have tried to avoid them." She fell silent. Johnny looked dubiously at the pile of fallen masonry. If there was anyone trapped beneath, he did not give much for their chances.

"You see," the girl went on, speaking quickly, "I know he would be round here now, if he was all right. He has to collect his money for the week from me. He wouldn't miss that for anything. I work for a group that tries to help people like Reg," she explained. "We provide food, clothing and shelter where we can. I've been coming to see Reg regularly and each Friday morning I bring him some money. I try and make him spend it on things he needs, but I think it generally ends up spent on drink," she added despondently. Johnny said nothing.

"What I wanted to ask," she said, "was whether you would let me have a few of your men to move some of that rubble. I can't do it alone."

"Look," Johnny said kindly, "in less than three hours' time the tide is going to come up to the top of the wall again, and unless I get this bank finished before then the town is going to get another river bath, and perhaps people will die. Now, if we keep working flat out, we may be able to prevent that, but until it is completed, I can't turn my men on to . . ." He paused, seeking another word for 'wild goose chase'. However, the girl had divined his meaning. Her jaw tightened and her chin went up determinedly.

"Very well," she snapped, "I am sorry to have troubled you. I'll do it myself," and she set off angrily.

Johnny swore under his breath. He liked the girl and the last role he wanted to play was that of the obstructive official. Behind him he was conscious of the sniggers and jokes of the men.

"Jack," he called to the foreman, "keep it moving here, while I take a look. If I can show her this tramp isn't buried in that pile of rubbish, maybe she'll go away." The big foreman waved a hand of understanding and pausing to pick up a crowbar and a torch, Johnny set off after the girl.

He caught her up when she was still several yards short of the building. Her head jerked around in surprise, on hearing him behind her.

"Here," he said roughly, "you'd better let me take a look for you. You'd never shift this mess." The girl gave a smile.

"Thanks," she said, the relief showing in her voice. "I wasn't looking forward to trying by myself. I'll give you a hand."

On closer inspection, Johnny could see that the building had collapsed inwards, as the outer wall had given way. Most of the upper floors now lay in a heap of smashed beams and huge fragments of cement and stonework that covered what had once been the ground floor.

Together, they scrambled over a mound of bricks and stood on the crazily tilted surface of an enormous slab of concrete that jutted out of the ruins. Johnny peered cautiously underneath. There was barely sufficient space to crawl through, but he was fairly confident he could manage it. Once inside, he might be able to see what remained of the interior better.

"I'm coming too," said the girl, when he told her of his plan. Johnny started to protest, but she stooped swiftly and had disappeared beneath the slab before he could finish. Johnny followed, taken aback by her agility.

He found her crouched in a small triangular space, the side of which consisted of a still-standing portion of a wall. His torch revealed a number of beams and large fragments of brickwork overhead. It looked highly unsafe, and at every movement, small showers of stones and dust fell, choking them. The floor had a shallow covering of water.

"Can we get any further, do you think?" The girl's face was pale and frightened, but she had lost none of her determination.

"I think so," he replied. "There's a hole underneath this beam. I might be able to get through. This time you stay here. Understand?" She nodded silently.

Lying flat on his stomach, Johnny inched his way along the side of an enormous iron beam; a girder which must have once held up one of the floors and which now helped to provide a narrow tunnel under the fallen debris. To his disappointment, it ended after about five feet, in a solid mound of bricks and plaster. As he began to wriggle his way back he heard a sound nearby.

"Was that you making that noise?" he called to the girl behind him. He heard her muffled voice saying "No."

He seized a piece of rock in his hand and tapped twice on the side of the beam. The sound rang out hollowly and a shower of dirt fell on him. There was a moment's pause and then he heard the sound again; a faint, but definite tapping in reply.

"Is anyone there?" he shouted. He heard another series of taps, but no word. There could be no doubt, someone was trapped there.

"You're right," he told the girl, when he had crawled back, "there is someone there and we've got to get him out fast."

Chapter Two

With the calling of the first warning at 6:45 a.m., a complicated and highly detailed plan swung into action.

Working steadily down the list in front of him, Peter began dialing the home telephone numbers of the city's senior officials. The call-out system worked on progressively expanding chains of communication. Thus Peter's first job was to call Derek Thompson, Carswell, the Flood Coordinator and Francis Whyte, Director General of the Greater London Council. Each of these three had a short list of numbers, which they would dial before setting out. These included some of the people at the top of Peter's master list, thereby providing an inbuilt check on the system. As soon as this was completed they would promptly leave for County Hall.

Alan Carswell was a small, sandy-haired man with neat precise movements and an almost intimidatingly efficient manner which, though tiresome to work under in ordinary circumstances, was invaluable in an emergency. It took only a few seconds for him to awaken and answer Peter's call.

"I've called the chief engineer," the young officer told him. "He's out at a repair job on the Isle of Dogs. He has confirmed that he is coming in at once. I don't think there is any point in your calling him to check."

"Agreed," Carswell replied, holding the receiver to his ear as he got out of bed and began undoing his pajamas. "Continue with the call-out for the first flood warning. I presume you've heard from the flood room already."

"Yes, Alan, I have, thanks. I'm doing my bit now. I'll be in at once. Right?" Neither wasted time on pleasantries. Quickly replacing the receiver, the Coordinator immediately dialed the numbers of his two senior deputies. In each case they answered promptly and their response was fast. He had been fortunate, he thought, as he turned away and began to dress himself hurriedly. The names on his list were senior officers, trained and ready for an emergency such as this. Further down the echelon, he knew the reaction would be slower. Tests had proved that to awaken a sleeping man and make him understand his duties could take as long as five minutes, and seldom took less than two or three.

In the meantime, at County Hall, Peter was experiencing exactly this problem. He had already abandoned the attempt to contact one of the liaison officers for the Electricity Generating Board and was telephoning his backup instead. He waited for what seemed hours, before an irritated voice answered and cursed angrily when told the news. "Hell, it's my day off. O'Neil's the one you're supposed to get today."

"I'm sorry, I can't rouse Mr. O'Neil. My instructions are, therefore, to contact you. Can you come in, please?" Peter spoke carefully; despite the gravity of the threat the city now faced, it was a fact that neither he nor any of his superiors in the Council possessed the

power to order the man in. The Coordinator and his
team were exactly what the words implied: they could
coordinate, they could urge, advise and request, but
they could not give orders. They had no statutory authority at all. Fortunately, the man proved reasonable.
"O.K.," he said wearily, "I'll come, but the sodding
river had better do its stuff this time."

Downstairs, in their office, the two night duty men
were performing the same function as Peter. At this
stage, the primary objective was to rouse and bring into
their posts the people who manned the Central Flood
Coordinating Room for the Greater London Council
itself, and the similar operating rooms that would be
set up by every London borough, besides the major
public services, such as the Post Office, Gas and Electricity Boards and London Transport. Once these men
were in place and liaison had been established between
them, it would then be possible to begin calling out the
second line of defense; the actual men and women,
whom the officers in the widely scattered control rooms
had to direct and organize into action. Then, and only
then, would it be possible to start warning the general
public. At all costs the system had to be ready to go
into action the moment the final alarm was given; one
hour before the water began to pour over the embankment walls in central London.

Peter looked at his watch. It was already a quarter
past seven and, as yet, he doubted if even the first officers on the call-up lists had reached their respective
buildings. The Coordinator would go to his office on the
ground floor, in the main County Hall block, just across
the river, but Derek Thompson would certainly come
to the warning room. Ultimately, it would be on Derek's
recommendation, as Chief Engineer, that the decision
as to whether or not to alert the public would be taken.

The teleprinter continued to churn out information
on sea and weather conditions, as the scientists at
Bracknell examined every detail for the slightest clue as

to the behavior of the storm. There was still a chance that the winds might change and for the depression to start moving across the central European continent, as had happened on all the previous occasions when the warnings had been issued. He glanced at the reports from East Anglia and Lincolnshire: severe gales, widespread damage to seawalls and defenses; it was the same story all along the coast. Great Yarmouth had suffered huge waves pounding the front and the sea had risen a foot above the harbor wall. Similar conditions were being reported at Lowestoft, with the majority of the trawlers, which had taken shelter there, damaged or capsized and parts of the town without power. The water level in the port had exceeded the capacity of the tide gauge and terrific winds were still being reported in all the other ports: FORCE 10, FORCE 11, GUSTING 85 PLUS, GUSTS 88 M.P.H., the last from Harwich at 6:00 a.m. The storm has lost a little of its strength in its journey south.

By 7:50 a.m., Peter had completed most of the calls on his list and was about to begin writing out a review of the situation for the senior officers to examine on their arrival. On the basis of this review, they would have to decide if the danger was serious enough to put the emergency services, the police, the fire brigade and ambulance service, on standby.

In Peter's opinion the situation was highly alarming. Although the winds had abated slightly, the storm was now less than one hundred miles from London and still advancing at an extremely fast rate. It was true that the damage along the east coast had not been catastrophic; a few square miles of farming land inundated in Lincolnshire, some local flooding in Mablethorpe, Yarmouth and other ports, but it was more likely, he knew, that the extent of devastation would not be apparent until later. At night, with appalling weather conditions and, therefore, communications being very difficult, any assessment would be a haphazard guess.

Besides, the threat to London was of a totally different nature. The most worrying factor in the reports he had read during the night had been the number of places recording an abnormally high level in the sea. In Peter's mind there was no doubt that a major sea surge was approaching the capital and, at its present speed, it would enter the narrow confines of the Thames on top of a high tide.

* * *

Among those who received early notice of the flood warning was one of the city's youngest councilors, Miles Wendoser. Miles was thirty-six years old and a clever, ambitious man, skilled in the devious art of city politics. It was characteristic of him that his first thought, on hearing the news, was not concerned with the safety of London and its inhabitants, but with the state visit of the American president, who was due to arrive in London that morning. He recalled the arrangements swiftly; a ceremonial drive past Westminster, down Whitehall, past the Horse Guards into Trafalgar Square, left up The Mall and into Buckingham Palace. Then, and to Miles this was the most important part of the events, there was to be a reception at which he himself would be present, with a large number of distinguished guests.

A flood alert now would not only call for the cancellation of the ceremonial drive, but it would also put an end to any hopes that Miles might have had of going to the Palace; and he had taken a great deal of trouble arranging that invitation. Instead, he would have to stay in the flood control room, where it was his duty, as chairman of the Public Safety Committee, to take overall command of the situation. What made it all the more infuriating was the knowledge that the alert was bound to be called off in two or three hours, which would be just too late for him to go to the reception.

Each year several alerts were called; there had been one six weeks ago, and they were always canceled a couple of hours before the flood was due. Ironically, one of the reasons Miles had taken over the position was in order to try and cut down the number of alerts and the cost of these turnouts.

Miles went into the bathroom and began to shave. His face was smooth and good-looking, marred only by a slight plumpness around the jaw; a hint of the occasional indulgence he allowed himself. He shaved carefully, turning over the situation in his mind. Perhaps there was material here that could be turned to his advantage?

Miles had been a councilor for six years. There had been a time, before that, when he would have considered such a post beneath him; when he would have accepted nothing less than a seat in parliament itself. A decade ago the name of Miles Wendoser had been a familiar one in the country, as leader of the youth wing of his party. A favorite both with the media and the party hierarchy, his brand of well-mannered radicalism had proved acceptable to a nation which was tired of the increasingly violent demands of student politicians. Miles had managed the movement with a flair for publicity which made him the darling of every journalist and television anchorman in England. Whenever they wanted a calculated, but outrageous, criticism of an old tradition, or a shocked denunciation of a new intrigue, Miles was always available and ready with the appropriate words.

Within his own party, the feelings of his fellow politicians were mixed concerning Miles. There were many who resented his sudden rise to fame and arrogant assumption that he was inevitably destined for high office. The majority, however, accepted him at the popular evaluation, and argued that he was just the caliber of man needed for the future. Their noise was sufficiently powerful to ensure that at the following parliamentary by-election, Miles was chosen as the party's official candidate for the seat.

The campaign was waged in the full glare of intense publicity. There was little other news at the time, and both the newspapers and television succeeded in wringing out the maximum controversy and public interest of the affair. Major personalities from both the government and opposition entered the battle, speaking on behalf of their candidates and appearing with them on the stands.

Miles fought the election with every skill and trick he knew. He was indefatigable; he was seen everywhere, interviewed constantly, gave opinions on every subject, from birth control to nuclear defense, and toured the constituency with a retinue of pressmen, advisers and professional hangers-on. He was the subject of interviews and profiles of his personal life, and views were run in several magazines, even his style of dress and the clothes he bought became a subject of great interest. "Daring, forceful, flamboyant, a new man with new ideas, the sort of man the nation needs to cut away the shackles of outmoded concepts" was how one editor described him; how could Miles possibly fail?

But that was exactly what he did. Whilst Miles had been working and living in a haze, blinded by the unquestioning adulation of those with whom he was in immediate contact, his opponent, a quiet, respectable, middle-aged man who lived in the district, had been devoting most of his time to his constituents. Unusually, the media had misread the mood of the people. A reactionary wave had set in against any form of radicalism, and in particular the radicalism of the flamboyant, arrogant type of young man such as Miles Wendoser. All his tactics during the campaign served only to reinforce this view. The local populace resented their homes being invaded by presumptuous strangers from the "big city", who treated them with patronizing disdain. They were angered at the failure to concentrate on, or even the attempt of any interest being taken in, local issues and problems. When the election results were counted, Miles was found to have converted the small but adequate majority of his predecessor into a stunning loss.

The magnitude of the disaster having become apparent, Miles found himself without a friend in the world. Furious at being betrayed, the press and his own party turned on him with a vengeance. His failures and shortcomings were dissected and held up as an object lesson to prospective members of parliament, on the dangers of abandoning traditional methods. From having been a more than welcome guest at dinner parties, Miles became socially unacceptable overnight, ostracized by society.

His parliamentary dreams shattered, deserted by his friends and forgotten by acquaintances, most people would never have given Miles another thought. There were very few people who could ever hope to recover from such a disaster; least of all Miles. However, this was to prove a very mistaken estimate of Miles. Besides the showmanship and bravado which he had so openly displayed, he was also possessed with a degree of dogged persistence and considerable ruthless cunning. When other men would have relinquished all hope and abandoned politics altogether, Miles did not; he returned to the bottom of the scale and started afresh at local government level.

It was hard, depressing and soul-destroying work, with none of the assistance he had formerly been accustomed to and with none of the glamour of his previous work to allay the nagging boredom. Finally, however, his persistence began to pay off; he was elected to the Greater London Council. This time he was careful: careful to put his name only to policies that he knew would succeed, and careful to side only with those people who held real power. He studied the machinery of government and the characters of those men involved.

He learned the rules and the tactics that could be used to outwit and outmaneuver his opponents.

During his six years in the Council Miles had remained loyal to his old party, resolutely supporting all its major policies, but consistently avoiding involving himself with anything controversial. Instead, he had concentrated on working his way into a position of power, from which he would be able to secure a return to the parliamentary seat he coveted. Since he had failed to make it on the strength of his charm and radical ideas, he was determined to succeed by wheeling and dealing behind the scene. He set out to make himself indispensable to his faction on the Council and took care, at the same time to be as agreeable as possible to the senior men who sat in parliament.

There could be no doubt of Miles' ability. Within a surprisingly short space of time, he had managed to make a name for himself again as a useful man and someone who could get things done. Several awkward assignments, within the Council, were entrusted to him on the party's behalf. He probed scandals and highlighted inefficiency, he became a champion of economies in local government. He made himself unpopular with the city's employees and was distrusted by his fellow councilors, but he had almost achieved his aim.

He now had another opportunity to show how essential he was: a state visit by the President of the United States jeopardized by this false flood alert.

Miles smiled grimly to himself as he began to dress. The thought would be causing many people to panic, important people, and they would be sincerely grateful when Miles Wendoser stepped in to settle the whole ridiculous problem.

His first move was to telephone the senior forecaster at Bracknell and ascertain the background to the situation.

"Are you quite positive," he demanded, "that this

time the surge risk is genuine? We've seen these storms in Scotland many times before and they never last long enough to pose a true threat to London."

The forecaster paused for a moment before answering; he had come across Wendoser before; on an occasion when the weather center had stuck its neck out and assured everyone that there was a serious flood risk. When the surge failed to materialize at Southend there had been many complaints and Wendoser had made life extremely difficult for the center. He decided to be cautious.

"At this stage, sir, it is impossible to say definitely what will happen. Weather conditions during the night were very bad in some parts of the north and tide patterns along the coast have been irregular."

"I know that," Miles snapped, "but are you aware that the President of the United States is making a state visit here today. I don't suppose you want us to cancel half the arrangements for a false alarm? In your opinion, are the present conditions definitely going to persist long enough to flood the city, or will they fade out, as they usually do?"

"Well, sir." The forecaster felt unhappy. At the moment the danger was real enough, he knew, but he also knew that the councilor was right; alerts never came to anything, they were always canceled because the weather improved in time. "I suppose it's true that the storm should ease fairly quickly now; as you say they always do. In fact the latest figures we've received for pressure and wind speed indicate that this may already have started."

"So in other words, although the situation gives cause for concern, it is unlikely, in view of past experience, to develop into a serious risk?"

"Yes, I think you could say that," the forecaster agreed, hesitating slightly. After all, he told himself, when Miles had rung off, it was true that the storms always moderated or altered course, and the alerts were always called off. However much he tried to persuade himself that this was so, he was still left with a nagging uneasy feeling in the back of his mind.

Miles set off for County Hall feeling pleased with himself. Thanks to him Bracknell would now play down the flood danger, giving him an opportunity to call off the alert, just when the government would be panicking about the American visit. It was all most satisfactory.

*   *   *

Although the rain during the night had washed the streets clean of the snow that had lain there for the past two days, the journey back to Westminster took Derek longer than he had expected. There was a surprising amount of early morning traffic, and in the East End heavily laden lorries added to the congestion. Only when he reached the embankment did the stream of cars begin to thin out, allowing him to speed up.

The flood warning had come at a thoroughly inconvenient moment, he decided, but then they invariably did. It meant that instead of getting on with his normal work, apart from having to deal with the urgent problem of the bank failure on the Isle of Dogs, he would have to spend the entire morning watching the state of the river, pulling his juniors off the tasks they were engaged on and sending them out to patrol the walls for leaks. Then the alarm would be called off a couple of hours before zero hour and the emergency apparatus would be stood down, but not before the whole day had been wasted.

The trouble was, he thought reflectively, that there was no real warning system. The very nature of the threat precluded it. Every time a big storm started to move down the east coast, raising a tidal surge, there was a danger that it might keep going until it reached the Thames estuary. The difficulty was that it was impossible to ascertain when a surge was going to come up the river until it hit Southend, by which time it was only an hour away from London.

This meant that it was only possible to give the capital one hour's warning that flooding would certainly take place and, since this was obviously not enough, the authorities had to go to emergency action stations whenever a surge came within four hours of London. As a result they experienced, on average, three false alarms every winter. The great barrier project at Woolwich was designed to prevent all this, but since it had been paralyzed by strikes, it was now two years behind schedule, which was probably fortunate since there was almost certainly not enough money to finance it anyway.

He glanced sideways towards the river on his right. A sluggish snake of brown greasy water, its surface choppy from the wind. It was incredible how harmless, almost docile, it looked. No wonder, he thought, the inhabitants of the city persistently refused to believe that the Thames, which had always been a part of their lives, was also a potentially terrifying threat to their existence.

On these occasions Derek regretted that the offices of the engineering department were separate from the main buildings of County Hall across the river. It meant that he would have to make three or four trips, back and forth, between them, during the course of the morning, and judging by the weather forecasts, there was a strong likelihood of having to do so in the rain.

The warning room operated by the Council came within his jurisdiction, since the engineers were the only people who could be expected to understand how the river worked. The control room, from which the authorities would direct operations in the event of a flood was, in effect, a separate organization with its own staff, located in the main County Hall building. Not unnaturally, this arrangement involved a considerable amount of two-way traffic between the two offices. To add to the complexity of the situation, the control room staff switched to a secret underground center in Holborn Kingsway, at an early stage in the emergency, since their rooms in County Hall would be inundated if flooding took place.

When he reached the warning room Derek found Peter Collins still engaged in calling up the names on his list. Another engineer arrived at the same time and Derek set him to work on the same task.

"So far no real problems," Peter told him. "I haven't been able to reach a few people, but their backups are coming instead. A couple of our own men are down with flu though, and we can't replace them."

"Make do as best you can," Derek told him. "If we find we are short I'll send in some replacements." The boy nodded as he started to make another call.

"O.K., sir," he said. "I've put copies of all the tapes on your desk, and also the figures from the tide gauges."

Derek went into his office and began to study the reports. His secretary appeared and put a cup of coffee in front of him. Derek looked up in surprise.

"How did you get in so early, Liz?" he asked. "Don't tell me you got an emergency call too?" Liz smiled back. She was plump, gray-haired and the far side of fifty. Derek had discovered her with relief two years ago, after a series of pretty, but empty-headed, girls had brought him to the limits of sanity. Liz never lost anything, never made a mistake and never got in a muddle, and she managed to do this without putting anyone's back up.

"I heard the forecast at seven o'clock and it sounded pretty bad, so I rang in to check," she said. "How does it look?"

"Like you say, it sounds bad: one hundred mile an hour winds, torrential rain, flooding from the sea along half the east coast. The question is, how long will it keep up? Your guess is as good as mine."

"What does Bracknell think?"

"They're playing it close. 'There are some indications that the wind may be veering at Southend, but it's impossible to draw any positive conclusions', but what can you expect? Last year they stuck their necks out and swore there'd be a seven-foot surge, so we ring all the bells, and it didn't even reach Southend. There were a lot of sore necks in Bracknell that day. This time they're being careful."

"Alan Carswell's been on, there's a meeting for the second phase of the alert at eight o'clock. I've told him you'll be there," said Liz. "Do you want me to call Georgina for you?"

Derek glanced at his watch. It read 7:48 a.m.

"No thanks," he said, "she'll be getting the kids up in a minute. I'll call her myself, after the meeting." He returned to his study of the reports.

Derek's mind went back to a meeting that had been held four months ago to decide the future of the barrier. Ostensibly it had been billed as a 'situation review' at which reports on the progress to date would be heard and assessments made, but from the very first he had known it would be more than that.

He had presented the facts to the committee. The Director General, Miles Wendoser, Carswell, the Flood Coordinator, and three other councilors were there as well as himself; at the start it had all gone smoothly, too smoothly, he realized later.

The barrier was going ahead. Since the last formal meeting they had made considerable progress and in particular had virtually succeeded in overcoming most of the problems that had been experienced in sinking the piles supporting the massive structure in a chalk bed, that had proved to be extensively faulted. Very soon they would be able to start work on the construction of the gate sills, the next major step in the program. It had been at this point that Miles had interrupted.

"I understood," he remarked, "that there was still a considerable amount of design testing to be done on the gate pivots. Is it wise, therefore, to embark on this next and extremely expensive phase of the operation, before the results of these tests are known?" He smiled suavely at Derek and looked round the room for confirmation.

"Most of the testing has been completed," Derek replied, "the tenders for the sills have been received. If we decide on those we could start work at once and make up for much of the delay we lost on the piers."

"And through strikes," interjected the Director General.

"Yes, and through strikes, as well," Derek agreed. The labor record at the barrier had become a bad joke at County Hall.

"In other words, what you are saying," the Director General went on, filling his pipe methodically as he spoke, "is that by altering our original plans we could begin building the sills while the design work on the pivots is still going on, instead of waiting for that to be completed; advance the second phase of the program?"

"That's correct," Derek acknowledged, "the contractors are confident they can handle it and by the time the designs are required they will have been finished." There was a moment's silence in the room, then Miles spoke again.

"This is all rather unexpected," he said. "You are suggesting a speeding up in the rate of construction at a time when no provision for this has been made. It would mean providing additional funds on a large scale." He paused. "And the scheme is already over the budget." There were nods and murmurs of agreement from the others present.

"Yes, but the funds have already been earmarked

for this project and under the original plan they would be needed now anyway. Also, the government has committed itself to supporting the barrier and contributing towards the additional cost," he retorted. He was conscious that he was fighting a hopeless cause, yet he could not think why it should be so. "Surely, it's in the public interest for the barrier to be completed as soon as possible," he said.

"Quite so, Derek, nobody would deny that for a second," the Director General said, "but a lot of other factors must be taken into account. We don't want to rush into a series of expensive mistakes. For instance," he continued casually, "there is this question of the strikers trying to turn the barrier project into a second Barbican affair." He puffed at his pipe and looked hard at the engineer. Before Derek could answer, Miles was speaking.

"There is also the new policy of restraint in public spending. It would hardly assist our relationship with the government if we were to demand another large sum at this present moment, simply in order to put forward a long term scheme of this nature. Nor could we very well begin cutting back on other projects at this stage, to find the money."

So this was it, Derek realized. The government had been promised that no new funds would be requested during the coming year and the Council intended to keep that promise. It would suit them if the barrier went ahead slowly and perhaps some of the money that would have been spent on it could be used to keep other projects going. The theory of a serious strike threat, like that which had paralyzed the redevelopment at the Barbican, was another highly convenient excuse. Softpedal the project for a year and the trouble with the unions would have blown over. He was determined not to give up without a fight, however.

"The flood barrier was originally scheduled to become operational by the end of 1978," he said, looking at them all, "it is now 1976 and the latest completion date is 1980. Unless we speed up the rate we won't even make that. How do you assess the extra risk to the capital during that time?" He turned to Carswell, who so far had said nothing. "Alan, you know what would happen if a surge came up the river. How do you feel about this?"

"Well, I don't really know," Carswell hedged, looking acutely embarrassed. "I admit it worries me, but we can still finish the bank raising program below Woolwich, can't we, and that'll be a help?"

"It'll be a help, all right. It'll help the surge come right into the center of London. Raising the banks downstream without closing the river off with a barrier is worse than doing nothing at all. It just contains the water so we get the full force of the flood where it can do most damage. In case any of you have forgotten, I'll remind you that the odds against a major overtopping are thirty-four to one and there hasn't been a big flood for twenty-three years. By the time we're ready for it, we will have cut the odds pretty fine."

*   *   *

"I might as well have saved my breath," he told Georgina, that night, when he got home. "They had made up their minds before they even went into the meeting. We keep going just as we are. The Director described it as 'taking advantage of an inevitable delay'."

Georgina nodded and handed him a drink she had mixed him. "Why didn't Alan Carswell support you?" she asked. "He knows the danger as much as you do." Derek sighed resignedly.

"Carswell's worried about the future. If and when the barrier is ever finished, he will be out of a job, so he has to follow the official line or he'll be offered nothing instead."

"And Miles is against you and the flood barrier in

general?" Georgina sat back in her chair and sipped her drink, regarding him thoughtfully.

"Miles is the government's fixer on the Council. He's in favor of anything they like. At the moment they don't want to have to pay out on their share of the project, so Miles has arranged for it to stand still for a year. I tell you I've had this city, had it right up to the teeth."

"Time for another move?" Georgina asked lightly, but her tone was serious. She had sensed her husband's growing disillusionment for some time. In twelve years of marriage they had worked in three different places. She had hoped this one would be a little more permanent. Derek gave her a reassuring smile.

"We'll see," he said, "I know you don't want to move."

"I like London. The kids are happy at school, and we have a nice house here. There's the studio. Maybe you could get another job?"

"Unless we get that barrier finished soon, there won't be a London for much longer. We're on borrowed time as it is, and the danger is getting worse every day."

*   *   *

He and Miles Wendoser had been enemies since the first day they had met. He had disliked the councilor for his suave slyness, his cynicism and his indifference to everything except his own career. Perhaps, he admitted to himself, there was also a tinge of envy in his feelings; envy for the sophisticated, well-bred manners, the inherited wealth, the smart friends, and above all, the arrogant assumption of superiority, that Miles displayed to those about him. Derek had never known poverty but his father, a small farmer on New Zealand's South Island, had had little to spare for the frills of life and his son had always had to work hard for a living.

For his part Miles had resented the engineer's out-

spokenness, his relaxed and casual attitudes towards
distinctions of seniority, and his refusal to be brow-
beaten or manipulated in matters he considered to be
his responsibility.

The confrontation over the flood barrier had been
building up for a long time, and for the moment it
looked as though Miles had won a round; for the survival of the city it was essential that he be prevented
from winning another.

*   *   *

Derek left his office and crossed the bridge in a hurry,
arriving in the control room at exactly eight o'clock. On
his way he considered the facts of the position. He felt
worried, far more so than he had admitted to Liz or
any of the others in his department. The storm bearing
down on the city was far in excess of anything he had
ever experienced before. It was nothing short of a hurricane, with winds exceeding one hundred miles an
hour. The devastation left in its wake had been very
widespread and so too had the damage along the sea-
shore from the immense waves battering the harbor
walls. So far there had been little surface flooding, certainly nothing on the scale of the disaster in 1953,
twenty-four years earlier. However, this could be due
to the fact that the sea walls in most places had been
greatly strengthened since then.

There was little doubt in his mind that unless there
was a last minute alteration in either the direction or
the strength of the winds, then London would be inundated by a catastrophic flood from which the city might
possibly never recover.

*   *   *

Peter Collins was already in the control room. In normal circumstances he should have been on his way
home after spending the night on duty, but the absence
of several members of the department meant that they

were short-staffed and Watson, the senior officer in the warning room, had asked him to stay on.

"Can you go over to the control room at County Hall," he asked, "and liaise with us from there? I'm afraid I've no one else to send. If this thing runs for any length of time, we shall really need a capable man there."

Peter left the building and walked across the square, past the Houses of Parliament and over Westminster Bridge. The morning was cold and gloomy; the dark clouds he had seen at dawn now covered the whole sky like a great black curtain and rain was falling. The wind, he noticed, had already risen and was now blowing strongly from the northwest, buffeting and pulling at his raincoat as it swept down the river. The first of the commuter traffic had begun to filter into the city, the street was noisy with cars and buses, and people were hurrying from the entrances of the underground station by the bridge. Many of these were walking in the same direction as himself and were obviously some of the seven thousand staff who manned the enormous headquarters of the Greater London Council, whose vast neoclassical facade rose above the buildings on the opposite bank.

Once over the bridge, Peter turned left and passed through an archway on the west side of the building. The entrance was marked "Members Only" and, for once, the security guards in their cabins on either side of the gate were checking the identities of everyone who entered. Peter showed his pass and went on through the doors and down the steps to the ground level where, he knew, the flood coordinators worked. At once, he was conscious of the unusual atmosphere in the great building. Men and women were hurrying past with anxious, purposeful expressions; some carrying messages and documents. Others, mostly the younger men, were moving chairs and furniture in order to prepare the committee and conference rooms for their emergency planning meetings. Instead of the usual, almost leisurely, pace, there was an air of urgency.

A desk had been set up outside the coordinator's office and a clerk noted down Peter's name before allowing him to go through. Inside he met a scene of frantic activity. The desks, usually scattered in various directions in the open-plan office, were now pushed together into three or four groups with chairs set round them. They were occupied by the coordinators and liaison officers who, between them, were attempting to answer a score of constantly ringing telephones, while at the same time they were themselves dialing other numbers, as the city's emergency systems were progressively brought into action. Messengers went to and fro, passing situation reports and information requests between the groups. Behind the chairs and round the series of maps that had been erected stood numerous senior officials. Peter recognized police and military uniforms among the figures of the Council staff, and also men from the public services. For a moment he wondered whether the second stage of the alert had been called and the military services put on standby, but then he realized that these were only the first circle of liaison officers called into position, ready to handle their respective orders when they came.

Seeking out Carswell, Peter handed him the summary from the warning room and told him of Watson's instructions.

"Fine, you've done a good job, Peter, we're all very grateful. Take over that seat there will you?" Carswell indicated a nearby chair. "Your chief is on his way over."

There was no denying that under Carswell's direction the planning and preparation for this eventuality had been extremely thorough. In front of him lay a neat pile of papers containing clear, unambiguous instructions for each phase of the alert. There was also a special telephone book giving all the numbers to be used while the alert was on. In a few seconds he had established contact with the office he had just left.

"Hello, Phil," he said, recognizing the voice of one of his colleagues, who had arrived a few minutes before his departure. "It's Peter here, at County Hall Coordination. What's the latest situation?"

"Pretty much the same," was the reply, "there's still no change in the river gauges and Southend is still four feet below danger point, with the wind at force seven from the northwest. It doesn't seem to have veered yet. Harwich is beginning to have trouble. Waves breaking over the harbor wall in places. Winds force nine, gusting force ten, pressure nine hundred and seventy-two." He was evidently quoting from the tape. "The estimate at the moment is that the water will rise at least another foot. Much the same goes for Walton-on-the-Naze and Colchester. That's all since you left."

"Right, Phil," out of the corner of his eye Peter had seen Derek Thompson enter the room, "the chief has just arrived. I'll be needing a full situation report in a few minutes. They'll want to know whether to call the standby alert."

"O.K., Peter, we'll have that ready for you as soon as we can."

Peter scribbled down the figures and noted the time. It was now 8:11 a.m.

*　　*　　*

The first person Derek saw when he entered the County Hall Control Room was Miles Wendoser. The councilor was standing in the center of a group of senior officials who were examining a large map of the east coast. On seeing him, Derek groaned inwardly; he was only too well aware of Wendoser's attitude towards the flood alert program; in the past the two men had crossed swords on several occasions.

"Ah, Derek, glad you've been able to get here." The speaker was a large, heavily built man with a sparse amount of hair above a rudely-veined face. His name was Francis Whyte, and he was the chief executive of the Greater London Council, with the title of Director General. "We would all like your opinion on the situation at the moment."

He motioned Derek forward and the group gave way to allow him through. He saw at a glance that most of the top men were present, besides the Director General and Miles. There was Carswell, the Room Controller, a police liaison officer, and another councilor, in a blue suit, called Hogarth. They looked at him expectantly.

"It seems simple to me," he replied. "A major storm passed into the North Sea last night from the Atlantic and has traveled down the east coast reaching Lowestoft. Wind damage has been extremely severe, judging from the few reports we've seen, and several places have experienced flooding. The most important factor is that a storm surge appears to be running and if it continues at the present rate, it will come up the river estuary on the high tide." He paused, waiting for a reaction to his words. The others looked at him seriously.

"So you consider we should go ahead with the alert?" the Director General asked.

Derek stared at him with surprise. "Why, yes, of course," he answered. "What possible reasons can there be for not doing so? The system is designed for just this situation."

"Don't you think the storm will blow itself out?" It was Carswell who spoke. "We would normally expect the danger to pass during the next two hours."

"Yes, maybe it will," Derek answered, "but it doesn't alter the fact that at this moment the danger is still very much with us, and we can't afford to take the risk. What happens if the storm doesn't fade and the surge keeps coming?"

There was a moment's silence, then the Director General spoke again.

"So what you are saying is that the next phase of the alert should now be called," he repeated slowly, "that we should put the emergency services on standby?"

"Yes," Derek replied succinctly.

"Tell me something, Derek," Miles spoke for the first time, "have you discussed the situation with Bracknell? I thought not," he said disdainfully, "but it so happens that I have had a talk with the chief forecaster." He paused to let his listener absorb the full impact of his words. "It seems that this storm you are so worried about has already started to slacken. Wind velocity is falling, pressure and temperature are both up. Even the coastal flooding appears to have ceased." Derek faced him angrily. The sight of Miles' cool, elegantly dressed figure and the air of sophisticated arrogance with which he treated those around him, never failed to annoy him.

"Bracknell can't possibly be in a position to be sure of what the storm will do yet," he said tightly. "We all know that conditions can vary widely even near a storm center. At the moment there simply isn't the data available to make an accurate prediction. As for the flooding, the reason for the apparent falling off in the report is because the surge has moved on to the East Anglia coast, where the sea defenses are the strongest in the country. After the '53 disaster, the walls were raised there for hundreds of miles and many of them rebuilt altogether. They can withstand surges of water that London couldn't begin to cope with."

"Derek," the Director General interrupted soothingly, "don't you think you may be overestimating the risk. We've had these storms before after all?" There was a murmur of agreement from the others.

"The winds over Scotland, last night, were the fiercest ever experienced in the country," Derek replied. "Everything; seas, waves, pressure, wind velocity, temperature readings, were far in excess of what was expected. None of that matters to us. All we have to worry about is whether a surge has been caused. It has and it's now less than three hours away and the winds driving it are still in the region of force ten. All right, I agree, they probably will die out, or veer away, and the surge won't reach us, but if it does, remember four feet of water might come over the walls."

"Yes, but we have surges every year. They never amount to anything, just a lot of false alarms, if you ask me." It was Hogarth, the councilor, who spoke. "Why should this one be any different?"

"This time may be exactly like all the others, but in case it isn't, I think we should follow the plans. They were drawn up for exactly this kind of emergency."

Miles spoke again. "There are other factors to consider this time," he said smoothly. There was a pause. No one spoke. Derek looked from one to the others.

"What other factors?" he demanded.

"What Mr. Wendoser means," the Director General explained, "is that there is a state visit today by the President of the United States. It will be difficult to call a full alert, without causing considerable disruption."

"That's certainly true for us," the police officer interjected. "Virtually every man we've got will be on crowd control and security duty. I doubt if we could cope with a flood warning as well."

There was a point in this. Derek had to concede that he had forgotten about the visit. The government would be unlikely to allow the alert to interfere with the President's reception, yet the absence of police participation rendered much of the procedure pointless. It was the police who carried out the tasks such as sounding the warning sirens, street patrolling, the provision of clearways for official vehicles and their radio network formed a major part of the communications coverage for the city, which the military and civilian networks could, at best, only supplement.

"The decision as to whether to allow the police and other services to join the alert is a governmental one, but I don't think that should stop us from calling the second phase. At least, then we will be in a position to take action if the flood does strike," he said.

"And I think we should consult with senior members of the government before we make a move, which might prove highly embarrassing," Miles replied shortly.

The Director General had lowered his massive head on to his chest and was staring at the floor, deep in thought.

"We shall have to compromise. We'll commence the next phase of the alert," he said at last, when he looked up. "The staff have been called out, and the control room made ready. There is not sufficient evidence of an easing in the weather to stand them down yet, so we must continue. We will place the emergency services on standby and activate the Kingsway flood control room. Apart from any other considerations, to do that will lessen the risk of confusion with the arrangements for the President's visit. But I'm afraid," he said, with a glance at Derek, "that we will have to accept that the police will not join in, unless the danger becomes considerably greater. In the meantime, I shall ask Miles Wendoser if he will contact the government departments concerned to discuss with them the best way of dealing with the situation."

Thus it was that the second stage of the alarm, the emergency services standby, was issued at 8:17 a.m.

*   *   *

The dawn had seen the start of a massive search for the trawler *Ross* in the sea off the Firth of Forth. The Royal Naval destroyer *Lowestoft* which had been quartering the area with her radar for the past two hours had so far been unable to locate her. The savage weather meant that any kind of visual search was virtually impossible; the waves were still running in excess of forty feet, easily sufficient to hide a boat the size of the

Ross completely. The North Berwick lifeboat had been launched and had been forced to turn back but a R.A.F. Nimrod antisubmarine search aircraft of Coastal Command took off at first light to fly reconnaissance patterns over the *Ross'* last radioed position.

On board, the situation had deteriorated during the night. The most serious development had been the discovery that the twisting motion of the waves had strained the propeller shaft, and twice before dawn broke, the engine had seized and stopped. On the second occasion it had taken nearly an hour to free it, during which time the *Ross* had rolled helplessly before the storm. The skipper and crew had done what they could do prevent her from broaching, by trailing warps over the stern, while down below the engineer and his mate cursed and prayed as they reassembled the drive shaft.

Every one of them knew that if they should lose power completely it would only be a matter of time before the *Ross* succumbed to the huge seas running down upon her from the north, which already threatened to capsize her or simply force her under by the sheer weight of water crashing down on her deck.

All they could do was to keep transmitting distress signals in the hope that before long the coastguard and rescue service would be able to get an accurate fix on their position and direct other vessels to their aid. But the nearest available ship, a Swedish freighter only fifteen miles away, estimated that in the current weather conditions it would take her seven hours to reach them.

Chapter Three

Derek was standing by the window in the flood control room, staring at the blank wall of the building opposite. It was typical, he thought wearily, that this of all rooms should be denied a view of the river. The well-meaning people who had set up the warning system were honest and hard working, but to all of them it was still only an exercise. Diagrams, plans, communications charts, telephone messages. They had been through the routine a hundred times, but scarcely any one of them had any real idea of what a tidal surge would do to their city. Most of them pictured a few streets knee deep in water, some flooded cellars being pumped out, a couple of days' confusion and then everything would return to normal.

None of the staff at present engaged in academic conversations with similar people in other offices about ambulance movements, stores of blankets and food, the supply of official armbands and similar vital issues, had any conception of what they might be faced with.

Back in New Zealand, when he was young, Derek had seen a village that had been inundated when a nearby river burst its banks and sent a wall of water crashing through its center. Afterwards, it had been impossible to see where some of the houses had once been. The village had had to be abandoned, and was remembered only as the graveyard where twenty-seven people had died in less than four minutes.

Sixty square miles of London would be flooded if the Thames overflowed, and in that area were the homes and offices of one and a half million people. There were also fifteen power stations, fifty-six telecommunications buildings, seventy underground stations and half a dozen hospitals. There were sewage plants, pumping stations, generators, computers, gas mains and power lines. The water would stretch from Acton Vale and Shepherd's Bush to Barnes Common, from Earl's Court and Buckingham Palace to Clapham Junction. Lambeth, Camberwell, New Cross, Stratford, West Ham, Dagenham, Plumpstead Marshes, mile upon mile of streets, homes, factories, offices, shops. In some of these streets the water would be nearly twenty feet deep.

The damage to property would be catastrophic; its effects radiating far beyond the boundaries of London. The south of England would certainly be paralyzed for weeks, perhaps months. Half of its electricity supply came from the London generating stations; the southern region trains relied totally on electricity from the city. Plant and stocks normally supplied to a vast range of firms throughout the country would be lost. Unemployment, whether directly or indirectly caused by the flood, would be appallingly high, as companies fell into liquidation.

Nobody had wanted even to hazard a guess at the possible casualties. A thousand, five thousand, fifteen, fifty! There had been over one hundred and fifty dead in Canvey Island alone in 1953 when the walls failed. There must be thousands of old and infirm men and women who would never be found and taken to safety within the sixty minutes between the final alarm and the coming of the tide up the river. If the winds held, they could keep the surge piled up in the estuary for hours, perhaps even days, blocking the escape of the outgoing tide. Even when the river did finally retreat, huge areas of ponded floodwater would remain trapped behind the walls where they might stay for weeks. Cut off from all aid; wet, cold, without food, power and some without drinking water; the weak, the old, the sick and the very young would have little chance. The casualties would be high enough even without any major disaster incidents and God knows, there were potentially plenty of them. The collapse of a wall, a fire or explosion; in a modern city such as London, there were lethal menaces in every street.

The order, putting the emergency services on alert, was in many ways meaningless. As far as the ambulances and fire brigades were concerned, it simply meant that they prepared to remove all their vehicles from the flood zone. For the police and military forces, the same applied, except for those few personnel necessary who would remain behind and attempt to warn an unsuspecting public that the Thames was about to fall upon their city. For the most part though, the rescue units were to be pulled back out of danger so that they would at least be able to give help when the water had begun to recede. While the flood rolled inland the people were on their own, and with twelve hundred police on security duty that was now more true than ever before.

Remembering that he had not yet told Georgina where he was, he walked over to a desk and dialed his home number. When she answered, he told her briefly what was going on.

"Oh, hell!" she said crossly, echoing the sentiments of numerous others that day, "does that mean I can't go into the studio today? I've got to, there's a very important client coming in this morning. I told you about him."

Derek sighed. Georgina had a share in a studio housed in a former wine vault, near the Barbican, which had now been turned into a craft center. She went in most days to work in stained glass. A client, any client, was a big event for her.

"Look," he said, "call me again at nine o'clock and I'll tell you if it's safe to go or not. With luck the alert will have been canceled by then."

"O.K.," Georgina replied, "will the house be safe?" she asked anxiously. "I mean is there anything I ought to do?"

"You'll be quite all right where you are." This was true, the Thompsons' house was well above the highest level the water would reach. "If there is a flood, you may have some trouble with the drains, but most of that should be in the garden at the back. Otherwise you should keep your gas, electricity and water. There's a camping gaz stove in the cupboard under the stairs, if you need it."

"What about the children? Should I stop them going to school? They could stay here, or come into the studio with me even."

"No, no," Derek told her at once. He had a vision of Georgina wandering about in the flooded streets, with two children clinging desperately to her. "Their schools will be perfectly safe as well. You may have to walk up and collect them if there are no buses, but that's all. Make sure you call me before you go into the studio, though."

Georgina, on the whole, sounded more amused and excited than worried, he thought as he rang off, which was probably just as well. He looked at his watch. It was time to check how Johnny was getting on on the Isle of Dogs.

* * *

In the final analysis, after all the planning had been done, all the central committees set up, the coordinators chosen, the lines of communication laid down, when the warning system had been designed, and the special equipment installed, the vast bulk of the work, both of making the ordinary people aware of the peril that was threatening them and of giving them aid when it happened, fell upon the local borough councils. There were twenty-eight and the river ran through sixteen of them. For the purpose of the emergency they were divided into groups of five or six, so that each borough with a river frontage, which was therefore likely to suffer damage, would be supported by neighboring boroughs which would not be affected. Each borough had its control room, which would report to its group control, which in turn would contact the Greater London Council nerve center.

The planners had decided, quite rightly, that the people most at risk, apart from those in the obvious places, like underground trains, for whom special arrangements had been made, were the elderly and the sick. Each council had drawn up comprehensive lists, which were frequently updated, of all those unlikely to receive or understand the alert, or unable to respond to it if they did. It was this problem that was bothering David Cox.

Dave was a social worker for Wandsworth Council. He was a tall, thin, ungainly young man of twenty, and still more than a little bewildered by the morning's events. At half past seven the telephone had rung, just as he was shaving, and a voice he did not know had told him to get down to the borough offices at once. This he had done and had found himself in a scene of wild confusion. Despite the efforts of the emergency planning officer, who was probably better at his job than most of his opposite numbers in other boroughs, it was taking a long time to make the preparations to meet the situation. Dave was sent down to the basement, where a control room had been established among the boilers, and told to distribute sheafs of instructions. Then he was ordered to stop doing that and report to a ground floor conference hall for orders. Notices were appearing on doorways bearing cryptic titles that he had not seen before. Several of these had been wrongly placed, adding to the confusion. There were, he noticed, two signs pointing in different directions for "transport control". Eventually he made his way to the correct room, where he found a large group of other social workers and welfare officers, all equally bewildered. After a few minutes, during which everyone speculated busily on what was happening, and what they would have to do, the senior welfare officer entered to address them.

"You have been told in the past what to do, but in case there are any doubts I will recap," he said, speaking quickly. "You will each be given a list of names and addresses, in the areas you normally cover. These belong to old or handicapped people who we consider to be at special risk. If the final warning is given you will go to these addresses, tell the people what to do and make sure they understand. If they need help, you will either see that they get it from neighbors, provide it yourself or call control. It's going to be a long job and I'm afraid you won't have a lot of time." He paused. "Are there any questions?"

"Yes," said one person. "Do we stay with these people until they move to safety?"

"No," the officer shook his head. "No, I'm afraid there won't be time for that, you will not have more than an hour and a quarter at the outside, and you'll find you have a lot of addresses to cover. Your job is only to warn and, if possible, ask the neighbor to help, otherwise, as I said, call control here. O.K.? Right, now collect your lists from the ladies at the back of the room."

The organization here was remarkable, Dave

thought, as he collected his list. It contained several typed pages stapled together. As he moved away, a supervisor approached him.

"Cox, you have a special problem," he was told, "you have to cover addresses in the South Battersea area. That's part of what we call the pond. Do you know why?" Dave shook his head. The supervisor smiled grimly. "The ground in that area ranges from sea level to five feet above it," he said, "while the river banks and much of the surrounding area is a good deal higher, which means," he went on, "that the houses and flats in that area could have twelve to fifteen feet of water round them for a week or ten days."

Dave gaped with surprise, "I never realized it was that bad," he exclaimed.

"No," replied the supervisor, "nor do most people, but there it is. Now, as well as checking all the people on the lists, I want you to visit the caretaker of each of the tower blocks there. They have been given leaflets like this." He handed Dave a sheet of paper headed "Thames Flooding", which was covered with instructions. "The caretakers have been contacted by telephone and told to give these out, if the sirens go. You must make sure they have grasped that."

"Do we start now?" Dave asked him. He was anxious to telephone his wife and let her know what was going on.

"No, we can't start until we are sure the flood is coming. You will set off at about nine-thirty, ready to begin when the sirens sound at ten; if they sound that is. In the meantime, do what the others are doing; check your lists to see if anyone has been missed."

One of the names on Dave Cox's list was that of Oliver Pole. Oliver Pole was an old and very sick man who lived with his wife on the first floor of a council block in North Battersea. He was ill with asbestosis, which he had caught during a lifetime's work in a large asbestos plant. Most of the day, Pole sat in a chair and listened to the radio. He seldom went out, except in the summer, when it was very hot and his wife would hold his arm, as he gasped and staggered along the road to the park, where they would sit on a bench together. Pole's symptoms had first appeared six years ago, but he had kept on working to retirement age, by which time he was very ill indeed. The union had taken up his case, along with several others, and now, after protracted negotiations, the company was paying a pension of nine pounds a week, a paltry sum and one which had never been enough to enable his wife to stop working even after her seventieth birthday.

Their flat consisted of one bedroom and a sitting room, with a tiny kitchen leading off it, and though they had little furniture, they were comfortable. The flat was warm and certainly more pleasant than some of the other places they had lived in. The block too, gaunt and functional though it was, suffered less from the problems usually found with such buildings. The Poles were friendly with the occupants of the flat next door, a young technician with the electricity board and his family, who occasionally looked in to see how the old couple were; they also knew several of the other residents.

Mrs. Pole worked for two mornings a week cleaning the Thompsons' house, for which she was paid five pounds a week by Georgina. The work was something in the nature of a charity, since Mrs. Pole was really too old and slow to accomplish much. Most of her time was spent drinking tea and complaining about the lack of attention paid to them by their only daughter, who had gone to live in Doncaster and who never wrote. Georgina did the housework herself usually, but she was fond of the old woman, so Mrs. Pole continued to turn up every Tuesday and Friday at nine o'clock.

As she fussed about making Pole's breakfast for him and seeing that he took the medicine the doctor had prescribed, they discussed the news they had listened to on the radio at eight o'clock. The major story of the day concerned the forthcoming visit of the American president to London and the preparations being made for his reception. Following this came details of renewed violence in Ulster and a lengthy feature on the Common Market agriculture talks being held in Brussels. Only at the end of the bulletin was there any mention of the storm:

"This morning Scotland is recovering from a night of the worst gales for over a century. In the Orkneys and Shetland Isles there have been winds of up to one hundred and thirty miles per hour. The crew of the ten thousand ton vessel *Southern City* were rescued after she had gone aground off the Butt of Lewis in the Outer Hebrides. All sea and air services between the islands and the mainland have ceased. In the North Sea men have been evacuated from a number of drilling rigs, in the face of mountainous waves, leaving only skeleton crews aboard. A helicopter is reported missing with two crew members off Aberdeen and coastguards have ruled out a search for survivors, until the weather moderates. Many districts are still without electricity due to broken power lines.

"In the early hours of this morning the storm moved into the north of England and there are reports of widespread damage, especially in coastal areas. In Durham a man was killed, when he was struck by falling timber."

The news was followed by the weather forecast.

"Gales are officially forecast for nearly all districts of the British Isles. In the north and northeast these will be particularly severe, but it is expected that these will die out during the course of the day. Rain will occur in most areas, with the possibility of hail in places."

"That sounds nasty," said Mrs. Pole, as she cleared away the breakfast, "I 'ope it doesn't come down 'ere."

"No, it'll be all right, dear," her husband reassured her, he coughed and settled himself more comfortably in his chair. "Forecast said it'd clear up in the a'ternoon." Mrs. Pole said no more on the subject and shortly afterwards she left the flat.

The entrance hall to the block was dirty and institutional. Its paint was badly cracked and there had been no attempt to brighten it up or make it more cheerful. The only form of decoration, apart from a notice board bearing a faded list of regulations, was a tattered poster, torn and scribbled over. Across the top was written in red: LONDON TIDAL FLOOD WARNING. Underneath it said in large black letters: YOU ARE IN A FLOOD RISK AREA. The poster gave instructions on what to do in an emergency. People were advised to warn their neighbors, get up to the first floor level or higher if possible, and listen to the announcements on the radio or television. "Above all," the poster urged, "do not try to travel away from the flood."

Mrs. Pole had never looked at this poster and was not even aware of its existence. In this respect, she was like everybody else in the building.

In the hall she met Eileen, the dark-haired girl who lived in the flat next to her own, coming in carrying a bag of shopping and her small daughter.

"You're early today, dear," Mrs. Pole remarked, "is everything going all right?"

"Oh, yes, luv," Eileen said, as she lowered the child to the ground. "I've just been to the shops. My Jerry's been called in to work early today. Somethin' to do wiv flooding, 'e said. Real nuisance, it was."

"He works with the electricity, don't 'e?" asked Mrs. Pole.

"That's right, luv," replied Eileen, "on the power station at Bankside. Must be gettin' on," she went on, "I've got a load of washing to do."

"Yes, dear, you do that. Goin' to be wet and nasty today, anyway."

They parted and Mrs. Pole set off, dismissing the

weather from her mind. This was mainly due to the delay in calling the emergency services standby. The order had been passed to the B.B.C. at 8:17 a.m., to enable them to prepare the broadcast emergency bulletins at ten o'clock. By the time the message had been received and handed to the program controller, and the gravity of the situation appreciated, the eight o'clock news and its accompanying forecast had finished. Consequently, these programs contained only the brief and unalarming references to the storm, which had been heard by the Poles. All over the country, this situation was repeated, as hundreds of thousands of men and women set off for the day's work, totally oblivious of what was to come. Miles Wendoser's actions were already having their effect.

* * *

With the calling of the standby alert, the decision was taken to activate the Greater London Council's secret flood coordination center, housed thirty feet underground, in part of the government's deep shelter tunnels in Holborn Kingsway. It was not the most convenient place for the purpose, but it was, at least, guaranteed to be waterproof.

The move was carried out in stages, so as to maintain close contact with the various groups. Peter went across in the second contingent. They were transported in buses and entered the tunnel through raised grilles in the center of the road, which gave access to flights of concrete steps. Inside, the control room consisted of a set of prefabricated offices erected in the tunnels. The main room was square and painted white. Its walls, like those of its counterpart at County Hall, were hung with maps and charts. Desks were arranged in a t-shape in the center, with others in the corners of the room. Rows of telephones with key and lamp switching units covered the surfaces. It had been decided to rely on the telephone network for as long as possible, and only use the radio as a last resort, when the cables failed.

A separate office housed the comprehensive wireless equipment manned by the army, police and Greater London Council, each of whom had their own separate networks.

Representatives from the army, water authority, police, London Transport and other organizations were moving to their appointed places.

Peter took his seat at one of the sets of corner desks facing the central table. Jo Pierce, the river engineer, whose place he had taken earlier, was already sitting there and greeted Peter warmly.

"What do you make of it?" he asked quietly, under cover of the noise and confusion, as the newcomers settled in. "Do you think we will get flooding?"

"The chief seems to think so," replied Peter. "Apparently there was a terrific argument because he wanted to sound the alert earlier."

At that moment Carswell called the room to order.

"No talking, please, except on official matters," he ordered, "and please keep your telephone conversations as brief as possible. We only have a limited number of lines and we have to make the best possible use of them."

The keyboard light started to flash and click rapidly in front of Peter, as the staff in the warning room began to route their calls through to the control center. In between calls Jo leaned over to him. "Where do you live?" he asked under his breath.

"Hammersmith," Peter answered, "Rylston Road."

"Ground floor?"

"No, first floor flat. What about you?"

"Basement in Fulham. That's why I was late, had to stop to take the carpets up. Only just bought the damned things."

*   *   *

Georgina Thompson had grown accustomed, during the course of her marriage, to having her husband called out in the middle of the night to return muddy and exhausted late the following evening.

For their first two years together, Derek had been building a hydroelectric scheme in Kashmir and there there had been a crisis almost every night. Even now, in London, where he held greater seniority, it was necessary at times. For the children, however, his absence was still a source of interest.

"Where did Dad go this time?" inquired her son Jake, between mouthfuls of cornflakes.

"The East End somewhere," she replied, searching her brain to recall what Derek had said as he left. "Part of the river bank collapsed."

"Like the dyke in that story about Holland and the boy?" Jake was eight years old and the tale had seized his imagination.

"Not quite so big, but that's the general idea. You might even see a little water in the streets today, if you're lucky," Georgina told him.

"Where?" he asked, "and how deep?" His sister Sarah looked up from a comic she was reading. She was six years old, with her brother's fair hair and blue eyes.

"Yes, where?" she demanded.

"Oh, only a little bit down by the river. It may not happen, but if it does, I'll take you down to have a look before tea. Now, hurry up, or you'll be late for school."

"Is this the flooding Dad talks about?" asked Jake seriously.

"Yes," Georgina answered, with some surprise. "It is."

"In that case," her son announced triumphantly, "the water will be fifteen feet deep. He told me so. Not in our road," he added, "only in the bits where the poor people live."

"Like Mrs. Pole?" suggested Sarah.

"Yes," said her brother, licking his spoon, "she's poor."

Georgina bundled them out of the door and off to school. Her children, she reflected, were more alive to distinctions of class and wealth than she had imagined. Perhaps it would not be such a bad idea to move away from London. There was a noise outside, the door opened again and Mrs. Pole walked in, breathing hard and wearing a green coat that Georgina had bought for her.

"Why, Mrs. Pole," she exclaimed, "I didn't expect you today, with all this talk of flooding."

"Flooding! What flooding? I ain't seen no flooding," said the old woman suspiciously. Georgina explained what she meant. When she had finished, Mrs. Pole looked upset.

"When's it coming?" she asked, her fingers clutching nervously at her bag. "P'raps I ought to go back. My 'usband doesn't like the damp. Makes 'im cough awful."

"It probably won't happen, Mrs. Pole. It's nothing to worry about, really." But once the idea had taken root, Mrs. Pole was not to be persuaded.

"Look," said Georgina kindly, when she realized the hopelessness of the task, "why don't you go back home. Take today off and stay with your husband. I'll still pay you, of course." She knew how important a day's wages were to the Pole household.

Mrs. Pole hesitated and dithered, but eventually agreed that it would be better.

"It's only on account of Pole, you understand. It's fer 'im I'm worried," she insisted. Georgina let her out and sat down to telephone Derek. If he said the danger was past, there was plenty of time for her to catch a tube and be in the studio by 9:45 a.m.

*   *   *

Having called the emergency services standby, it was now necessary to begin releasing details of the situation to the general public. Shortly after the message had been given to the B.B.C., Radio London contacted the Ministry of Agriculture, asking for a story on the flood danger. In doing so they were following the system in force the previous year, when the warning room had been under the control of this department, which was housed in Horseferry Road, whereas at the time of the disaster the Greater London Council had assumed control of the entire warning apparatus. This mistake caused some delay, nevertheless they eventually got through to the press office at the Kingsway control room and were given a report on the circumstances. This report was featured in their nine o'clock news bulletin, which referred to "possible flooding along the Thames in central London", and advised people to stay tuned in to their radios for further news and to listen for the sirens. At the same time the B.B.C. broadcast a similar story, but advised listeners that the danger was still only theoretical and that there was no assurance that the flooding would occur.

London Transport had already begun to withdraw stock from the danger zone and place warning notices outside the underground stations and delays in services, were also being extended to the buses, where inspectors were posting signs at bus stops and warning passengers. These factors, taken together with the broadcasts, managed to ensure that quite a large number of people became acquainted with the alert at approximately nine o'clock, though few of them had any idea of the scale of the threat.

Unfortunately it was typical of behavior in such circumstances that virtually everyone continued to go about their business, as though nothing was going to happen.

*　　*　　*

By nine o'clock the surge had advanced as far as Walton-on-the-Naze and was less than one hour from

Southend, the gateway to the Thames. During this last hour it had caused considerable havoc in Harwich, and inland as far as Colchester, where the Colne had burst its banks. The overflow had swept down on to a bungalow estate and had carried several of them away. Three people unable to get out, had been drowned as the water had trapped them. Essex police, alarmed by a number of breaches in the county's sea defenses, had begun advising residents in Canvey Island, the scene of the disaster a quarter of a century previously when one hundred and fifty people had died, to leave their homes and seek refuge on higher ground. At this stage, the full extent of the damage in many parts was not yet clear, so badly had communications been disrupted. Fallen trees and telegraph lines, and waves surging three and four miles inland in places, had totally cut off some sections of the East Anglian coast.

* * *

Miles returned to the control room in County Hall feeling thoroughly pleased with himself. His talk with the personal assistant to the Cabinet Minister concerned had been most satisfactory in every way, he reflected. His views had been in exact accordance with those of the Minister, who had been horror-stricken at the thought of curtailing the President's welcome on the grounds that the police guarding him were required elsewhere. The Minister had appreciated the way in which the business was being handled and would no doubt wish to thank Miles personally at a later date.

The only possible way for this clever exercise in public relations to go wrong would be for the city of London to be inundated, and this Miles believed to be extremely remote.

All but a few of the room's occupants had now left to man the Kingsway control room, taking with them their maps and the vast array of instruction pamphlets, emergency telephone listings and strategic diagrams. A skeleton staff remained behind, answering the telephone calls that still came through. One of them looked up, saw Miles and called to him.

"Mr. Wendoser, sir, have you seen Mr. Thompson in the building? It's his wife on the line."

"I think he's gone back to Great George Street," Miles replied. Mentally he recalled the chief engineer's wife as he had seen her at a cocktail party: slender and blonde-haired. She had been extremely pretty. On an impulse he reached for the receiver.

"Pass her to me, I'll talk to her," he said.

"Good heavens!" Georgina exclaimed in surprise, when he spoke to her. "How did I get you, Mr. Wendoser, I was trying to reach Derek. He said he would let me know if it was all right to go out yet, because of the flooding," she added.

"My dear girl," Miles responded patronisingly, "you've no need to worry at all. Of course it's safe to go out. There was never any real danger. I haven't even issued a full alarm."

"Thank God for that," Georgina replied with relief. "Now I can go into the studio. If you see Derek, tell him I rang will you?"

"Of course I will, but you know you really must persuade your husband to bring you round for a drink one day soon," Miles smiled smoothly. Georgina laughed politely. She did not like Miles in the least, but it was not a good idea to be rude to him.

With a sardonic smile, Miles replaced the receiver. Despite the chief engineer's stubborn insistence on the seriousness of the flood peril, even Derek Thompson's own wife had preferred to accept the true reading of the facts that he, Miles, had proposed. There was a kind of salutory justice in it.

*   *   *

Georgina wasted no time, pausing only to collect a book of sketches to show her prospective client she hurried out of the house and took a taxi as far as the underground station at Gloucester Road. Inside the booking hall a board had been displayed with a chalked message advising travelers that services might be cut because there was a risk of flooding from the Thames. Georgina did not notice it. She was thinking that it was a pity she had not telephoned County Hall before sending Mrs. Pole away. After waiting for a short while she boarded a Circle Line train running eastwards beneath the embankment.

*   *   *

Derek walked back to Great George Street, his thoughts preoccupied with the recent confrontation with Miles Wendoser. He felt annoyed at the outcome, but not surprised. As yet the authorities refused to accept that the city was facing a real threat. They would seize any opportunity to put off admitting the unpalatable facts. All the talk about the risk of a false alarm, the need to avoid panic, was merely an excuse for postponing what, to Derek's mind, was an inevitable decision. He considered it absolutely necessary to issue a full alert to the public.

In the office entrance, the porter had hung an "out of order" sign on the lift. Derek climbed the stairs, mapping out in his mind the order of things to be done to meet the emergency. Under the new phase of the alert he was required to send out engineers equipped with portable radios to patrol strategic stretches of the river, keeping an eye on the water level and sending back regular reports. In this way the warning room could build up an accurate picture of the state of the river as a whole. Finding the men for these patrols meant taking them off other jobs at the very moment when they were most wanted. Johnny Easton in particular needed reinforcements urgently.

Liz was waiting for him in his office. "This is the latest reading from Teddington Weir," she said, handing him a slip of paper. "Brian Watson's talked to them and they say the flow is one of the highest they've known and there's no chance of it letting up."

"What about the radio patrols, are they ready to go out?" he asked her, as he read the details. The meter at Teddington provided information on the amount of water draining into their main river from the upstream tributaries. If the flow was high, water coming in from the sea could not escape upstream.

"They'll be ready to go in fifteen minutes," Liz said. "We've had to close down the work on the Richmond job to get them through. Will you brief them, or shall I get one of the others to do it?"

"I thought we'd have to do that," he agreed. It was annoying because it meant there would be complaints later. Richmond was subject to local flooding on a minor scale, when the river was running high, as it was now. For some months the engineers had been laboring to construct additional storm drains in the district.

"I'll talk to them myself," he said. "I suppose you know about the state visit?"

"The American president, you mean? Yes, I was going to watch him go past."

"County Hall can think of nothing else. Half the Council must be lunching with him. You'd think Jehovah was coming with the ten commandments. I pointed out they might have to vary his route a little and Miles Wendoser hit the roof."

"Does he take the usual route?" asked Liz.

"For the final leg, at least. Westminster, Whitehall, up the Mall to the Palace. Flags flying, bands playing, the Household Cavalry, Coldstream Guards, crowds of sightseers, the full works. Only trouble is the timing. He's due at the Palace at eleven-fifteen. His last half mile will be under water."

"That must be why Larkin rang. He said he'd call back." Commander Larkin was head of H8 division of the Metropolitan Police, the division responsible for the maintenance of public order. Larkin's men took most of the load under the flood alert, but they were also dealing with the state visit. Derek decided to talk to him at once.

"How serious is it, do you think?" Larkin asked him when he got through a few moments later.

"Everybody keeps asking me the same questions," Derek replied with exasperation. "I'm not a fortune teller. Any fool can see the situation looks bad at the moment. There's a hurricane blowing out there, or has nobody realized it?"

"Easy, Derek," Larkin's voice came calmly back. Derek could picture him sitting at his desk, a large man with a pale heavy face and small bright eyes. Larkin never got excited. He dealt with emergencies every day and treated them all in the same phlegmatic way. "We just need to be sure that's all. My boys are badly stretched as it is. You know what it's like on these occasions. If you don't have a uniform every ten feet, some maniac gets overconfident and starts throwing things."

Derek took a deep breath. "Listen," he said carefully, "this state drive is going to have to be called off, unless you want the President and the Queen to swim back to the Palace. You know damn well how important your men are in these alerts. Christ, we're going to need every officer you've got and more as it is. So let's cut out this junk about Guards of Honor in blue helmets and get them out on the streets."

There was a momentary silence on the other end of the line, then Larkin replied: "The word here is that the storm will blow itself out during the next two hours. According to Bracknell the wind is veering already."

"Jesus Christ," Derek clenched his teeth in anger, "all Bracknell have said is that the wind may be veering. They still don't know if it will actually do so. They're playing safe because they got their balls chewed off for jumping the gun last time."

"Well, that may be so, Derek," said the policeman,

"but I've been ordered not to alter my program until we get a clearer indication."

"By which time," Derek remarked coldly, "it will be too late to do anything."

"It's not as bad as that," Larkin said. "We just want more evidence before we make fools of ourselves with the Americans. It's not my decision," he added. "It's the big chief's upstairs. You know that."

"Yeah, I know," Derek said resignedly. "I'll come back to you as soon as I get definite news."

He had hardly put the telephone down before it rang again. It was Johnny Easton. "Johnny," he said, "I was just about to call you. How's it coming along?"

"Bad news, I'm afraid," came the reply. Derek listened, as in a few short sentences the young engineer told him about the trapped man. "My boys are trying to dig him out now," he said. "Trouble is that the bank's had to wait while we do it. I've asked the police and Council for assistance but it's taking time. What's the latest on the weather front?"

"No improvement so far. You had better assume for the time being that there's an emergency in force, though I seem to be the only one to realize it so far." Johnny gave a chuckle.

"The President's visit?" he said, "I guessed that might cause trouble."

"You guessed right," Derek said grimly. "How much longer do you need to get the bank completed?"

"There's at least another two hours' work to be done," was the immediate answer. "Chief, unless you can let me have another team, there isn't a hope in hell of being finished. This tramp is buried beneath the entire building. They're having to use the excavator to shift the stuff."

"It might be better to finish the bank first. If the water comes in again, he'll probably drown. At least with the bank in place, you could carry on digging behind it."

"He'll drown anyway, if we wait," Johnny told him. "Water is draining down to where he's stuck all the time. I've put a pump in, but it's impossible to get at the worst of it. I'm worried that what's left of the ruin may collapse further. They're sending us a mobile crane, which will help."

"Johnny," Derek spoke earnestly, "I want your men back on the bank as soon as possible. I don't believe those sandbags will hold in the breach, and if they go suddenly, you could all be caught in the burst."

"I'll do my best," Johnny assured him. "Just keep me posted on the surge, will you?"

Liz had assembled a dozen junior engineers to send out on bank patrol. Derek found them waiting for him in the main office discussing the news excitedly. It was easy to see, he realized, that to these young men, an alert, with its release from the day to day run of humdrum activities, was something to look forward to. He found himself hoping that none of them would be called upon to perform their tasks in earnest.

"You all know what this is about," he addressed them from the front of the room. "So I shan't need to go over the details again. You've been briefed often enough. Draw your radios and get off to your areas as quickly as you can. When you arrive, check in to this station and with your local control room as well. You've been given the frequencies. Then examine the banks and walls for any signs of obvious weakness and report them. I want any rise in the river level mentioned and you will radio in the moment there is any sign of overflowing, spillage or bank failure. Understood?"

"What do we do if flooding does take place, sir?" a serious-faced figure at the front of the room asked him. Derek recognized him as one of the new recruits taken on in the autumn.

"When you've radioed your report in, keep moving, watching the banks for as long as you can. If you see that overtopping is occurring along the full length of the banks, contact your local control room and ask for orders. They will have particular points they need continuous reports on. One final point," he went on, speaking to the whole room, "your job is to watch the river, not to try and warn the public. Other people will be doing that. It is vital that you stay in position and call when we need you. O.K. Off you go and good luck."

He watched them file out of the door and then returned to the warning room. At any moment the teleprinter would be receiving news from Harwich and Walton-on-the-Naze in Essex with details of the tide levels. An hour from now the surge might be starting its run up the Thames, and the Queen would be welcoming the American president.

Twenty minutes later he was on the telephone again. This time to Alan Carswell in the underground control room at Kingsway.

"Have you seen the tape from Harwich?" he asked the Coordinator. "It still looks serious to me."

"Yes, it was shown to me a moment ago. I see the winds are moderating. That's a good sign."

"They've lost some of their speed, if that's what you mean. Yes, I agree. The wind speed gauges at the port were showing an average of seventy miles an hour, but the sea is still very high. They have a six-foot increase on the predicted range. You realize what that indicates?"

"That there is a six-foot surge running down the coast. Yes, of course, I do," Carswell replied petulantly. "The question is, will it keep on going? Personally, I don't think so, but we are taking the usual precautions."

"What about the police, though? According to Larkin, his forces are still committed to security duty alone."

"I understand that a decision on the matter will be taken in the near future. Apparently the police can move to their emergency positions in a very short space of time, if necessary."

"I hope to God you're right," Derek told him.

Getting up from his desk, Derek walked to the window and looked out on to Westminster Square. The gothic spires of the Houses of Parliament stood out starkly against the dull sky. Beyond, the river appeared brown and inert; a tug was towing a line of barges upstream, leaving a trail of white foam. In the square, he noticed men were busy stringing flags from the white poles that had been put up earlier in the week; the stars and stripes alternating with the familiar Union Jack.

Flicking the switch on his desk intercom Derek called Liz back into the office.

"I'm going over to Kingsway in a couple of minutes," he told her. "There's nothing more I can do from here, so all messages can be switched through to me there. What will you do," he asked, "if we have to sound the alarm sirens?"

"Oh, I shall be all right," Liz smiled cheerfully, "my flat's in a danger zone, but I'm on the fourth floor, so I'll be in no danger. The water won't rise to more than a couple of feet round me anyway. You told me that yourself."

Derek was silent for a moment, then he said, "Why don't you stay with us tonight. Our house will be well above the flooding and Georgie and the children will look after you?"

"Please," he went on as Liz tried to protest, "to be honest, I would be very grateful if you did. I shan't be able to get back until very late, if at all today, and you would be company for Georgie. Besides, we'd both like to have you."

"That's very kind," Liz seemed genuinely pleased. "It would be nice for me as well," she admitted. "I didn't much fancy being marooned in Pimlico."

"Good, that's settled then." While he was speaking Derek had already dialed the number of his home, and now he waited, listening to the steady double ring. He turned thoughtfully back to Liz.

"No reply," he said quietly, "which is odd. Georgie said she would call me before she left. Still," he made a wry face, "she's never been one for following instructions. You'd better take my key, Liz, you may have to let yourself in."

There was one final action to be taken, before he left for the bunker, as he always thought of the Kingsway center. He went back to the warning room and called Watson over to him.

"I shall be in the control room from now on," he told him. "You're equipped to keep operating here, even if the flood does come, but if the sirens go, I want you to send home anyone you don't need and who can be sure of getting home within the hour. Understood?"

"Yes, sir," Watson nodded, "of course, quite a lot of the staff have tasks allocated to them in an emergency anyway."

"They'll stay, of course, and carry out their new duties, but the rest, clerks, secretaries and so on, they can be allowed to go, provided they can be sure of reaching their homes in time; remembering there will be no tubes at all, and no buses in the flood zone."

"I'll see to that," Watson replied. "I've assembled all the reports and data to go to Kingsway with you." He indicated a bulky file on a nearby table. Derek picked it up. He then realised that the rest of the room was watching him and turned to speak to them. "We are now as far into an alert as we have been before," he said quietly. "I still hope it will be called off before very much longer, but if it isn't a great many people will be relying on your work. I'm sure you won't let us down, and with a small degree of luck," he added more cheerfully, "I should be back here shortly."

*   *   *

Johnny's first action on crawling out of the ruins of the warehouse was to call his men over and set them to work shoveling away the loose rubble. They attacked the job eagerly, cutting through piles of debris to get at the center of the mound of great concrete slabs and iron beams which had buried the old tramp. Leaving Jack in charge, Johnny went over to his car and radioed the news of the discovery to the police.

"We'll need a crane of some sort, to lift the heaviest blocks, and another excavator would be a help too," he told the inspector on duty.

"I don't know where we can get hold of one of those in a hurry," the inspector replied.

"Come on, it's not difficult. Try a local contractor on the docks, they must have hundreds."

"I'll see what can be done," the inspector said doubtfully, "and I'll send some men down to help anyway."

"Yeah, but will you make sure you get that crane because all the men in the world won't shift these girders with their bare hands."

"Can't you tunnel underneath or dig round them?"

"Jesus," Johnny shouted into the telephone, with exasperation, "what do you think this is, a sand pit? If one of these things slips, it'll bring the whole lot down on top of the guy and crush him to death. So stop fretting and get me a crane." Cutting the connection without giving the man a chance to reply, he went back to where the men were still digging.

The girl had joined them. He could see her straining to move a heavy boulder.

"You can be more help to me," he told her. "I want to put a pump into that hole we crawled down. There's too much water draining in."

The girl accepted this without a word and followed him silently to the river edge. At the breach a pump was still chugging away strongly, throwing a continuous stream of water over the sandbag wall.

"Is it safe to take it from here?" she asked as he jumped down to get the bottom end of the pipe.

"No, it isn't particularly, but I've got nothing else right now, so it has to be this one. Here, grab hold." He handed her up the muddy pipe and climbed out again.

Even for someone as strongly built as he was, the pump was heavy. Together they made their way slowly back.

"What's your name?" he asked her, when they had reached half way and had paused for a second, for him to alter his grip.

"Tilly Mallinson," she said. "I live in Greenwich," she added inconsequentially.

"I'm Johnny Easton," he said, heaving the pump off the ground again, "from Notting Hill." The two looked at each other and smiled.

"Will it take long to get him out?" she asked.

He shook his head, "No, it shouldn't take more than an hour. He's not very deep, and once we can lift those heavy pieces off him, it'll be easy. We need a crane, though."

"That machine you've got there," she pointed, "the excavator, couldn't that be used instead?"

"No, it would help, but it needs something that can lift the big blocks clear away, otherwise it might bring the rest down on top of him."

They reached the building and, with the help of two of the men, dragged the heavy pump into position. Johnny crawled underneath the rubble again and placed the end of the suction pipe in the water that had gathered in the furthest recess. When he emerged his clothes were half-soaked and his face worried.

"What's wrong?" Tilly asked anxiously, her eyes wide.

"There's too much water in there, that's what's wrong," he replied shortly. "It must have been running in a lot faster than I thought. Start that pump up," he ordered. "See it keeps going."

Jack, the foreman, came over, his spade on his shoulder. His face red and beaded with sweat.

"I reckon if we get the tractor bucket underneath the edge of that slab we could shift it back and maybe try getting in from the rear. It would take some of the weight off the rest, even if we couldn't." He pointed, with a stubby finger, to a wall which was almost intact, that lay lengthways among the wreckage at the back of the remains. Johnny followed his gaze.

"It's a bloody great chunk, Jack," he said doubtfully, "but it's worth a try. If we can't push it up, we'll fix a cable round and try towing it off that way."

At that moment a white-painted police land rover appeared, lurching over the muddy ground towards them. It drew up and an officer in uniform got out, with half a dozen constables in rubber boots carrying spades and other tools.

"Mister Easton?" he said, as he came across to them, "Sergeant Denny. I've brought all the chaps I could spare. Where's the trapped man?"

"I'll show you," Johnny answered. "What about the crane? How long will that be?"

"They're bringing one out of the docks. It will be here in the next twenty minutes."

*　　*　　*

Beneath the mound of debris which walled him in, Reg was beginning to experience panic once more. When he first heard the sounds of tapping on the beam above his head, followed by the noise of what was obviously rescue digging, his spirit had risen hopefully. He had no idea of the depth at which he was buried, but he felt sure it could only take a short time to reach him, then he would be safe.

Now he was less sure. Although the noises above had continued for some time, there had been no welcoming breakthrough of light into the cavity in which he lay. The sounds had not even grown louder, but had merely continued faint and distant, so that he had begun to wonder if he had truly been discovered. It might be that he was simply hearing the noise of the demolition gang going about their normal day's work.

What frightened him most, however, was the water which had now risen until it covered his legs and its continuous trickle was plainly and disturbingly audible. When the icy cold liquid had first begun to steal round his feet and lower legs, it had galvanized him into renewed efforts to free himself. For a long time he had struggled and twisted, tearing at the heavy blocks of stone and brickwork, which pressed upon him. One or two smaller pieces did come loose, but their removal made no apparent difference and eventually he gave up. His strength was fading fast now; the cold was making him shiver uncontrollably for long spasms. He tried desperately to raise himself out of the water, but the roof was too low, even for him to sit upright. Straining his ears in the dark, he listened to the sound of the water. It was entering in a frighteningly steady flow. Unless help came quickly, he realized, he would be drowned where he lay, like a rat.

* * *

At nine o'clock, a transporter arrived, escorted by a police car, and carrying a caterpillar-tracked crane. It also started to rain again, a steady, soaking downpour.

"Do you mind if I sit in your car for a bit?" Tilly asked Johnny. Her teeth were chattering with cold. "I don't want to leave until you get him out."

"Sure," he said at once, "give me a shout if the radio phone goes, will you? It's impossible to hear it in this racket." The crane engine spluttered and choked, and came to life as he spoke.

The addition of the police team, the crane and the crews of two fire engines, which had also arrived on the scene, greatly speeded up the rescue work. Despite the rain which rapidly turned much of the wrecked warehouse into a morass of glutinous gray mud, it proved possible to clear a way for the crane to get close to some of the larger pieces. Johnny was watching it lift an iron girder, when the sound of the car horn caught his attention. It was Watson in the warning room with the latest information. Johnny listened carefully, the look of concern on his face deepening as he did so.

"What's so important about the weather in Harwich and Southend," Tilly asked in bewilderment, "it's bad enough here, as it is."

"It's not the weather that matters, there's a kind of tidal wave moving down the North Sea and it might come up the river. At the moment it's just reached Harwich."

"Is it serious if it comes up here?"

Johnny gave her a gloomy look. "I reckon so," he replied, "if it keeps going the way it is now, in an hour's time this whole place will be under eight feet of water."

*   *   *

Out in the North Sea, the crew of the *Ross* had almost abandoned hope of survival. Exhausted by more than twenty hours of nonstop battle against the hurricane, battered and bruised from the continually pounding sea, and their clothes soaked to the skin by near freezing water, they were making a last ditch attempt to save the ship by streaming a drogue anchor from her stern. The engine had failed twice during the past three hours and twenty minutes ago the engineer had reported that the propeller shaft had locked solid. Crippled and helpless the *Ross* had rolled before the waves while the sea had forced her stern round till she was lying broadside to the storm, with the waves broaching over her.

At the stern a small group of crew members struggled to make fast the heavy warp of the drogue, in the face of the seas that swept furiously across the violently pitching deck, as the gunwhale disappeared beneath the surface at each roll of the boat. All around them the wind was tearing the crests of the waves into long shreds of foam, filling the air with driving spray. Visibility was no more than a few feet. There was only a faint chance, the skipper knew, that the drogue would be able to hold back the stern and enable the boat to ride the storm till help came, but it was all they had.

The storm denied them even this, however. Before they had paid out more than a few feet of the cable, a single freak wave, twice the height of the worst they had experienced, reared above them. Clawing futilely at the almost vertical slope the trawler slid downwards into the trough with terrifying speed, listing deeply into the water. She had barely begun to right herself when the whole weight of the wave fell upon her.

The men in the stern were wearing life lines, but these were pitifully inadequate against the avalanche of water that swept over them. Two were torn loose and flung bodily overboard to vanish into the raging sea. In the same moment the wave checked the boat's attempt to right herself and rolled her clear over, so that for a brief instant the copper sheathing of her hull was visible amidst the maëlstrom of white foam. Then she was gone, dragged under by the suction, and the wave thundered on while the dead hulk with its drowned crew sank slowly to the sea bed four hundred feet below.

Chapter Four

Every sixty seconds another aircraft thundered down one of the runways, jets screaming as they built up the thrust to hoist the lumbering giant into the sky. In the distance, others raced in against the wind to touch down, or taxied into position in the line-ups. Scores of airplanes, of every size and model, stood in rows round the terminal buildings, attended by groups of service vehicles and scurrying mechanics. Across the tarmac swept brightly painted buses loaded with passengers and luggage. It was nine-fifteen in the morning and the Charles de Gaulle airport, the gateway to Paris and pride of France, was working at near capacity.

Despite the cold temperature, the day was fine and the sky clear, except for the threadlike streaks of cirrus clouds, which were at a very high altitude. On the roof of the main European departure building crowds of sightseers stood watching the planes. Many of the children clutched small American flags which they were waving frantically. Their parents stamped their feet with the cold, their shoulders hunched into their coats, as they chatted desultorily among themselves.

Down below, the main car park had been taken over by several hundred demonstrators. They stood by the fence chanting and waving an assortment of banners with varying slogans. In front of them, within the perimeter of the runway area stood an almost solid line of C.R.S. riot police in heavy leather coats, equipped with submachine guns. Other squads of armed police were visible at strategic points around the buildings, and guarding the entrance to the V.I.P. departure area.

Out on the tarmac a section of the field near the departure gate had been tightly cordoned off by more C.R.S. Within this guarded area stood a huge Boeing. Its markings were those of the United States Air Force. Just behind the nose was the legend AIR FORCE ONE and in the center of the fuselage was painted the image of the round seal, in blue and gold, of the President of the United States of America.

Between the gleaming aircraft and the V.I.P. suite, a double rank of soldiers, in the uniform of the Presidential guard, had been drawn up. Two officers moved down the lines making a last minute scrutiny of uniforms.

All at once the figures of the waiting police stiffened into expectant watchfulness. From the demonstrators there rose a renewed hum of protest. Straining their ears the spectators on the roof caught the faint whine of police sirens approaching from the south. A minute or two later a flying wedge of white helmeted "motards" swept into the airport at the head of a procession of black limousines. The President of the United States had come to take his leave of his host for the past four days, the President of the French Republic.

* * *

Commander Larkin's office was on the eighth floor of the skyscraper in Victoria that was the new headquarters of the Metropolitan Police. It could easily have been mistaken for the office of any business executive with its large modern desk, swiveling, high-backed, mock leather chair and thick gray carpet. The view from the window was stupendous, across the rooftops to Parliament and the river. Today, with the rain pattering hard against the glass, Larkin had pulled down the blinds.

There was a tap at the door, he growled an answer, and a young, slightly built man with short black hair entered.

"Could I have a word with you for a moment, sir?" the newcomer asked. His name was Pellew and he was an inspector.

"I can guess what it is you want to know," Larkin said, waving him to a seat. Pellew was in charge of arrangements for flood control. "And the orders are still to concentrate on crowd control and security in the center of the city."

"I know that, Commander," Pellew replied. "The thing is I've been thinking and looking at the latest information from the teleprinter, and frankly it doesn't bode well. The meteorologists at Bracknell are still playing it down and they must know what they're doing, but all the same I feel we ought to be taking some action."

"How much longer till the flood strike?"

"Just on two hours, sir. That's the bare minimum for us to get even a token force into the danger zones, and, as you know, by rights we should have all our men in position by the time the sirens go. Also, if they confirm that the alert is still on during the next fifteen minutes, we are supposed to begin transferring operational control from here to Paddington Green." Larkin nodded thoughtfully; in the event of flooding, New Scotland Yard would be hit and its electrical systems put out of action. To overcome this plans had been laid to move headquarters up to the police station at Paddington.

"I've had Special Branch on the line just now," he said. "The President's plane has left Paris and they've picked up two students in the Mall, carrying cans of paint. So far there have been forty-two death threats and another eleven vague warnings of unspecified trouble."

"So what do we do, sir?"

"We do what we're ordered. Our superiors have decided that it's safe for this visit to go on. So at the moment we have to commit our men to protecting the procession route. If they change their minds and decide to put us on flood duty, they'll tell us."

"I was wondering, sir," Pellew hesitated, before going on, "perhaps you could talk to the chief engineer at flood control, Kingsway. He might be able to give us a better indication of what the picture is."

"Yes, well," Larkin said doubtfully, "I may talk to him, but whatever he may say, there's nothing to be done until we get fresh orders. Now stop fussing," he went on, "the experts at Bracknell and the Greater London Council know what they're doing. If there was any real danger of a surge, they'd tell us all right and frankly I'm glad they haven't. We've enough to do as it is."

Pellew stood up. "Very good, Commander," he said formally, "I'll continue watching the tape and I'll inform you as soon as there's anything to report."

Larkin dismissed him with a nod. It was strange that the alert had still not been called off. Presumably the authorities were playing safe. A telephone on his desk rang shrilly.

"Simmonds here, Commander. I'm in the operations room. Things are starting to hot up. Half a dozen coachloads of protesters have arrived from that American electronics firm that's closed. They're forming up in the park."

"Contact the nearest senior officer and tell him to get in touch with their leaders. He's to make it clear that only a small party will be allowed close to the procession route," Larkin told him. "I'm coming down to take control now."

* * *

Miles Wendoser had arrived at Holborn at approximately the same time that Derek Thompson started out from Westminster. Already the councilor's early confidence was being eroded by swiftly mounting doubts. Despite his assurances to the government, it had so far proved impossible to call off the alert, and he was now coming under strong pressure to request the cancellation of the ceremonial procession and the redeployment of the police. To have to do that would be disastrous, but unless they received some encouraging news during the next quarter of an hour, it was going to be all but impossible to avoid it. At the moment his only hope lay in the weather proving too bad for the procession to take place.

Carswell had got the control room functioning smoothly and was running the operation with his customary efficiency. On the big wall map, the plotters were busy marking in the positions of the group and local controls that were already in action, and the points where the river engineers were patrolling the defenses. From the desks came a constant stream of noise as the liaison officers kept up their work.

The first thing to be done, Miles decided, was to check the true weather situation with Bracknell. Using one of the three direct land lines he got through to the senior forecaster again. This time the man was clearly worried.

"I know I said before that I thought the winds were veering," he replied to Miles' questions, "but it doesn't seem to have happened now. You often get a lot of contraindications locally ahead of a big depression. In this case they don't seem to have meant anything. The storm center has kept right on coming and the winds are still force ten. Barometric pressure is still showing no sign of a sustained rise."

"What conclusions do you draw from these facts?" Miles demanded sharply.

"Well, sir, I don't see that anything is likely to stop the storm from reaching Southend during the next thirty to forty minutes. During the past hour we've been getting a lot of reports of abnormally high seas on the East Anglian coast. I would say that there is a definite surge running out there, and these winds will keep it moving right on to Southend."

"Have you any idea how high it is?" Miles felt a sense of foreboding as he asked the question.

"Impossible to say at the moment until we get a reading from the gauges at the estuary, but judging by what's happened at Harwich and Walton it could be as high as six feet."

Miles rang off and for a moment stood silently gazing at the map as the realization of the significance of the forecaster's remarks slowly sank in. Mentally he recalled the figures for the tide levels: high water would reach twenty-four feet, if on top of that there were a six-foot surge then the river would top the banks by a whole foot. Moreover, it was common knowledge that the height of a surge actually increased as it came up the estuary and the enormous volume of water was squeezed between the banks as the river narrowed. Three or four feet of water over the defenses, the consequences were unthinkable.

Carswell had been trying to catch his eye for the past few minutes, now he came over to where Miles stood.

"I don't see how we can delay calling on the police for help now," he said, speaking in an urgent undertone. "There's no sign of a let-up in the weather, we simply can't take the risk any longer." Miles turned on him fiercely.

"The responsibility is mine," he snapped savagely.

"I'll decide when or when not to bring in assistance. As it happens, I am going to talk to the government now and I shall naturally advise them of the seriousness of the position."

Leaving the controller blinking with hurt surprise at this rebuke, he stalked off into the small private office opposite the radio cabin, which had been built to enable senior staff to hold important meetings without disturbing the control center. Inside it was even more starkly furnished than the room which he had just left, with bare chipboard walls and a number of cheap wooden chairs grouped round a table. There was the familiar musty smell of a place that was never used.

Miles had had no very clear idea of what he was going to say to the Ministers involved in the crisis. Apart from any other consideration there was an obvious division of responsibility. His promise to prevent the alert from interfering with the President's arrival had been made to the Foreign Office, but a request for the assistance of the police had to be made to the Home Secretary. The first course was to contact the private secretary of the Foreign Secretary; to his surprise his reception was less hostile than he had expected.

"To tell you the truth, Miles, much as we appreciate what you've been doing for us, we shall have to cancel anyway. The weather's so frightful the whole business would be a farce. As it is his plane was barely able to land in this wind. Shall you be coming to the reception?"

"I'll try and make it. I may be a little late, though," Miles said.

"Well, try and get there if you can and I'll see you're presented. Oh, and by the way, do you have any influence with the people who clear the drains?"

"The ordinary street gutters are a local council job; main sewers are the Thames Water Authority's concern. I can probably produce some action though. What's the difficulty?"

"It's the chief's house in Kensington. None of the rain that's fallen recently has drained away properly and each time we have a succession of great lakes forming in the road outside. Apparently, the trouble is being caused by a river outfall and with your alert on nobody will go down and look."

"I'll try and have a team sent down now to see what's wrong," Miles assured him, "but they may not be able to do much until the rain stops."

"Fine, just as long as I can tell my chief that something is being done."

His next call to the Home Office was less well received and Miles had to suffer a long grumble of complaints about the lack of notice and conflicting instructions. The knowledge that he had the support of at least one Ministry, however, gave him the confidence to talk the matter out brazenly.

"I know it's difficult," he said, "but I'm sure you'll understand that we've only delayed this long in order to try and help everybody. I gather that the procession will be canceled anyway."

"It's all very well for you to talk of being helpful," was the crisp reply at the other end, "but it makes us look pretty stupid with the commissioners, changing our minds like this. It had better be worth it."

Leaving him to deal with that problem, Miles returned to the control room in a more cheerful frame of mind. Seeking out Carswell, he gave him the news.

"Thank God for that," the Controller breathed a sigh of relief. "How long before Larkin's men can be in position?"

"I've no idea, but I can't see that it can take him too long. Give him a couple of minutes for the new orders to get through, then call him."

Watching Carswell go off happily to attend to the new state of affairs, Miles permitted himself a brief smile. It looked as though he had successfully saved his reputation from a very tricky position. It only remained to inform the leader of the Council of the imminence of the flood, but that could wait until the police had confirmed they were starting to move. In the meantime, there was the question of the Foreign Secretary's drains. It would be as well to spare no effort which might bring him an ally and it should surely be possible to send a team down the sewer for a quick check. He went over to the desk of the liaison man from the water authority.

* * *

Larkin received the news of the results of Miles Wendoser's activities with incredulity.

"How the hell do they expect us to transport our men into their new positions before ten o'clock, let alone brief and equip them?" he demanded angrily. "I've spent half the morning telling my people not to worry about anything to do with flood warnings, and now suddenly it's all changed." Stubbing out a cigarette viciously, he bellowed for Pellew.

"Bloody fairground, this town," he growled, when the young inspector appeared. "Everybody changing their minds, first this and then that. Get down to operations. Cancel all security duty; the flood emergency program is to go ahead with maximum speed. I want every man in his new location by ten o'clock."

"But, Commander!" Pellew replied, aghast, "we haven't a hope. It's nearly nine-thirty already."

"I know what the bloody time is. Just do as you're told," Larkin snarled. The inspector fled hastily. Behind him Larkin began working out the best method of moving five thousand policemen into the danger zones in less than a third of the time allowed.

* * *

One of the first people to be affected when the first London warning was called had been Jerry Able, the young technician who lived with his wife Eileen, next door to Mrs. Pole. Jerry was on standby duty at Bankside Power Station, on the edge of the Thames opposite St. Paul's Cathedral. In the event of an emergency, it was his job to make up the team that would go in and prepare to shut down the station.

It was an indication of the degree of complacency that existed throughout London that neither Jerry nor any of his companions had any idea of the real nature of the threat. The station's emergency planning had been delegated to one of the chemical engineers, Alan Watts, who was already responsible for a heavy load of work. He had been allocated virtually nothing in the way of money, personnel, training time or equipment. He had simply received orders to prepare the station against flooding and had done the best he could with his own resources. The only assistance he had been offered in the five years since he had taken over, were three instruction pamphlets describing the flood danger in general terms, and setting out a rough guide as to what the authorities intended to do once it had happened. There had been no advice on the precautions that should primarily be taken.

Jerry was familiar with the usual procedure. Having arrived at the station he checked in and went straight to his position, watching the monitors for the number five furnace, where he expected to wait for the next hour or two. He was a short stocky man with fair curly hair which he kept very neatly cut. Mechanically, he checked the rows of dials; they were all working smoothly. The loads were running fairly high, but then that was to be expected. Eight o'clock on a winter's morning was a peak demand period as people switched on their electric fires, stoves and turned on lights all over the city. The southern region railway also took their power from Bankside and they too would be using a considerable amount of energy in order to generate the commuter trains. His thoughts turned to the reason for his call-out and he idly speculated on the possibility of the surge occurring.

The generating station was in reality a single enormous hall like the nave of a cathedral; a hundred feet high and about two hundred and fifty feet long. Down one half of this ran a line of four huge turbines; enormous cylindrical monsters, sheathed in yellow-painted steel plating, each with an attendant console of gauges and control panels. Beside these, and occupying the entire remaining half of the building, were the furnaces and boilers; the true giants of the station. From the basement, thirty feet below, their gray steel sides reached up almost to the roof, hot and quivering, burning nearly a ton of oil every minute. From these and from the boilers in the basement beneath the turbines, ran a fantastic complex of heavily insulated pipes carrying the steam at a pressure of fifteen hundred pounds per square inch to drive the turbine blades.

If water from the river came in in any volume, he knew the destruction it would cause would be staggering. The whole basement level would fill swiftly, drowning the lower part of the furnaces and the boilers. Even if they began shutting down the fires at once, they would remain dangerously hot for at least six hours. He could imagine, only too easily, the effect of cold water rising around superheated metal.

By nine o'clock several other men had reported in for duty, though none of these could give Jerry any news on the alert. A modern generating station requires a surprisingly small number of men to operate it; at Bankside a normal shift comprised thirty staff and technicians, many of whom spend their working day alone, communicating with each other by telephone. Consequently, Jerry was left wondering about the situation by himself. He paced up and down in front of the furnaces, watching the flames leaping behind the glass peepholes. Occasionally, through the grilles in the floor he caught glimpses of men moving equipment in the basement. They appeared to be taking small items of machinery up on to the main level. Jerry could see auxiliary motors, feed pumps and compressors being swayed up on the hoists. He wished the noise of the furnaces did not make it impossible to hear what they were saying.

At length, he saw the figure of Alan Watts approaching from the far end of the hall. The chemist was evidently making a tour of inspection, for he stopped to speak to all the other technicians on his way.

"Morning, Jerry," he said, when at length he reached him. "Everything O.K.?"

"Sure, no problems," Jerry replied. "What's the story about this flooding, though?" Alan smiled and made a worried face.

At thirty, the two men were the same age, but the chemist was taller and lightly built. "I've had regional H.Q. on," he said, "and it looks as though we may get some water in here this time."

"Jesus," Jerry whistled softly, "what the hell do we do? Shut down at once?"

"No," Alan shook his head, "I'm afraid they won't let us do that unless the flooding is certain. They'll know in about thirty minutes. After that we shall have an hour to shut down and get clear."

"We can switch off the turbines and cut the fuel easily enough," said Jerry. "That would take about twenty minutes, but what about the boilers and the steam pipes; they're over a thousand degrees. If the water comes in contact with them . . ." He left the sentence unfinished.

"I know," Alan said frowning, "but there's nothing one can do. We've also got a two thousand-gallon tank of sulphuric acid in the basement. Imagine what'll happen when the water reaches that."

"My God, it'll explode," Jerry exclaimed in alarm.

"Yes, well I'm going to try and plug the vents now,

but I doubt if I can make it watertight for long. Whereabouts do you live?" he asked, changing the subject abruptly.

"Battersea," Jerry told him. "Why, will it be bad there too?"

"I think it could be, are you on the ground floor?"

"No, first. It's a block of flats."

"You should be safe." Alan paused for a moment. He was obviously hesitating over his next words. "I am sending most of the others home, Jerry," he said at length, "but I'd like you to stay on. You're our best man on the furnace?"

"Stay till the water comes, you mean?" Jerry asked slowly.

"Yes, will you do it?" Jerry was silent for a moment. "All right," he said. "I'll do it. I'll stay."

*   *   *

At Southend that morning the major topic of conversation along the waterfront and in the harbor was the unusual state of the tide. High water was predicted originally at eleven-thirty, but this had been altered on the advice of Bracknell to ten o'clock in the morning. Sailors and fishermen noted that there had been scarcely no ebb from the previous night. Although most people had heard about the storms in the north of the country and there were a few who could remember the disaster a quarter of a century earlier, it was not appreciated that the sea was threatening an even more serious assault. The wind was blowing from the northwest with increasing strength and it was generally believed that the afternoon would bring bad weather and a rough sea. Boat owners began to secure their canvas covers and put extra chocks under their keels in preparation. A few townspeople with time on their hands walked out a short way along the pier, but the waves were starting to shake the wooden piles and in places

spray was breaking over the railway line that ran down
to the pier head.

*   *   *

Georgina's thoughts, as she sat in the tube, did not
turn to the possibility of the flood. As her husband had
remarked earlier, most people, even those, who like
Georgina, were close to the center of authority, could
not envisage the destruction of the city in which they
lived, a city whose size seemed so immense that they
took its survival for granted. It had, after all, existed
for two thousand years.

Much more on her mind, as the train roared and rattled along the Circle Line, through Victoria and Westminster, before turning to run beneath the embankment
beside the river, was the question of the new job that
had been recently offered to Derek. Georgina was, on
the whole, keen for him to accept it; the work would
involve more money, more prestige, and a different,
more interesting life; also she thought Derek needed a
change from the rather over conservative environment
of local government. In this she knew he agreed with
her. He was alive to the danger of growing stale, and
was reluctant to become bogged down in the day-to-
day running of the city. South Africa, though, was a
big step and maybe not the right one; perhaps they
should wait to see if a better position would be offered.

The train roared on. There were many passengers
about, mainly shoppers going in after the rush hour,
and the normal traffic of businessmen and those working in legal centers. There was the usual lengthy pause
at Aldgate, while the train waited for a new driver;
then on through Liverpool Street and Moorgate, before
finally pulling into Barbican Station.

Outside, Georgina shivered in the cold wind that
whistled down among the great towers and passageways of the vast new development built by the City

Corporation. She hated the new construction with its gray concrete walls and soaring apartment blocks, which had been erected in place of the narrow alleys and old houses that had crammed the area before the blitz of the Second World War devastated it. The rain was falling heavily now, and she hurried across the road and down a small side street.

The studio was an old wine vault that had once been used for storing casks of rum in the days before the East India Docks were built. The vast vaulted cellar, with its stone piers, had been turned into a center where a group of artists and craftsmen worked and displayed their products. There were silversmiths and jewelers, glass blowers and engravers, joiners, leather workers, a bookbinder and a screen printer; a complex assortment of talent and skill which generated an atmosphere which Georgina found stimulating. For many years she had painted, but recently she had become absorbed in the making of stained glass. Today she had a client coming to view her work and, hopefully, commission some pieces.

The studio was shut. On the door, a typewritten note had been hastily tacked up stating that owing to an electricity failure the management committee had decided not to open that morning. Georgina cursed and banged on the door with her fist. There was no answer, but a couple of men going down the street turned their heads and laughed.

Eventually giving up, she realized that she was rapidly becoming very wet. She looked round for a taxi, but there was not one to be seen. Cursing the feeble hearts of the management committee, Georgina sprinted back towards the shelter of the station and to her surprise, found a train drawing in. She leapt aboard and sat back with a sigh of relief. At least, she thought, she would now be back in Chelsea by eleven o'clock.

The tube was another Circle Line train. It pulled out of the station and rattled slowly into the tunnel. At

Liverpool Street a large number of people got on. Georgina did not find this strange, as she knew that the station served the mainline terminus for the east of England. Into her compartment entered several stockbrokers and a strikingly beautiful colored girl in a cream trouser suit. The stockbrokers were discussing the storm in East Anglia.

"I tell you," one of them said, a tall blond man still in his twenties, dressed in an immaculate suit, "I tell you, we had a chap in the office today whose wife called him at nine-thirty from Clacton-on-Sea to say the water was eighteen inches deep in the kitchen and what should she do."

"What did he say?" asked one of his companions interestedly.

"I'd have said get out quickly," said another, an older man with a velvet-collared coat.

"That's just it, he didn't get a chance to say anything. The line went dead before he could reply. Poor chap was in such a stew, we had to let him go home in the end."

"Eighteen inches of water wouldn't be so bad," someone remarked.

"As long as it stayed at that," replied the man with the velvet collar. "Perhaps she stopped speaking when the water went over her head." There was general laughter at this. The train continued its journey westwards, and for once there was no delay at Aldgate, but just before Tower Hill there was a pause of several minutes.

"It's the new system," explained one of the stockbrokers. "Because of this flood thing, they have to control the whole network individually and manually, instead of letting the computer do it for them. That makes it much slower."

"What do you make of this flood warning?" someone asked.

"Well they've been talking about it for years, but

nothing's ever come of it. You know what the authorities are like, they can't afford to take any chances, so the moment they think there is the remotest possibility of any flooding, they sound the alarm."

The train started forward with a jerk, causing people to lurch forward and grab hold of the overhead strap handles, as it continued slowly into Tower Hill station. The platform was deserted and completely silent. No one got out and after a minute or two the doors slammed shut again and the train set off. No sooner had they entered the tunnel again, when there was another abrupt halt and this time they remained stationary for a considerable time. As they started forward again, Georgina looked at her watch. The time was now ten twenty-two.

*   *   *

With Liz gone and the radio patrols despatched, Derek got into his car and drove up to Holborn. Kingsway had been sealed off to normal traffic, but at a glance at his pass, the police on the barrier waved him through. The gratings in the center of the road had been taken up, and beside them, blocking most of the street, were several large radio vans, some of them bearing military markings. Around these was parked an imposing array of official cars and service vehicles. Outside the barriers a small crowd of on-lookers braved the rain to watch the strange activities.

There was another policeman at the entrance to the tunnel who consulted a list of names before permitting Derek to proceed. The concrete stairs were slippery with rain and he descended gingerly.

"They intended to put up an awning, sir," the policeman told him, "but it wouldn't hold in the wind. Mind the wires!" He pointed to a sagging bundle of cables that were wound round into thick coils inside. Derek thanked him and went inside to look for Carswell.

The Coordinator was glad to see him. "It doesn't look good, Derek," he said. "The wind is increasing overhead and Bracknell say the storm center will be on us in an hour."

"Have they released the police from crowd control?" Derek asked.

"Yes, Miles has just fixed it. The military are coming in too, under Operation King Canute. The state drive has been canceled, the Queen will meet the President and take him back to stay at Windsor, while the alert is in force. They'll try and hold the ceremonies tomorrow."

"What's the official attitude now?"

"Miles Wendoser is getting a Cabinet Minister to come down and take charge. He will make the final decision, or at least approve it."

Derek went on to talk to Peter Collins at the liaison desk before going into the radio cabin. It was imperative to check that his river patrols were in position. He was relying on them to watch the progress of the surge up the river and build up an accurate picture of its effects.

Personally, he no longer had any doubts that there would be severe flooding. He was thankful that Miles had at last had the sense to call the police in to do their job. The military too would be a help, though they would probably not be able to bring their forces into action until after the surge had struck.

Contacting the patrols took some time. Several of the men had still to get into position. Derek was still at it when Carswell came hurrying in.

"The warning room has just been on," he said at once. "It's Southend. The tide will reach the second warning bell within the next five minutes."

Derek thought for a moment, as his mind raced over the calculations he had worked out a hundred times before in practice. The second warning bell at Southend was the limit at which the danger signal was flashed to the warning room. Any rise in the water level, above this point, meant water over the banks at some point in London. The question was, how far would the water rise after it had passed the bell?

"You'll sound the sirens as soon as the bell goes, I take it?" he said.

"Well," Carswell hesitated. He seemed almost flustered, Derek noticed. For once, his immaculate hair was disarrayed, as though he had been running his hands through it. "The thing is," he went on, "we've been advised to wait until we are quite sure there will be substantial flooding, so as to avoid any false alarms."

"False alarms! Are you out of your mind, Alan. There's an eight-foot surge at Southend and a bloody hurricane blowing, and you're worried about false alarms!" Derek cried in amazement. "Who thought up this bright idea?"

Carswell made frantic calming sounds. "Keep your voice down," he hissed, "it's the Minister. This is a government decision." With one hand he indicated a small knot of people standing by the big wall map, among them Derek recognized the Home Secretary. "The thing is," Carswell explained, "the government wants to be quite sure before they ask for the emergency powers. It's a very delicate matter."

"Listen, Alan, you know as well as I do that a state of emergency can be called by the Queen in Council. It only takes half a dozen people about ten minutes. The only problem is getting Parliament to agree if they want it extended, so what's the panic?"

"I've just been asked to wait a while, that's all, until it becomes clear that there will be large scale flooding."

* * *

Since nine-thirty the tide gauge in the warning room at Westminster, which repeated the movements of a similar gauge on the pier at Southend, had been showing a marked and steady rise. For the next thirty minutes the staff watched anxiously, as the automatic pen drew its thin trail of black ink silently across the paper drum, gradually nearing a bright red line three-quarters of the way up, and which marked the level at which the sea would overcome the defenses of London. Using one of the open telephone links, they maintained a constant link with Peter Collins in the control room at Kingsway, as the pen climbed gradually towards the line.

At 10:08 the two crossed, and instantly the room was filled with the urgent clamor of an electric bell. Watson switched it off and the rest of the room watched in silence as he picked up the telephone.

"This is the warning room," he said formally. "The tide at Southend has reached the danger point for London and is continuing to rise. We are sending the details over the teleprinter now."

* * *

Derek was now listening to the same argument from the Minister himself. He was a small, portly man with a disagreeably pompous manner. Miles Wendoser was dancing in attendance.

"It has been decided at Cabinet level," he informed them, "that we should seek to avoid a premature sounding of the alarms, that is to say, the sirens and so forth, in case it appears that this, er . . ." the Minister paused groping for the correct terms, "this surge tide, as you call it, will not, in fact, come up the river as far as central London. You will appreciate, of course," he continued, "that all the necessary arrangements are being made to provide aid and assistance to the city, and I am in a position to tell you that preparations are at hand to declare a state of emergency, under the terms of which the officers of this establishment," he waved a pudgy hand at the control room, "will be granted statutory powers."

"Just how much of a surge do you need to see before you let us call the alarm?" asked Derek icily. "I mean do you want one foot of water in the streets, or two or ten?"

"I find that remark offensive," replied the Minister.

Miles broke in hastily, "I am sure Mr. Thompson didn't mean quite that, Minister, but naturally he is concerned."

"We are all concerned," said the Minister, "to take the best care of the interests of both the people and of the nation. I am not suggesting a long postponement, I merely wish to be sure that what you describe is really going to take place."

There was a noise at the door and Peter Collins put his head round; seeing Derek he handed him a sheet of paper. Derek took it and handed it wordlessly to the Minister, after he had read it. It was taken direct from the teleprinter and read simply: SOUTHEND 10.06 HRS. FINAL FLOOD ALARM SOUNDED—WATER CONTINUES TO RISE—ESTIMATED RATE ONE FOOT PER 8.5 MINUTES.

"For your information, Minister," he said, "a rise of one foot at Southend means about one and a half feet at London Bridge."

The Minister swallowed, blinked and looked round the circle of grim faces.

"I think you had better sound the siren," he said, in a small voice. "Will you please give me a moment to inform the Prime Minister."

*   *   *

Minutes later, at New Scotland Yard, Commander Larkin left his office and went into the operations room, where shirt-sleeved officers were directing the movement of five thousand policemen, as they took up their emergency positions. At his entrance silence fell over the room, and all eyes turned expectantly towards him.

"Gentlemen," he said, "I have been ordered to sound the warning sirens. We are to expect a major flood within the next sixty minutes. We will begin emergency procedures as from now." Crossing over to the far side of the room, he went to a small table on which stood a gray metal box with a red handle. It was covered with a clear plastic case. Larkin removed the case and pulled the handle down, it made a single sharp click and instantly a red light on the box began to wink rapidly.

The time was exactly 10:10 a.m.

*   *   *

The sounding of the final warning was the signal for the start of a second and more secret call-out of officials. In Cheltenham, a hundred miles away from London, peremptory telephone messages summoned hundreds of men and women from their homes and offices to an R.A.F. base a short distance from the town. The maneuver was accomplished quietly and without fuss, and attracted very little notice. Casual observers, near the gates of the base, remarked on the unusual number of arrivals, and on a marked increase in the number of security guards on duty, but failed to attach any significance to these facts. They did not see the newcomers enter one of the buildings far from the perimeter fence, where banks of high speed lifts conveyed them swiftly downwards to an intricate complex of tunnels more than two hundred feet below the ground.

For here, comprehensively protected against attack from anything from nuclear bombardment to civil insurrection, was the country's chief regional seat of government, the secret alternative capital from which the nation could be controlled in the event of a breakdown of normal parliamentary rule. A series of similar bunkers spread across Britain, linked by a special microwave radio network, whose tall concrete towers could be seen at intervals round the country and whose function often puzzled curious local inhabitants. From these R.S.G.'s, as they were known, the military and civil services would be controlled by regional commissioners, under the authority of the emergency power act. Cheltenham, with its excellent road and rail links to London and other parts of the country, and its high proportion of retired former civil servants and military personnel, whose reliability was assured, had been chosen as the central point of the system.

The Prime Minister had only just greeted the President on his arrival from France when he received the telephone message from Kingsway, to the effect that flooding on a large scale within central London was now certain. The President had at first offered to leave for America straight away, thus sparing the government the added complication of a state visit, but eventually they agreed that he should lunch at Windsor Castle with the Queen and then come to London to discuss the situation.

The activating of the R.S.G.'s had been carried out by the Civil Contingencies Unit at the Home Office, and was an automatic response to the flood threat. On ascertaining the facts the Prime Minister decided that the central government would continue to operate from London itself, using the underground Defense Ministry complex beneath number 42 High Holborn, round the corner from the flood control room at Kingsway, as a headquarters. This was well provided with communications facilities and living quarters and was more convenient than the second alternative government center located at Hendon. Nevertheless, in view of the serious social and economic consequences that might follow a prolonged inundation of the city, the R.S.G.'s were ordered to remain on alert and during the interval before the surge, several train loads of senior civil servants occupying positions considered essential for the survival of the nation, were dispatched to Cheltenham and other centers, in conditions of utmost secrecy.

Chapter Five

Mrs. Pole was not finding it as easy to get home as she had expected. Normally, she was in the habit of taking a bus as far as Wandsworth Bridge Road and then walking down to her home in Battersea. Today it seemed, however, that hardly any were running. She waited in the rain for an hour for the first bus; even then it was crowded with people, all complaining about the service and the weather, and so she was forced to stand all the way. Mrs. Pole paid no attention to their grumbles. She was well used to difficulties of this nature. When she got off there was an inspector waiting by the stop.

"I should hurry, Missus," he said kindly, "we've orders not to run vehicles into Battersea and Wandsworth, 'cause of this flooding."

Mrs. Pole tied her scarf more tightly round her head and set off grimly in the direction of home. She walked slowly, trying to keep up a steady pace. At length she neared the bridge and turned down into Battersea. The road was a busy one, cars and trucks thundered past, in a never-ending stream of traffic, their tires showering her with spray. At several of the main intersections she observed detachments of police moving about. They appeared to be stacking the metal barriers used for blocking off roads. Mrs. Pole wondered if there had been an accident. If it had not been raining so hard she might have stopped to ask. As it was she kept going; she was half way home when the sirens sounded.

The sirens were all set off simultaneously at 10:16 a.m. There were one hundred of them, the majority reconditioned models that had last seen service in the Second World War, scattered throughout the areas that were thought to be in peril from the river.

That Mrs. Pole heard the sound at all was surprising; northwest winds were now blowing through the city at speeds in excess of forty-five miles an hour, shifting the noise away from the riverside towards the high ground. The continued rumble of traffic drowned much of the sound, rendering the warning either inaudible or incomprehensible to most. Mrs. Pole was one of the lucky few.

Twelve one-minute blasts at fifteen-second intervals. To the old lady they seemed like a continuous wail that was lost now and then in the wind. It was not the sickening rise and fall of the air raid sirens she had listened to in her youth, but a steadier moaning rate. She had no idea of the reason for it; she had never read the posters or leaflets, nor had she seen the periodic article in the press or television on the subject. Nevertheless she was frightened; the sound had an eerie, foreboding quality. There were too many strange things happening that day. She remembered Georgina's talk of floods, and the remark of the bus inspector. At the next junction there were no police, but the metal barriers had been placed over part of the side road together with a large sign which said: FLOOD EMER-GENCY CLEARWAY—EMERGENCY SERVICE VEHICLES

ONLY, and when she got to the traffic lights, she saw police directing the traffic off the main road and into the side streets.

She was nearing Battersea Park when she heard the familiar shriek of police sirens behind her. A long convoy of vans was following the flashing lights of a white police Jaguar; within a few seconds they shot past and disappeared ahead of her. A short while later three ambulances passed her traveling in the opposite direction, on their way to the depots on the high ground to the south. Every major junction now had the familiar barriers and signs ordering normal traffic to divert elsewhere.

With increasing anxiety Mrs. Pole hurried on; her one desire was to get back home as quickly as possible and away from these disturbing new events. She had crossed over the street and had moved off the clearway, when a car went past, stopped and drew up in front of her.

"Hey, Mrs. Pole," the driver called through the window, "what are you doin' 'ere, 'aven't you 'eard about the warnings?"

"Warnings," Mrs. Pole answered breathlessly, as she panted up alongside, "I don't know anything about no warnings. Is that them hooters then?"

"Yeah, that's it," the driver replied. He was a young man in his twenties, good looking with long black hair and very white teeth. She recognized him as he lived in one of the top flats in Beran House. "You'd better be getting 'ome quick," he told her. "Come on, jump in and I'll give you a lift."

"The guv'nor sent us 'ome early," he explained cheerfully, "he got a warning from the Council saying the river might overflow. Made us put up boards an' sandbags an' that, had to take up the dynamos too. Soon as we finished, 'e says get along home."

"But what's goin' to 'appen?" Mrs. Pole asked. "Why

should there be a flood. There's never been no flood before? Is it the rain?" She looked anxiously at the drops splashing in the puddles.

"Reckon it must be," the driver answered, "there's a big storm coming too, caused a lot of damage in the north. You'll be O.K.," he said reassuringly, "you're on the first floor, aren't you? Be sitting pretty. It's the folks on the ground will have to watch out."

When they reached the flats the young man let her out.

"I'm taking my car up the hill," he said, pointing to the high ground beyond the railway line. "I don't want it getting full of water. See you later."

Inside the Tower, a number of residents were gathered in the entrance hall talking to the caretaker, who was handing out leaflets.

"Those living on the ground floor," he was saying, "must either move up an' stay with people 'igher up, or go off to safety somewhere else. The water could be twelve feet deep round the block here."

"How long will it last, Mr. Prentice?" someone wanted to know.

"It could be two weeks," the caretaker replied. "Or even longer," he added ominously. Mrs. Pole could see he was enjoying his new found importance. "Come along now, you haven't got long, you know," he called out.

Eileen was standing on the edge of the group. Seeing Mrs. Pole she came up to her.

"I'm worried about Jerry," she said anxiously. " 'E's down at Bankside, and that's right on the river."

"He'll be all right, dear," Mrs. Pole said sympathetically. "They'll take care of 'im, won't they? They always do, these big firms. It's government, really."

"Yes, but what about me an' Marlene, stuck in 'ere, without 'im, all by ourselves. Two weeks, Mr. Prentice said the water could stay, and we'd be trapped here all that time. Still," she added vaguely, "I expect they've got boats an' things."

Pole greeted his wife with relief. He had obviously been fretting in her absence.

"There's a terrible flood coming from the river," he said, agitatedly. "It's been on the radio and the caretaker's been round. Did you 'ear the sirens."

Mrs. Pole nodded weakly. "What's it say on the radio?" she asked. Her husband went over to the small red portable radio he kept near his chair and switched it on. There was a crackle of static then they heard the clear tones of the announcer. "This is the B.B.C. Here is a special announcement . . ."

The message that followed repeated the warnings of the posters and leaflets, except in so far as it made no mention of the depth of water to be expected, or the length of time it might last.

"That Mr. Prentice, the caretaker, said to fill the bath and basin with water to drink," her husband said, "so I did that. We ain't got a lot of food to eat though."

"No, we ain't got enough for a week," Mrs. Pole agreed. "I wonder if I could go down to the shops." She was thinking that they only had Georgina's five pounds to last them until the flood went down, and in fact they had almost nothing at all in the house.

To her relief, her husband refused to allow such a dangerous course. They were still wondering what to do, when there was a knock at the door. Outside stood a woman from the floor above.

"I just came down to see if you were all right," she said, "and to see if you needed any help or anything. I know your 'usband doesn't get about so well." Mrs. Pole told her about the food situation. "Don't you worry," the woman said, "I'll send Harry down to the shop on the corner. I want some things for myself anyway. What would you like me to get?"

This offer, kind and well-intentioned as it was, upset

Mrs. Pole more than any other feature of the alert had done so far. She found it difficult to decide what they needed at such short notice, and was reluctant to admit how little they had to spend. Eventually, the woman realized something of the problem.

"Look," she said, "I'll tell Harry to get a whole load of stuff in, then if you run low, you can pop up to see me and take what you want. You can settle up with me later. I think that would be easiest, wouldn't it?"

When she had left, the Poles sat in their chairs and looked at each other. They felt less lonely and afraid, but it all seemed utterly incomprehensible. Neither of them could understand how this crisis could have built up so suddenly and without any apparent warning. Outside, on the stairs, they could hear the sound of feet and noises of people carrying heavy objects, as those who lived on the ground floor and basement moved up to stay with friends, taking their possessions with them. The children were enjoying the excitement and raced up and down, chattering and laughing. Pole switched on the gas fire and they settled down to wait.

*   *   *

Less than two miles away, Dave Cox was able to hear the sirens without difficulty, since one had been placed on the roof of the new building at the borough offices. Immediately after the final orders had come through, he and six others had been sent off in their cars to the Battersea district and told to get on with their task of warning people on their list.

Now that the alert had begun, Dave realized that he felt distinctly uneasy about the entire operation. To begin with, his list contained eighteen names and addresses, allowing him, he calculated, a little over three minutes in which to find the house or flat, arouse the occupants, explain the danger to them and tell them what to do. Dave had no illusions about the sort of difficulties he would encounter. A week ago he had been detailed to assist on an outing for twenty residents of an old people's home in the borough. It had taken over an hour to bring them out of the home and load them on to the coach. This had not been because the old people had dawdled or forgotten things, or because they had not been ready. It had taken that length of time because they simply could not move any faster. Old men and women with arthritic limbs and those needing walking aids were very slow.

While they had been waiting at the Council offices Dave had talked to one of the policemen who had been helping in the building. To his amazement he had learned that no loudspeaker cars were being sent out to broadcast the news of the alert to people who had not heard or understood the sirens.

"We don't have loudspeakers on the cars nowadays," the sergeant had told him. "The public didn't like them. We've got half a dozen loudhailers, of course, but they're not much use, especially in this weather."

"Well, we'll have to hope most people hear the sirens," Dave had replied cheerfully. The sergeant had smiled at his optimism.

"Listen, lad," he said, "you may not know this but we held a siren practice last year in Lambeth. It was a bloody joke. In the area we selected, three-quarters of the people either didn't hear the sirens or else they didn't know what they were for, and of the ones that did, three-quarters of them didn't have any idea of what to do. If you lot think you'll find a population fully aware that there is a danger of imminent flooding, you couldn't be more wrong. There are over a hundred thousand people in this borough; if as many as ten thousand of them know what's going on, you'll be lucky."

The sergeant was correct in his assumptions, although he had given a rather biased view of the position. In fact a surprisingly large number of people were aware of the danger by as early as half past nine. This was largely due to the deployment of the emergency services, and the restrictions in public transport. When the sirens went and the warning had been put out on B.B.C. radio and television as well as on local radio stations, the effect was cumulative; as more people heard the news they began to leave their jobs, or at least telephone their wives and families, spreading the circle of awareness further.

Unfortunately, this awareness was patchy. Certain districts found nearly the entire population alerted, and, if not prepared for what would happen, at least ready to react. Others, however, had been completely passed by; they had missed the sirens and either not noticed, or not realized the significance of the activity around them. To these the first inrush of water was to be an overwhelming shock.

The truth behind the sergeant's words became evident as soon as Dave Cox set to work. The first address on his list was a basement in a dingy cul-de-sac on the edge of some derelict ground. The occupant was described on the paper as a woman of eighty-two in good health. He hammered on the door for four minutes before she appeared; a tiny old woman in a brown dress who peered at him shortsightedly.

"Mrs. McCann?" he asked.

"Eh, yes."

"I'm from the Council. I have come to warn you that there is a danger of flooding and this means it will be necessary for you to leave your home for a while. Do you have any neighbors you could go to who live on the first floor or higher?"

"Eh, what's that?" she asked. Dave repeated the question. The noise of the wind and rain was now so loud it was difficult for the old woman to hear unless he shouted right into her ear.

"Flooding," she said querulously, "there's never been no flooding 'ere. It's damp all right, but no flooding. You're not getting me out with talk of flooding."

"Please, Mrs. McCann," Dave urged, "it really is most urgent that you go to safety. Do you know anyone nearby?"

"Go away," Mrs. McCann shouted at him sharply, "go away. I don't want to hear no more about it, go away an' leave me in peace." Stepping back inside, she banged the door in his face. For a moment Dave was at a loss as to what to do. He rapped on the door and called, but the old woman stubbornly refused to reappear. He climbed back up the steps to pavement level and looked round. It was a depressing enough street at the best of times, but even to his inexperienced eye it was a death trap. Mrs. McCann's basement was near the bottom of the street where a high brick wall joined the two rows of houses. Any water coming down would back up and spread out rapidly into the surrounding houses.

Seeing a man coming down the street, Dave ran up to him and asked his help.

"I can't stay," he explained. "I've got a long list of people to see, but could you try and make sure Mrs. McCann gets up to safety?" The man looked dubious.

"I dunno," he said, moodily, "what about my own folks? I oughter be looking after them."

"Well, find someone else to help the old lady," Dave yelled at him as he hurried off, "before she drowns." Worried and upset by the encounter, he continued on his round.

Two streets away, he found another old woman, but to his relief, a band of her neighbors were already looking after her. "We've got all her stuff out," a man told him proudly, "even her cooker and carpet. She's staying with us on the top floor till it's all over."

This pattern was repeated twice over; in both cases watchful neighbors and friends had turned out immediately to help someone they knew to be in difficulties. People were laughing and joking cheerfully as they lugged furniture up out of harm's way and barricaded doors. One woman offered him a cup of tea and told him it was "just like the blitz."

In Culver Street, he came back to earth with a crunch. An old man living alone refused even to come to the door. Dave could hear him inside, moving about and muttering to himself. He pushed one of the Council's notices through the letterbox and rang the doorbells of neighboring houses before he got a reply.

"It's no good," the stout woman who answered the door told him, "he's mad, that man. Never comes out except at night and won't let anyone go near him. Meals on Wheels tried to get in a few times, but he wouldn't open the door. There's nothing you can do."

Resignedly he set off again through the rain, the weather getting worse every minute. The leaden gray cloud which had covered the sky since early morning had darkened perceptibly. The storm center was now less than twenty miles away.

The next address was a blank. There was no one at home and the flat was obviously deserted. There was now less than twenty-five minutes left in which to complete his mission and he was still only a third of the way through his list. At this rate the last four or five addresses would not be reached in time, and he had no doubt as to the fate which lay in store for the occupants. Old and frail, utterly bewildered they would be swept to their deaths, trapped and drowned in the rising water. Mentally he tried to picture the street he was in as it would look after the flood had struck. The experts had said the water would be twelve to fifteen feet deep, perhaps more. It was almost unimaginable.

* * *

While Dave Cox and his colleagues were doing their best to accomplish an impossible task, the police were experiencing their own difficulties. All over London cars and vans were hurrying towards the flood zones with men drawn from the safer areas. Officers were being pulled from their patrols and daily routine work to begin the massive job of attempting to warn the hundreds of thousands of people who were as yet unaware of their peril. Round the city, at strategic points out of reach of the water, a ring of command posts was being established; canteens and stores were being set up, vehicle depots organized; while on the streets the traffic division was attempting to open up a system of clearways for the emergency forces.

The original plan was for all units to be in position by the time of the final alarm, but owing to the conflicting orders less than a fifth of the men had arrived by this time. The delayed cancellation of the state visit meant that several of the busiest roads around Westminster and Buckingham Palace remained closed almost until the sirens were sounded, causing traffic congestion in other roads, some of which had been designated as clearways, and this hampered the movement of the reinforcements.

However, by straining every resource at his command, Larkin finally managed to get the majority of his men into their new positions by ten-thirty. After assigning police for duty at the new command posts, and others for setting up the clearways, there were less than three thousand left who could actually go out into the streets and warn the public. By then, however, much of the impact had been lost. Many people had forgotten about the sirens or lost interest when nobody had explained their significance and were continuing with their ordinary business as though nothing had happened. Those others who had appreciated the position had taken to their cars in an attempt to get home.

* * *

In the operations room Inspector Weaver, the officer in charge of traffic control, was experiencing particular difficulty in keeping the clearways open, as desperate drivers ignored the signs and drove round the barriers.

At ten-thirty he reported to Kingsway flood control that the Albert Embankment section, opposite Parliament, was jammed solid with cars.

"I'm afraid there's very little we can do, sir," the police liaison officer reported to Carswell, "we can't spare the men to patrol every exit and entrance, so they're pouring on to it from all sides. It is completely blocked at the Vauxhall Bridge roundabout and there's a tail-back for two miles."

"They must be mad. What do they think they're going to do when the river starts to overflow? You must clear it."

"I'm sorry, sir," the officer shrugged his shoulders helplessly. He was fair-haired and very young, Carswell noticed. "Our men have been trying to warn them, but nothing will make them leave their cars."

"What do you think?" Carswell asked Derek, when he had told him the news. "The police estimate that there may be as many as ten thousand people down there. It'll be a massacre."

"Yes," Derek agreed, without looking at him, "it'll be exactly that." He took a telephone from Peter and spoke rapidly to the warning room. "I want the figures for the river tide gauge," he said. There was a moment's pause, as he listened, then "O.K., thanks," he said and handed the receiver back. "It's coming fast," he said, walking over to the wall map. "The water is level with the banks already at Tilbury and there's been local bank failure, according to the port authorities. It'll hit Thamesmead during the next quarter of an hour. By then we should know what height of water to expect." Taking a chinagraph pencil he drew a thick red line down each bank at the mouth of the estuary.

* * *

Police Constable Charles Partridge was angry and worried. He was also very cold and wet. The steady rain in which he had been standing for the last half an hour had begun to penetrate beneath the folds of his waterproof cape and the patches of dampness were slowly spreading. He was standing beside the road on the Albert Embankment with his back to the river. In front of him, locked immovably in the vicelike grip of a monstrous snarl up, was a seemingly endless line of stationary cars that sat nose to tail with their motors running.

Partridge had been drafted into the central area, together with a large number of his colleagues from Notting Hill, to assist the forces in the danger zone, and had been detailed to patrol the embankment which was designated as a clearway. Almost immediately the wail of the sirens had been heard and they had begun putting up the steel barriers and turning back private cars.

There had not been enough men, however, to police every entrance. Cars began pouring into the area as news of the alert spread and thousands upon thousands of office workers streamed over the bridges in an effort to get home before the floods struck. As they went they were joined by equally heavy traffic coming westwards, up the river; men and women from the industrial factories of the south bank making for their homes in Lambeth, Battersea and Wandsworth. At first the police had attempted to stem this flow of vehicles but, as more and more filtered through on the unmanned side roads, they had eventually given up in despair. The sergeant radioed through to traffic control that the clearway was impassable. So Charles Partridge had stood about in the rain for the last twenty minutes, watching the alternately crawling and stationary cars, and waiting for orders. He was beginning to wonder if he could find some shelter anywhere, when the sergeant came up.

"Right, lad," he said morosely, "new orders. You're to start asking this lot," he waved a hand at the lines of cursing drivers, "to leave their vehicles and seek safety at first floor level or above. That clear?"

"But Sarge," Partridge protested, "tell them to abandon their cars! You must be joking. We haven't a hope. They'll just tell us to get stuffed."

"I know, lad," the sergeant said patiently. He was a big kindly man and popular with the men under his command. "I dare say most of them will tell you to jump into the blasted river, but we have to try."

The young constable looked around him. As far as he could see the main road was one solid queue and every side road was jammed with drivers trying to cut in. At a guess it would be the same story on every street in the vicinity, he thought.

"How long have we got?" he asked, and the sergeant made a wry face. "They said originally it would start overflowing at eleven o'clock, but your guess is as good as mine. Don't you worry, though, we'll get orders to pull out before it goes over your head." He gave a laugh and went off down the road to inform the rest of his squad.

Partridge looked over the embankment wall, the river was about six feet below the top. A muddy brown sea of choppy water, flowing swiftly upstream. He heaved a sigh of resignation and walked over to the nearest car.

* * *

Thirty feet below the pavements of Chelsea Pat Gouch and Andy Hayward were in trouble. Pat was a senior repairs foreman for the water authority, a gray-haired man of fifty, who had spent the whole of his working life in the thankless task of keeping the capital's sewers operating efficiently. His assistant, Andy, was ten years younger, a small, lithe, cheerful individual, who kept up a constant stream of conversation as they went about their work in the dark, brick lined tunnels. With them was a young trainee.

Very few people were aware of their activities. Most Londoners never gave a thought to the enormous system of pipes and conduits that networked the city, carrying away the waste of its seven and a half million inhabitants. Yet Pat and Andy's work was vital. Without them, the constantly flowing channels would have swiftly blocked up and raw sewage have backed up in the pipes with disastrous consequences for the drains and lavatories above.

The reason for the men's presence underground at such a hazardous time, when the volume of rain alone was sufficient to keep out the normal repair crews, was to unstop a blockage in a storm weir leading to a river overflow. It was this operation that their chief had been given special instructions to carry out by Miles Wendoser.

During the downpour earlier in the week it had been realized that the outflow from the weir in the old Fleet tunnel had become blocked, preventing the excess water from draining off, and causing congestion further up the system. After Thursday's particularly heavy rain, the road gullies themselves became blocked and water flooded across some streets in Kensington. Pat and his two helpers had been sent down to clear the obstruction.

They had entered the system through a manhole in the main intercept sewer and had then walked for half a mile to the weir chamber. It was hard work for the water level, swollen by the recent rains, had risen to cover the narrow ledge that ran along the edge of the channel and the three men had to wade through water thigh deep. No one spoke during the journey, partly because the effort of forcing a passage through the swirling liquid was so great, but also because all of them were anxious to get the job over as quickly as possible. They were well aware of the dangers involved. Owing to the short pause in the rain which had taken place during the night, the water level in this part of the sewer network had fallen just enough to permit an inspection, but this was only a temporary respite. Even now, on the surface it was raining again. Within a short while the water would begin to pour through the drains filling the tunnel they were in almost to the roof in a very short space of time, since there was such an enormous volume of water on the roads.

They waded on in silence. The lamps fastened to their safety helmets shone brightly, revealing the damp encrusted brickwork of the great tunnel, streaked green and yellow by the nitrous atmosphere. All about them the noise of water was magnified and distorted by the tunnel, and ahead the distant roar of the weir sounded ominously.

The noise grew steadily until, suddenly, almost without warning the arched roof of the tunnel disappeared and they were standing at the entrance to an immense underground chamber sixty feet across, its roof supported on ornate iron pillars that straddled the water course. As they entered, the young boy, Billy, pressed forward excitedly.

"Blimey," he exclaimed in awe. "I've never seen anything like this before," he took the lamp from his helmet to inspect the further recesses of the chamber.

"Aye, they built big, the Victorians, and they built to last," Andy mopped his face. Despite the clammy dampness, the exertion of the trip up the tunnel had left him pouring with sweat.

"I remember when I first saw this place, twenty years ago, and how I felt the same way." While the other two talked Pat was examining the chamber carefully. The weir itself was unblocked. The level in the main channel was still not quite high enough to reach it, though now and then a stream of water spilled over and down towards the vast gates that protected the entrance to the river. These gates were the most impressive feature of the chamber, four colossal flaps of iron set in two tiers, one above the other, each the height of an average man. They were designed to allow the excess flow out into the river, entering at high water.

Turning his gaze to the left of the chamber, Pat soon realized what was wrong. Water was gushing down the stepped spillway that marked the junction of the old sewer with the main channel. The flow was swift, as it always was, due to the drop involved, and the stream was white and broken with foam where it passed over the steps. It was this which was making the noise that reechoed through the vaultlike chamber. He called the others over.

"What do you make of that?" he asked. Billy remained silent, but Andy realized what he meant at once.

"The flow should be much higher down there," he said. "We expected to find the weir covered, didn't we?"

"That's what I was thinking," Pat said quietly, "so if there is a blockage . . ."

"It must be up the old tunnel somewhere," Andy finished the sentence for him.

All three men peered up at the entrance to the old sewer. Their torches seemed scarcely able to penetrate its black interior. It had an oddly sinister air about it, and not one of them relished the prospect of venturing down it.

"Well," said Pat, at length, "I suppose we'd better take a look now, now that we're here. I'll go first and you two follow, but watch where you put your feet," he said warningly to Billy, "this place isn't like most of the others you've been in. It's very old and the brickwork's dodgy in places."

A stairway had been cut in the slope leading up to the entrance and an iron rail had been built into the wall for support. The three clambered up and stepped gingerly into the tunnel mouth.

"Careful now," Pat said, "it moves fast here, don't lose your footing." Slowly they moved ahead, wading down the middle of the stream. The water was shallower than on their first trip, reaching only their ankles, but the tunnel was smaller, so that they were forced to stoop. For what seemed to Billy an eternity they continued in this fashion, their lamps casting queer shadows on the moist lichen-covered walls. Here and there he saw patches where the brickwork had almost collapsed, eaten away perhaps by fungus or worn down by the constant flow. In front of him the two older men were discussing the state of the sewer in low tones, their voices magnified and hollowed by the tunnel, while behind them the roar of the spillway had sunk to a low rumble.

The obstruction, when they finally came to it, loomed up with startling suddenness. One minute they were moving on into an endless black void, the next they were faced with a great plug of white gray material that filled the entire tunnel from the roof to the surface of the water. They examined it curiously, puzzled by its appearance and size; for some reason they felt reluctant to touch it.

"What the hell's that?" Andy asked, shining his lamp on to its surface. Billy's first thought was that they had stumbled upon one of the enormous outcrops of fungus growths of which he had heard, that were said to abound in the older passages of the system. Pat prodded the surface with a pick, the metal point grated sharply.

"You know what it is?" he said, peering at it more closely. "Cement, Portland bloody cement. Some bugger must've tipped a load down one of the shafts, and the stuff's seized up solid." With a laugh he swung the pick, it bounced off the unyielding stone with a dull booming sound. "See that, hard as bloody rock. Take a bomb to shift it."

The relief in discovering such a simple, if unusual, explanation to this strange phenomenon set them laughing and joking among themselves. The cement was surprisingly strong and withstood repeated blows from their picks and hammers, without yielding more than a few splintered fragments. Pat spent some time examining the lower portion which was hidden by the water. Evidently the cement had been unable to seal the channel entirely.

"It must have come down when the water level was right up high," he theorized, "and set firm when the level dropped, all except that bit at the bottom, that never had a chance to get dry."

"I reckon this is what's causing problems up the hill," Andy observed.

"Aye," Pat agreed, "there's probably a fair bit of water behind there. They'll have to stop the pipe further up before they try an' do anything about it."

Their job done, the three men turned and began the return journey. They walked swiftly, aware of the danger of lingering unnecessarily below ground when a flood alert was in force. With the flow behind them the walk was less tiring, and soon they heard the noise of the weir chamber ahead.

It was some moments later that they felt the first signs of danger. A tremor seemed to run down the tunnel, as though something large and heavy had fallen far back inside. They paused for a second to listen. To their horror, there followed a roaring blast of sound that shook the walls around them.

"Run," Pat screamed to the other two. "For God's sake, run!"

As the appalling realization of what had happened burst upon them, they began a desperate stumbling race through the water that dragged at their boots. They had almost reached the mouth of the weir chamber when the torrent hit them.

Younger and fitter than the others, Billy had just reached the entrance. Lungs bursting, the blood pounding in his head with the effort, he flung himself through, clutching with desperate strength at the hand rail as his feet slipped from under him on the slimy steps. Behind, he heard a tremendous boom of thunder and a single piercing scream of animal terror, before the water burst from the tunnel mouth like an erupting geyser.

Clouds of spray vomited forth, half blinding him, and a solid column of water raced outwards, across the

chamber, on to the weir, with the momentum of an express train. Dimly, in the now almost total darkness, he
saw the figures of his companions flung down into the
maëlstrom that now seethed around the iron gates. By
some freak of chance their lamps still worked, and he
could see them fighting uselessly against the raging
strength of the water.

It seemed only seconds before the flow had risen
waist deep, even in the highest parts of the chamber.
In a vain attempt to help his friends, Billy relaxed his
hold on the rail; instantly he was sucked downward
and swept away. Reaching out frantically, his fingers
managed to grasp the bottom-most rung and he clung to
it with a strength born of terror.

Pulling his head clear to the surface, he looked down
towards the weir where a yellow glow in the water still
marked the struggles of one of his friends. Then abruptly the figure was tossed to the surface for a second. In
the momentary gleam of light from the upturned helmet, he recognized Andy's panic-distorted face. As he
watched in horror, a great chunk of debris from the
burst cement shot from the tunnel, bounced crazily on
the crest of the weir and smashed into the helpless man.

Though stunned by the shock of what had taken
place, Billy could see that his own position was no less
critical. The weir chamber was now nowhere less than
chest deep and the level continued to rise, with frightening speed. His only chance, he realized, was to reach
some place of safety, where he might be able to hold
on until the level dropped again, provided the two tiers
of doors still operated to prevent the water reaching the
roof.

Seeing that the flow had become less violent, he abandoned his hold on the railing, once more, and struck
out for the gate. At one side he had noticed a ladder
leading to a narrow gantry built presumably to enable
the engineer to service the hinges and locks. If he could
reach that he would be safe for a while at least.

Kicking off his boots, he swam out awkwardly, trying to hold his face out of the filthy liquid. The tunnel mouth was now completely submerged, but water was evidently still flowing in for the current carried him toward his goal, pitching him up against the doors with a crash that jarred his bones. The iron surface was pitted and covered with slime; fighting to get a grip on its surface he began to inch himself slowly towards the ladder.

It seemed to take a lifetime, slipping and sliding with the water pulling him first one way then the other, and at times pinning him so firmly that he could scarcely move. He was still two feet from safety when a tremor ran down the door and above the noise of the water there came a slow harsh grating of metal. Looking upwards, the boy, now paralyzed with fear, saw that the iron hinges were starting to turn. The pressure of the water was opening the gates to the river. He made a last desperate attempt to clutch at the ladder, his fingers touching its rungs, then with a dull clang that rang through the chamber the giant doors slid open and the whirling current swept him through the gates.

The flood had claimed its first three victims.

* * *

Tilly sat in the car watching the cumbersome movements of the crane which was attempting to hoist up one end of an iron girder. The dark figures of the rescuers stood out clearly against the heaps of gray brown stone. It had started to rain again and the drops splashed hard on the wind-screen, distorting the scene. She had offered to help once more, but Johnny had told her briskly to stay out of the way and handle any messages that came over the radio phone. Squinting through the glass she could make him out; guiding the crane operator from a crazily tilted section of wall. It was a complicated and difficult maneuver; the girder had to be extracted from the rubble with the least possible disturbance, otherwise the whole pile might collapse, falling inward on the trapped man below.

The crane ceased its lurching crawl, and evidently was now correctly positioned. She saw the massive hook lowered to be grasped by two of the waiting men. There was a moment's pause, then the jib gave a jerk as it took the weight. Johnny was still in the same position, his hand waving the operator steadily on. All at once he leapt down, to be lost from sight for a second, reappearing where the lower end of the girder had been dragged free. Tilly saw him pulling it round towards him, swinging it clear of the surrounding wreckage. She could only guess at its weight; the engineer's strength must be tremendous.

The beam came away, the crane edging backwards on its tracks. The growl of the engine reached her even through the loud drumming of the rain. Her eyes strayed round towards the river. On the far bank, almost obscured by the downpour, she could just distinguish the shapes of those houses in Greenwich. A large black barge was towing a line of covered barges upstream. The tide was coming in fast and the wind was raising broken waves on the swiftly flowing water. She had never given a thought to it before, now it seemed menacingly high.

Her thoughts were interrupted by a new sound. High above the noise of the rain and the machines, she heard the steady wail of a siren. At first she dismissed it as something to do with the docks and scarcely noticed when it stopped. Then it came again, and this time she listened. Six long blasts. She was still puzzled over their meaning, when the radio telephone beeped. Leaning down she picked up the receiver.

"Is Johnny Easton there," demanded a voice. "I must speak to him."

"I'll try and get him for you," Tilly said. "Wait a second."

"Please hurry," said the voice urgently, "it's vitally important that I talk to him now."

Tilly sounded the horn, but she saw Johnny was already on his way over. He grabbed the receiver from her without ceremony. "This is Johnny Easton," he said. "I've just heard the sirens."

When he finished listening, he replaced the telephone carefully and turned to Tilly.

"The surge is definitely coming up the river. You've just heard the warning sirens. It'll be here in about forty-five minutes, but I doubt if this bank will hold for more than twenty. You had better get home while you can."

"I'm not leaving here till you get Reg out," she said stubbornly.

"There's nothing you can do," Johnny replied angrily, "and you are in danger here. I'm going to stay and get him out, so don't you worry."

She glared at him. "Do you think I'm a child? If I want to stay, I'll stay."

"Listen," Johnny said, "this place is a death trap. There'll be precious little left above the water. If you stay here you are in great danger, and we shall have you to take care of as well. If you hurry now you may be able to get back to Greenwich."

"But what will you do?" Tilly asked. "When will you go?"

"I'll be O.K.," he grinned. "If necessary, I'll swim back home."

Tilly got out of the car and began to walk towards the foot tunnel that ran under the river to Greenwich. At the edge of the site she stopped and looked back. Johnny was back with the rescuers, but he saw her and waved. She wondered when she would see him again.

Chapter Six

Once the initial excitement had died down, the atmosphere in the Kingsway control room was surprisingly calm. The Coordinator and officials got on with their work, answering telephones, taking down reports, relaying messages and issuing advice with an air of unhurried efficiency, as though they were taking part in another exercise. It amazed Derek to see the team of girls marking the inexorable progress of the surge on the master plan of the capital, with a total lack of concern. They might have been playing some complicated kind of game instead of charting the slow destruction of the city that was their home. They had been chosen for the job from the police force, and presumably they found it no more nerve-racking than plotting traffic accidents and car chases.

The first situation reports from the lower reaches had just come in, and the girls were busy with grease pencils and colored markers, altering the picture to show the new position. Already the land on both banks around Tilbury and Gravesend, as far as Purfleet, was marked in red. These were the Essex and Kent marshes; the traditional flood plain of the river since before history was recorded. Recent generations had reclaimed this land, building dykes and walls in a determined effort to hold back the sea. So far the map showed that the water had penetrated only a short distance inland; evidence that the walls were holding, with only small-scale overflowing and the occasional minor breach. Any major bank failure would be instantly felt as the sea raced in to inundate the vast area of flat ground behind.

From time to time either Carswell or one of his assistants would call out fresh data to them to be plotted. LIMITED OVERTOPPING WEST THURROCK—LOCAL FLOODING ERITH MARSHES—RIVER INGREBOURNE REPORTS BANK FAILURE, WATER ENTERING DAGENHAM SEWAGE WORKS. The messages charted the progress of the flood up the river. Gravesend, Thurrock, Purfleet, past the Wennington and Rainham marshes with their massive new defenses, and on towards the densely populated east end, Barking and East Ham, Woolwich and Silvertown. ILFORD PUMPING STATION, LEVEL OF RIVER RODING CAUSING CONCERN. The unusually heavy flow in the Thames creeks was backing up and causing problems some way from the immediate flood zone.

"How are we doing, Derek?" It was the Director General at his side. Despite his bulk, he was light on his feet. "It looks as though the new walls are standing up to the strain."

"They should do, they were designed to take this kind of pressure. The banks will contain most of the flow till the surge hits Woolwich, apart from some localized spilling here and there," he replied.

"Well that's good news, at any rate," the Director General beamed at Derek, with cheerful optimism.

"No, it's not good news. It is exactly what we expected," Derek replied, crushingly. "Personally, I would rather see the marshes flood as much as possible. It might take some height off the surge."

"You mean let the flood exhaust itself in regions that don't matter?" the Director General said.

"They still matter; a lot of people live there, and there are factories, refineries, gas works and there's some good farming land too with a lot of livestock, but I would rather see that go than let central London take the full brunt of the surge. However, unfortunately, we don't have any choice."

"A rather negative attitude, I think, Thompson," said a smooth voice at his side. It was Wendoser, who had evidently been listening to the conversation. "I am only surprised you didn't recommend that we knocked down those carefully raised walls so that Canvey Island, Barking and Thamesmead would be inundated as well. Such a pity for them to miss it all."

The councilor gazed down at Derek disdainfully, rocking to and fro slightly on the balls of his feet. His plump, self-confident face angered Derek, but he managed to control his temper.

"No, Miles," he said equably, "I simply told you to build a flood barrier, remember?"

"It was a pity you didn't tell us how much it was going to cost, while you were about it. But there is no point in worrying over past mistakes." He went on hastily, before Derek could reply. "Will you come over here, please. I want a word with you." Without waiting for an answer, he stalked off into the conference room. Derek followed; the room was empty. Wendoser took up a stance in the center and glared at him arrogantly.

"Shut the door," he snapped, "I'd rather keep this between ourselves at this stage."

"What is this I hear," he said, when Derek had complied, "about you sending council staff off home, when they should be attending to their duties?"

"Certainly, I ordered that those people whose jobs were not vital should go home, if they could be sure of reaching safety in time. I imagine most sensible people would do the same. Do you have any objection?"

"Objection! I most certainly do have an objection," Wendoser hissed. "The rules state perfectly clearly that all personnel are to remain at their posts, and yet one of your staff turns up at a school in Lambeth before the sirens are sounded and takes her daughter away, while at the same time telling the headmaster that he had better get out before he drowns. Allowing your own staff to start taking precautions before the public have been warned is a most serious matter. I dread to think what might happen if the press were to get hold of this."

Derek's jaw tightened angrily. "Frankly, Miles, I couldn't give a damn. This isn't some public relations exercise we've engaged in. Any minute now the North Sea is going to come into the center of London; the lives of hundreds of thousands are at stake. If this woman has had the sense to realize that and make sure she and her child are safe, then she's doing the right thing."

"Haven't you considered the risks involved?" Miles was almost beside himself with rage. His usual icy calm had deserted him. "What about the panic that can be spread by sending people off without proper instructions or knowledge of the situation. The alarm and confusion that will have been created at the school by this woman turning up and demanding her child, before the sirens were sounded, and where the staff are aware that she works for the council and has access to special information. It's exactly the kind of thing that starts panic." Miles was breathing hard, his face flushed with anger.

Derek eyed him squarely. "I don't know why you are so worried by the idea of panic," he said. "If panic will get people out of the danger areas, then I'm all for it. If my girl managed to persuade the teachers to close the school down and send the children home, well and good. There will be panic enough when the sea water begins to come down the streets, only by then it will be too late. By far the greatest danger at the moment, is being caused by people in authority who are still treating this business as though it's some kind of game."

Wendoser gave a contemptuous snort. "Sentimental idiocy," he snapped. "I hope, for your sake, that no ill consequences result from your thoughtless actions. In the meantime, I should be grateful if you would consult your superiors before you make any more humanitarian gestures."

He stalked out, leaving Derek pale with fury. It was unbelievable that, at a time of national crisis, men like Wendoser could be concerned about petty details of procedure, worrying about the possible consequences of some minor irregularity, when disaster was staring them in the face. Even at this stage few could accept the true state of affairs. Like a chicken with its neck wrung, they continued to behave as though nothing had happened. There was a certain ironic humor in his thought of these officials swimming for their lives as their city drowned beneath them.

There was a knock at the door, Peter came in. He looked tired, but still alert.

"Michael Jarratt is calling in on the radio from Woolwich, Chief," he said, "I told him you'd want to speak to him." Derek smiled at him. "Thanks," he said, "I'll come."

Jarratt was one of the radio-equipped engineers patrolling the banks. This station at Woolwich Ferry was crucial; it was here that the surge would first reach the poorly defended, upper section of the river; the section that the uncompleted barrier had been supposed to protect.

"Is there any other news?" he asked. "What about Thamesmead? I would have thought they would be awash by now."

Peter shook his head. "Officially, there's no change

from the last bulletin you heard. Overtopping along the whole length of the wall, but no serious problems so far. But I gather from the Water people that they are having difficulty in contacting the sewage plant down there, so the situation may be worse than we think."

This was the trouble, Derek thought, as he went into the radio room. Too often one only learned of a major incident through the casual reference in some other message. The river would encroach on the dry land at varying speeds and depths. What might initially appear no more serious than a few inches of wetting, could well turn into an inland lake, as water entered from points further upstream. The residents of Thamesmead might believe that they could cope with the overtopping of the river wall in front of them, particularly since the estate had been built with this danger in mind; they might be unaware of breaches above them which would let the river in from the rear.

Inside the radio office, one of the operators handed him a headset, the microphone clipped to the earpieces like those used by airline pilots. Derek picked it up, and as he did so the second engineer on duty placed a slip of paper before him. Glancing down he saw it was a summary of the latest information from the tide gauges.

"Hello, Mike," he called into the microphone, "what's it like down there?" There was a loud crackle and Jarratt's voice came on. It was clear, but Derek was conscious of a good deal of static on the air.

"The river started to come over the top in the last five minutes, sir." Jarratt was obviously shouting, to make himself heard against the wind. "It has been breaking over the top stones for some time, but now it's simply pouring over the whole length of the wall, as far as I can see and streaming down into the road. God, what a sight!" There was a pause for a moment and then Jarratt's voice came on again, speaking quickly. "It's unbelievable. The river must have risen a foot since I called in. Water coming over in torrents. It's almost impossible to see where the wall begins. It's as though the river's come right up to the road all of a sudden. There was a man trying to drive through in a mini, but he has had to give up and get out. The water is now level with the windows. He was only just in time. The noise is terrific, can you hear it?" The voice stopped, but Derek was unable to separate the confusion of sounds in the background. "There's now one enormous expanse of water running into the road and through the houses and shops. I'm on the fourth floor and I can't see any dry ground anywhere."

"How deep do you estimate the water to be in the road, Mike?" Derek asked urgently. "Is it still rising, or is the water moving through at the same depth as before?"

"It's hard to tell," came the answer, "but I think it is maintaining a depth of about three feet, judging by that car I mentioned, but it's still pouring . . ." his voice broke off. Clearly audible over the air came a dull, thunderous rumble, like a distant explosion. When Jarratt spoke again, his voice was high pitched with excitement.

"It's the wall," he shouted, "the wall's gone! It's given way! A great wave just swept forward into the houses. It's like a bloody avalanche. Incredible, the car's gone; submerged or rolled over maybe. I can't see. The windows on the ground floor of the houses around have gone and one, two, at least two doors are broken down. You can see where the breach is. The river's rushing through a gap fifty yards wide. Jesus, there's a man, I think, in one of the houses! What's he doing. He's mad . . . he's gone. No, there he is!"

There was a confused babble of sounds and voices, as though several people were speaking at once, then Jarratt's voice came back more clearly, and speaking with a new, slower note.

"There was a man trying to get out of a house, but the water knocked him down, he nearly got up, but I think he's definitely had it. The water is surging through the houses now."

Derek put his hand over the mouthpiece. "Can you switch this to the loudspeakers through there?" he asked the operator, with a jerk of his head towards the door. The man nodded silently and his hands moved to the switches and levers in front of him. A few seconds later they heard the sound of Jarratt's voice in the control room.

Derek had been correct in his earlier assumption that the majority of the men and women who staffed the control room had very little clear idea of what major flooding of a city the size of London would entail. True they had read the scientific data and seen the documentary films. They had looked at the maps and heard the figures, but none of them had thought of what the streets they lived in would look like with twelve feet of water in them, or of how they would attempt to cope without light, heat or power for a fortnight.

The surge tide was virtually an academic conception, a red line on the charts, a series of annual exercises on which artificial reports of flood damage were read out and telephone lines tested. Even after the final warning had been issued the real meaning had not yet gone home.

Among the senior staff present there was a tendency to encourage the belief that somehow the worst might somehow be avoided. There was still reluctance to admit that the situation had gone too far. For this reason Miles Wendoser was received with encouragement when he read out the latest weather forecast from Bracknell, which suggested that the storm had lost a degree of its former strength.

"Wind speed at Southend is still only force ten," he told them, "and there are signs that it may be dropping. Barometric pressure is better too. It looks as though the worst is over." His remarks were received with murmurs of relief and there were smiles on many faces.

"Of course," he continued, "I am told by the experts that this won't make a great deal of difference, but even so it's good news." Miles beamed at their hopeful faces and turned away to talk to Carswell.

"I think I'll let the boys from the press have a sight of this," he said, waving the report. "It's important to make sure they see the positive side of things." It was at precisely that moment that the loudspeakers cut in.

The effect was instantaneous and dramatic. Conversation ceased and silence fell as every head turned toward the sound.

"I can't see if anyone else was caught by the wave, but they wouldn't stand a chance . . . The water is nearly up to the top of the doorways, flowing at a tremendous speed. There's a brick wall collapsed, a couple of splashes and it has gone . . . It isn't Woolwich any more, it's just river everywhere as far as I can see."

The distorted metallic voice echoed round the room. The grins and smiles faded, to be replaced by expressions of shocked disbelief as realization of the disaster sank in. Even Wendoser was stunned. Seeing that he had made his point. Derek turned back to the radio operator. "O.K.," he said, "that's enough." Jarratt's voice ceased abruptly. Derek looked at the roomful of nervous faces. "Right," he said quietly, "now we all know what this is really about. So, no more pie in the sky optimism; let's get on with the job."

*   *   *

A short time earlier, a column of cars had pulled away from Westminster, heading northwest. It consisted of three limousines escorted by a police car and four motor cycles. The sirens and flashing lights succeeded in clearing a path through the heavy traffic around Hyde Park Corner and Knightsbridge and the convoy passed rapidly down the Cromwell Road in the direction of Hammersmith. At the flyover, there was a delay. The cars closed up and the police driver forced his way through the reluctant vehicles. At the traffic lights the man on duty waved them past, and they continued on towards Slough.

Once on the motorway, the convoy went into the fast lane and stayed there, traveling at over seventy miles an hour, despite the rain and slush. Other vehicles moved hastily out of the way to let them pass. Inside the three limousines the passengers spoke scarcely a word to each other. There were eight altogether, each a senior member of the government. They included the Lord Chancellor and two Ministers. Their destination was Windsor. The cars left the motorway and sped through the approaches to the town, towards the great castle that dominated the skyline. A small crowd of curious onlookers watched from the shelter of their umbrellas as they entered the main gate and continued on into the inner yard. Above the enormous bulk of Henry II's round tower the bright red and gold sovereign's standard flapped in the wind.

Inside the castle, the Ministers and their colleagues were led into one of the state apartments of the upper Ward. The room was magnificent, even those who had made the journey before were awed by the sumptuous furnishings. The ceiling was painted by Verrio, the carving by Grindling Gibbons and above cabinets of rare porcelain hung paintings by Rembrandt and Van Dyke. Some of the men exchanged whispers of appreciation.

At the far end of the room a door opened with a soft click. A slim elegant man with silver hair and an erect military bearing entered, his shoes falling soundlessly on the thick carpet. Advancing towards them he greeted the Chancellor.

"Her Majesty is ready to begin at once, My Lord," he said quietly. "The necessary preparations have been made. Will you please follow me to the Council Chamber."

Exactly six minutes later the eight men, seated at a

polished oak table, watched as the Queen placed her
signature on an Order in Council under the authority of
which the government proclaimed a state of emergency.

*   *   *

To his surprise one of the first calls Derek received at
Kingsway after the final alert was from Liz. Her voice
sounded concerned.

"It's a personal matter really," she told him, "and I
wouldn't have worried you, but I think you ought to
know."

"Don't stall with me, Liz. What's gone wrong?"

"Nothing, I hope," she replied quickly, "but Miss
Marchant has been on the phone. Your children's head-
mistress," she explained as Derek failed to respond to
the name. "Because of the flood warning they are sending all the children home. The school is earmarked for
an emergency center by Wandsworth Council. Anyway, she hasn't been able to contact your wife, so she
telephoned the office. I explained where you were and
she's sending the children off with one of your neighbors, a Mrs. Sarah Bentham."

"Yes, I know her," Derek admitted, "the kids are
always going round there to tea. Did you try and contact Georgina?"

"Yes I did. There's still no reply."

Derek rang off, puzzled. It was unlike Georgina to
be as scatterbrained as this. Even if she had been unable to reach home she would almost certainly have
telephoned the school once she had heard the sirens.
She might only have gone off to do some last minute
shopping, but equally she might have tried to get up
to her studio, in which case she could face a lot of difficulty in getting back across the river, especially with
the Wandsworth Bridge road area severely flooded.

Moreover, once the surge reached the city center,
knocking out of action most of the telephone system,
there would be no means of finding out when she did

at last make her way home, and she would be unable
to contact him in any way. Even if he took the car he
would have to drive out as far as Kingston before finding a bridge across the Thames that was still usable.

"Problems?" Carswell queried when he returned to
the map table.

"It's Georgina," he said. "She seems to have disappeared temporarily." Briefly he explained what had
happened.

"She's probably out shopping and on her way back,"
Miles suggested. He was standing nearby and had
heard the conversation.

"Yes, I know," Derek agreed. "It's worrying that's
all. I particularly told her not to go out without telephoning me first."

Miles looked at him sharply.

"Maybe she did and couldn't get through." Derek
shrugged.

"I just hope she hasn't got stuck anywhere near the
river," he said. "She could be trapped for days if she's
not careful." A fresh batch of messages were placed
on the table beside him and he began reading one.
Miles seemed ill at ease, he thought, and kept glancing
at him oddly. Perhaps he had at last appreciated the
true seriousness of the position they were in.

*   *   *

When Tilly had finally disappeared, Johnny called Jack
to him. "You know what those sirens mean," he said.
"I'm going to stay and try to get this man out. If any
of the men want to keep me company, I'll be glad of
their help, but I shan't mind if anyone wants to go."

"They'll all want to stay," the foreman replied unhesitatingly. "Do you want us to try and finish the
wall?"

"No, Jack, there's no time. All we can do is try to
get that poor bastard out of there, as soon as we can."

"It's going to take time. There's a hell of a lot on

top of him." Together they turned their attention to the ruins once more. The recent work with the crane had barely made any impression on the fallen building.

"It'll take all day, dragging bits out piecemeal like this. We'll have to try another way," Johnny said. "Remember I told you that when I crawled in and heard him tapping, there was another of those girders sticking out from below? Well, I think if we could get the crane on to that and hoist it up a little, it might lift the wreckage enough for me to get through underneath."

Jack looked at him with a frown. "That's a hell of a chance to take," he said seriously, "most likely the lot will come down on you."

"I know, but it looks like the only way we may have of pulling him out, before the water gets him. Those sandbags we put up will never stand up to any pressure. Anyway, we'll try it."

It took some time to maneuver the crane into the correct position and to locate the other end of the girder. Eventually, it was managed and very slowly they began lifting. At first nothing seemed to happen, the crane engine roared, the jib jerking with the strain, and gradually the rescuers saw the iron beam begin to rise, carrying the wreckage with it.

Johnny had removed his heavy jacket in readiness. As soon as he saw the girder lift enough to give him the clearance he needed, he signaled the operator to stop.

"Johnny, take care," Jack said to him pointlessly, as he bent to crawl inside. "I don't know how long it will hold. If we have any trouble out here, I'll bang on this beam we're lifting. You do the same if you get stuck."

Wriggling his way down the narrow cavity into which he had been before, Johnny found, as he had expected, that the moving of the girder had exposed a small gap in the debris at the end. By lying full length in the liquid mud that lay inches deep at the bottom, he was able to start digging at the rubble with his hands. The going was easier than he had expected. It was mostly soft dirt with a few chunks of stone and brick, and in a few minutes he had made a hole big enough for him to push his head through.

At first, his torch revealed only a confused tangle of beams and fallen brickwork. He had evidently come through into one of the lower rooms, into which the floors above had collapsed. As far as he could see, it was only the presence of the iron girder that was preventing the whole lot from coming down further.

The tapping he had heard had come along the iron, so the tramp must presumably be at the far end. Johnny began to widen the hole he had made, scraping away more of the debris that blocked his way. Above him he could detect the strain on the massive girder as it took the weight of the surrounding rubble; every now and then small pieces of dirt would shower down on him making him uncomfortably aware of the risk he was taking. It took some time to scrape a way wide enough to allow his great shoulders to pass.

Scrambling through at last, he found himself kneeling in over a foot of water that lay on the floor of the room; evidently the place was filling up rapidly. He flashed his torch round once more and called out, his voice sounding oddly hollow in the confined space. Hearing no response, he called again, and to his relief was rewarded with a faint answering cry coming from the far side of a pile of splintered timbers.

Johnny crawled forward at once with renewed energy, but was brought up short at the obstruction. Examining it carefully he saw that it was the result of the fall of the ceiling above, and that the slightest attempt at moving any of it would result in an avalanche. Since one end of the blockage was against a wall, the only way to get beyond would be by going under the girder that supported the other side. To do so, he saw, would mean lying flat in the water and trying to drag himself through while he held his breath.

For a moment he hesitated, the danger was only too

clear. He had no means of knowing what was on the other side; he could be trapped under the wreckage and drowned helplessly, or he might bring the rest of the roof down upon him. Moreover, the smallest slipping of the great beam would crush him to death instantly.

Praying that his torch would remain watertight, he took a deep breath and ducked under the water, feeling ahead of him with his hands. The water was freezing cold, numbing his body as though he had turned to ice. He fumbled with his hands, feeling the surface of the girder above him, and pushed himself forward with his legs and elbows. Clouds of debris had been stirred up, and he felt the particles of dirt against his face.

His fingers found the edge of the iron beam but immediately beyond they encountered a solid obstruction. Fighting back the instinct to pull back he twisted sideways in the blackness and to his relief his hands broke the surface unhindered. With a rush he scraped through and came up for air, but even as he opened his mouth to draw he struck his head violently on some object in the dark above him.

Panic gripped him instantly, with the horror of being trapped in a tiny space with water only a few inches from the roof. If his need for air had not been so great he might well have tried to make his way back. As it was he steeled his nerves and found that he had about a foot and a half of head room. His torch he had clipped to his belt, bringing it up he flashed it around him.

He had come out in a space about the size of a cupboard underneath a stairway and almost the same shape. In front of him, the girder he had followed disappeared into a pile of bricks that partly covered the legs of the old man, whose white face with a pathetic expression of terror and relief, gazed into his own a few feet away. The water that surrounded him was up to his chest and the low ceiling meant that he could not even sit up.

Johnny scrambled out from under the beam and into the center of the cavity where there was room enough for him to kneel. The old man clutched his arm desperately as he approached.

"Help me," he whispered hoarsely. "For God's sake help me. Don't leave me here."

"We'll have you out in a minute, don't worry," Johnny told him. "Are you hurt?"

"My legs, they're caught," the old man raised a hand from his chest and pointed. "Can't feel anything there."

Johnny began working swiftly to move the bricks that pinned the tramp to the floor. Originally they must have been supporting part of the weight of the girder, but with this now eased, he found they came away without difficulty. He gave Reg the torch to hold. It was amazing that he had managed to survive for so long, lying in the water. Even after a short time, Johnny found himself shivering uncontrollably with cold.

With most of the bricks removed he started to ease Reg out. One of his legs looked very bloody, but Johnny hoped the injury might be less serious than it looked. The old man was appallingly weak and stiff, however, and Johnny virtually had to lift him out. His skin had gone clammy to touch and his breath was coming in short irregular gasps.

"The only way out, is the way I came in," Johnny explained to him carefully. "We've got to crawl under this beam, through the water. It's not deep and not more than about three feet long, but it's the only way. I'll go first and I'll pull you through by your feet. Just don't fight it and you'll be O.K." The old man nodded dumbly. In his shrunken face, his eyes appeared unnaturally large. Johnny set him in position and started to slide himself backwards under the girder. Then he reached forward and grasped Reg by the ankles; at this point the tramp gave a horrified scream and flung himself to the side, dropping the torch into the water and plunging them both into darkness. Johnny yelled out at him to come back and pulled himself forward out of the hole. At that moment there came an echoing clang from the girder that vibrated hollowly about them. It was followed by another, and, as the echoes of that died away, there came a third stroke.

* * *

Outside in the rain Jack had been waiting for a sign of Johnny's progress. As the minutes passed he became increasingly worried. The tide had begun to rise rapidly, already it was two-thirds of the way up the wall of sandbags they had erected and water was beginning to come through in ever-growing spurts as the pressure built up. The men, he noticed, were beginning to grow nervous, looking over their shoulders at the river behind them. He looked at his watch; already Johnny had been nearly twenty minutes inside the building and the surge was due in a quarter of an hour.

He was on the point of going into the wreckage himself, convinced that something had happened to Johnny, when the sandbag wall collapsed with frightening suddenness. To the horrified cries of the watching men, the wall bulged, split, and finally burst apart, spilling a foaming inrush of brown water across the ground once more. With incredible speed, it raced over the site to the second defense bank, traveling swiftly down its length until it reached the uncompleted section, from where it began to pour down towards the rescuers.

Jack wasted no time. Roaring at his men to get clear, he seized a hammer and struck the girder three hard blows. Then, without waiting to see if these produced any effect, he began to crawl into the ruins after Johnny. Behind him the water was already streaming among the piled rubble.

* * *

Johnny had guessed the significance of the signal at once. He could hear the old tramp splashing about in the darkness and shouted to him to calm down, but the long incarceration had finally unhinged a mind that must always have been weak. There was a stream of incoherent gibberish and then the sound of weeping. Cursing himself for getting into such a mess he scrambled towards him once more and succeeded in dragging him back to the hole. When he realized what was happening, the old man suddenly began to struggle and fight with a strength Johnny would not have believed possible. Boney hands clutched at his throat, squeezing until he choked, and in self-defense he struck out. At once Reg went limp; with no time to worry whether he had hurt him or not, Johnny seized the inert body and dragged him into the water behind him.

The return journey under the beam was far more difficult than he had anticipated; inching his way frantically backwards through the water while all the time keeping his grip on Reg's legs. At one point they seemed to have snagged on some hidden obstacle, but at last, when his lungs had almost reached bursting point, he was through and pulling the old man clear.

At the hole he had made on the far side of the room he met Jack.

"Hurry!" the foreman told him urgently, "the wall's gone again and the water's coming fast." Together they hoisted Reg through and started to drag him up the narrow tunnel. Water was beginning to stream down in alarming quantities. At any moment, Johnny thought, it would start bringing down the precariously balanced masonry above them. Slipping and sliding in the mud and slush under their feet, they struggled to get out. As they reached the open air the great girder that had protected them shivered and moved slightly, and behind them came a long rumbling crash, as the roof fell in in a shower of bricks and broken joists. Soaked to the skin, covered in mud and dirt, they staggered out into the rain.

An ambulance had been standing by and Reg was at once placed on a stretcher and carried off. Soon the strident note of its siren was fading into the distance.

"How do you think he seemed?" Johnny said to Jack, as they stood looking at the torrent pouring through the breach. The latter shook his head.

"Not too good," he said. "It's a miracle you got him out at all."

At the first sign of the renewed flooding the fire brigade crews and the police rescue teams had pulled back to assist those in the surrounding houses. Johnny and his team were now the only men left on the site.

"I want everybody out of here," he told the foreman. "Get them into the truck and up towards the north. The surge will be on us in a few minutes, and there's nothing more we can do here. If you get cut off by the floods, leave the vehicle and try to get up on to the mud chute."

"What about you? Aren't you coming with us?" Johnny shook his head.

"The Chief will want someone watching this part when the surge hits it. I've got a portable radio in the car. I'll take that and stay down here."

"You'd better get some dry clothes then," Jack grunted. "We've got some in the truck." Johnny looked down at the filthy mud-soaked things he was wearing.

"Let's hope they fit," he said. "Dry clothes are going to be scarce around here from now on."

It took only a few minutes to dispatch Jack and the men. Johnny waved the barrellike Irishman off with regret; there were few people he would rather have with him in a crisis than Jack with his immense physical stamina and uncompromising practicality.

The crane driver and his assistants were still loading their machine on to its trailer; he had advised them not to bother, but they had been determined to go ahead.

Only sheer luck had saved the crane from being caught when the wall burst. If that had happened he and Jack would be dead now; the thought made him shiver momentarily and abruptly he turned away to examine the state of the tide.

There could be no doubt now that the storm center had reached the city. Gusts of wind blowing into the open site from the river were strong enough to make his progress through the slippery mud a demanding effort. Flurries of torrential rain swept around him continuously, stinging his unprotected face and hands. There had scarcely been any point in changing his clothes, he thought wryly.

When he finally made it to the bank the sight that met his eyes surpassed anything he had expected. The usually tranquil Thames had swollen into a wide sea of white-crested waves, which were already lapping the top of the defenses. It was unbelievable that the river could be so high. Only a few more inches and the main bulk of the water would come spilling over; even at a quick glance he could see that it was already appreciably higher than the dry ground behind him. The far shore was almost totally hidden from view by rain and flying spume, with the raging wind and the waves surging beneath his feet, drenching him with spray. Where the bank had given way, the river was boiling through the gap and down into the town, carving out what was virtually a new channel for itself. The breach had widened considerably and even as he watched, another section of bank slid suddenly down and was snatched away instantly by the current.

Johnny leapt down from the wall and began running along it, towards the tip of the Isle. He was searching for other weak points, places where the defenses might crumble without warning before the awful pressure, and send waves racing inland in advance of the main flood.

There was still a chance that the predicted surge might rise only a few inches above the walls, causing

damage and confusion, but not the catastrophe that
would result from total inundation.

Near the public gardens he found the first danger
spot. A blind alley ran between the entrances to neighboring wharves, ending in a wall of granite blocks.
Solid as this seemed, water was already spurting between the joints in the stone and trickling down the inside of the wall. The river here was relatively protected by wooden pilings serving the wharves. Even so,
spray was being thrown up to fall in the roadway. Un-
clipping his radio he called up the local control room,
at the same time hurrying back the way he had come.

Round the corner he careered straight into someone
running the other way. It was not until he was trying to
lift her to her feet that he realized it was Tilly.

"What are you doing back here?" he demanded angrily. "Don't you understand what's about to happen?" The girl shook her head.

"I couldn't get through the tunnel," she gasped. "I
tried to find a taxi or bus, but there's no way to get
back. So I came back to see if you could give me a lift."
In place of the smart, self-assured young lady he had
seen earlier, there was now a badly frightened girl,
though judging by the firm set of her jaw, she would be
the last to admit it. Her face was really very beautiful,
he thought, looking at her; big eyes and delicate
bones.

"Come on," he said, "let's get you out of here, while
we still can."

"Is it definitely coming, this tidal wave, surge, you
called it?" Tilly asked. In answer, Johnny took her to
the corner of the road he had just come down. At the
far end, thirty yards away, the water had begun to slop
over the wall, splashing on to the tarmac below. Even
as they watched the splashes turned into a single wave
that curved over and completely hid the wall. Tilly
raised a hand to her mouth, shocked disbelief showing
on her face.

"Come on." Johnny took her by the arm; before they could move, however, there came a noise like the roll of thunder and the incoming torrent seemed suddenly to leap towards them in an explosive burst of foam.

Together they ran to their left, down a street lined with warehouses, interspersed with massive wooden gates and shuttered windows protected by iron grilles. The area appeared deserted, several of the buildings had obviously been abandoned. The high brick walls shielded them to a great extent from the noise of the wind, but the rain still poured down with undiminished vigor and in the rear they could see the flood water spreading across the street, advancing swiftly after them. All at once, Tilly slipped and fell heavily. Johnny stooped to help her up and she scrambled quickly to her feet again, only to give a cry of pain as she put the weight on her foot.

"I'll be all right," she said. "I'll just have to go more slowly."

Johnny looked back, wiping the rain from his face. The water had not gained appreciably on them; presumably the main flow was seeking the easier path downhill, on to the low ground. Then, glancing ahead of them, his eyes encountered an ominous sign. The girl saw his expression change and followed his gaze. A few yards away a pair of high green wooden doors barred the entrance to a wharf. From the narrow gap under these water was trickling over the pavement. The meaning was clear; the river had already entered the buildings behind.

He slipped an arm round her waist and, half carrying her, set off again. Fifty yards away he saw a gate standing partly closed, and on the far side he knew there was open ground where the houses behind had been cleared for redevelopment. By cutting through there they might find a way up on to the high ground of the mud chute.

"What's the mud chute?" Tilly asked as they passed the ominously leaking doors.

"It's an artificial hill between Cubitt Town and Millwall, made out of the muck dug out from the docks, about thirty feet high." He did not add that it was a barren, weed-infested plateau, virtually without shelter. Johnny held no illusions about the conditions they would have to face if they remained in dockland. The whole area was going to be cut off and drowned. It was not impossible that the Thames might alter its course, slicing through the loop and turning the tongue of land into a true island. There was a plan of sorts, he remembered, to evacuate the people who lived here, using the pleasure steamers that, on normal days, ran tourists between Charing Cross and Greenwich. It had sounded farfetched when he had first heard about it, and in present conditions, with high winds and a river which had swollen to hide its banks, it would be impossible for the boats to get near enough for anyone to reach them.

The doors they had just passed gave a loud creaking sound, as though a heavy weight had been leant against them. Tilly was wincing at every step but he forced her on. They had almost reached their goal, when the doors burst open with a tremendous crash.

As though struck a violent blow, they broke apart, literally flying off their hinges. A solid trough of water, five feet deep, tore through and across the street to break against the far wall, in an immense arc. Instantly, as they stared rooted in amazement, the flood was boiling about their feet. Desperately, they splashed towards the gates. Johnny pushed the girl through and tried to force them shut. Already the street was filling rapidly, the water was a foot deep and exerting a savage pressure against him. Using all his great strength, he gave a tremendous heave and succeeded in driving the bolts home.

"That should hold it back for a while, at least," he

said. "The flood will take the course with the least re-
sistance, down the street." There was still a certain
amount of liquid trickling through. Tilly had lost her
hat in the road and her black curls were now soaked
and dripping with rain. She smiled at him.

"My God, I've never been so wet in my life." Using
Johnny's arm to steady herself, she removed her boots
and emptied out a stream of water. Both of them
laughed, an expression of the relief at their narrow
escape breaking through.

Johnny looked round at the place they were in. It
was a cleared site, of about ten acres, much like the
one he had been working on, except that it was barricaded in all round; on three sides, by the remains of
the original brick walls, and on the fourth, running at
right angles to the river and the street they had just
come down, by a corrugated iron fence. Ahead of them
the mud chute rose above the surrounding houses, like
the brow of a hill.

*   *   *

Details of Johnny's last radio message were passed to
Kingsway from Tower Hamlets Control, where they
were shown to Derek by Peter Collins. The Chief
looked tired, he thought, and the strain was showing
on his face.

"You shouldn't still be on duty, Peter," he said. "I'll
try and get you replaced."

"I'm quite happy to stay, sir," Peter replied quietly.
"I'd like to see it through." Derek smiled briefly.

"Get back to Johnny on the radio," he ordered. "Tell
him that the surge is running at over thirteen feet. He's
to pull out at once."

Hearing Carswell call his name, he went back to the
plotting board.

"We're starting to receive information concerning
flood penetration in the Canning Town district," the
Controller said, in his pedantic manner. "I understood

that the defenses there were sufficiently high to prevent such an occurrence."

"The water's entering from the rear," Derek explained patiently. "The new defenses were outflanked at Silvertown where the barrier ought to be. It'll be coming into Canning Town from the west via Bow Creek. A major failure there could flood the whole of Newham. I've done the calculations based on the results at Woolwich," he added. "The crest of the surge is thirteen and a half feet high giving a total river height of thirty-eight and a half feet." Carswell fingered his moustache nervously.

"That's nearly ten feet higher than the walls," he said hoarsely.

"The Isle of Dogs will soon be taking the full weight," Derek went on. "There's nothing we can do there to help, but you'd better get on to Lewisham and Southwark and warn them that they too will face flooding from the rear to begin with. I think the river will cut through at Deptford, near the cattle market, past New Cross into Peckham, Camberwell, Brixton and Kennington. By then, the banks will be overtopping in Rotherhithe and Bermondsey, and water will be coming down into Southwark Park, the Old Kent Road and Walworth Road. It will be deep too; six or seven feet, double that in a few places."

The door of the conference room opened. Miles and the Director General came out with the Minister.

"How are we doing, eh? Holding our own still. Marvellous, you chaps are doing splendidly," the Minister boomed, with false joviality that set Derek's teeth on edge. "Mustn't give up hope, that's most essential."

"I think our Chief Engineer is inclined to be a trifle, er, pessimistic, don't you agree, Director?" Miles said.

"Must be optimistic," the Minister replied, before anyone could speak. "Too easy to look on the black side. Now, tell us, how will it go from here?" He looked encouragingly at Derek, who returned his stare, tight-lipped.

"We'll begin losing services very soon," he said. "The sewage farm at Crayford Ness is in difficulties already and the flooding will probably block the northern outfall sewer in Newham. Blackwell and Brunswick Wharf power stations will have gone by now. Barking is already in trouble and Deptford will be under water within the next ten minutes, followed by Bankside."

"They can transfer power from elsewhere on the National Grid, though, can't they?"

"To a limited extent," Derek told him, "but by then you will have lost virtually all the main London generating stations and a lot of sub-stations. The same goes for gas."

A police liaison officer came up and touched Carswell's arm.

"All policemen are being withdrawn from the flood zone in Lewisham and Southwark, sir," he reported quietly, "and I'm afraid the Albert Embankment is still blocked, but they have managed to clear all vehicles from the bridges."

"Port of London Authority evacuating West India and Millwall docks due to floodwater," announced a voice behind.

"Overtopping in Deptford," said another. "River engineer estimates rate of rise as one foot every four minutes."

"I know I am not an expert, but that sounds pretty fast to me," said the Minister, after the last remark.

"The surge has only just reached us," Derek told him, "and it'll keep on rising at that rate for another half an hour before we see the crest."

* * *

Johnny and Tilly were crossing the open site as quickly as Tilly's twisted ankle would allow. Days of rain had turned the ground into clinging mud which slowed their progress. The wind and rain and the effort of keeping their balance made talking pointless. They were about halfway across when they heard a noise like a dull rumble.

"What was that?" Tilly asked, raising her voice above the wind. "It sounded like something falling over." Johnny shook his head.

"More walls giving way, I should think," he said, "I'm not sure what direction it came from, though."

They had walked on for another few paces when all at once a colossal wave crashed through the corrugated fence on their left and thundered toward them along the entire length of the site, a huge roller of foaming water carrying before it fragments of the wreckage it had destroyed in its path. The iron sheeting and timbers that had formed the fence vanished instantly; Tilly saw one sheet tossed high in the air by the leaping breakers. She caught a glimpse of the river beyond, now stretching on in an apparently limitless expanse as far as she could see and for one terrible moment it seemed as though the sea itself was falling upon them. Then she was running, running as she had never run before, for the far wall.

The flood caught them even as Tilly gathered herself to leap for the top of the wall. With terrific violence it burst over them, flinging them down and surging over their bodies. In its midst were vast quantities of debris and mud which battered savagely against their helpless bodies.

Breathless and numbed by the cold and sudden shock, Tilly fought desperately to lift her head clear as the level round her rose with frightening speed. Through the foam and spray on the surface she caught a momentary glimpse of Johnny. The big engineer had managed to regain his feet and was struggling toward her; she heard him call her name. Then before her horrified eyes, an enormous baulk of timber swirling along on the crest of the flood, bore down upon them. With a sickening crunch it struck him full in the back, pitching him forward to vanish into the water.

Tilly opened her mouth in a scream of anguish at the sight, but as she did so she was sucked under, choking on the dirt laden liquid. For a second time she tried to recover her footing, but the flood was very deep now and she was weaker. Other pieces of swiftly moving debris cannoned into her, knocking the breath from her body. A red mist swam before her eyes, an agonizing pain tightened in her chest, then everything fell away into darkness and her body sank downward to join Johnny's.

Chapter Seven

By contrast with the speed with which the Isle of Dogs had been overrun, the inundation of Deptford and New Cross was a much less dramatic affair. There had already been serious flooding in South Woolwich and the Blackwall Tunnel, fortunately cleared of cars, had filled completely. The gas works on the point were also out of action. Moving into Greenwich, the surge entered the Palace and swept up the High Road where it joined water spreading outwards from the creek. The high ground of Shooters Hill and Blackheath, however, formed an effective barrier and it was not until it reached the cattle market at Deptford that the river was able to find a way down on to the old flood plain of Bermondsey.

The overtopping took place slowly at first, and even after the surge had risen to over a foot above the defenses, the maze of twisting streets between the riverside and the park delayed the onslaught for a while. Eventually, however, the pressure behind drove the flood out on a broad front, through New Cross and into Peckham.

At first the water was nowhere more than two feet deep, but this increased rapidly as the flow built up with the approach of the surge crest. Despite the efforts of the police and the sounding of the sirens, many cars and people were still about and many shops were doing business. The first inrush of the water, sweeping down the streets, caused an immediate stampede.

Screaming women ran before the flood clutching terrified babies. Husbands and wives searched frantically for each other and for lost children, among the fleeing crowds. Car drivers mounted the pavements and drove among the people in their attempts to escape. What contributed most to the alarm was the fact that the water seemed to approach from several different directions at once. It seemed impossible to escape; mobs of frightened men and women rushed into first one street then another, only to be met by the greedy water advancing toward them.

Many people first encountered the flood when it entered the shops they were in and here some of the most horrifying scenes of panic took place. In one small supermarket, still busy with shoppers, a tide of water surged in, heavily laden with dirt and debris collected in its course. Within seconds it was knee deep in the confined space, sufficient to threaten the lives of children. In the confusion that followed a number of women lost their heads and made a terrified dash for the exits, trampling over anyone who got in their way. People slipped and fell, were knocked down and a glass door was shattered. When order was finally restored, an old woman had died as the result of a head injury and a weeping mother was feeling through the black liquid for the body of her three-year-old daughter.

The Surrey docks were also overrun, but since these had largely been abandoned this scarcely mattered; but the river was now overtopping the whole length of the defenses in Bermondsey and pouring into Southwark Park, Tower Bridge Road and the Old Kent Road. The whole of this vast, densely populated area lay at the mercy of the water. The police and Council officers had done their best, but it had been an impossible task to alert all the inhabitants. Like those in Deptford the vast majority were taken totally unawares.

As the water worked its way inwards, the gutters and drains beneath the streets filled swiftly; the pressure built up with the enormous volume pouring into the district and before long this caused manhole covers to lift some way in front of the advancing tide. Heavily contaminated water burst forth, forming a barrier in the path of refugees fleeing from the area, in which the open manholes remained as deadly traps beneath.

The authorities had assumed that the natural instinct of everyone would be to get up above the flood level and remain there until the water retreated. In this they had underestimated people's urge to get home. Husbands became desperate to reach their wives and families, mothers to get back to their children. Everywhere people struggled to get through the water; to their friends and relatives, to help their neighbors or simply to rescue their belongings. It was from these that many of the casualties came. Caught in basements and back rooms they were trapped by the sudden descent of the flood and overwhelmed before they could climb to safety. Many of the elderly lost their lives in this way; staying too long to salvage their few possessions, they then lacked the strength to get back through the water.

On the north bank the situation was far less serious. Wapping and the London Docks were badly affected but the latter had been closed for some years while the inhabitants of Wapping and the nearby districts had been accustomed to the dangers of the river and obeyed the warnings. Though deep, the water did not penetrate far inland, allowing rescuers to reach those in need quickly.

Around Tower Hill, the story was much the same. The surge caused overtopping, a few streets near to the river were drowned in a foot or so of water and tourists watched incredulously as the moat of the Tower of London slowly filled once more. As the crest came up to Tower Bridge, the river penetrated the main Underground railway system for the first time. A cascade of water poured down the steps and ventilation shafts and began draining down through the tunnels toward Monument and Cannon Street.

* * *

At Kingsway, the river's assault on Deptford and Southwark was the signal for an immediate increase in the volume of messages to be relayed to the center.

The engineers patrolling the banks were the first to call in with reports of overtopping. Derek listened to these messages, monitoring the water's advance, and his expression became gradually more severe as he heard the news. They were followed by the local flood controls with the latest situation reports and messages relayed through the separate police networks. Everywhere the story was the same; the river was breaking through all along the defenses and penetrating rapidly into the heart of one of the most densely populated sections of London.

At ten fifty-two the alarm bell rang on the tide gauge at Tower Pier. Derek noted down the details and made some quick calculations.

"The surge is coming up river faster than I expected," he told Carswell. "It's running about eight minutes ahead of schedule. The winds over the sea must be near their peak still."

"I'll see all the control rooms are warned," Carswell replied. "The water seems to move over the ground at much greater speed than has been anticipated," he went on. When he returned, "We've lost six hospitals so far, four generating stations and the sewage plant at Crayfordness, and the crest of the surge hasn't reached us yet. Frankly, I don't mind admitting it is terrible to see this sort of thing really happening."

Derek fought an impulse to smile; even after years of living in England, men like Carswell still surprised him. The Tannoy crackled abruptly.

"Attention, attention. Overtopping at London Bridge now expected at ten fifty-six. Repeat. Overtopping at London Bridge now expected at ten fifty-six. Advise all controls immediately." There was a flurry of activity at the liaison desks as the announcer switched off.

Derek looked down at the map. The picture was changing all the time. Groups of red markers indicated the furthest extent of flooding reported so far. Confronting them, lines of similar markers colored blue, showed where the rescue services, police and military units were retreating before the advance of the water. Already it was obvious that some of these would be cut off before they could reach safety; the flood was pushing out sudden tentacles ahead of the main front and using the drains to leap-frog beneath the streets into pockets of low ground. As he watched a plotter moved one of the red markers on to London Bridge Station and another on to Guy's Hospital next door.

"Kennington Park Road—water entering from northeast," called out the officer in charge and another marker was moved up. The pattern was becoming clear; the surge had spilled over in Bermondsey and was cutting across the bend in the river into Lambeth. By the time the tide overtopped on the other side, along the Albert Embankment, people trying to escape southwards would find themselves trapped with the river at their backs. His thoughts were interrupted by an urgent shout from Carswell.

"Derek," the Controller's face was pale with dismay,

"it's the Underground," he said in an unnaturally high voice. "They still have passengers in the tubes."

* * *

Georgina had come to the end of her last cigarette. She ground out the stub angrily with her shoe. Around her the other passengers were displaying signs of similar irritation as they had been waiting in the tunnel for twenty minutes. The stockbrokers discussed the matter between themselves and the consensus of opinion at first blamed the flood alert, but as the delay continued others suggested that the train had broken down. For the most part, however, the passengers sat or stood in silence, ignoring each other.

After the train had been stationary for twenty-five minutes the connecting door at the far end of the compartment opened and a young colored guard stepped through from the carriage beyond.

"We apologize for the delay to passengers," he announced, when he reached the middle of the carriage. "This is due to the failure of a preceding train."

"How much longer will we be?" demanded the velvet-collared stockbroker authoritatively.

"Not very long, sir," came the reply. "The engineers are working on it."

"You should have asked him about this flooding," someone said after the guard had left. The other shrugged his shoulders. "He probably knows no more than you or I, less if anything. He spends his day traveling round and round in the bowels of the earth. What does he know about the weather outside?"

"All the same I shouldn't fancy being down here if the river does burst its banks." Georgina looked up sharply at this, and the man saw her and smiled.

"Don't worry," he said kindly. "I don't imagine London Transport would let their passengers actually drown."

"It doesn't worry me, really," she told him. "It's just an unpleasant thought, that's all. Anyway, the alert was called off," she explained briefly about Derek and her conversation with Miles.

"That's good news, at least," replied the man, offering Georgina a cigarette from a gold case, "but in that case, it's odd that the train went straight through at Temple, without stopping. There was nobody waiting on the platform either."

"There's probably a bomb scare," speculated another passenger. "Only they don't want to frighten us. That's why we didn't stop."

"You mean the bomb is here on this train, with us?" said Georgina with some alarm.

"That's right, that's why they cleared the station too."

"Nonsense," the stockbroker remarked scornfully. "If that were so they would have made us leave the train and walk back along the lines."

* * *

In the central operations room at London Transport's headquarters the head supervisor was listening to the superintendent for the Circle Line Division.

"I've still got two trains in the tunnel, east of Charing Cross," the superintendent reported. He was a thin, fair-haired man with glasses. "The lead train has developed brake failure and is blocking the one behind. They've sent a team of engineers down and I understand they should have the trouble cleared up within the next ten minutes." The supervisor glanced at the clock, the time was ten forty-seven.

"There is still twenty-three minutes to go before the flood is due, I'll let you keep the men down there for exactly ten minutes longer," he said. "After that, if the trains are still stuck, you'll have to order the crews out and bring them up through Charing Cross. I take it that

neither train has passengers aboard?" The superintendent shook his head emphatically.

"The defective unit came up from Aldgate East after
the alert had been sounded," he said. "They sent it
last in case it broke down. The other one came round
from Liverpool Street at the last minute."

"Right, carry on then, but remember, no more than
ten minutes."

* * *

The name of the guard who had informed the passengers of the reasons for the delay was Sandy Cotton.
Sandy was a cheerful, high-spirited boy, nineteen years
old, who had joined the Underground service six
months ago. He went down the whole length of the
train and let himself into the driver's cabin.

"Anything doin' up ahead?" he asked. "Those people
back there," he jerked a thumb in the direction of the
passengers, "are getting mighty fed up with waiting."
The driver shrugged his shoulders and peeled a stick
of chewing gum, offering one to Sandy. He was a thickset man in his forties, taciturn but not unfriendly.

"The engineers are still on the job," he said, "I
talked to Charing Cross on the telephone an' they say
no more than ten minutes." The cab window was open
and Sandy could see a pair of telephone leads had been
hung out and clipped on to the two copper wires that
ran down the side of every tube tunnel carrying communications between one station and the next. The
driver spoke again.

"What do you reckon about this flooding then?" he
asked. "Are we still under special restrictions?"

Neither of them knew the answer to that. As the
stockbroker had remarked earlier, the train staff were
virtually isolated from the rest of the world. They
waited silently together, looking out into the dark of
the tunnel ahead, where they could just make out the

rear lights of the train in front of them. All at once the telephone gave a loud, piercing ring. The driver picked it up.

"This is the line superintendent," said the voice on the other end. "The flood warning has been put forward. You are to contact your guard, abandon your engine and proceed at once on foot to Charing Cross, where the flood gates will be kept open to let you out."

"Yes, sir!" the driver exclaimed. "How long · have we got?"

"You have fifteen minutes, fifteen minutes, no more."

"What?" the driver yelled down the telephone, in surprise, "fifteen minutes, I have got a full load of passengers back there. There is no way they are going to get out in fifteen minutes."

The superintendent's consternation was audible even to Sandy, on the other side of the cab.

"For Christ's sake, get them out immediately and start them walking. I'll send some men back to help. We thought you were running empty."

Inside the carriages there had been sufficient speculation among the passengers on the possible disaster that could befall them for the order to leave the train to cause considerable alarm. The driver and guard did not tell them the reason for the course they were taking, judging rightly, that to do so would only make their task more difficult. Instead, they informed everyone that the engineers were finding it impossible to repair the train in front.

There were eight coaches in the train. Some three hundred and fifty passengers in all and it took over ten minutes to persuade them to leave their seats and step out into the dark, sooty tunnel. People seemed to have a dread of treading on the rails, even after they had been assured that the power was turned off. They picked their way carefully along the edge of the track towards the front of the train, tripping and stumbling as they went. They were met by anxious men from the station carrying torches who began leading them down the tunnel. Sandy and the driver brought up the rear, trying to hold back the fear that rose within them. The column seemed to move terrifyingly slowly, there was over a quarter of a mile to go before they reached the station, and at any second they expected to hear the sound of water behind, bursting upon them out of the blackness. Sandy looked at the luminous dial of his watch, the hands stood at five minutes past eleven. The hair on the nape of his neck began to crawl with panic.

* * *

At Bankside Power Station Jerry and the other men on emergency duty had started to shut down the generators and turbines as soon as the sirens were sounded. The process was not particularly complicated and could have been accomplished within twenty minutes if necessary, had Alan Watts not ordered them to take it more slowly to avoid straining the switch gear. At the same time they had cut off the supply of fuel to the furnaces, putting out the fires and opening the valves to release the pressure in the boilers. Soon the great hall was filled with hissing clouds of steam.

On the third furnace bank, Jerry shut the tap that pumped the oil and watched the flames in the glass portholes sink and die. The usual deep roar of the furnaces gave way to sharper sounds of escaping steam and banging of metal as the technicians opened up the valve handles. He checked that his furnaces were completely dead, before climbing up to do the same to the remaining furnaces.

He had just returned to the control panel and was watching the gauges when Alan Watts came round again.

"How's it going?" the chemist shouted above the blast of the nearby valves.

"O.K., I think," Jerry pointed at the dials whose hands were slowly swinging back towards the left. Watts ran his eye over them.

"Fine," he replied, "can you leave them and help the man on number one boiler, his release valve has jammed?" Jerry nodded and took a last look at his gauges. By the time any water entered the building the pressure level would be well down below the safety mark.

Number one boiler was the oldest in the station, at the end of the hall nearest the administration floors and the central switching office. Jerry found the operator, a gray-haired man in his fifties called Smallpage, wrestling with the heavy iron wheel of the valve.

"Can't budge it at all," he gasped. "It must have seized up somehow." Jerry motioned him out of the way, and wriggled into position behind it.

"Careful," Smallpage called out to him as he grasped the wheel, "it's hot." Jerry snatched his hands back with a curse as the metal seared his palms, and put on the gloves the older man handed him. The valve had no reason to be so hot; he examined it carefully, looking for signs of a leak or rupture, but could find nothing unusual. Gripping the wheel carefully, he gave a sharp heave. The valve remained firmly locked in position. Jerry braced himself and tried again, and then a third time, using every ounce of his strength, but the wheel remained immovable. Smallpage regarded him with satisfaction.

"Pass me up a hammer," Jerry called to him irritably, "and some oil to put round the joint."

* * *

Alan Watts had gone to check with the man he had stationed on the fuel wharf to watch the state of the river and keep him informed of the height of the tide. He returned to the main building half soaked despite his raincoat and closed the door on the wind and rain outside thankfully. However unpleasant the station might be in summer, he reflected, there was no denying it was a good place to be in during the cold. He went straight up to his office and called the Electricity Control Center for the latest information on the tide.

"A message has just come in from Kingsway saying the surge will reach London Bridge at two minutes past eleven," he was told. His eyes flicked up to one of the clocks on the wall.

"That's in about ten minutes' time," he said with disbelief. "Are you positive about this message? I went down to look at the river myself a short while ago and the level was at least three feet below the top of the wall."

"I'm afraid that's all we know here. We'll let you know as soon as we hear anything new."

Alan went immediately to the main switching room, a large glass-fronted box which projected outwards into the generating hall. From here the whole installation, with the exception of the furnaces, could be controlled remotely from the enormous banks of dials and switches set in green-painted consoles round the room. A row of television monitors enabled the supervisors to watch every section of the station.

"Everything's going according to the book," the duty supervisor told him. "The turbines are all off, the furnaces have been shut down and the boilers opened up, with the exception of number one, which they are still working on."

"I certainly hope they get it fixed pretty soon," said Alan, "it's going to cause enough trouble when the flood water meets those boilers as it is, with the temperature they'll be at. If one of them is still carrying high pressure, things could be very nasty." The supervisor pointed to one of the dials in front of him.

"If that happens," he said quietly, "it will be a lot

more than nasty. She's carrying ten thousand pounds per square inch. That could tear the whole building apart if it fractured."

*   *   *

While the passengers were being led through the tunnel to Charing Cross, in the station above, desperate last-ditch attempts were being made to protect the tube entrances from flooding, before they could be brought out. Sandbags had been filled and were being laid in the ticket hall, but only enough were available in the stores to make a barrier four feet high across the entrance nearest to the river. In the meantime, the staff did the best they could with planks and boarding and prayed that the flood gates below would hold.

The passengers were only halfway along the track before the operations room at St. James's Park was calling the station master at Charing Cross urgently with the news that the District Line, east of him, had begun to flood. At almost the same moment the men he had sent to keep the river opposite under observation reported that overtopping had started.

The water came over with extraordinarily little hurry or excitement. For the whole of the past hour the two men had watched as it gradually crept up the banks until it was within a foot of the top, and the lower parts of the nearby bridge were covered. Neither of them had been unduly alarmed about this, although passersby had remarked on the needle fine jets of spray coming from cracks in the wall in several places.

Occasionally splashes of water shot over the wall, as the wind whipped up the surface, and before long the pavement was covered with spreading puddles. The increasing frequency of these splashes was the first indication that the river was continuing to rise. Then the water was no longer splashing upwards but had begun to dribble down the back of the wall, first in widely separated trickles, then in rapidly growing streams, until with terrifying suddenness the river seemed to swell up and pour across the full length of the wall in a limitless cataract.

Surprisingly, with the exception of a small band of television newsmen and some reporters photographing the scene from the relative safety of Hungerford Bridge, there were few people about to watch it coming. The area was one in which the police had succeeded in diverting the traffic, owing to the small number of side roads, and the majority of buildings were either Government or institutional offices of some kind; Somerset House, with its registers of births and deaths, the Temple Chambers of the barristers, the Savoy Hotel and the squat turrets of the Ministry of Defence. The rain, the icy wind and the general unpleasantness of the wet pavements had combined to keep away the sightseers who might otherwise have crowded down.

Once the river had begun to spill across in earnest, the speed and volume of the flood was devastating. By the time the two watchers had blurted out their news to the stationmaster the water was lapping six inches deep round the booking hall and the oozing cracks in the barricades were being frantically stuffed with rags. The sight of the river streaming down into the roadway, as though over an enormous weir, was an awesome spectacle. As far as the eye could see, the whole embankment was being inundated.

* * *

The control room at Kingsway was preoccupied with the situation of Charing Cross, when news of trouble at Bankside came in. Derek, Miles Wendoser and Alan Carswell were talking on a conference line to the operations controls at St. James's Park, who was relaying the details from the stationmaster in the Underground.

"A certain amount of flood water is entering the station," he reported, "but so far the staff are able to cope with it."

"How deep is it in the roadway on the embankment?" asked Derek. There was a short pause, then, "About eighteen inches, but it is coming over the wall extremely fast and the level is rising." Derek's face tightened.

"How long before you can get the passengers up?"

"We estimate not more than five minutes, they have nearly reached the platform."

"What about the position in the remainder of the system?" Carswell asked.

"Tower Hill and Monument on the District Line are both flooded, how badly we don't know since our staff have been withdrawn. Cannon Street is still dry, but reports are coming in of water moving down the tunnels from the east. Blackfriars is also unaffected so far and Temple is presumably much the same as Charing Cross, but there is no one there to tell any longer. It's the same at Westminster. Elsewhere the east London section was hit some time ago as you know. London Bridge, Borough and Elephant and Castle are all taking water and so is Waterloo. So far we haven't seen any flooding here at St. James's Park."

"They should be just in time," Carswell said, when they had rung off. "The river won't have risen much more than another foot by the time the passengers reach the surface."

"What are we doing to help?" demanded Miles.

"There's very little we can do," Carswell replied. "I've asked the police to send over as many sandbags as they can, and Derek has ordered a reserve team of engineers up from the depot in Kensington, but by the time they arrive it'll be too late to do any good, if the passengers are still below ground."

"They could use pumps, couldn't they? They could pump out any water coming in?" Miles looked angrily at the Controller.

"All the pumps in the world won't do any good, unless they get there instantly," Derek said to him. He had taken out a large-scale map of the area.

"Look at this," he said spreading it in front of them and smoothing it flat. "Between Blackfriars and Westminster, the Thames is held back by a wall four and a half feet high and nearly two miles long. It's built of stone and concrete blocks and at the moment it's being overtopped by more than a foot of water along its entire length. A terrific strain is being placed on it and the overtopping increases that enormously. If any part of that wall should break . . ." he shrugged expressively. The others were silent.

It was at that point that a police liaison officer interrupted them. "Excuse me, Controller," he said to Carswell, "but we are getting reports of an incident at Bankside Power Station. An explosion of some sort, quite a big one apparently. There seems to be a lot of damage."

In two quick strides Carswell was at the side of the Central Electricity Board representative. Derek saw the man shake his head helplessly.

"No good," Carswell said when he returned. "He lost all contact with Bankside some five minutes ago. He's been trying to raise the Board's offices across the road, but without success. All telephone lines in the district are out of action and their radio doesn't appear to be working. Two other generating stations have reported that their power links to Bankside have been interrupted though."

"I don't see that a bit of water on the ground should cause an explosion in a building the size of a modern power station. After all they've been told what to do and given plenty of time to switch off," Miles said. The hot atmosphere of the room was making him sweat and he was beginning to look worried.

"That's fine if everything goes according to plan," Derek replied shortly, "but if it doesn't, you've got boilers carrying white hot steam at high pressure, meeting cold water very suddenly. Which is one certain way of getting a bang," he added. The councilor gave him a cold stare.

"Well, find out if that is what did occur and start doing something about it, instead of standing there speculating." He turned his back on them and began examining the master map.

"Doesn't he know there's nothing we can do, even if there has been an explosion?" Carswell's face was pale with anger. "Does he think we can work miracles?"

"Forget it, Alan," Derek told him. "At the moment, the problem to concentrate on is getting those passengers out of the tubes. I'm going to see if my engineers have got there yet." He looked down at the map again. "Try and get hold of a team of divers. We may need them."

Crises were coming fast upon one another now. Already a large part of the city was under water. Miles of streets and houses flooded. With power and communications badly hit, it was no longer possible to have a clear idea of what was happening, quite apart from directing the rescue services properly. Now they faced a potential catastrophe in the tubes, an as yet unknown disaster at Bankside and there was still no word from Johnny.

*   *   *

Bankside was in trouble. The surge had heaved the river over the defenses by London Bridge at exactly the predicted time and at the same moment, the man Alan Watts had stationed at the fuel wharf had dialed the switching room to say that water was coming in and he was abandoning his post.

Inside Jerry was still working to free the trapped valve in a vain attempt to release the pressure in number one boiler. Smallpage, whose job it should have been, had given up completely and Jerry could scarcely blame him. For the last quarter of an hour they had been hammering at the unyielding metal, but it was becoming obvious that no amount of physical effort was going to prove sufficient. It was quite probable, Jerry thought, that the valve had corroded inside or else been distorted by the twelve hundred degree heat within. Judging from the look of the valve wheel now, all he had succeeded in doing was bending it further out of true.

He paused to wipe the sweat from his face. It was still very hot near the boilers and the heat would not fall appreciably for another couple of hours at least, owing to the heavy insulation. For the first time, he was conscious of the great silence which had fallen on the station. Even the hissing of steam from the remaining boilers and pipes had ceased. He had become so used to the constant roar and vibration from the furnaces and turbines that it felt strange now to be able to hear the sound of men's voices at the other end of the hall.

The silence was shattered abruptly by the urgent clamor of the alarm bells. Even though he had been expecting the sound at any moment for the past hour, nevertheless, it took him by surprise. Leaping down the ladder, he ran to the rail and looked down into the basement. There was no sign of any water, but he could see Smallpage hurrying toward the stairway, from the direction of the fuel wharf, carrying a large spanner.

"Water's coming in fast," he said as he climbed towards Jerry. "We haven't much time. I brought this wrench to see if we could unscrew the safety valve."

"Any idea how long before it reaches the boiler?" Jerry asked, but Smallpage shook his head.

"Hard to say, it's pouring into the lower basement mighty quickly though. A few minutes at most, I reckon."

Jerry grabbed the spanner as he came leaping up the stairs and set to work.

"It's no good," he called down a short while later, "she still won't budge. Pass me up that hammer again."

He struck the tool hard several times, and on the last stroke he thought he detected a slight movement. He heard Smallpage calling him and rested for a moment. At once he was aware of new sounds filling the hall. The trickling and splashing of water pouring in among the pipes and furnaces beneath his feet mingled with the explosive hiss of steam as the freezing cold liquid met the still red hot metal.

"For God's sake," Smallpage cried out, "come on down and get out, it's nearly reached the bottom of the boilers." Jerry peered down through the tangled maze of pipes; the basement floor was completely covered in a pool of black water. Even as he looked, he saw that the level was rising swiftly. He gave a last furious blow with the hammer. There was a ringing crash and the spanner shaft snapped clean into two. Jerry slipped forward, made a frantic grab at the ladder, missed, and fell heavily to the floor.

The drop was not more than ten feet, but he landed badly, sending pain shooting through his right leg and hip. At once, Smallpage ran to him and tried to help him to his feet. Wincing with agony, Jerry managed to pull himself up, clutching at the stair rail for support.

"We'd better get clear," he gasped to the older man. "I didn't free the safety. She'll blow any minute."

With his arm supported by Smallpage's shoulder, Jerry began to stagger over the turbine floor, towards the door. All around him, the air was full of roaring vents of steam and the splutter of hot metal. As the flood rose to touch the lower pipes there came sharp retorts from the fracturing steel. They saw one long span of asbestos-wrapped ducting collapse suddenly into the water that simmered below. One thought was paramount in their minds; how long before the level reached the boilers.

They had passed the turbines and were almost at the doors when fresh blasts of steam told them their worst fears were realized. Great gouts of vapor spiraled up-

ward, toward the roof; the noise of spluttering and bub-
bling filled their ears. Forgetting the pain of his injured
leg, Jerry ran forwards, looking back over his shoulder
as he went. He was still thirty feet from safety when
the boiler fractured.

Like a colossal bomb the fifty-foot boiler exploded
with a stunning blast of sound, tearing a gigantic hole
in the station roof. Fountains of steam belched outwards, filling the hall. Huge pieces of wreckage crashed
down and the air sang with vicious shrapnel. The blast
lifted the turbine floor, curling back the metal as though
it were tin foil. Before the two men's feet, a wide gap
opened up, revealing the flooded basement below.

Through the torn metal Jerry saw the white two
thousand-gallon tank with its load of sulphuric acid tilt
slowly from its mounting and slide into the water. For
a second, it vanished from view, then the surface
erupted in a violent reaction, hurling a tremendous
spout of toxic liquid towards the roof. Clouds of choking gas rose through the floor, the water boiled furiously and a rain of acid droplets fell about him, burning
his clothes and searing the exposed flesh. Crying out with
pain, Jerry tried to drag himself back away from the edge.

As he did so there came a terrible scream from
Smallpage. Turning toward the sound he saw the technician clinging to a section of floor badly shattered by
the explosion that was about to break off into the inferno below. He had caught the full force of the acid
spray, his clothes were half burnt away and his face and
hands covered with red scars. Already the tilt of the
floor was so great he was starting to slide downward,
his fingers clawing desperately at the steel surface.

There was a sound of tearing metal, the floor lurched
and dipped sharply, and Smallpage slithered to the
edge; for a moment he hung there, then with a last
desperate cry, he fell back into the center of the boiling
water below.

Jerry crawled back toward the middle of the hall.

The floor was covered with wreckage from the boiler; beads of acid clung to the metal. Half fainting with agony, he tried to ease the burning on his skin with water from the nearby boiling pools that lay among the debris. From overhead there came a rending crash and another shower of debris fell into the hall. He looked up; towering towards the sky, the gray bulk of the station's massive chimney was visible through the gaping roof. With a shock, he realized it was leaning perceptibly. There was another crash, a tremor shook the building and more pieces of roof hurtled down. The chimney was leaning at an impossible angle now. A great crack opened halfway up and he saw a shower of bricks tumble out and fall toward him.

The base of the chimney slipped forward, dissolving into a crumbling avalanche. More cracks appeared in the shaft; the soot stained cap broke off; with one last frantic effort Jerry staggered to his feet and began to stumble futilely across the floor . . .

Then the falling tower blotted everything out in a roar of devastation.

*　　　*　　　*

Georgina had begun to think the tunnel would never end. For what seemed like hours she had been stumbling through the darkness along the rough path beside the rails, half crouching to avoid the curve of the roof, tripping and falling over unseen obstacles. The only light came from the feeble glow of half a dozen flashlights carried by the men from the station, and they had to walk holding on to the person in front.

At first, it had taken all her attention just to keep going, but after a while she started to wonder what was happening again. There was a note of urgency in the behavior of the guards, as they hurried the passengers along in the direction of the station. A woman who had tripped and fallen had been picked up at once, without ceremony, and told briskly to keep moving.

The possibility that the surge might, after all, be taking place, had already occurred to Georgina and she could not put it out of her mind. As far as she could remember from what Derek had said to her earlier, the flood was due at eleven o'clock and she knew it could not be far off that time. The thought of being trapped underground in the tunnels, with the river pouring in, nearly paralyzed her with fear. Her imagination was vivid and she pictured herself struggling frantically in the darkness, as the level rose to the roof, and the last terrible seconds before the water choked off her life.

The angle of the tunnel changed; they were walking up a gradual slope. To Georgina's intense relief, a tiny circle of light appeared in the distance. She felt a ripple of elation pass down the line of passengers, at the sight of their goal. She hurried forward with the others. There were still a couple of hundred yards to go when she stepped off the path and her foot slipped into a puddle between the rails. With a shock, she drew back and looked down. A torch flickered up the tunnel towards her and by its light she could see water oozing over the floor of the tunnel, glinting menacingly among the rails.

A wave of renewed terror swept over her and she broke into a run, but before she could take more than a few steps, a hand grasped her by the arm.

"Easy, lady." It was one of the men from the station ahead. "If we panic this lot, nobody's going to get out." His voice was slow and reassuring. Still holding her firmly he walked with her to the end of the tunnel.

"We often get a bit of water down here, when there's been some rain," continued her companion. "It's the drains, you see, they can't take the extra." His words did not convince Georgina, but his manner was so calm and unworried that her fears subsided a little.

At long last they embarked, blinking in the glare of the station lamps and the daylight coming in through the open roof near the end of the platform. At this point, she recalled, the District Line ran at surface level for a while, passing over the deeper Northern Line tubes. Where the roof ended thin streams of water were splashing down on to the platform. Georgina noticed this with alarm. The station seemed totally empty and very quiet, with no signs of normal traffic. The voices of the guards rang strangely loud after the confined space of the tunnel. She looked back and saw that more water was following them out of the tunnel, trickling swiftly among the dust and litter beside the lines.

"Is the river flooding?" she whispered to the man at her elbow. He gave her a quick smile, but did not reply. He was about forty-five, she judged, short and stockily built, wearing a donkey jacket.

The railway staff began shepherding the passengers off the platform and down the stairs on their left, which led to the main station concourse. Here a confusing array of passages and stairways linking four lines and six different platforms joined the exit routes to the surface. Normally, this place was full of people streaming to and fro from one platform to another or up to the streets above. It was one of the busiest stations in London. Now it was completely deserted, and the loudest noise, the steady grind of the escalators. There was something unreal and frightening about it. Georgina found herself hanging back, unwilling to go on.

"Come along, lady." Once again, it was the man beside her who took her arm and began steering her in the direction of the exit. His voice, she noticed, had a trace of a Welsh accent. At the escalators, the passengers bunched together as those in front stepped on and began to ride up. Georgina waited nervously. From above there came sounds of hammering and men's voices shouting. One or two of the people around her were talking quietly among themselves. In another couple of minutes they would all be safely out.

*   *   *

1117 HOURS L.T. OPERATIONS CENTER TO FLOOD CONTROL KINGSWAY: Passengers leaving Charing Cross. Flood level on embankment two and a half feet. Escalators and electrical systems still functioning. Rescue team standing by in Strand. End.

1118 HOURS FLOOD CONTROL METROPOLITAN POLICE TO FLOOD CONTROL KINGSWAY: Urgent. Reports indicate extensive damage Bankside Power Station following explosion. Main roof and chimney collapsed. Unconfirmed four dead eleven injured. Requesting immediate medical assistance. End.

1120 HOURS FLOOD CONTROL KINGSWAY TO FLOOD CONTROL METROPOLITAN POLICE: Rescue teams from Sawyer Street Fire Station and Guy's Hospital attempting to reach Bankside. End.

1121 HOURS FLOOD CONTROL METROPOLITAN POLICE TO FLOOD CONTROL KINGSWAY: Urgent flash! Flash! Flash! Major wall failure Victoria Embankment Northumberland Avenue. Estimate thirty yards plus. End.

1123 HOURS LONDON TRANSPORT OPERATIONS CENTER TO FLOOD CONTROL KINGSWAY: Urgent. All contact lost with Charing Cross Underground. Please assist. Please assist. Urgent. End.

*   *   *

The failure of the wall further down the embankment had been apparent at Charing Cross only as a low rumble like distant thunder and not a single person below ground was prepared for its devastating effect.

The water raced across the road and flung itself upon the station from the rear, smashing aside the hasty barricade at the entrance as though it had been built of paper. Georgina had just mounted the escalator; jerking her head up at the sound, she saw the flood burst through at the top of the stairs in a storm of spray, flinging men and women backward to the floor below,

as an avalanche of roaring water swept down the stairway towards her.

In an instant she was hurled from her feet and
dragged over the passage to the far side. Gasping for
breath, she struck out desperately; her hand struck an
iron pillar near one of the escalators and she clung on
with all her strength. The water was pouring into the
station from every direction, another torrent was rushing down the steps from the platform they had just left.
All around her, people were struggling and screaming
with terror as they were swept away helplessly, tossed
about like pieces of debris, by the raging flood.

By some miracle the lights remained on. She saw the
man who had helped her in the tunnel, not far away.
Clinging to the wall he pulled himself over to her.

"Follow me, this way," he shouted to her above the
noise, seizing her wrist, as she shook her head and
held on to the pillar. "You'll drown if you stay here."
Breaking her hold, he dragged her over to the escalator.
The water was already surging round their thighs and
racing in a torrent down the stairway. Georgina cried
out in fear and tried to tear herself free.

"For God's sake," the man cried, "it's the only way.
There are flood doors down there." Two more men
struggled through the water toward them and still holding her arm the man plunged down the stairway.

They fell slipping and sliding in the water, desperately holding on to each other and to the sides of the
escalator. At the bottom was a narrow chamber, now
waist deep. The flood was surging through a small doorway, over which hung a heavy steel shutter. The man
dragged Georgina through and on to the platform beyond, out of the way of the water which was pouring
down on to the tracks. Behind them came two colored
men; she recognized one as the guard from her train,
the other was the driver.

Her rescuer seized hold of a heavy chain hanging
from the roof and began to pull on it. The flow had

risen until it nearly filled the doorway. Suddenly, there was a confused thumping outside and two more figures tumbled through the gap, to be thrown down on to the track.

The chain made a steady clanking, as though a ratchet was being worked, and the heavy shutter began slowly to close over the doorway. The stream of water narrowed, spurting fiercely with the pressure behind. Abruptly it ceased altogether and the platform fell quiet.

At the same moment the lights went out.

Chapter Eight

The messages lay in a small pile on the table in the conference room. The Minister finished reading the last one and dropped it soundlessly on top of the others.

"How many?" he asked quietly.

"We are not sure." It was Carswell who spoke. "We think about three hundred and fifty, perhaps four hundred. The trains were very full."

"Four hundred," the Minister repeated the figure, shaking his head in disbelief. "What an appalling thing to happen. Those poor people." He was talking to himself. The rest of the group, Miles, Derek, Carswell, Reeves, the police officer and London Transport's liaison man remained silent.

"What is the figure of the total casualties to be expected?" he asked suddenly. The others looked embarrassed. No one met his eye. "Well?" demanded the Minister sharply. Eventually Miles answered him.

"We haven't liked to make any official estimate," he said smoothly. "It is impossible to make a truly accurate forecast, and in any case these things can be utterly misleading if taken out of context."

"Will you please tell me how many deaths you expect to occur as a direct result of this flood." The room had gone very silent, everyone tensely waiting for a reply, but Miles still hesitated, and in exasperation the Minister turned on Reeves.

"You, Inspector, you must know what your people think."

"Well, sir," Reeves was clearly unhappy about the effect of what he had to say, "we have taken a percentage figure of the total number of people in the affected area . . ." he paused.

"Go on, man," the Minister glared at him.

Reeves swallowed and continued. "Based on this we have prepared disposal plans for up to one hundred and fifty thousand fatalities." The Minister gaped at him incredulously.

"A hundred and fifty thousand dead!" he exclaimed.

"Of course, that is an outside figure," Miles interjected hastily, "based on suggestions made in the House of Lords during a debate on the barrier in 1970. We don't expect to reach half that number."

"Is there any chance that some of those passengers might have survived and could be rescued?"

"It's just possible," Derek said, "a few people might be lucky enough to find an air pocket somewhere, where they might survive for a short while. A team of rescuers is attempting to reach the station now."

"You don't sound very hopeful, Mr. Thompson."

"Minister," Derek replied wearily, "the only certain fact we have at the moment is that none of the passengers reached the surface. This means they were somewhere down in the tunnels and passages below ground when the flood hit them. Those tunnels are the first place that the water drains into and the last to be pumped dry. Even if there were some survivors, we would never find them in time."

"They have flood gates in the Underground, though," it was Inspector Reeves who spoke. "Wouldn't those help?"

"The flood gates are relics from the war time," the liaison officer replied, "designed to protect the system in the event of a German bomb blowing a hole in one of the under river tunnels, so the biggest ones are at Charing Cross and Waterloo, on each side of the Thames. They're not honestly that much use in this kind of situation. Our experts tell us that sixty miles of tunnels will be completely flooded."

Miles sat down at the desk, pulling a sheet of paper toward him. He began to cover it with an efficient shorthand. It was just the kind of petty skill that he would possess, Derek thought, as he watched. After a while the councilor laid down his pen and looked up.

"Tell me, Carswell," he said, "why didn't you obtain positive confirmation from London Transport that all trains were empty?" The Controller stared back at him, in surprise his jaw dropped.

"I, er, I don't know," he stammered, "there was no provision for it. That was left to the supervisors at St. James's Park."

"I see." Miles's tone was icy. "And it didn't occur to you that their actions should be monitored from here, which after all is the main function of this room." Carswell began to splutter a reply, but Miles ignored him and continued to write. Again he paused and this time it was Derek's turn to be interrogated.

"Were you aware that the flood gates in the underground were insufficient to protect the system from inundation?" he asked, "and that consequently passengers were at risk?"

"The passengers were at risk because no flood barrier was there to protect them," Derek retorted angrily, "not because the gates in the underground were too old."

Miles sniffed in thinly veiled contempt and added

some more lines to the cryptic symbols on the paper.

"We shall see when all this is over," he said, standing up. The rest followed him back into the main room. At the door Carswell caught Derek's arm.

"I want to talk to you," he said under his breath. "Stay behind for a moment."

"You realize what Wendoser's up to?" he said urgently, when the others had gone. "He's going to make scapegoats out of you and me for all this." He waved an arm in the direction of the control room. "We are going to have to take the blame for everybody's mistakes."

"Come on, Alan, this business is too big to be laid at our feet. We've all been wrong about it from the beginning and we've all made mistakes."

"Oh yes, then what about the delay in turning out the police? Whose fault was that?" Carswell did not wait for Derek to reply but hurried on, his face flushed with emotion. "Wendoser's looking for people to blame for what's gone wrong so as to take the pressure off him. If you don't believe me, think about this. He's put in a memorandum claiming you are responsible for the deaths of three sewage engineers."

"What the hell are you talking about? I don't know anything about sewage engineers. They are not under my control."

"That's right." Carswell leant over the table, "But when Miles asked if men would be in danger in the sewers, you told him they would be safe provided they came up before the tide was due. Well, these three weren't. They were trapped. A report came in half an hour ago, but you never saw that because Miles Wendoser took it and didn't tell you about it. He doesn't intend you to find out until they call an inquiry."

*   *   *

In the aftermath of the disaster at Bankside, Alan Watts was attempting to search the ruins of the station for sur-

vivors. In what remained of the administration floor he
had set up an emergency command post from where he
was organizing the few members of his shift who still
remained.

The fall of the chimney had caused colossal damage.
Surveying the wreckage Alan doubted whether the station could ever be repaired. The huge shaft had crashed
right through the roof on to the turbine floor which had
collapsed into the flooded basement, taking the two
hundred-ton turbines with it. The northern end of the
administration floor, together with the switching room,
had been destroyed by the top piece of the chimney,
which had plunged right through them like an enormous missile. The furnaces and boilers were now
twisted heaps of metal, unrecognizable amid the debris
of the roof. When the chimney fell, huge blocks of
masonry had been flung outward, smashing the walls
and machinery around them. A great swathe of destruction had been cut right through the heart of the
station.

So far they had managed to recover two bodies, a
third, that of Smallpage, had been seen to fall into the
basement when the number one boiler exploded, and
the remains of Jerry were presumably somewhere beneath the tangle of half-submerged rubble in the basement. Behind him Alan could hear the faint moans of
the twelve injured men they had managed to pull from
beneath the wreckage. Four of them were very badly
hurt; one, who had been half crushed by a steel joist,
had horrifying injuries. All the station's medical equipment had been lost, the board's offices across the road
had been able to supply bandages and a few other simple items, but that was all. With the emergency radio
destroyed, Alan had been forced to despatch two men
to try and reach Guy's Hospital at the other end of
Southwark Street.

The water appeared to have stopped rising, he noted
with relief, having reached a level two feet above where

the turbine floor had once been. The fall of the roof and smoke stack had choked most of the interior of the station with rubble leaving comparatively little open water visible on the surface. It was not until one went outside and saw the water chest deep in the road that the full extent of the flood became apparent.

There was a sound of footsteps outside in the corridor and another man entered. He was one of the technicians Alan had sent off earlier to try and reach the hospital. He was filthy and soaked to the skin, his clothes dripping water on to the floor. A fresh white bandage around his head made a startling contrast against the grime that covered his face. Wearily he slumped down on a chair.

"We couldn't get through," he said. "It's impossible. The water's over your head in Southwark Street. We found a copper though, and he radioed a message to Scotland Yard. They're trying to organize some help for us, but unless they come by boat they won't make it."

"Could they get through the back way, do you think?" suggested Alan, "the ground's a bit higher there."

"Jesus!" the man swore tiredly, "there is no back way I tell you. The water's too deep to stand in, you have to swim in most places, and it's moving fast. A man gets swept about all over the place. It's useless trying to get anywhere. The flood is full of muck and dirt; there are abandoned cars and wire that catches your feet, and God knows what else. The fuel from our bunker is starting to come out as well, and it's pelting with rain."

Alan nodded absently as he tried to think of a course of action. The station held twelve thousand tons of heavy oil in a bunker beneath the lawn outside. Since it was slightly lighter than the water around it, the flood was effectively pumping it out into the surrounding streets. It was thick and treacly and stuck to everything it touched; by nightfall there wouldn't be a house or building in the district whose ground floors would ever be usable again.

"I'll go and talk to the policeman," he said. "Did he come back with you?"

"Yeah, he's on the floor below with the others. We weren't sure where you'd be. How about the guys in there?" He pointed in the direction of the injured men. "How are they doing?"

"Hadfield is in a bad way; he can't last much longer without help. He is still unconscious, thank God, and I've done what I could for him. All we can do now is wait for a doctor to get here." The other man gave an angry snort.

"And how long before that happens, and how long before they can get him to a hospital, a hospital with power and light? He needs surgery and intensive care and so do most of the rest if they're not going to die within the next few hours. Why the hell has no one made any preparations to cope with this kind of flooding? Where are the boats, the helicopters? What are the authorities doing? Why did nobody ever tell us what was going to happen?"

"I think a lot of people must be wondering that right now," Alan replied quietly.

*   *   *

Beyond Charing Cross, on the north bank of the river, the surge had spilled over into Whitehall and Westminster, where it filled the ground floors of every single government department to a depth of four feet and flooded the Houses of Parliament. The strength of the storm overhead was more in evidence in the wider streets and open spaces here than it had been in other parts of London. Clerks and secretaries who ran from their offices before the flood were drenched by rain as they sought the safety of the high ground at Piccadilly. Savage gusts of wind tore through the parks, driving the water toward Buckingham Palace. In a short space of time, Trafalgar Square, the Mall and Downing Street were inundated, and in St. James's Park there was soon more than ten feet of water.

Orders had been given that all offices of government were to continue functioning normally, where this was possible, using radio links to communicate when the telephone failed. As the magnitude of the disaster became apparent, however, large numbers of officials began to leave their posts and join the crowds fleeing out of the area. Once again their instinct was not so much self-preservation as fear for the safety of their families. In a large measure this flight was due to ignorance. Whereas in the past, both the authorities and the general public had tended to dismiss the dangers of a flood, there was now an over correction resulting in a swing the other way. The river was credited with a speed and power it did not possess. Even people with homes in outlying suburbs became worried. Unable to contact their families on the telephone, they immediately assumed the worst and joined the rush. All sorts of wild rumors sprung up. That the capital was being evacuated. That martial law had been declared. That the flood water was so heavily contaminated it was dangerous to touch it, and a dozen others.

After a lifetime of complacency, it was an appalling experience for many people to see the institutions where they worked drowned feet deep in water, and to watch familiar streets become part of a swiftly flowing river. Some were numbed with shock and wandered about as though in a daze, utterly bewildered. The river had dealt the heart of the city a crippling psychological blow.

On the opposite side, on the Albert Embankment, the situation faced by the traffic police became no easier during the final few minutes before overtopping began. Following his sergeant's orders, Constable Partridge had begun warning the drivers of the cars that jammed the

road to abandon them and clear the area at once if
they could. The reaction had been predictable. Each
driver had looked towards the embankment wall, seen
that it was still holding firm, and stayed where he was.
One or two allowed passengers in the car to get out but
that was all. Partridge had lost count of the number of
windows he had tapped on when his personal radio
gave a squawk.

"Overtopping is expected in your sector within ten
minutes," he was told. "You are to leave your present
position and report at once to Vauxhall Bridge, where
transport is waiting to evacuate you. Repeat: abandon
your position and go at once to Vauxhall Bridge."

The young constable did not wait to ask questions.
He left the road and ran down the pavement as fast as
his legs would take him. Already, waves were starting
to break over the crest of the wall and spill down on to
the pavement. He could see other members of the squad
racing ahead of him to the bridge. A line of vans was
parked there, engines running, and lamps flashing. As
he reached them an officer checked his number and he
saw his name crossed off a list.

"Right, on to the front van, quickly now." He leapt
in; half a dozen men were aboard already and others
tumbled in behind him. Someone slammed the doors
shut and the van took off with a jerk, siren screaming
and shot up the bridge to Victoria.

Behind him on the embankment, the sudden departure of the police coupled with the first signs of water
splashing over the river wall, had at last convinced the
car drivers that they were in danger. A few in the line
got out into the rain and ran to the wall. One quick
glance was enough, then they were running back,
weaving through the cars, shouting at the others to get
out and follow. Within the space of minutes a thousand
vehicles had been abandoned and their owners were
hastening down the road in the direction of the bridge,

or into nearby side streets. Even as they did so the surge swelled across the wall in earnest.

Different reasons were given later to explain why the wall should have failed at such a point. It was said that a slight narrowing of the channel caused a sudden increase in the pressure, or that the stonework had been damaged by a road accident earlier in the week. Whatever the reason, after only a few moments of overtopping a fifteen-yard section opposite Black Prince Road broke apart without warning, releasing a devastating cataract on the fleeing mob.

One knot of a dozen people, all but two of them men, was passing right in front of the breach when it occurred. They died quickly. Overwhelmed in the first rush of the water and battered by heavy lumps of stone, they were dragged under nearby cars, trapped and drowned. Fortunately, for many others near by, the abandoned vehicles absorbed much of the initial impact of the inrush, and they were able to keep their feet as the water swirled round them, waist deep, and began to travel down toward Kennington Road. Several climbed on to the roofs of cars and stayed there helplessly, while the flood rose around them.

Those who had been attempting to escape by either Lambeth or Vauxhall Bridge soon realized that this was impossible. The flow over the walls had cut the approaches and was streaming into Vauxhall in a solid mass. The only way out lay by running ahead and this they did, through the maze of small roads that lay between the embankment and Kennington Road.

These streets were already full of cars that had been trying to find a way round the jammed main roads. Their drivers were for the most part quick to realize the significance of the crowds fleeing past them and left hastily, but a number remained obstinately where they were and refused to move until they saw the reason for such chaos. By the time they did so, it was too late.

Moving swiftly beneath the cars, hidden from view until almost the last minute, the water rose suddenly around them. Before the occupants could react it was too deep for the doors to be opened and with grim persistence was rising to window level.

Frantic scenes now took place, with men and women struggling desperately, screaming to those outside for help. Windows jammed shut or were broken. People fought their way out, scratched and bleeding, some pushing their children out, hoping that they would be saved. Others stayed huddled inside in the belief that they could survive until the flood subsided. Many went wild with terror, flailing about, yelling incoherently and fighting with their fellow passengers.

The people living in these streets had received warning from the police and had made some preparations, but even so they were stunned by the sheer volume of the flood and the speed with which it pushed its way into their homes and swamped their rooms. Many were caught in the act of removing possessions to the security of the first floor and were forced to make a dash for the stairs. Some gave shelter to people outside or joined in the efforts to rescue those trapped in the cars. The flood was maintaining a depth of four feet or so; in part due to the obstructions in the streets which held back the water and kept the level high. This in itself was sufficient to drown young children whose parents were unable to hold them up or who slipped and fell in the current. The elderly, too, had little chance, even when they succeeded in escaping from their cars, and were swiftly overborne, their bodies disappearing into the dirt-laden liquid.

The water had penetrated more than forty streets, before it burst through into Kennington in strength. Here, too, there were roads bearing heavy traffic, as refugees fled out of Bermondsey and Newington before the surge that had entered from the east. The meeting of these two confluxes resulted in massive confusion over a wide area and panic set in with the realization that there was no longer any way of escape.

Even as the crowds were hurrying this way and that through the streets looking for a road leading to safety, only to find others approaching from the opposite direction with the same object, the manhole covers in the tarmac lifted and water began gushing up beneath their feet. Surrounded, cut off, and convinced that death from drowning was imminent, hundreds ran blindly on in screaming hysteria or hammered frantically on the doors of nearby homes, begging to be let in.

The water closed in pitilessly. Checked at length by the rising ground, Brixton Hill and Denmark Hill in the south and Lavender Hill to the west, the level began to deepen. Silently and steadily it crept upwards, swallowing cars, hedges, gardens, breaking through windows to pour into the rooms beyond, carrying with it the mud and stench of the river mixed with filth from the drains. There was nothing that anyone could do but sit upstairs and listen to the water lapping at the stairs.

*   *   *

Dave Cox was in York Road, Battersea heading towards Clapham Junction, where two of the six remaining addresses on his list were located. The rain was lashing down as it had done for most of the day and the wind had increased strongly; gusts were rattling the slates on the roofs and shaking the hoardings beside the road. It was an hour since he had heard the sirens go off and he was growing apprehensive. The idea of being caught in the open when the floods started did not appeal to him. He was thankful that his own flat was the other side of the Common, well out of reach of the water. He thought about his wife; Angela would be safe enough he decided. The Council would see she got home all right, or else keep her behind at the Town Hall. She might start worrying about him though. For a moment he was tempted to try and tele-phone her but decided against it.

There were very few people about, he noticed, and even fewer cars. He knew about the clearway system, but as far as he could remember York Road was not part of it. Presumably the alert was responsible. He peered through the windscreen looking for the turning he wanted. With a bit of luck, he thought, he might be able to drop by his flat when he had finished and check that everything was all right. He could also leave a note for Angela. She might even be there by now.

Dave was unaware that the flood had already entered the area from the northeast at Nine Elms, where the Thames winds round past Pimlico on the opposite bank. With the exception of a small section of land around the power station, the whole of Battersea lies below the normal high water mark. The park, with its gardens and lake, was in fact created out of what had formerly been a swamp. As had happened a few minutes earlier in Bermondsey and Southwark, the flood was streaming in from the rear, even as it commenced slipping over the banks.

The ground between the road and the river was heavily industrialized. A variety of large firms had premises and factories here; petrol companies with distribution depots, packaging firms, a distillery and a glucose plant. A number of sites had recently been cleared preparing for redevelopment, and near to these lay the heliport. On the other side of the road were small streets of mean houses, old tenement blocks and charity dwellings. There was real poverty and hardship here. Wandsworth was a large borough with a heavy social security burden and a severe housing shortage, despite much replacement of slum buildings. In among these were dotted sporadic groups of tower blocks, that stood out like white sentinels among the surrounding sprawl.

The road curved slightly, bending leftward in the direction of the river. He was driving past a disused warehouse. Its gaunt grime-encrusted sides rose five storeys above him. A fading sign invited offers for disposal of the premises. The doors and lower windows were boarded up, and covered with scrawls and fly posters. Behind this facade of strength the flood, unknown to those outside, had already broken through.

The waterfront at this point was old and badly in need of repair. One set of owners had begun the task but had gone bankrupt before completing the work. The Council had been reluctant to undertake the expense themselves since to do so might have affected the wharf facilities and it was thought more sensible to wait until new owners came forward and the job could be undertaken jointly. So the flood entered without difficulty, spilling over the wall, crumbling away the old brick and lifting the rotten timber piling. Once inside it surged through the rear of the building, on this side doors had been left unlocked and windows uncovered. The land sloped slightly back from the bank and soon the water was rising against the street wall.

The surge came up the river fast. More and more water poured into the site, inside the building it was over five feet deep. Trickles began coming under the main gate but they went unnoticed in the rain. So too did similar oozings from the windows. Elsewhere in the area flooding in the streets near the river had begun; here, it was held back temporarily while the pressure mounted.

It was a window that gave first. To Dave's horror and amazement he saw a column of water spout suddenly from the wall in front of him, leaping clear across the pavement to fall into the middle of the road. The sight was so incredible that for a moment he could not react at all, but stared open-mouthed in shock, gripping the wheel. Then the car slowed abruptly as it met the water racing to meet it.

Pulling himself together he put the wheel hard over

and swung the car across the road into a side street opposite. The flood was dragging at the tires, threatening to stall him. From the corner of his eye he saw a second window had burst open, spurting more of the pentup lake behind into the roadway, then a third went and the whole surface of the street had vanished in a swiftly moving sea. Dave wrenched the gear lever down and pumped the accelerator hard; the car lurched forward, tearing itself free and shot off. Another car had appeared from nowhere straight in front of him; he swerved again and they missed by inches. There was a momentary vision of the other driver's horrified face, then they were past.

At the end of the street he slammed on the brakes and drew to a screeching halt. He was faced with a choice: the sensible course would be to turn right and drive up to Lavender Hill, safely out of reach of the advancing flood. On the other hand, his sense of duty prompted him to turn left and try to warn the Poles and an old man, who had flats in tower blocks a couple of streets away. After the warning he had received about the depth of flooding that would be expected in this district, he had doubted if he would still be able to get out of the area without a great deal of difficulty, even though he felt unhappy at the thought that the old people might be caught unawares. He hesitated for a moment, then overcoming his instinct for self-preservation, he turned to the left. Two children were standing near the corner looking down the street, apparently oblivious to the danger. He hooted at them and waved furiously as he drove past up the hill. The time was exactly eleven twenty-two.

In Bevan Tower the caretaker had begun to organize the moving of the Poles' furniture and possessions to the upper floors. There were plenty of willing helpers, people who had come down from the flats above with offers of space and assistance in carrying. The television had gone already, also the fridge and the electric fire. With a great deal of sweating and swearing, the sofa had been manhandled up to the third floor, and two men were in the process of taking the bed apart. Mrs. Pole was very confused, she had no idea of what to do and had begun to pack all their clothes very carefully. It upset her to see other people entering their flat and taking down curtains and rolling up the rugs. She was sure things were going to be missing and kept running in and out of the bedroom trying to keep track.

A scene of complete chaos greeted Dave's eyes as he entered. The hall was full of bits of furniture and heaped bedclothes. Nevertheless, he was relieved to see that the residents had had enough sense to start taking precautions. The Poles were obviously being looked after, and he was about to leave without further delay when he remembered the orders he had been given to check that the caretaker understood what to do.

After a fruitless search on the ground and first floors, he finally tracked the man down in the basement, where a young man with long hair was helping him to remove the last of his things from his tiny flat. He was a thin, worried-looking individual with a shock of white hair, who was very evidently thankful to see someone in authority.

"I've 'anded out the leaflets, like they told me on the phone," he said, in response to Dave's questions, "an' I shut off the lifts and locked 'em up at the top."

"Good. The leaflets are the main thing. They tell everyone exactly what to do. You had better hurry, though, as the flood will be here in a few minutes," Dave told him. Even as he spoke, his ears caught the sound of splashing outside. Hurrying back to the passage, he saw that water was pouring into the well of the window at the far end. At that moment the lights in the building failed.

Realizing that he stood in danger of being caught in the Tower, Dave ran up the stairs without waiting to see more. He emerged into the hall in time to see the flood spreading across the open ground, and at the same time boiling up from every drain and manhole, to the excited cries of those watching from the windows.

His first thought was for his car. The water was only a few inches deep and there was still a chance, he thought, that he might be able to drive it out and up to the hill. Pushing aside a group of residents clustered by the door, he ran out, down the shallow steps into the roadway and splashed his way to the car. The coldness of the flood was a surprise, so too was the strength of the flow around his ankles, and it felt oddly absurd to be wetting his shoes and trousers in such a way.

Reaching his car, he flung open the door and saw to his dismay that the level had risen above the sill and water was spilling through to the interior. He climbed in hastily and tried to start the engine. For a few moments, it seemed as though he would succeed; the car gave a series of coughs and splutters as though it was about to fire and Dave pumped the accelerator frantically to get it going. But the sounds died away as the lower part of the engine became submerged and he found himself sitting impotently in the midst of a fast deepening lake.

Stepping out into the water again he found it now reached almost to his knees. The entire expanse round the buildings was covered and the whole area was losing its identity as the flood swallowed road, concrete and grass with the same featureless surface. He began wading back to the flats, reaching them just as the water began to stream over the top step.

The caretaker shut the doors straight away and placed a hastily improvised sandbag against the sill. The residents clustered round and watched the flood rise. The door was glass reinforced with wire, but through it they could see the depth about them increase with a calm, unhurried rate, gradually covering the line of little pillars that protected the grass in front of the block and the bonnet of Dave's car that still remained parked opposite.

No one spoke until, with a sudden exclamation of surprise, a woman jumped back.

"Agh," she cried, "it's coming in!"

The others looked down; from beneath the doorway a thin trickle of liquid was oozing into the room. The caretaker began feverishly trying to mop it up, but it was coming in too fast. Outside it was more than three feet deep and the pressure forced spurts of water through the join in the doors.

"Will they hold, d'you reckon?" a man asked the caretaker. He shook his head doubtfully.

"I don't know," he said. "That glass is pretty strong and I've shut the bolts down, but I don't know about the lock." Even as he spoke, there came a series of ominous creaks from the steel frame and the seepage increased noticeably.

"Everybody back from the doors!" but the caretaker had no need to give the order, the others were already running back to the stairs.

"You, Mr. and Mrs. Pole, you'd best get upstairs, while the rest of us get everything up to the first floor," Dave instructed. "We don't want you getting caught if this door goes suddenly. Some of you men give a hand here."

They worked quickly with an eye always on the menacing brown sea beyond the glass. The ground floor was now completely covered in water, which was now seeping in from the rear as well. Gusts of wind were blowing furiously against the door, causing further frightening sounds of strain. Before long one of the men, a lanky youth barely out of school, called a halt.

"This is crazy," he said, "I'm not staying here, risking my life for someone else's junk," and he disappeared in the direction of the stairs. The others hesitated for a second and then followed.

The last up was the dark-haired mechanic who had brought Mrs. Pole back. He had barely reached the safety of the landing when there came a shattering crack below that echoed round the building, and the sound of water surging in among the ground floor rooms. Huddled on the stairs, they listened to the noise of breaking glass and odd thumps and bangs as the flood poured in among the remaining furniture. At length all became quiet except for the sound of lapping water and the bluster of the storm outside. A sickening damp stench came up the stairway.

Dave descended to the bend in the stairs and peered down at the scene below. Returning after a moment, he gave a helpless shrug of his shoulders.

"I think it's about five feet deep," he said tonelessly. "It's hard to tell. It's very dark down there." Nobody spoke and Mrs. Pole began to cry. Eileen took her by the arm and led her gently into a nearby room.

For the next hour everyone in the block gazed anxiously out of the windows, looking for signs of a slowing down in the rise of the flood, or else hoping to catch sight of rescuers and help from the outside. Instead they saw nothing but the water slowly swallowing everything that lay around them. The car outside had vanished completely, so too had others once visible in nearby streets from the upper windows. Where there had formerly been views of small gardens, a playground and the park, busy roads of traffic, there was now only a single dismal sea, from which buildings, the tops of trees and lampposts projected like toys.

* * *

The Thames is a busy river. Each day numerous vessels of all shapes and sizes, ranging from private launches to heavily laden barges and one hundred and fifty ton oil carriers, pass upstream on the incoming tide on their journeys from the docks to the depots and wharves along the higher reaches. Then too, even in winter, there is a considerable traffic of pleasure steamers from the piers at Westminster and Charing Cross to the tourist attractions at Greenwich. When the final flood alarm was given an hour earlier many of these craft were caught some way short of their destinations and were forced to make for whatever berths they could find.

The river police did the best they could in the time available to make sure that every boat was firmly tied, with sufficient slack on her warps to allow for the expected rise in the tide, but the surge crest was greater than any of them had thought possible, and though most skippers took the time to secure their vessels properly, there remained a number whose only thought was for their own safety.

Between Westminster Bridge and Lambeth Bridge, the gothic towers of the Houses of Parliament and the gaunt black wings of St. Thomas's Hospital faced each other across the swollen inland sea, which had enveloped them both. Along this stretch, a train of six barges lay attached to a mooring in midstream, directly opposite the hospital, loaded with cement for the Portland works in Fulham, their two hundred-ton bulks moving uneasily in the choppy waters, while the wind tore at the stiff canvas tarpaulins that covered their cargoes.

The police had kept the bridges clear of cars until the final minutes before the flood in an attempt to encourage motorists to turn away from the riverside and to permit the movement of emergency vehicles. On the south bank, the tailback from the jam on the Albert Embankment reached as far back as Lambeth Palace, and, realizing the hopelessness of staying where they were, a number of drivers pulled out of the queues and drove on to the bridge even as the river began to spill down on to the pavement below. Although a few succeeded in crossing into Millbank, most found the northern approaches already inundated and became marooned on the bridge crests, with the waters rising around them.

At first the occupants felt only relief at escaping the fate suffered by those who had remained on the embankment and who were now being compelled to swim for their lives in the face of the torrents sweeping inland; but by eleven-fifteen it had become plain that the surge would submerge even the bridges themselves and they began to look frantically for some means of escape from their rapidly shrinking island. At this point, with the embankment walls many feet below the surface, and the bridge roads awash, a new and deadly menace became apparent.

Out in the midst of the swollen river, the strain on the warps holding the barge train to the rusty iron mooring buoy was enormous. The depth had increased to a point where the barges were being forced under water because of the insufficient length of the cable and in addition to this the violent gale gusting up the river and the strong current of the incoming surge tide were causing the heavy vessels to swing upstream, increasing the strain.

The warps finally parted at eleven twenty-one, but the fact was not immediately evident to those on the bridge, peering through the pelting rain. At first the barges hardly moved, but bumped and ground together in the swell. Then the wind caught all but one of the six and began driving them toward the bridge. Within an incredibly short space of time the clumsy vessels had gathered momentum until they were bearing down on the bridge with frightening speed.

Over one hundred people were now packed on to the central portion of the bridge. Some standing on their car roofs or clinging to the parapets, trying to stay above the water. Already terrified by the catastrophe they were witnessing around them and which threatened to engulf them and all they possessed as well, they saw, through the rain, the looming barges drifting down upon them. Many ran desperately to the far side or began wading into the water in an attempt to get to the end of the bridge. Others crouched behind cars and clung to one another, as they waited for the collision.

The leading barge struck the middle of the bridge with a ringing crash that echoed out across the river above the noise of the flood and the howling wind. Its two hundred ton weight encased in heavy wood and iron, designed to withstand the frequent shunting and jostling of its trade, tore deeply into the center arch, throwing up a great gout of spray, in which chunks of masonry and flying debris were visible. The force of the impact tossed men and women off the parapets and hurled a number of cars into the water. The bows of the barge split open flinging out a cloud of gray cement powder, covering the bridge and staining the water around it. A section of the roadway sagged into the river, spilling half a dozen cars just as a second barge smashed into it, crushing them like toys and riding up on to the crest of the bridge until its bows pointed skywards.

The third barge of the train struck the bridge further over towards the southern end, where it was almost completely submerged, and though it did considerable damage, much of this was concealed by the water, whilst the fourth collided with the rear of the leading vessel, causing both to begin sinking rapidly. A large part of the central span had collapsed and vanished beneath the turbulent water that swept around the piers. Those who still survived clung to what remained, helpless and unable to escape from the destruction being wrought around them. Many had been badly injured, crushed by falling stones and iron work, and were screaming in pain and fear.

From both sides of the river, from the upper windows of the Houses of Parliament and the tall buildings on Millbank, from St. Thomas's and the Bishop's Palace, horrified onlookers watched as the fifth barge was carried towards the bridge by the wind and tide. It was just possible, through the driving rain, to make out the figures of people clinging to the wreckage and struggling in the water.

The massive barge hit the bridge only a few yards from the point of the first blow. At the last moment it had swung in the current so that it struck almost broadside on, smacking against the battered stonework with terrific force. Bursts of spray rose, hiding the scene. When it subsided the watchers saw that the bridge had gone. The parapets and the lines of lampposts had vanished and the river was foaming through the gap. A car floated for a few moments, bobbing against the hull of one of the sinking barges, before disappearing. But of the people who had been trying to cross before the flood there was no longer any sign. In less than four minutes over a hundred men, women and children had been swept to their deaths.

*　　　*　　　*

From a window on the first floor of St. Thomas's Hospital, looking out over the Thames, Jane Goodwin, turned away, sick with horror at the sight. The events of the past hour, the steady rise of the river, the first overtopping of the wall in front of the hospital, the rapid flooding of the ground floor, the inundation of the surrounding buildings and now the destruction of the bridge had left her shocked and bewildered. It was impossible that such things could be happening in the places that she knew so well, that streets she had walked down, the shops which she went to every day, could be lying under feet of water.

Jane had been a staff nurse at the hospital for the past two years. She was an attractive girl with thick light brown hair and a ready smile, popular with patients and staff. Since the start of the morning she and the other nurses had been furiously at work, moving patients and equipment from the vulnerable lower regions of the hospital to the upper floors. Despite all their efforts, however, there had been much that it had been impossible to carry off or protect. Many costly and vitally needed items had been abandoned and lost. X-ray machines, radiation equipment, operating theaters, painstakingly assembled research laboratories. Years of effort and work wiped out in a few minutes.

She looked round the room, it was a women's surgical ward. The patients seemed unworried, she thought, even by the appalling catastrophe which had just occurred and which those able to walk about, or with their beds near the windows, had seen and described to the others. One or two had been worried about the safety of their families, but Jane and the other nurses had reassured them without difficulty. She wished she could dispel her own fears as easily. Her mother and younger sister lived not far away in a small house in Vauxhall, and at this time of day her mother would be on her own.

Her thoughts were interrupted by a cry from one of the patients near the windows, and she hurried over. A middle-aged woman in a floral dressing gown was peering out and calling excitedly to the rest of the room.

"That other boat, the one that was still tied up. It's broken loose."

Looking out Jane saw that the woman was right. The last of the barges, which had previously seemed to have remained firmly attached to the mooring buoy, was drifting freely in mid channel. Several other patients rushed to the windows and joined in the chatter of this commentary.

Jane watched in silence, the memory of the recent horror still too fresh in her mind to share their excitement. The river stretched before her, across to Westminster and beyond, completely hiding the banks, and disappearing out of sight amongst the crowded buildings on the opposite shore. Beneath her she could see the tops of the embankment lampposts, apparently standing in the middle of the river.

"It's coming over this way!" The cry caught her attention and she looked back at the barge. Caught by some freak combination of wind and current the squat vessel was being pulled in towards the bank. She saw the blunt bows swing round until they pointed straight at the hospital. For nearly a minute nothing seemed to happen, then a furious gust of wind shook the windows and at the same time the barge began to quicken its pace and move towards them, growing larger by the second. So unexpected was this development, that it was several moments before anyone realized its significance and the barge had reached the line of the embankment walls before Jane screamed at the others to get back from the windows.

Behind the river wall and the pavement beside it, the ground rose slightly before running down into the gardens in front of the building. Now all these were deeply submerged and the barge, grounding slightly on the crest of the bank, rushed on towards the hospital without slackening speed and struck the center of the wing in which Jane's ward was situated.

The vessel, with its enormous weight traveling at such a rate, had gathered a terrible momentum; besides which the building was designed to withstand far lower stresses than a bridge, and the impact was devastating. The barge buried itself almost twice its own length in the ground floor, carrying away the whole of the end wall and fifty feet of one side. Half the floor above collapsed into the gap in an avalanche of bricks and rubble, which caused eighteen people, most of them patients still in their beds, to fall into the seething destruction below. This was followed immediately by the barge, tossing and turning in the tumultuous swell of water, smashing against the walls inside the narrow confines of the building and bringing down further falls of debris from above.

The first shock had fortunately hurled Jane backwards across the ward and away from the window.

Half-stunned and covered in dust and pieces of plaster, she picked herself up. She almost fainted at the sight which met her eyes. Half the ward had vanished. Where the wall and windows and floor had been at the end of the room there was now only an immense hole through which she could see the tossing surface of the river and the colossal heaving shape of the barge smashing the lower floor around it. The air was full of dust and rain blowing in through the open wall and amidst all this confusion could be heard the awful screaming of the injured. In the churning water below she could see scattered red hospital blankets, but worse than all this were the broken figures of some of those who had been standing next to her a moment earlier, which she could just make out, lying among the wreckage.

Another violent shock shook the ward and a section of the floor dipped precariously and then fell into the seething waters below. An appalling cry rang out nearby and Jane saw a bed with its patient shrieking desperately for help, slide down toward the gap and topple crazily downward, spilling sheets, blankets and pillows. She closed her eyes to shut out the fall of the body.

Pulling herself together, she began to force the stunned survivors out of what remained of the ward, while she and another nurse tried to help those unable to walk. It could only be a matter of moments, she knew, before the whole room collapsed. One woman lay badly hurt beneath a pile of fallen rubble near the very brink of the gap. Jane began pulling the bricks away, heedless of the woman's moans of pain. A doctor from another ward near by ran in and started to help, as ominous cracking noises rang from below.

A shiver ran through the floor. Jane and the doctor seized the woman's arms and dragged her free, pulling her over the floor and running with her towards the door. As they made it through to safety, the entire room behind them and the ceiling above crashed down upon the barge, burying it and with it the bodies of its victims.

* * *

Dave went up to the rooftop of Bevan Towers and looked about. The storm raged overhead, filling the sky with driving rain. In the distance to the south he could see Lavender Hill, standing dry above the surrounding water, elsewhere the river stretched in every direction. The capital had vanished totally, in its place remained only endless scattered groups of buildings like drowned villages. Where the Thames had once been it was now impossible to tell. In some places the lamps of the bridges still showed above the water level; the final signs of the river's existence.

It was a dismal, dismaying spectacle, made all the more so by the total absence of any sign of life. With the water still streaming in from the banks, movement of any kind was as yet impossible and in any case he was looking at one of the most deeply flooded areas of all, where the level had passed ten feet in some places and was still rising. To all intents and purposes he might be looking at an abandoned city.

Returning inside he found the caretaker waiting for him. "The water's still coming up down below," the latter told him. "Do you think we ought to get people out of the first floor yet?" With an effort, Dave recalled the instructions he had been issued for this situation.

"Yes," he said, "better get them up. Will you see to it, while I go round the block to check who's there?"

Starting at the top he worked his way down the block, repeating to each family the information he had been given. The flood could be expected to last for several days so they must take care to ration whatever food they had. Electricity would be off for a considerable time to come, and gas supplies too would probably be cut.

"What about the water," he was asked frequently. "We've filled our baths like you told us to, but is it safe to drink the tap water still?"

"Yes," he told them, "but there won't be much more from the taps. They draw supplies from a tank on the roof and that's filled by an electric pump. Try not to flush the toilets if you can help it, there's a danger you'll cause overflows in flats beneath if you do."

As he went he checked off the names on a list and added details of food and provisions. When he reached the bottom he found he had one hundred and ninety-one out of two hundred and forty-seven residents present. The rest, like Eileen's husband, had not been able to get back from work in time. Most people seemed unworried by their predicament. For years now they had been used to periodic cuts in power and lighting. The full impact of what it would mean to be confined in the block for a week had yet to be fully realized. Moreover, as high-rise tenants they were less upset than most about the possibility of damage to their homes, though a number of the men he saw were found looking anxiously at their insurance policies.

He spent some time with the Poles, who had now been moved to the second floor. The old woman seemed to have recovered her spirits and was chatting with Eileen, but her husband appeared upset about the few pieces of furniture they had lost. He kept creeping down the stairs to look at the swamped floors below. The water had only in fact just reached the first floor. The rise had slowed slightly, but it was still increasing; climbing the stairs, step by step. Dave took him back to his wife.

"Why don't you listen to the radio?" he suggested. "You've got a portable."

"Leave off," Eileen told him scornfully. "There's nothing on 'cept the same old message: 'You are advised to remain calm and stay above the water until help can reach you.' What's the good of that?"

"D'you think it will really last a week, this water?" Mrs. Pole asked.

"Yeah, imagine being stuck here all that time." Eileen shivered. "It's getting cold too. I'm worried about my 'usband. He won't be able to get near in this."

"The Council said it would be a week before the flood went down, but I reckon they'll have help for us before then," the caretaker said reassuringly. "They've got boats and things," he added hopefully. "They'd get to us before we ran short. But you'd better go easy on the food and water in the meantime."

"What about my Jerry?" Eileen asked insistently. "Do you think he'll be all right?"

"Of course he will, love." It was Mrs. Pole who answered. "He's with the electricity board, isn't he? They'll look after 'im. He's probably better off than the rest of us right now."

At that moment the door opened and the caretaker entered. "Can I have a word?" he said quietly to Dave. "There's something I think you should see.

"You can see from up at the top," he continued, when they were out in the passage. "It looks like a big fire by the riverside, and I think it's coming this way."

*   *   *

Eastwards of Wandsworth Bridge on the south bank, the river is lined with wharves and delivery depots for the petroleum industry. Rows of storage tanks holding thousands of tons of fuel oil and petrol stand among the factories of packaging companies, distilleries and other hazardous processes. In normal circumstances they are safe enough, protected by comprehensive fire-fighting devices, and readily accessible to the vehicles of the fire brigade. The flood, however, changed all that.

It was never afterwards discovered exactly where the fire began. The most likely cause was attributed to the breaking loose of an empty barge which then collided with the submerged river wall. Smashing through the brickwork like a monstrous battering ram, it continued on to the yard of a fuel depot where it sliced through the fragile metal of a storage tank with contemptuous ease, knocking over the entire structure and drenching the wall of a neighboring building with spirit. From then it needed only a spark from a circuit shorted by the water to start a conflagration.

Once the fire had taken hold it spread with a terrifying swiftness. The flood had already lifted a number of tanks of inflammable liquids from their bases. Oil and petrol from a dozen ruptured pipes had leaked into many of the surrounding buildings. Ordinarily much of this would have been too diluted to burn but the advancing flames raised the temperature to a point where it too caught light. Soon the heat ruptured further tanks in the complex, sending balls of exploding flame into the air and spreading the fire into the neighboring distillery.

The consequence of the inrush of a petrol-oil mixture, burning at intense heat, into a plant of this nature was catastrophic. Within seconds the entire area was a sea of flames, in which high pressure tanks exploded with devastating blasts of fire that tore apart whole sections of the complex and freed more fuel to feed the inferno.

Fanned by the winds, and borne onward on the still overflowing river, the flames swept down on neighboring premises. In the space of a mile there were three large fuel depots, the already blazing distillery and a number of smaller concerns with stocks of paint and inflammable chemicals. Once the fire caught hold there was nothing to prevent it spreading through the closely packed installations that filled the area.

In Battersea the huge clouds of smoke rising from the river, and the periodic booms of the exploding tanks, had begun to alarm the inhabitants of houses nearby. Although the open expanse of the main road protected them at first, the overall movement of wind and water was toward them, and before long patches of blazing oil were drifting down on them. With flood water too deep to wade in, they searched desperately for some means of escape before they became trapped between fire and flood.

* * *

The borough control rooms were the main centers of action against the disaster. More makeshift in appearance than the Kingsway center with its sophisticated communications equipment, its teleprinter and its military style plotting technique, they were less concerned with monitoring the behavior of the flood than with taking immediate steps to relieve the hardship it caused.

During the short period before the surge struck an immense amount of work had already been done, both in warning those people and institutions who required special attention, and in making preparations for the care and feeding of the thousands of homeless.

Schools and church halls formed the backbone of the emergency accommodation and it was a tribute to the organization that lay behind the plans that in nearly all cases the relevant authorities had been prepared in advance for such an eventuality. Headmasters, priests and caretakers all over the London area had begun working to instructions sent to them during the past three years and updated ever since. While their children were sent to other schools or home to their parents, they started clearing rooms and preparing to receive the first influx of refugees. At the same time, government, military and social service depots were opening their doors to an ever growing fleet of vans and trucks which arrived to load up with the blankets, warm clothing, oil heaters, camp beds and other items needed to cope with thousands of wet and homeless families.

Once the flooding had commenced the control rooms began directing the rescue resources at their command to the spots they were best able to assist. The plan that had evolved was for police, firemen, troops and the like to work on the edge of the flood zone, pulling people out from the shallower areas and advancing slowly toward the more deeply inundated parts as the water receded.

Such, at any rate, was the plan. In some boroughs it was easier to put into practice than in others. Wandsworth in particular found itself faced with a number of insoluble difficulties. The borough was a large one, both geographically and from the point of view of population. It was also poor, with large numbers of Council house tenants and low income families. Such people tended to suffer most in the flooding and yet possessed the smallest reserves of food, clothing and money, on which to fall back. Consequently they were forced to turn to the authorities for aid. Moreover, large parts of the district were extremely low lying and now held upward of ten feet of water, which the engineers said would remain for at least a week. The control room was therefore engaged in drawing up plans to feed twelve thousand trapped in these areas, mainly in high-rise flats, at the same time as it organzed relief for the rest of the borough.

Details of the fire in York Road were first reported to Wandsworth flood control in the basement of the town hall. The general layout here was similar to that of Kingsway though on a simpler scale with greater improvisation of equipment. The officials manning it were also less detached and impersonal in their attitudes than their equivalents in Holborn. They were familiar with the streets and buildings into which the flood had moved. Many of them lived near by, some had listened to reports of water in their own homes, and all of them felt a high degree of personal interest in the tragedy. Some, like the housing officers, could see their work being set back ten years in front of their very eyes.

After the pronouncement of the state of emergency,

the chief executive of the Council had taken command of operations in Wandsworth. He was a tall spare man with thin sandy hair, named Simpson, who habitually went about the office with his jacket off and his sleeves rolled up.

"Do we have any idea of the true extent of the blaze?" he asked the police officer who brought him the news.

"No, sir. I'm afraid not. Our information comes from an observation post set up in an office block to the east. They report that a very large area is on fire and that it is spreading down into the houses, but the smoke is obscuring their view."

"What's the opinion of the fire service? Where's their man?"

"Here, sir," a middle-aged man behind the sergeant stepped forward. "It is the worst possible place it could happen, I'm afraid, sir. Heavily industrialized with very large quantities of inflammables in storage. Across the main road the houses are old and in poor condition to resist fire."

"Won't the rain and water put out the flames?" Simpson questioned him.

"Eventually yes, sir," the fireman replied, "but the fire could keep going for a long time if it's getting sufficient fuel from the oil tanks. I've been on to H.Q. and they are going to see if they can send the fire boats down to help. Nothing else can get through."

"Will they be able to put it out?" asked a councilor who had been listening to the conversation. The fireman shook his head worriedly.

"Frankly, sir, I don't think they will be able to do very much. The range of their pumps is limited and it will be difficult for them to get in close with the banks hidden."

The chief executive turned back to the police sergeant. "We have some boats somewhere around," he said. "I want as many as possible sent down to the fire area and I want an accurate report on the extent of the blaze. I shall contact Kingsway and see if they can assist us at all."

A short while later he was talking to Alan Carswell in Holborn on the radio. "We shall do all we can," the controller assured him, "but it's not much. Lambeth may be able to send you some boats and as soon as the wind drops the military will see what they can do with helicopters."

"Look, I've got thirty thousand people in the area threatened by this fire. If the flames keep spreading we're going to need every boat in London. What about the fire ships?"

"Only one can reach you, but it's coming. There isn't sufficient clearance under the bridges for the others to get through."

When he returned to the main room the sergeant was waiting for him. "I've ordered all available boats into the area at once, they'll start ferrying people up to the hill," he reported, "and two men with a radio are taking a dinghy in to make a full reconnaissance of the situation."

"Good, how many boats were you able to send?"

"Eleven, sir, that's all we have at the moment. We're hoping to get some more, though," he added lamely.

"Eleven boats," Simpson repeated quietly, "eleven boats to evacuate thirty thousand. I hope you believe in miracles, sergeant, because it looks as though we are going to need one."

* * *

With the withdrawal of the police detachments from traffic control duty on the bridges and approach roads, and the first signs of overtopping by the river, large numbers of people, both in cars and on foot, sought safety, as those at Lambeth had done, by going on to

the bridges and consequently became trapped when
the water behind rose to cut them off.

Although the appalling tragedy at Lambeth was not
repeated, none of the bridges were high enough for
their roadways to remain above the level of the flood,
and several were totally submerged. By 11:30, when
reports of the destruction wrought by the barges had
been received, urgent appeals were being sent to the police and army to try and rescue these stranded groups.
With the Thames now more than a mile wide, the
chances of their survival, clinging to the parapets and
ironworks, and in many cases up to their necks in freezing water, unprotected from the wind and rain, until the
tide retreated, were nonexistent.

Rescue, however, was not possible in most cases. The
police had organized supplies of boats for the emergency and some two thousand two hundred were earmarked, but only a small fraction of these were available in the first hours of the flood. Many of the others,
as the authorities in Wandsworth were discovering,
were in shops and storage depots and boat clubs many
miles from the center of London, and even those on
the water were far from the main river. Moreover,
many were too small to be of much use in the open
river, which had now taken on the appearance of the
sea, with waves caused by the storm rolling swiftly inland. Yet the larger boats could only work within a
restricted area, since they were no longer able to pass
beneath the arches of the bridges.

Near the site of the Battersea Heliport the fire boat
Firefly had gone to the aid of a small group who had
tried to escape from the sudden flood that had drowned
Battersea, by crossing the railway bridge on the line
from Clapham Junction up to Olympia. As the river
had risen to cut them off, they had been forced to climb
up the frameworked iron sides, to avoid the water.
There were less than a dozen of them all told, and the
Firefly took them off without great difficulty, for the

bridge itself afforded some protection from the strong winds that were blowing.

Firefly was the biggest of the city's two fire boats; sixty-six feet long with a beam of sixteen feet and a crew of eight. Her twin hundred horsepower Foden diesels gave her a top speed of nearly ten knots and she carried two high pressure diesel fire pumps, each of which could supply seven hundred and fifty gallons of water per minute, at a pressure of one hundred pounds per square inch, through fixed piping to the four monitors on her decks which were fitted with self-inducing foam generators as well as to eight other delivery heads. In addition, she was equipped with separate foam generators on both her port and starboard sides which fed foam spreaders designed to protect her from oil burning on the water, and beneath the forward deck were tanks holding nine hundred gallons of foam.

What concerned the skipper most at the moment was what to do with his passengers now he had them on board. The fire boat had limited accommodation and very little room below decks. Most of the interior was taken up with the engines, pumps and fuel, or by the three large tanks of foam for use against oil fires. Hoses, breathing gear and other equipment occupied the remaining space. The rescued men, cold and wet after their ordeal, crammed into the crew's locker room.

"You're lucky we were on this stretch at all," the skipper told them. He was a slow speaking, thickset man, with grizzled black hair, named Coulson. "We were up at Chiswick earlier on today, and were trying to get back to our headquarters wharf at Lambeth, before we were stopped by this bridge. The question now is where am I to put you off? The banks are all covered and I can't get past Wandsworth Bridge." He was still thinking about the problem as he went up to the wheelhouse.

"I was just going to call you," the mate told him, as he stepped through the narrow hatch. "It looks as though we've got a big blaze upstream." He pointed to where a column of greasy black smoke was billowing skywards.

"I reckon that's oil," he went on. "Could be one of the depots on the riverside." The skipper peered at it through the binoculars for a moment.

"We'd better take a look," he agreed. "Pass the word to headquarters, will you?"

Before the message could be got off, however, they received an urgent order to make for the scene of the fire with all possible speed. The flames had already taken a fierce hold on the waterfront storage tanks and had set the nearer streets ablaze. Some tenement blocks were virtually surrounded by volatile installations and the inhabitants of these were dying horribly, many leaping from their burning homes to perish in the lakes of fire that spread across the water.

The scene that came into view as the fire boat sailed upstream, surpassed anything the crew had ever experienced before. Not since the great incendiary raids on the docks and East End had such a conflagration been known in London. For more than half a mile the riverside was alight with flames leaping from the buildings, sometimes spurting high into the air in balls of fire as another tank or container exploded, feeding the blaze further. Clouds of smoke and steam curled up, towering hundreds of feet above the fires. Flying sparks and fragments of red hot debris showered up by the blasts, fell back hissing into the water. The furious roar and crackle of the flames mingled with the crash of falling beams and the sudden boom of the explosions mercifully blotted out the cries of the families caught within the inferno.

Coulson took his ship down the length of the blazing shoreline, examining the situation critically. He was careful to keep well away from where he estimated the walls lay beneath the surface for he was conscious of the danger to the *Firefly* if she should strike some submerged object close to the fire. Even at a distance the heat was unbearable and the flames filled the interior of the wheelhouse with a lurid flickering light.

"I don't like it," he confessed to the mate. "Unless we go in dangerously close our pumps won't touch the fire, and it's impossible to see where the walls lie on this stretch. If we get too near we could hole the boat or snag a wire and that'd be our lot." The mate nodded.

"I've never seen anything this bad before," he said. "What can we do by ourselves? I reckon the rain's more use than we are an' that's starting to ease up. And we've still got those passengers below," he added. The skipper shrugged his shoulders beneath his yellow oilskin.

"We'll have to do what we can," he replied. "Radio headquarters that we're going in as close as we can get."

Slowly and very cautiously he maneuvered in towards the shore, while on deck his men, swathed in heavy protective gear against the fierce heat, made ready the monitors in the bows and stern, and fitted hoses to the delivery heads forward of the wheelhouse. At a signal from the skipper they started the foam spreaders and began laying a protective film of chemical about the boat. When they were about ten yards from where he estimated the wall had once been they turned on the monitors. There came a deep powerful drone from the pumps, then the jets of water hissed skywards, arching outward across the intervening space to fall among the burning remains of a warehouse. Clouds of steam shot up, but though the jets drenched the outer walls of the building, the terrific volume seemed to have little effect on the fire. The flames still belched out furiously with undiminished energy. After several minutes the skipper turned to the mate again.

"It's no use," he called out, above the noise, "we'll have to go in closer and bring the hoses to bear as well."

"If we go any nearer we'll hit the bank. There's no way of telling what's underneath the water. There could be crane jibs, steel fencing, concrete pillars, anything just below the surface," the mate shouted back.

"We have to take the risk. There's no other way," the skipper replied.

"What good will we do even if we do go right in?" the mate demanded. "We can't begin to touch a blaze this size with what we've got, and anyway the wind is carrying it away from us inland?"

"I know that, damn you!" the skipper said angrily, "but what the hell else can we do? There are people dying in there in hundreds!"

Putting the wheel over he brought *Firefly* around on a new course that would take her in close under the walls of the blazing buildings. The ship's draught was a little over four feet and though the water over the banks was almost certainly deeper than this he knew that the mate had been right about the danger of hidden projections just below the surface.

He had to come within five yards of where he guessed the banks lay, before the hoses could be brought into action. At this range, the heat was so intense that the paintwork began to bubble and blister and the men on deck had to use face protectors to enable them to work. Coulson scanned the river anxiously for the least sign of a submerged obstruction.

Fortunately, there was less oil on the water here than he had feared. The wind and currents were carrying the burning lakes inward to spread the flames among the houses beyond. A sudden shattering explosion, fiercer than any other they had seen, sent a shower of small debris hissing down about them. He saw a fireman turn his hose briefly on to the deck for'ard, washing off a scattering of smoldering fragments.

Ahead of them the rear wall of a building toppled suddenly outward, collapsing into the flood in a roar of steam as the red hot bricks touched the water. Coulson swung the wheel over sharply to clear it, and instantly there came a confused clatter and grating sound from the stern, and a violent tremor shook the boat. Abruptly it ceased as the engines cut out.

"Jesus!" cried the mate, "what's that?" He looked round in fear towards the stern.

"Something must have snagged the screws and fouled them," the skipper's voice was harsh with alarm. "I'm going back to see what's happened. Tell the men to get the life raft ready and get those survivors up on deck. As soon as we get free take us out into mid-channel."

"Aye, aye, sir." The mate reached for the Tannoy microphone, as he did so he saw the bows had started to swing round towards the line of blazing buildings.

On the opposite bank, some workers from Fulham Power Station had been watching the scene from an upper-floor window, through binoculars. For the past half hour they had noted the rapid spreading of the fire, until the whole shore appeared to be ablaze, and the unsuccessful endeavors of the *Firefly*. They had seen the hasty mustering of men on her decks but only when the boat turned stern on to them did they realize that something was wrong and that she was lying dead in the water. For a short while she seemed to drift sideways with the stream and men could be seen clustered about the life rafts. But before anything could be done she was caught in the grip of a savage current and drawn inwards towards the inferno. For a second she appeared silhouetted blackly against the orange flames, then with a rush she was swept across the walls. Screaming with terror some of the crew leapt into the water in a vain attempt to escape, as the fire boat shot into the heat of the raging flames and was lost to sight.

* * *

By one o'clock the rapid influx of flood water into the district of North Battersea was complete and at Bevan Tower the level finally ceased to rise, having reached

a point two feet below the ceilings of the first floor.
Those inmates who, like Dave Cox, went to the top of
the stairs and looked down at the black scum covered
surface could only guess at the damage that had been
caused in the inundated flats. Beyond a few broken
sticks of furniture which had floated up from below
and a steady number of slowly rising bubbles, the water
remained undisturbed and impenetrable.

Yet despite this outwardly passive appearance, a new
and potentially catastrophic danger to the building was
building up unseen, concealed by the flood. During the
hurried efforts to remove furniture and fittings before
they could be spoiled by the river, an attempt had been
made to shift the stove from a flat on the first floor.
The attempt had been abandoned when the climbing
water level had threatened to cut off and trap the men
as they worked. They fled for the stairs, leaving the
stove where it was, pulled out a little way from the
wall.

The speed with which the flooding had occurred and
the confusion that resulted meant that there was no
central direction for these matters. No one had stopped
to consider whether the gas should be turned off at the
mains before such tasks were started, or what the result
might be if they were left half completed. Where the
stove had been so hastily moved the coupling to the
main pipe in the wall had fractured, allowing gas to
escape into the room. This fact had passed unnoticed in
the panic and throughout the afternoon a deadly pocket of gas built up between the surface of the water and
the ceiling above.

The threat posed by the pressure of this explosive
mixture was infinitely more serious than might at first
be imagined. Bevan Tower, like many other recent
high-rise buildings, was constructed of prefabricated
sections which were hoisted into position by cranes and
fixed in such a way that walls and floors were tensioned
together throughout the entire structure. This gave the

block tremendous overall strength and enabled the builders to do without a massive internal skeleton on steel girders on which to support the fabric. The wall and floor units thus acted as their own skeleton by virtue of their tension with each other.

While this system brought many benefits it also meant that severe damage to a number of these interdependent sections could result in a disastrous loss of strength throughout the structure. Indeed, in theory it was possible that if sufficient sections were destroyed, the tensions elsewhere in the building might literally tear it apart.

Chapter Nine

Georgina had never before experienced darkness as total as that in which she now found herself. She stood rooted to the spot, terrified even to move. All around she could hear the noise of water moving, in the background she was aware of the creaking of the steel flood doors and faint confused echoes from the holocaust above. It seemed as though her worst imaginings were about to be realized, that she would drown horribly in the dark when the tunnel flooded.

There was a soft click and the beam of a torch flashed over the platform. It was held by the railway mechanic who shone it slowly round, taking in the situation. By its light Georgina could see the other survivors from the station looking at each other silently. Two of them, the velvet-collared stockbroker and the pretty colored girl in the trouser suit, were picking themselves up from the tracks on to which they had been thrown by the torrent.

They were, she realized, on the southbound platform

of the Northern line Tube. Ahead of her, where the tunnel mouth should have gaped open, a solid steel barrier had been dropped across the entrance. Opposite on the white tiled wall were the familiar destination maps and advertising posters, just visible in the faint light. The far tunnel was still open, though she could make out a pile of machinery and equipment standing on the end of the platform.

The driver and guard began helping the other two out of the rail pit and up on to the platform. The man who had led them down took no notice of them, he was inspecting the gateways, through one of which they had just come. There were four of them, narrow shafts leading through to the escalators beyond. Three of these, Georgina saw, were sealed by heavy flood gates of the kind that they had closed behind them, but the fourth had been blocked off by what appeared to be a makeshift barrier of iron sheeting reinforced by wooden beams. The man was examining this construction very carefully, and the rest of the group of survivors gathered slowly about him. As they did he looked up.

"Hey," he called out to the driver, "try that emergency phone down the platform will you. We may still be able to make contact with Leicester Square."

He flashed the torch round the others. "Is anyone hurt?" he asked. "More than bruises that is?" They all shook their heads. "Good," he went on, "well now we had better try and find a way out of this place." He flicked the torch in the direction of the open tunnel. "Up that way."

The train driver came hurrying back down the platform. "I don't know," he replied in answer to the unspoken query of the mechanic. "I think maybe I got through for a second, but then the line went dead."

"Let's hope they heard you anyway. What's your name?"

"I'm Jo Clark," replied the driver, "and this is Sandy, he's my guard," he indicated the youth beside him.

"My name is David Rees, and I'm chief mechanic in this station, or rather," he grinned, "I was. What about the rest of you?"

"Douglas Russell," the stockbroker answered first. Georgina and the other girl, who was called Angelica, gave their names in turn.

"This is what we have to do," the Welshman told them. "We can't go back the way we came in, and that," he jerked a thumb in the direction of the sealed tunnel, "leads right under the river. So the only direction left is to walk up the tunnel and try to reach Strand station or Leicester Square."

"Is it O.K.?" asked Jo, the driver. "There'll be water coming down that way, won't there?"

"There'll be water coming down, that's certain enough," replied Rees. "We might be able to make our way past."

The stockbroker interrupted. "Presumably," he said, "we have no choice. If we stay here and water comes down the open tunnel we will be trapped here. There's no other way out."

"Maybe we could put up the gate at the other end," suggested Jo. "Looks like the stuff is all there." Rees shook his head.

"We were working on that gate when we went to help you lot," he said. "The lifting gear has jammed, and we could never get her off the ground. It weighs four tons. In any case," he added, "we couldn't stay in here, this doorway will not last for very much longer. The pressure above must be enormous. We had best be starting on our way at once."

Reluctantly, the six men and women moved up the platform and stepped down the slope into the tunnel. On their way they found another torch left behind by the team that only a short while ago had been working down there.

"Hey! There's water coming down from inside!" exclaimed Russell. They all paused and looked. Sure enough, among the rails pools of liquid glistened in the torchlight. They drew back afraid, but the Welshman drove them on with a snort of derision.

"That's nothing more than seepage from the drains and cable shafts," he said scornfully. "No need to bother your heads about that. You'll know about it all right if the water does break through."

They walked on in silence. All about her Georgina could hear the soft sounds of water trickling into the tunnel. Several times she stepped into puddles in the dark. The struggle on the stairs had left her clothes soaked and now she ached with cold.

"We'll be starting to go downhill very soon," Rees said to her.

"Downhill?" she repeated in surprise. "I thought the tubes were all straight."

"No way, lady. They slope away from the stations at each end. It gives the trains more braking power when they draw in and a quicker start when they leave."

"What you're trying to tell us," said the stockbroker, "is that the tunnel we are in goes down to a dip in the middle, so that is where we will find deep water if there is any."

"But why should there be any deep water at all?" asked Georgina anxiously. "The Strand is much higher than this, and the flood won't reach there, surely?"

"No, but it probably will reach Trafalgar Square, or so we were told, and there are connections from there into the Strand, and in any case there's another tunnel running parallel with this one that is almost certainly flooded, the Bakerloo Line. Water could run down from there into Trafalgar Square and then through into this place."

The slope the mechanic had predicted was gradual and at first they scarcely noticed it, but after a while they realized they were definitely walking downhill. The going seemed rougher, there was more water about and their feet stumbled frequently. Georgina found she was becoming bitterly tired. She looked at her watch; to her surprise the luminous dial was still working. It was 11:45.

All at once Rees stopped dead, and behind him the others came to a halt. Georgina peered forward to see what was wrong. In front of them the tunnel stretched away into darkness, still sloping downward, but the rails were now hidden by a silent black pool that covered the whole width of the tunnel and disappeared out of sight. In the feeble light of the torch there was no way of telling how deep it eventually was.

"Wait here, all of you," ordered Rees, and he began splashing on down the tunnel. They could see the water rising about his legs as he went. The light of the torch dwindled slowly till he was no more than a faint glimmer. After what seemed like an age he returned.

"It's no good," he said wearily, wading through the last few feet. "I went in up to my waist and still didn't get to the deepest part. I reckon it must be nearly to the roof in the center of the dip. The flood must have broken through from the new workings in the Strand."

"You think there's no chance of getting through?" asked Russell, his face expressionless in the torchlight.

"Not a hope. The water is still rising. If we went on we should most likely be caught in the middle."

"Hell man," it was the driver Jo who spoke, "it doesn't look that difficult to me. That dip can't last for more than a few hundred yards, an' we should be able to swim through that."

"Maybe," responded Rees tersely, "but what will you do then. You can't get out to the surface at Strand because that's where the water's entering from so you'll have to go on up to Leicester Square. That means another dip, and that one will certainly be blocked by now."

"So what do we do now?" The colored girl Angelica spoke for the first time.

"We go back to the station we've just left and try to close that flood gate at the mouth of this line. Then if we're lucky we can just wait until they pump out the stairs above us and let us out."

The driver looked doubtful. "I still say we should try an' get through the water," he said. Beside him the young guard watched the exchange with anxious eyes.

"I've told you it's impossible to get through," Rees snapped angrily. "We've enough trouble on our hands, without committing suicide."

"Seems more like suicide to go back to Charing Cross," the driver retorted. "What you goin' to do there? Wait till the water comes up the tunnel and drowns you like rats. I tell you this is the only way." Without waiting for any response from the Welshman he waded into the water.

"You comin' with me, Sandy?" he yelled over his shoulder to the guard, "or you goin' to stop behind and drown with this guy?" The youth hesitated for a moment, then with a helpless glance at Rees he set off after the driver.

The young girl gave a whimper of fear as their torch faded out down the tunnel, and started forward to the edge of the water. Rees pulled her back by the arm.

"Let them go," he said gently. "When you're lucky enough to have someone with you who is an expert, it's best to follow his advice."

"But that man said the water would come in and we'd all drown," the girl said plaintively, and burst into tears. Georgina went up and put her arm around her.

"Easy now," Rees told her, "I'm hoping we'll be able to get that flood gate into position behind us. If we can do that we shall be sitting pretty. Those two will be coming back to join us before we get back to the platform, you'll see."

They were still some way from the end and had only just reached the level part of the track when a sudden cry, hollowed and distorted by the tunnel, echoed down towards them. Instantly they halted and looked back. There was no sign of movement or light in the darkness behind them but the cry ended abruptly with what sounded unpleasantly like a choking cough. They stared towards the noise, expecting any moment to see the driver and his guard struggling toward them, driven back by the flood.

For a few seconds there was not a sound, then there came a prolonged gurgle, a noise like a kind of liquid belch, and suddenly water was streaming about their feet. Horror-struck at the thought of the fate which must have befallen the two men, and which now only too obviously faced themselves, Georgina and her three remaining companions fled up the track in the direction of the platform.

Sandy had not been over enthusiastic about the idea of attempting to force a way through the water that lay between him and safety, but he greatly respected Jo, his driver, and if Jo said it was the best thing to do that was good enough for him. The stubborn driver had proved himself sensible enough in the past, and Sandy trusted his knowledge of the underground system a lot more than that of the Welshman David Rees, whom he had never seen before.

All the same he did not relish the idea of wading on into the ever-increasing depth before them. The water was freezing cold to a degree that he would not have thought possible, it seemed to grip his chest in a paralyzing iron hand, turning his body numb. They made slow progress, fighting their way through against what they could feel was a strong current. Somewhere ahead of them in the darkness more water must be flowing into the tunnel. Sandy prayed it was not overtaking them. He was trying to keep to the raised side path but every so often he would slip off and fall into the deep central trough.

The depth increased steadily, and soon they were swimming rather than walking, with the water surging round their necks. Jo was trying to hold his torch above the surface as he thrashed along, but this was not easy and periodically they were plunged into total darkness.

"We'll have to go back, Jo. It's too deep," Sandy cried out.

"No, it'll be O.K., only a bit further," the driver called back, but even as he did so Sandy felt the ground beneath him slip away altogether; then his head was under the surface and he was fighting and gasping for air. The depth had risen sharply; he kicked out frantically trying to touch the bottom, but the light had gone out again and his mouth was full of grit and dirt from the water. Once more his head went under and this time, when he rose for air, he struck himself violently against the roof of the tunnel.

Seized with panic at the thought of what this signified, Sandy screamed out for Jo, but there was no reply and the light did not reappear. He screamed again, water entered his mouth, leaving him choking. The roof was now barely inches from the surface. Totally lost in the dark, he pulled himself along with his fingers on the roof without any idea of the direction he was taking. His one aim was to preserve the tiny space of air that now meant life to him. For a short way this shrank terrifyingly so that he had to press his face flat against the bricks of the roof to draw breath.

Then, just when he had virtually lost the strength and will to go any further the gap began to grow wider, and almost before he realized what had happened, the roof had lifted away and he could feel the ground beneath his feet once more. Able to stand again for the first time in minutes, he rested for a moment and called out to Jo, hoping to hear an answering cry, and perhaps catch sight of the welcome glimmer of the torch. Instead however he heard only the sound of water lapping against the side of the tunnel and the quick rasp of his own breathing.

When he finally concluded that he was alone, Sandy's first assumption was that he had somehow become confused in the darkness and turned about, to come out on the same side of the water as he had gone in. With the light to guide him, Jo had presumably been able to make it through to the safety on the other side. Expecting any minute to find himself on the platform he had recently left he began to wade along the tunnel as fast as he could.

It was the current flowing against him that finally brought home to him his true position. By rights, if he had been heading back towards Charing Cross, it should have been moving with him, as the water flowed outwards into the tunnel. Yet there could no longer be any doubt that the source of the flow was still ahead of him. With a shock he realized that he was cut off from the others and was now wandering alone in the immense system of half-flooded tunnels with very little chance of being able to find his way out before they filled totally and he was drowned. In a daze, without any clear idea of what he was doing or where he was going, he waded on.

At one point, he was conscious of the tunnel having opened out and knew that he must have arrived at a station. The sound of water entering was much louder than before, and came from somewhere on his left, but the overall level of the flooding was lower and he found it easier to walk. He must have reached the Strand, he decided, the source of the water he had come through. The station had been temporarily closed while it was being rebuilt and the flooding was presumably flowing in through the workings. He debated whether to follow the flow to its source and thus try to make his way to the surface but decided it would be too risky. The chances of being trapped in a narrow passage in the dark where he would be unable to find a way out were too great.

Beyond the station and its influx of water, the depth of flooding grew markedly less, until at one point it practically ceased altogether. Sandy, stumbling on in the darkness was no longer capable of noticing the fact. Shivering with cold, exhausted by the journey through the flooded portion of the tunnels, fingers scratched and bleeding from the rough brick, he kept going like an automaton. The next dip in the track was upon him before he knew it and, scarcely realizing, he was once again wading chest deep.

*   *   *

Fresh messages and reports were entering Kingsway in such volume that the staff were hard pressed to maintain a semblance of order. The heat and noise in the confined space were terrific. Smoking had been banned and the air-conditioning turned up, but there were upwards of forty people seated at the desks or milling about between the radio office and the plotting tables, and the atmosphere was almost unbearable. Most of the men were working in shirt sleeves, adding a further touch of unreality, Derek thought, glancing at the latest weather summary with its reference to 55 m.p.h. winds heavy rain overhead and freezing temperatures.

The girls on the plotting team were working flat out to keep pace with the continuous stream of instructions being called out to them. The main gap was thickly dotted with incident markers, colored arrows indicating the movements of service units and rescue crews, and ever expanding patches of red that showed the parts of the city now submerged.

The broad pattern of the flooding was becoming apparent, very much as the engineers had predicted. On the northern side of the Thames, with the exception of

Newham and Tower Hamlets in the east and Hammersmith in the west, which were heavily inundated, the
flooding was confined to a narrow strip, a few streets
wide, along the border of the river. Only in Westminster had the surge penetrated inland for three-quarters
of a mile.

In the south the picture was very different. Between
Wandsworth Bridge and Woolwich, the flooding lay in
a broad belt up to three miles in width. Huge tracts of
Lewisham, Southwark, Lambeth and Battersea had
been drowned; in some places depths of nearly twenty
feet had been reported. In these areas the rescue authorities were being placed under tremendous strain, attempting to cope with thousands of urgent appeals for
help, many of which they were being forced to turn
away or ignore. Draining this ground, more than forty
square miles of it, so far, he estimated, would at least
take several days, at the worst some streets would still
be under deep water in a fortnight's time.

Against the background of noise and chatter Derek
was trying to plan the dewatering operation. It would
be no easy task. As he had explained to the Minister
earlier, even when the winds died away and the tides
ebbed, allowing the sea to retreat, they would still be
left with huge areas of ponded water, trapped behind
the defenses, which would have to be mechanically
drained or pumped dry. At the same time the dozen
major breaches in the walls and a host of minor ones,
would have to be temporarily filled in order to prevent
more flooding taking place at high tide.

Then there would remain the unbelievable task of
repairing the damage and clearing up the mess. Half
a million homes and buildings would be left with their
lower storeys rendered uninhabitable by a thick coating
of slime, river mud and the filth from the city's streets
and sewers. In some cases, oil and chemicals from nearby stores would have done irreparable damage. Everywhere it would take months to pump them dry, shovel

out the dirt, cleanse the rooms, before starting on jobs like replacing electric wiring and rebuilding. Nor would the damage be confined to those districts which had experienced actual flooding. Raw sewage would be backing up in the pipes for miles around, blocking drains and lavatories, and welling up into houses out of reach of the floods.

His thoughts switched to his own home. He wished there was some way of knowing if Georgina was safe. The children, he had no doubt, were being looked after and were probably in the middle of eating lunch, unconcerned by the absence of their mother and father. Georgina might have decided to go anywhere but her most likely destination would be the studio, in which case she would then have found herself unable to cross over into Wandsworth. The thought that she might have tried to beat the surge back by taking a tube as far as Fulham had already occurred to him, and he forced himself to discount it. Georgina was well enough aware of the danger of being caught in the tubes to risk traveling when the sirens had gone. The odds against her having been one of the passengers on the disaster train were astronomical. There must be hundreds of other men in the same position as himself at this time, trying to carry out their duties efficiently and yet worried about their wives and families. At least his actual home was in no serious danger, to that extent he was more fortunate than many others.

A sudden commotion in the group round the map drew his attention and he went over to see what was happening. Carswell was on the telephone talking urgently but Miles was there, his mouth tight and compressed.

"A big fire has broken out near Wandsworth Bridge," he said, the strain of the past two hours evident in his manner. "They say it's out of control and spreading." He looked questioningly at Derek as though seeking a solution to their problems. Beside him a plump, dark girl with short hair leaned over and placed a triangular white plastic marker with an orange flame painted on it, at York Road. Derek said nothing, there was nothing to say until they had more facts, and even then, there was little enough they could do. To describe fire as out of control was meaningless. With several feet of water in the surrounding streets and no fire brigade or equipment to fight it, there was nothing to be done except hope the flames went out of their own accord.

He realized that Miles was still speaking. The councilor appeared strangely ill at ease and embarrassed, unlike his normal suave self. Taking Derek by the arm he led him to the side of the room.

"There's something I should like you to know about," he said speaking quickly and keeping his voice low, "a personal matter." Derek's face registered his surprise. "I believe you were expecting your wife to telephone you at around nine o'clock this morning," he paused uncomfortably. Derek made no reply. Miles was perfectly aware of this fact. He had been present when the message from the school had come through, and had been part of the conversation that had followed.

"Well," Miles continued, "I am afraid she did telephone. The call was put through to County Hall after you had left, it was about 9:15, and so I took it."

"My God." Realization dawned on Derek. "What did you tell her?" he demanded fiercely. Miles went red and stammered.

"Nothing really, nothing important. It was still very early then. I told her not to worry, that the alert would probably be called off. I forgot about it till now . . ." he finished lamely.

"You stupid . . ." Derek groped for words to express his fury. "You did to her exactly what you did to the rest of the city. You made her believe it was safe to go out less than an hour before we let the sirens off. The one thing I had been telling her not to do." Miles backed away from him, his face sweating with anxiety.

"I'm sure she'll be all right," he said. "She's probably only having to make a big detour to find a bridge over the river."

"You'd better be right," Derek replied savagely, "because, so help me, if anything happens to Georgina because of what you did I shall drown you myself."

Miles continued to apologize, but his groveling display, a sharp contrast to his usual arrogance, sickened Derek and he left him standing. The councilor was a lot more frightened underneath than he appeared at first sight. He was witnessing the collapse of everything he had lived for, and none knew better than him what that entailed. Miles had been foremost among those who had pretended the danger did not exist, and the majority of people had believed him and had been deceived. Things would not go easy with Miles when the flood was over.

Georgina's actions were easy to predict now. After speaking to Miles at 9:15 her first thought would be that she could get to the studio and see her client. The sirens would have sounded shortly after her arrival, leaving her desperate to get home to the children. By now she could be anywhere.

It was even hotter by the maps, thanks to the triple row of arc lights that hung over the table. Derek pushed his way through the scrum of officials who were clustered about.

"What's the position on this fire?" he asked Carswell.

"To be perfectly honest, I don't know. Nobody has been able to get close enough to report yet. As far as we can make out, something like half a mile of factories and oil depots are alight to the east of Wandsworth Bridge and the flames have started to spread down into Battersea."

"That's a diabolical place for a fire," said a police inspector. "I know it well. Old buildings crammed to-

gether, narrow streets, tenement blocks; if the fire gets
a hold there we'll have a devil of a job putting it out.
Flood or no flood."

"I'm asking all neighboring boroughs to send in rescue boats, as well as the army and police. The local
control are trying to pull the inhabitants back to Lavender Hill and Clapham Common."

"What about reconnaissance flights by helicopters?"
suggested someone.

"Impossible in these winds," responded an army officer. "They couldn't even take off." The borough liaison men began shouting details of incoming messages.

"Richmond sending eight inflatable boats by truck."

"Southwark reports no boats available."

"Kensington and Chelsea have sent all their spare
boats to Hammersmith."

Another army officer came forward. "We can let you
have our reserve unit of six boats stationed at the Duke
of York Barracks in Chelsea," he informed Carswell.

"Yes, thank you, Major. Will you all contact Wandsworth direct please, but keep a note of what goes
where." This was what Carswell was best at, jiggling
men and resources between different groups, meeting
each emergency as it came. At that moment the voice
of one of the police liaison team interrupted.

"Mr. Carswell. Paddington Green Central are being
asked if you have ordered the evacuation of West Ham
because of the broken sewer?"

"The evacuation of West Ham?" Carswell echoed in
surprise. "I've made no mention of West Ham in any
order." His moustache twitched indignantly and he
glared about him as though challenging anyone to deny
it, "And what's this about the sewer?"

The officer turned his back to his telephone, then
called something back, but the words were lost in the
crossfire of orders and messages.

"Please," Carswell shouted to the room in general,
"can we confine remarks to essential matters only, and

then quietly." The noise in the control room subsided a fraction.

"The Northern outfall sewer has fractured, sir," the policeman repeated his message. "Sewage is draining into West Ham. Apparently a rumor's been started that compulsory evacuation has been ordered."

"Evacuate people where? West Ham is one of the most heavily flooded points on the map. The water's more than six feet deep. There's no possibility of evacuation from there at this juncture. If there is serious contamination, the residents will have to boil their drinking water."

"Yes, sir," the policeman replied, "but about boiling the water, sir. Our men there have been told to pass the word on not to light the gas. The board say there's a danger of explosions."

There were a few chuckles round the room at this. It was the kind of ludicrous conflict of orders which could only arise in a situation like this, Derek thought, but at least it broke the tension.

"Well, tell them to do the best they can," Carswell ordered. "If they decide to evacuate later on, of course we'll give them assistance but so far we have definitely not given such an instruction." He turned to the Water Board's desk. "What is this about the sewer breaking? Why wasn't I told earlier?"

"I'm very sorry, sir," the senior representative replied apologetically, "we haven't heard about it ourselves. We've lost contact with many of our stations in that area."

"Is it possible that the sewer has fractured?"

"Quite possible, I'm afraid. It runs above ground at that point, traveling overland to the Beckton outfall. We're checking now."

Carswell seemed satisfied with this answer. In the confusion that existed generally it was certainly too much to expect that the central control would be kept informed of all developments. He turned his attention back to the fire. Miles, however, had come on to the scene and was less easily pleased.

"Look here!" he said, "if the Northern outfall has broken we shall have to do more than tell the residents to boil their water. Half London's drains empty into that pipe. We could face a massive outbreak of epidemics, typhoid, dysentery, you name it. If that sewer has broken there will be no choice but to evacuate the area."

"Of course, of course. I wasn't suggesting that we do nothing. But there is no point in our telling West Ham to evacuate when we haven't prepared any facilities. If the local medical officer considers it necessary he will give the order and we will then assist. It has to be that way round or there is chaos."

Miles appeared to have recovered from their recent interview and Derek saw him stiffen at the rebuff. He was prevented from continuing the argument, however, by more insistent calls for the Controller's attention.

"Report from Bankside generating station, sir. They still request urgent medical assistance. No help has been able to get through to them."

"Wandsworth control ask when will the fireboat be ready? The blaze is still spreading rapidly."

Derek went back to his desk. There was little he could do to assist with these major incidents. Nor, for that matter, did he think the others would achieve a great deal but even so the effort had to be made. For his part the most important task was to marshal men and equipment ready to start dewatering the moment the river went down. Already under his direction dumps of materials, sandbags, timber, steel piling, sheeting and such items, were being established in Green Park, Clapham Common and a number of other strategic points. From here teams of engineers and workmen would set about making temporary repairs to the river walls. At the same time other groups would be assisting the drainage engineer to unblock the gullies and drains around the perimeter of the flood zone. When the waters first rushed in they scooped up a vast quantity of rubbish and debris as they advanced which settled gradually, blocking the outlets to the drains. These had to be cleared to allow the sewerage system to play its part in removing the water.

He was still engaged on this when he felt a hand on his shoulder. It was Carswell.

"I've just heard from London Transport," he said. "They sent a rescue team into the tunnels at Leicester Square to see if there was any chance of recovering some of the bodies from the tube disaster and they found a man alive. What's more he says there are others down there." He paused for a moment, then went on, his face grave. "I'm afraid he says one of them is your wife."

* * *

Dave's first reaction on returning to the roof was amazement that such a large fire could have built up with such speed. Clouds of dense, oily black smoke were belching towards the sky in a pall that seemed to stretch over most of Battersea. Around its base tongues of fire were visible, licking through roofs and walls. As he stared in horrified fascination there came the rattle and boom of an explosion and a fresh gout of flames shot out from the edge of the conflagration.

At present, the fire seemed a long way off. It was hard to tell even if it had spread to the houses nearest the main road, but he thought it probably had. The caretaker's voice interrupted his thoughts.

"What do we do if it comes this way?" he asked.

"Keep your voice down!" Dave warned him. There were several others on the roof now, staring excitedly at the blaze. "It's not going to cross all this water, is it?"

"That's an oil fire, look at the smoke. It's burning on the water, you can see it. What'll happen once it gets in among the houses?"

Dave did not reply. Instead he began petulantly ordering the other residents off the roof. To his relief they obeyed without argument. He had no clear idea of what to do, the instructions he had been given merely told him to see that the people in the block kept calm, and that help would be brought when it was needed. He supposed vaguely there were boats available to rescue them if the fire came too close. He was unaware that at that moment a desperate appeal for boats and rafts of any kind was being put out to every town and village in the south of England and that trucks carrying them were being diverted to Wandsworth, regardless of their original destination, and given priority over all other traffic.

He was making his way back downstairs again when Eileen came rushing up. "Oh Mr. Cox," she cried, "come quick. Mrs. Pole's 'usband's fallen in the water."

Ever since the flood had first entered the flats old Pole had felt unhappy. It had not been possible to bring all their furniture upstairs in time and a few items had been lost. In themselves they were of little consequence; a couple of wooden chairs, a cupboard and a chest of drawers. But in the bottom of a drawer in the cupboard Pole kept his savings, one hundred and seventy pounds, put aside to use in an emergency, or, his recurrent nightmare, to look after himself if his wife should die before him. No one else in the world knew of the money and he had not told the men who had cleared the flat to move the cupboard, for fear they should guess its secret.

So he hovered anxiously at the water's edge, peering into the darkness below, wheezing and coughing in the damp air. When at last he actually fell in, he was fortunate that Eileen was passing on the stairs and heard the splash, for the shock knocked the remaining breath from his body and left him unable even to shout for help.

By the time Dave arrived on the scene he had been

dragged out, semi-conscious, the wet clothes stripped off him and his wife was sitting beside him as he lay in bed.

"What he needs is a 'ot water bottle," said Eileen, "but we'll 'ave to use the gas. D'you reckon it's safe?"

"We'll have to risk it. We've no other choice," he told her. The old man's skin had gone pale and clammy, as he lay in the bed staring up glassily at the ceiling and breathing in short irregular gasps.

Eileen went back into her own flat to boil the kettle for Mr. Pole's hot water bottle. Turning on the ring of her stove, she was relieved to hear a faint sound of escaping gas, but the pressure was very low. The pilot flame had gone out and she had to strike a match to light it. Leaving the kettle on the stove she went to find herself a cigarette and sat down in the sitting room to wait for it to boil. She was still worried about Jerry, despite old Mrs. Pole's assurances that the Electricity Board would look after him. It was quite possible that he might at that moment be trying to get through to her, or was himself trapped in some building by the tides. The sheer magnitude of the flood was beyond her comprehension; she had never thought of herself as living near the river and she now pictured the whole of London drowned twenty feet deep.

There was a knock at the door and one of the other women in the block came in.

"Sorry to worry you, dear," she said, "but I think your Marlene's gone up to the roof."

"God, the little pest," Eileen swore. "I told her to stay where she was. I'd better go and get her."

"How's that kettle coming on?" asked the woman.

"Oh, the gas is really low. I turned it full on an' it still keeps flickering," Eileen told her. "If it starts whistling before I'm back, can you get it?"

"O.K. dear, I'll listen for it." The two women went out, shutting the door behind them. The kitchen door was already almost closed, but the action sent a draught eddying across the top of the stove. The blue flame sank away to nothing and flickered out. Eileen began climbing the stairs resignedly, towards the roof, calling out to her daughter. She had reached the next landing when the pressure in the gas main increased suddenly. An audible hissing rose from the stove and gas began to filter into the room.

*　　*　　*

The fire was now spreading among the houses and flats with a vengeance. Streams of blazing oil licked out from the burning factories, carrying the flames right inside the building. Amid the closely packed rows of slum dwellings the fire caught hold with frightening speed, spreading from house to house down the narrow streets.

The panic that ensued among the inhabitants was indescribable. Men and women flung themselves from upper windows into the water, swimming desperately ahead of the flames, or attempting to use tables, boxes, items of furniture, even their own front doors, as makeshift boats. Many were hampered by screaming children, who hung back, more terrified of the water than of the roaring flames behind. Women swam, pushing their babies in front of them, in boxes, even saucepans. In some streets the flood was sufficiently shallow to enable people to wade, and here many were able to make good their escape with the help of police and rescue crews who had rushed to the scene. In those areas where this was impossible, however, the only choice was to swim.

Weighed down by clothes, and hampered by obstructions in the water, thousands splashed frantically along once familiar streets that had now turned into death traps. They held on to floating pieces of wood, bits of furniture and anything else that would give them buoyancy. They swam in short agonized bursts from one house to another, from one projecting wall or shed roof to another, bobbing like rats among the debris of the flood.

As always, it was the men who survived best. The women, the young children, the elderly, swallowed water, choked and slipped under, often before they had gone half a street's length. The cold, too, was more than many could withstand. They clung to some temporary handhold until numbness overtook them and they fell back into the water, too weak to stay afloat. For many it was more than they could do even to wade once they reached the higher ground. Exhausted and frozen they made for the nearest haven, and collapsed.

The sending of boats into the streets near the fire had little effect. Initially the dozen or so available were too few in any case to do more than make a token effort. Moreover, it proved extremely difficult to prevent them from being swamped by crowds of frantic swimmers who clung to the sides, crying out for help.

By one o'clock Wandsworth control reported to Kingsway that the situation was disastrous and begged for urgent assistance. The fire was still raging and rescuers returning from the area put the number of dead at over a thousand, some of whom had been caught in patches of flaming oil and been burned alive. Many times the number had been injured or needed urgent treatment for shock and exposure.

They were told that every single boat that could be found would be sent to them, regardless of needs elsewhere and that forty inflatable dinghys were already on their way from Richmond. The smoke from the fire now spread over a large part of the southwest of the city in a dense pall.

In fact the Borough Council was finding increasing difficulty in imposing order on the situation. The fire was still burning, but it had ceased its advance, having consumed most of the oil in the depots. In several places it had reached stretches of water too wide for it to leap across. Boats, however, were now reaching the area in large numbers and it was decided to attempt a partial evacuation of the worst hit areas. The sudden emergency had generated a staggering amount of orders, counter orders, messages, urgent requests, reports and the like, many of which had been acted on at once and the control not informed until some time afterward.

This problem was experienced throughout London once the volume of message traffic built up, but Wandsworth had more difficulty than others in this respect. Apart from anything else, there were, at the height of the fire, numerous rescue units working who were not strictly under its authority or else unaware that they were. Consequently messages went astray and remained unanswered. This was especially true where radio was being used. The G.L.C. radio stations were seldom used in normal circumstances and only during the annual flood exercise were all thirty-five permitted to transmit and receive simultaneously. Throughout the city long delays and confusion resulted as undertrained officers strove to cope with the enormous volume of signals.

None of this was any consolation to Mrs. Pole, waiting anxiously by her husband's side, nor to the refugees who crowded into the flats and waited for boats to take them to the relief centres on dry ground. The same was true for the men in what was left of Bankside Generating Station waiting for doctors to attend their injured. All over London groups of men and women watched hopefully from windows for help that did not come.

Chapter Ten

Derek stood on the footpath of Hungerford Bridge and looked down into the dirty brown water below. The Victoria Embankment, in more normal times one of the main highways of London, no longer existed in recognizable form. Only the stalks of the street lamps and the protruding branches of trees marked its outline. Further down it was possible to make out a slight swirl in the flood at the point where the bank had been breached. Judging by the little that could be seen of the underground station at the foot of the bridge, the water here was at least seven feet deep, with little prospect of a decrease during the next few hours.

No trace remained on the surface of the disaster that had overtaken the tube train, three hundred and fifty of whose passengers now lay entombed within the passages and tunnels below. Nor was there anything to suggest that his own wife was trapped down there sixty feet below the pavements in a platform that was rapidly filling up with water.

He had had some vague ideas when he set out from

Holborn about sealing off the station entrance at Charing Cross and attempting to pump out the tunnels underneath. One look at the scene had been sufficient to
show him the impracticality of such plans. It was
doubtful whether it would even be possible to reach the
entrances, let alone seal them. As for pumping the
station dry; with more water pouring in from the open
Circle Line tunnels it would mean emptying the entire
system before the level in the station underneath was
seriously affected.

No, if there was a way, and there had to be one, of
reaching Georgina, it must be from another direction.
He walked back up the bridge toward the main line
station. The most important question to be decided
first of all, was the exact position of the remaining passengers now, following the failure of their attempt to
break out in the direction of Leicester Square with the
young guard. It was essential that any rescue attempt
be able to locate them with the minimum of effort.

The ground rose sharply in front of him, coming up
to meet the bridge and forming an effective barrier to
the river. He paused and looked back again at the
sunken embankment. It was unbelievable to see London in this state even though he had pictured it often
enough in his mind. Somehow it was worse, after spending time in the control room, listening to the various
districts describing their gradual inundation, then to
come out and see it all there before one's eyes. Floods
always gave the same air of desolation and hopelessness,
he thought, in that way they were more depressing than
other natural disasters.

Inside the main line station, the silence was startling.
Without the crowds and the constant noise of trains
pulling in and out, the huge hall seemed almost op-
pressively empty. Only the pigeons remained, strutting
unconcernedly about on the empty platforms. Regardless of which point they chose to start the rescue from,
this was the most convenient place to use as a head-

quarters. There was plenty of room to assemble the equipment, the pumps, hoses, sandbags, diving gear, that would be necessary for an assault on the tunnels. Already a truck was pulling into the station and disgorging a team of men and the stores to back them up.

Directing the movements of these was a slimly built man about five years younger than himself, with short dark hair and a neatly trimmed beard. He wore a white turtleneck sweater and rubber boots with the tops turned down. Catching sight of Derek, he came over.

"Was it any good?" he asked with a jerk of his head in the direction of the bridge. Derek shook his head.

"No, you were right, Pat, it's hopeless this end; until the tide falls back we'll have to come from above."

"I've got the plans you wanted inside. We can take a look if you like." Pat Murdoch was one of the Underground service's chief safety engineers and this was very much his operation. Nevertheless he was honest enough to realize that it had to be tackled in a variety of ways simultaneously, and he had welcomed Derek's offer of help. The two men went into a nearby office.

"You can see here," Pat explained pointing to one of the multicolored diagrams, "how the Northern Line platforms can be shut off and isolated from the remainder of the station. The doors are wound down over the platform entrances. They weigh about four and a half tons."

"What about the tunnels themselves?"

"They are sealed by ten-ton flood gates. One is in position on this part of the line," he indicated the end of the tunnel facing the Thames. "And there's another at the other end by Waterloo." He gave a dry chuckle, "The two passages under the river must be about the only stretches of track not in danger of flooding."

"Why wasn't the northern end of the line blocked off as well?" Derek asked. "I understood there was a gate there as well."

"There is, or rather there is supposed to be, but according to the guard they fished out an hour ago, it isn't in place. Something had gone wrong with the tackle that lowers it into place and they weren't able to repair it before the water started coming down the stairs."

"So at the moment the survivors are on the southbound platform with one end of the tunnel blocked by a flood gate and the other open, and through which water is presumably now beginning to enter the platform."

"Yes, that's true, I'm afraid. We weren't able to question the guard a great deal but he did tell us that water was flowing into the tube from Strand. Presumably it is coming through from Trafalgar Square via the new passages that have been cut to link the stations."

"Can we do anything to stop that?" Derek queried. Pat shook his head.

"Unfortunately there are no isolating shutters on the Bakerloo Line which runs through Trafalgar Square. So even if we could stop the surface entrances there, we would still be left with the flow draining in from the embankment."

Derek was silent, he was examining the plans in detail. Whatever they decided, a rescue attempt, if it was made, must take place as soon as possible. Even as they stood here talking the flood was percolating through the tunnels into every corner of the system. As he had told the Minister in the control room, the Underground network was the first place to fill and the last to be pumped dry. He had little guessed then that Georgina might be trapped within it.

"I think," he said at length, "that our first priority must be to slow the rate at which the tunnels are filling, particularly this northern one in which the passengers are sheltering. If we seal the entrance at Trafalgar Square and put in a high volume pump we should at least draw off some of the flow from the Bakerloo

Line. If necessary we can do the same at the Strand. That way we should give ourselves a chance."

Before Pat could reply the door of the room opened. The two men looked up. The newcomer was a short, stoutly built individual with a scowling face and thick black hair partly concealed beneath a red woolly hat. His age appeared to be about the same as Pat's.

"Ah, Paul, come on in," Pat welcomed him. "This is Paul Frean," he explained to Derek, "who led the search party that found the guard." Paul Frean sat down heavily on a chair opposite Derek and looked at him searchingly. His face was fat and ruddy complexioned.

"So it's you that has your wife down in the tunnels," he said at length. "I'm sorry about that."

"We're in the process of seeing how we can best get her out," Derek replied, "and the others with her."

Paul leaned forward on the table and produced a battered packet of cigarettes and a packet of matches. With slow clumsy movements he lit one and drew on it gratefully; his fingers, Derek noticed, were crusted with remnants of mud and dirt. "I've just been down the Piccadilly tunnel west from Leicester Square," he said looking from one to the other. "It's not deep yet, but it's rising."

Pat made a wry face. "I was afraid that would happen," he said.

Derek shrugged. "We've known all along that the central section of the network would fill," he said. "Once it gets in at one point it's only a matter of time before the rest goes."

"Aye, that's true enough," Paul agreed heavily, "and the Northern Line tubes are the deepest sections of the whole bloody system."

The problem was obvious enough. At the moment the survivors, assuming they were still alive, were at one end of the tunnel, protected from the floods above them by the steel doors and gates. All the time, however, water was draining down into the system and spreading round through the vast interlocking network of tunnels, passages and stations. Even if they succeeded in halting the flow entering at the Strand it was still only a matter of time before the flooding moved against them from the rear.

"We can put in pumps at Leicester Square," Derek pointed out, "which will slow down the advance. We might even be able to rig some kind of barrier to hold it back."

"The water's coming up from the east as well," Pat said softly. "We can't fight everywhere." The faces of both men showed concern as they faced Derek across the table. It was not difficult to see how they rated Georgina's chances of survival.

"Listen," he said to them both, "I can see the difficulties and they are very great, but I still believe that we can get into that tunnel and bring the remaining passengers out alive; provided we do it at once before the tubes fill up behind us."

"That's quite a demand you're going to have to put to any rescue team," Pat shook his head slowly and pursed his lips. "I can't see myself ordering any of my own men to make that trip."

"I'm not asking anyone to do anything I'm not prepared to do myself," Derek said firmly. Paul Frean gave a final puff at his cigarette and ground the stub out in a glass ashtray.

"Have you any idea what it's like down there?" he asked. "The water is chest deep in some places already, and it's up to your waist in most others. Moving through the tunnels is very slow on account of that. You can't see where you're treading and half the time you're having to wade with your arms over your head to keep the torches dry. How long do you think it'll take a rescue team to get from Leicester Square, which is the only possible way in now, to the platform where the passengers are?" Without waiting for Derek to answer he went on, "I'll tell you, it would take at least an hour, by which time the level in the tunnel will have risen to the roof and cut off the way back."

"Do you have any better suggestions?" demanded Derek angrily. "I'm not going to sit back idly and let my wife drown. If nobody's willing to come with me I'll go by myself."

"I can't order any of my men to go with you, you understand that?" said Pat. He shot a quick glance at Paul.

"Just give me a couple of spare breathing sets and a diagram of this part of the system and I'll manage," Derek snapped.

"You really think you can make it by yourself?"

"I've no idea," Derek was getting really angry now, "but it looks as though I'm the only hope those people have got. So the sooner you two stop listing the problems and let me get started the better."

"Not quite the only hope." Pat gave a slow smile. "Paul," he said, "do you think you can find a couple of volunteers from among your lads?"

"I guess so," the other replied heavily. "There are always plenty of fools about. Like me," he added pointedly. "I'll go and see."

"Right, I'll collect the breathing sets and equipment. We'll start as soon as we can."

Derek looked about him in amazement. "But I thought . . ." he exclaimed.

"I told you we wouldn't order a team down," Pat said with another smile, "but a party of volunteers now, that's different. Besides, we couldn't have let you go wandering about in our tunnels by yourself. You might have got lost or broken something."

Twenty minutes later they were standing on the Northern Line platform beneath Leicester Square. About them lay all the paraphernalia of rescue. Neophrene wetsuits, heavy boots, tanks of compressed air, torches, cutting gear and a special two-way radio set, designed for just this kind of operation and capable of transmiting through solid rock.

"Wonderful jobs," said Pat, exhibiting it to Derek. "We first used them on the big Moorgate crash two years ago. Before that we had to rely on standard telephones."

Derek struggled into his suit; it was similar to that used by skin divers, but thicker and more durable. There was a thin film of water covering the tracks and in the background he was conscious of the steady note of a pump engine.

"We've put the biggest pump we can find into the bottom of the ventilation shaft and we're getting rid of about ten thousand gallons per hour," Pat told him. "So far that seems to be holding it down to this level."

"Let's hope it stays that way till we get back," he eyed the breathing sets that lay in a row by the wall. "How long under water do those things give us?" he asked.

"Thirty minutes maximum." It was Paul who answered. In the black diving suit he looked even more grotesque than he had before. "Anything longer would be too bulky to manage, and we each have to carry a spare set for the passengers as it is."

"Let's hope it's enough," Derek said.

"It should be, with any luck we won't have to use them till we reach the central portion of the track between Strand and Charing Cross embankment. Also we expect to find the final portion of the tunnel clear as well."

"Yes," said Paul drily, "or there won't be any point in our making the trip."

Hastily they completed their remaining preparations. Pat had managed to find them each a protective helmet with a lamp attached like those used by miners.

"I thought these would make the first part of the

journey easier," he said. "I don't know how they'll stand up to getting wet so we will carry hand torches as well." He introduced Derek to the two other men who had volunteered to come along. Both were tall and strongly built with an air of self-reliance and dependability despite their youth, which he put at the early twenties. One was called John; he had very fair hair Derek noticed. The other was darker with gray eyes and named Bruno.

"Thanks for coming along," he told them. The young men grinned back nervously.

"It's nothing," Bruno said. "We enjoy these trips."

"Yes, they make life more interesting," added his friend. "A change from the usual work."

They made a final check of their own and each other's equipment. With his own breathing set on his back and a spare for one of the passengers strapped across his chest, as well as other accoutrements like knives, lengths of rope and first aid supplies which had been distributed among them, Derek felt weighed down and bulky. It would be even worse once they reached deep water. Pat Murdoch gave some last minute instructions before they climbed down on to the track.

"Keep close together, as much as possible," he said, "particularly in the deep parts, and always check the positions of others in the team. Try not to use your air for as long as you can help it. You may need it all on the way back."

Together they set off into the mouth of the tunnel. They walked in two groups on each side of the track. It was the first time Derek had ever been in one of the tubes on foot, and at first the novelty of it interested him. They walked ankle deep in water that lay in the bottom of the tunnel and as they went Pat explained the built in system of slopes that characterized the network.

"They vary from line to line, depending of course on

the date of construction, but on this line they've a standard hump design. The slope is one in thirty away from a station and one in sixty on the approach."

"What's the construction of the tunnels themselves?" Derek asked.

"Cast iron lining, bolted together in sections. The width is twelve feet, widening out to twenty feet in stations. This is one of the deepest parts of the system. We are at approximately sixty feet."

The tunnel took on a slow curve towards the left, and at the same time Derek noticed the ground had begun to slope. The water level grew deeper at once and it became an effort to walk with it dragging at his legs. The beams of the torches reflected eerily off the ponded surface ahead of him. It was still and inky black, its surface marred only by an occasional piece of floating wood or rubbish.

"See that?" Paul commented as his torch picked out an entire sleeper drifting gently towards them. "Jarrick wood, hard as bloody iron. It's a wonder it can float."

"How badly has the Underground been hit, apart from simple flooding like this?" Derek asked. Pat gave a snort.

"In a word, we're paralyzed," he said. "I've been telling them for years that this would happen, but nobody took any notice. For a start, all these will have to be redone." He pointed to the line of wires and cables that ran along the walls. "None of the wiring will stand up to prolonged immersion. We produce our own electrical power as you probably know, but one station is in Greenwich and another is at Lot's Road in Chelsea, and both these have been flooded, so we're left with Neasden. Also our biggest substation is in Charing Cross, and that's gone."

"What about the control systems?"

"Most of the really sophisticated equipment is above the water level at St. James's Park or at the emergency control center at Chalk Farm. We lose a certain amount of signaling devices though. It will take us six months to get working again at the very least."

The effort of talking while at the same time wading through three feet of water grew too much and they went on in silence. Derek's mind was on Georgina and the others ahead of them. All the time they had been getting ready he had been desperate to get on. Now they had started he found himself almost dreading what they might discover once they finally reached Charing Cross. It was very possible that the five survivors were already dead, drowned as the level rose in the platform and surged over their heads. He pictured Georgina staying afloat, swimming for a few terrifying minutes before the water reached the roof.

Pat halted for a moment, unslung his radio and unzipped its waterproof case. "We have traveled an estimated quarter of a mile." He spoke in the curiously formal abbreviated speech of radio operators. "We are approaching the lowest portion of track before Strand. Water level is three foot six and rising."

"Very good," came the reply at once. "Your position noted. The level at Leicester Square has risen slightly but the pumps are still coping. Good luck."

"I don't like the sound of that last bit," remarked Paul, flashing his torch into the darkness of the way they had come.

"It may be nothing," Pat said. "Probably just a temporary increase. They would have told us if there had been a significant change."

"Maybe they don't want to worry us." It was Bruno who spoke. "I reckon we had better push on as fast as we can."

The going worsened rapidly now. Within a few yards the tunnel seemed to have shrunk to a third of its size as the water rose up the walls. For the first time Derek was struck by the cold. The open cuffs and ankles of the wet suit allowed a thin layer of freezing water to creep upwards against the skin. After a while he knew, his body would have warmed it up, creating an insulating barrier to prevent further heat loss. In the meantime, however, the sensation was far from pleasant.

The level rose further till it reached the top of his chest. They were walking single file now with Pat in the lead. He halted again and held up his hand. "Check your breathing sets are ready," he ordered, "and be prepared to use them if you have to. I think we should be able to get through without using them, but we'll see."

They went forward once more. It had become so deep that Derek found himself swimming more than he was walking. It was abominably difficult to make any sort of headway at all. His feet kept bobbing off the ground leaving him thrashing with his arms. Around him he could see the others experiencing the same difficulty.

In front of him, Bruno's helmet lamp flickered for a moment and then went out. Above the noise of his own splashing he heard him swear. The water was up to his chin now, any further and he would have to use his air tank. Presumably Paul was already doing so. The couple of inches in their heights would be all important here. Gritting his teeth he struggled on. For the first time he understood what it would mean to be caught in a tunnel like this without the means of escape that they carried. He thought of the guard making the trip alone and without even a torch. Judging by what Pat had told him the next dip, the one between Strand and Charing Cross, would be even worse than this one. A good stretch of that must be totally filled and they would have to swim, though swimming might be easier than this infernal walking.

At last, just when Derek had begun to think that something must have gone wrong, that they must have missed their way or gone right through the station, the ground began to level out again and the flooding dropped back. With relief at being able to walk properly again, they pushed forward into the shallows. Pat stopped again to radio a report of their progress.

"Well done," replied the operator at the other end. "You must be close to Strand station now."

"Are the pumps there working yet?" asked Pat. "They should be by now."

"They reported that two pumps had begun work a few minutes ago," came the reply, "but so far they appear to be having no appreciable effect on the level of water within the station."

"What about the situation at your end?"

"The water level in the bottom of the ventilation shaft has risen by a few inches, but so far we see nothing to worry about unduly."

"It looks as though the combined effect of pumping from three different places at the same time is managing to hold down the levels," he said, turning back to the rest of the group who were standing listening. "If they can keep that up we may be in with a chance."

"Assuming there are no unpleasant surprises up ahead," remarked Paul. "This pool is getting deeper by the looks of things. I suggest we hurry if we want to find anybody still alive at the other end."

The tunnel had straightened out after passing the center of the dip and it now stretched away before them into nothingness. For the first time they became aware of sounds in the darkness other than the noise of their own feet sloshing through the flood.

"That's water pouring in up ahead, or I'm no judge." said John. "It must be coming from the new workings."

"What's being done to this station that involves so much work?" Derek asked.

"It's due to become the new Charing Cross," Paul

explained, "and what you now call Charing Cross will
become Embankment. It's all to do with the new Fleet
Line."

"I don't fancy the chances of that being completed in
a hurry after all this," said Bruno. "I reckon London
Transport's going to be a bit strapped for cash for the
next couple of years."

The noise of water ahead grew louder until it seemed
as though they must be approaching a waterfall. A
glimmer of white appeared on the edge of their torch
beam. In a short while it resolved itself into a torrent
spurting out from a hole in the wall at the very end of
the station.

"It must be meant for a pipe of some kind running
through the station, probably sewage or gas." Pat examined the wall carefully. The flow was not violent and
they passed through without difficulty.

"That can't be the main inflow," said Paul, pausing
for breath. The platform inside the station was exactly
level with the top of the water and he sat down on the
edge with a sigh of relief. He made an absurd picture,
Derek thought, like some kind of insane holiday snap-
shot.

For an answer Pat pointed silently down the platform with his torch. Slightly over half way down their
eyes caught a glint of movement on the concrete. From
a doorway on the right water was sluicing out on to the
tracks in a wide river. Further down still was a second
doorway spilling out a second torrent. They walked
slowly towards them. The flow was over two feet deep
where it left the arch but it spread out to cover a wide
area of the platform and slip down to join the rest of
the water with scarcely a sound.

"Could we block these off maybe?" suggested John,
shining his torch up into the passage that lay behind
the doorway. "There seems to be plenty of materials
lying around," and he gestured to the heaps of bricks

and baulks of timber that dotted the platform. Pat shook his head.

"No, it would be a waste of time," he said, "and I doubt if we could make a barrier that would hold. We'll just have to trust to the pumps."

"It's flowing in at a hell of a rate, Pat." It was Paul who spoke. "I can't say I'm thrilled at the idea of going on with this at my back."

"The sooner we get going, the sooner we'll be back. It's not much further to go now," Pat replied.

They approached the end of the platform. There were still signs in place bearing the station name and the familiar tube maps but all were covered in thick coats of dust and surrounded by piles of building materials and rubbish. It gave the place a curious air of abandonment and desolation. Before they stepped into the water again Pat made another call to Leicester Square.

"How's the level back there?" Derek asked him when he had finished.

"Still rising but no cause for alarm. They're putting a second pump into operation to hold it. The irony is," he continued as they reached the mouth of the tunnel, "that there should be a flood gate here, one of the main ten-ton efforts, but it's been taken down temporarily while the rebuilding is going on."

"I thought the gate was at the entrance by Charing Cross?" Derek said in surprise. Pat shook his head, the lamp beam flickering jerkily as he did so.

"No, what they've got there is a kind of steel diaphragm that can be erected by hand. There are several of those at station entrances. They're designed to stop local flooding in the event of a burst sewer or water main. Of course they're still pretty heavy, they weigh several tons, and they have to be hoisted into place with lifting tackle, but I doubt if they could hold a big flood for long."

"That's the one they were working on when the train broke down."

"Yes, and lucky for the survivors that they were. Because of that one of the section gates shutting off the platform was up and they managed to crawl through. I doubt if they would have been able to raise it in time otherwise with the water rushing in on them."

"It must have been horrific down there," Derek said, his throat dry at the thought of what Georgina must have gone through, what she must still be going through.

Pat gave him a reassuring smile. He must have read his thoughts. "Don't worry," he said, "we'll get to her in time."

That the second leg of the journey was going to be harder was apparent from the outset. The water was waist deep as the platform disappeared behind them and the sounds of the falling torrent faded in their ears. They waded slowly, puffing with the effort, leaning forward to use their weight against the resisting water. Derek tried to decide if he was feeling warmer. His body seemed to have settled into numbness, failing to respond to any kind of temperature. The weight of the two breathing sets seemed enormous.

"It's not so far, this stretch," Pat remarked and sure enough he noticed the by now familiar changes in the level almost at once. When the water began to get really deep, Pat called a halt.

"I'm going to fix a rope here," he said, "to give us a guide on the way back if we need it. Remember the water probably goes right up to the ceiling here so we may have to swim for part of the way."

There was sound of hissing air as everyone checked their breathing sets once more and they set off. The level rose rapidly once more and Derek fancied he could detect the pressure of water flowing past him from the rear. A moment later Bruno's voice confirmed his suspicions.

"Something's happening in the rear," he called out. "I can feel a hell of a current in this water."

"I know," Pat shouted back, his voice flattened by the confined space about him, "we'll just have to hope the pumps can take it," and he plunged onward into the water that now swirled round his chest. Derek followed close behind, he had nothing but admiration for Pat's determination but even so he felt a twinge of doubt. The air they carried was only sufficient to get them through two or three stretches of submerged tunnel. It would not last long enough to get them back if they had to swim for the entire distance back to Leicester Square. In fact it was doubtful if they would get more than halfway in such circumstances. By going on when there was a strong possibility that the tunnel behind them had begun to fill rapidly despite all the efforts of the pumps, they were taking a tremendous chance.

Pushing forward he caught up with him. "Are you sure you know what you're doing?" he asked. "It's fine for me to go on, I have a wife in there, but what about the others?"

"They know the danger as well as you do, probably better," Pat replied. "In any case I doubt if we could just go straight back now even if we wanted to, the levels behind us must be nearly up to the tunnel roof."

"What happens when we get to the passengers then, how do we get them out?"

"I'm hoping," Pat's breath came in gasps as he struggled through the water, "I'm hoping that we'll be able to open the flood gate at the other end of the platform in Charing Cross. That will mean a lot of this water will be drawn off into the tunnel under the river. With any luck that will give us the clearance we need to get back."

"Can the gate be opened by hand?"

"Yes, but it takes a lot of effort to do so. That's probably the only reason the passengers haven't tried to do it already."

By now the water was once again too deep for talking and Derek was forced to concentrate all his attention on fighting his way forward. Ahead his torch showed the tunnel roof sloping down to meet the surface of the flood. Pat had already put on his face mask and was adjusting the mouthpiece of this breathing set. He looked round at the others and gave a thumbs up sign before switching off his lamp and diving abruptly beneath the surface. A stream of bubbles marked his progress. Stopping only long enough to adjust his own equipment, Derek followed him.

The inky blackness in which he found himself totally surpassed anything he had been prepared for. It was as though he had been suddenly struck blind. The water was gritty and thick with filth, he coud feel small particles washing past his face. He was conscious of the roaring noise of his own breathing in his ears. His helmet grated against the tunnel roof, bringing him to a halt. With an effort he forced himself downwards and began to swim properly. This was easier than he had expected; in some respects easier than wading in deep water, but the extra equipment he carried hampered him. He had been swimming for what seemed a lifetime and still there was no end to the flooding. He was seized with a sudden unreasoning panic that he might have gone wrong already, perhaps he had turned the wrong way as he dived and was even now heading back the way he had so laboriously come.

Compelling himself to think calmly he dismissed the thought and continued on his course. To occupy his mind he attempted to calculate the length of the tunnel that had been navigated under water in this way. The distance between the two stations was something like an eighth of a mile, in which case not more than two hundred yards could be flooded completely. The thought of making the trip a second time with Georgina in tow appalled him.

They seemed to have been swimming for hours,

bumping and scraping against the sides of the tunnel, when he felt his head break the surface suddenly. Testing the depth carefully, he found it was just possible to stand with his head completely clear of the water. He could still see nothing, the darkness around him was as intense and unrelieved by any glimmer of light as it had been beneath the water.

There were sounds beside him of another swimmer surfacing then a blaze of light filled the tunnel and hurt his eyes. Ahead of him Pat was holding a rubber torch, looking back, checking the safe arrival of the remainder of the team. Derek looked about him, the heads and shoulders of the others glistened wetly in the torch light, as the men pulled off their masks and switched off the air from their tanks. Next to him Paul Frean spat to clear his mouth, and swore at the dirt in the water. Everyone appeared to have survived the passage without incident.

When the remaining torches had been produced and lit, they went forward again. By some extraordinary lucky chance two of the helmet lamps still worked, evidently their mechanisms were better sealed than they had realized. They had only gone a few steps when Pat stopped suddenly. "There's something under the surface here," he said, "my foot caught on it. I couldn't tell what it was." He groped about in the water for a moment, feeling with his hands, then he straightened up with a jerk.

"What is it?" they all looked at him. He held his hand up against the glare of the torches.

"I think it's a body. Give me some help here, one of you." Paul waded forward. Together the two of them dragged out the upper portion of a man's corpse. He was middled-aged and appeared to be wearing a dark blue jacket.

"He must be the driver who tried to get through and didn't make it," said Paul eyeing the grisly figure.

"Yes, he was trapped when the water came up and couldn't get back in time," agreed Pat.

"What do we do with him now. We can't leave him lying here in the tunnel."

"No, we'll tow him up to the station and leave him there on the platform. There's hardly any distance to go now." He shifted his grip on one of the dead man's sleeves and began to forge his way slowly ahead. The others followed as they began the final section of the journey.

* * *

The situation in Kingsway control had eased a little now that the special emergency created by the fire in Wandsworth appeared to have lessened and the staff were able to concentrate on the backlog of reports and messages that had built up.

Carswell was going through a thick pile of photocopies of messages received during the previous hour. Wandsworth were having a hell of a time, he noted, trying to cope with huge numbers of displaced people from the flooded parts of the borough. Their control was still appealing for help in reaching twelve thousand people marooned in high-rise flats by water that was expected to remain ponded for at least another week.

"What are the total projections for boats available within twenty-four hours?" he asked one of his subordinates near by. "You had better ask the police desk, they are handling that department."

"Met. Pol. say they hope to have twenty-two hundred boats in use within twenty-four hours," the assistant reported back a short while later. "Apparently they are all definitely promised and the owners are bringing them in. They say the total could be as high as three thousand with others that they don't know about."

Three thousand boats was better than he had expected, but all the same some boroughs would be appallingly stretched over the next three or four days. They would have to provide transport for food into the stricken area, as well as bringing out the injured and, in certain areas, conducting complete evacuation. As Miles had said earlier, districts like West Ham were running serious risks of massive epidemics breaking out unless prompt action was taken to remove the population from the contaminated waters. Yet at the moment there simply weren't boats available to evacuate upwards of twenty thousand people, nor were the support facilities in neighboring boroughs ready to handle them yet.

It was a great pity that the old Civil Defense apparatus had been cut down so completely, he thought. As a result, there were no easily available resources of disciplined manpower, with stocks of equipment, trained and ready to go into action within a few hours of an emergency. True, the government maintained the Civil Service Home Defense College, where senior government and borough officers could receive training in how best to cope with these situations. There had also been the recent setting up of committees to coordinate the emergency services of the fire brigade, police and ambulances in the event of a major peacetime incident such as an airliner crashing in the middle of London, a serious accident at one of the main railway termini, or some similar disaster. There was very little, however, available to cope rapidly with a catastrophe on the scale of the one they were facing now.

One of the reports in front of him indicated that the authorities were taking steps to throw a cordon round the flooded areas in order to prevent people from entering. Ostensibly the reason given for this was to protect the public and prevent more people from getting into danger. In fact it was a measure designed to prevent looting and maintain order during the crisis. Only those who could show a valid reason for doing so would be allowed to cross the police lines into the prohibited areas. Thousands of special constables and territorial army reservists were being called up to carry out this task, as well as performing the vital job of keeping the clearways open. As it was, he noted, considerable traffic congestion was building up in northwest London around Ealing and Acton as a result of the cutting of the M4 by flood water at Hammersmith.

There were unending urgent appeals for medical aid, most of them, judging from subsequent messages, unanswered, though since Kingsway received only those reports which related to major incidents, it was not always possible to tell. A large number of hospitals had been flooded out, especially on the south bank. For the most part they had managed to cope in time, moving patients upstairs, but a great deal of very expensive equipment had been lost. Some of the older institutions had experienced great difficulties. One home for the mentally handicapped was thought to have lost most of its ninety patients when the flood swept into its single storey wards.

The big question now was how long would they have to wait before the surge retreated and the worst of the flooding began to subside. This was especially important for places like the Isle of Dogs, which to all intents and purposes no longer existed as dry land. That was one area that would certainly have to be evacuated, along with West Ham next door. The government, he knew, were anxious to be able to tell the people something optimistic and helpful. The Prime Minister was scheduled to broadcast to the nation at six o'clock and it was hoped that by then he would be able to say that the water level in the streets was falling. Miles had been attending to that business; Carswell looked round for him, but could see no sign of the councilor anywhere in the room.

In fact, Miles was in the conference room next door, where he had shut himself away for the past half hour. He was reading through a letter he had just finished writing and which now lay on the table in front of him. It was a letter of resignation.

Ever since the moment when Derek Thompson had switched the radio transmission from Woolwich into the control room's loudspeakers, Miles had realized that his career in politics had been finished. He had taken a risk and persuaded the city and the government to economize on the flood barrier during a time of financial hardship, and so avoided cutting back on less essential but politically more sensitive items. At the time it had seemed an easy way out, a sensible solution even, and one which might have earned him considerable credit.

The flood had changed all that. Miles was now discredited so thoroughly that there was no possibility of his ever being able to live down the event and return to favor. With the aftermath of the surge would come a demand for scapegoats. The public would want to know who was responsible for the disaster that had taken place, and Miles was under no illusions as to whose head would be offered up to the mob.

Alan Carswell had been right in thinking that Miles had intended to throw the blame on to the shoulders of other members of the administration if he could. A cold analysis of the recent events however had shown him how pathetically little he could offer to balance against the weight of his own errors. Nearly every person involved in the preparations for the surge had been guilty of small mistakes, but Miles knew perfectly well that no amount of these would be sufficient to save him. No doubt, others would also face criticism of their actions but none of that would divert attention from him. He was finished and he knew it.

He folded the letter deliberately, placed it in an envelope and addressed it to the Chairman of the Council in his precise neat hand. Inside he had put a clear and dispassionate assessment of his own actions and the lessons that were to be drawn from them. Afterward there would be a searching enquiry into what had gone wrong and Miles liked to think that his opinions would be listened to even then. Putting the letter in his pocket he picked up his briefcase and went through into the control room.

"I'm going over to Charing Cross to take a look at what's being done there," he told Carswell. "I don't imagine I shall be very long."

"I hear the rescue is not going too well," the controller replied. "The tubes are filling up fast. The pumps can't hold it."

With the river still pouring in over the city's defenses that was only to be expected, Miles thought, as he climbed the long flights of steps that led to the open air. The tube disaster was the climax of a whole series of errors whose causes were in the main attributed to him. Not only had it cost the lives of several hundred people, but almost certainly by now, as a direct result of his actions, it had claimed the life of Derek Thompson's wife, and probably of Derek, too, if he had indeed been one of the rescue party that was now in the tunnels. It had been this personal involvement with the tragedy for which he was responsible that had made him decide on what he was about to do.

His car was parked near the top of the road and he drove left into New Oxford Street. It was strange coming straight from the flood room with its reports of widespread havoc, and seeing the normal life of the West End carrying on as though nothing had happened. It reminded him of a remark he had once made to Derek, "Even the very worst flood," he had said, "would only touch a tenth part of London." If he had had any idea then of what that would mean, none of this would probably have happened.

He was tempted to drive down towards the river and take a look for himself at what the surge had done, but decided against it. He knew well enough from reading the reports in the control room what to expect and the sight would only be depressing. Expanses of muddy water lapping through people's homes, and the hopeless, despairing faces of refugees staring out resentfully at the unafflicted visitors who had come to watch.

London had fallen victim to its own success in a way. The explosive growth that had turned it into the first industrial capital of the world had carried its boundaries beyond the safe high ground of the original city and left it vulnerable to the river's attack. It had seemed so vast and secure that they had all believed that nothing could shake it. Yet within less than the space of one hour it had been dealt a mortal blow by forces of nature against which the city was powerless.

How long, he wondered, would it be before the damage could be put right and London restored? A year would probably suffice to repair the most obvious and immediate injuries. The tubes would be pumped dry, the wrecked cars towed away, the drains flushed out, the ruined houses condemned and torn down. By then, with superhuman effort, it might be possible to rebuild the power stations, relay the telephone and electrical lines and restore normal services to the city. But there would still be enormous unseen damage lying below the surface, just as the worst of the wreckage lay concealed by the floods at the moment. No amount of aid would bring back the dead passengers of the train, or those who had lost their lives in the fire at Wandsworth, or been drowned when the river burst into Kennington. Nothing would compensate the injured and the bereaved for their loss, or the men whose jobs had vanished when the factories that employed them were destroyed.

In its present economic condition it was doubtful if it would take less than a generation for the scars to disappear; just as it had for the last traces of the bombing to be erased. The two occurrences were directly comparable.

He drove past the top of the park and swung down into his own street. There were pools of water in the roadway. Evidence that the flooding was not very far away and had caused rain water to back up in the drains. The sight reminded him of the sewage workers he had sent to their deaths. It was as though the consequences of every thoughtless action were returning to haunt him.

There was nobody at his home when he arrived, to his profound relief. The house was quiet and showed no signs of having been affected by the flooding, though he did not bother to check the bathrooms. He went straight up to his study on the first floor. On the mantelpiece, by the clock, stood the gold-embossed invitation from Buckingham Palace, the President's reception. Idly he took it down and ran his finger over the heavy gilt. When would they hold it now, he wondered, and where? Derek Thompson had been right all along the way and he, Miles, had been wrong. There was nothing that could be done about it now. He placed the card carefully on his desk and put the letter of resignation beside it. In a way he supposed it was a comment on his marriage that he had written nothing to his wife.

There was a decanter of malt whiskey on a table by the door. He poured himself a generous glass. From a drawer in the desk he took a bottle of pills and began to swallow them mechanically one after another. When he had finished them he sat down at the desk and looked out into the garden and waited. It was a pity, he thought, that it was not spring: the garden was really quite beautiful then.

Chapter Eleven

Georgina's feelings on returning to the Charing Cross platform were a mixture of relief at being at last out of the claustrophobic closeness of the tunnels and despair at their failure to escape. The platform was a dank, oppressive place to wait for rescue she thought, looking about at her surroundings, but at least the white enameled tiling and the colored posters were a welcome change after the never ending darkness. She wished she could stop feeling so cold even for a moment. Everything she wore was soaked through, her skirt clung wetly to her legs, tripping her at every step. The others were in the same position she saw. Angelica did not even possess a coat and Russell had given her his, though that too was sopping. All four of them were shivering continually.

For the moment, at least, they were out of the flooding, but it was obvious that this state of affairs would not last for much longer. Water streamed steadily through the entrance of the tunnel, building up on the track below the platform. Judging by the speed with which it was coming they had not more than an hour left before their refuge became their grave. The only other exits were the doors leading to the escalator down which they had come at the beginning. All four of these were shut fast but small patches of oozing dampness about their sills were a clear indication of the weight of water above. The door furthest away which was blocked by an improvised barrier was leaking badly. If that gave it would only be minutes before the whole platform filled.

Rees and the other man, Russell, were working on the hoisting gear for the flood gate. If they could get that into position and close off the flow of water entering from the tunnel their chance of survival would be greatly improved. There would then be nothing to prevent them from waiting till the floods in the streets above went down and rescuers could pump out the station. Assuming that was that one of the stairway doors didn't burst open, or that they didn't die of pneumonia first, or run out of air. Georgina tried hard to remember all Derek had told her about surge tide. As far as she could recall one of the points that he had considered most important had been that it would be a very long time before the flood retreated. Besides, she thought, there was no reason for anyone to know that they were down here at all. The authorities would most probably assume that everyone who had been below ground when the water entered the station had been drowned. If the flood was as bad as Derek had said it would be there would be enough for the rescue services to do without worrying about a thousand to one chance of there being survivors from such an overwhelming catastrophe.

With only one torch between them, and that up at the end where the men were working, there was almost no light in the central portion of the platform while the far flood gate was completely invisible. Georgina walked back up to talk to Angelica who was fiddling with her cigarette lighter.

"I can't get the damned thing to light at all," she complained as Georgina approached.

"Maybe one of the men has one that still works," Georgina suggested. "The man with the coat, he smokes I think." Angelica gave a rueful smile.

He lost his lighter when we came down the stairs. It must have fallen out of his pocket I guess. It doesn't matter much anyway, my cigarette's got to dry out first." She gestured to where a line of limp white tubes lay carefully arranged on top of an upturned fire bucket. They looked extraordinarily unappetizing, Georgina thought.

There was a bench near by and the two women sat down on it, huddling together for warmth. For a while they stayed quiet listening to the sounds of the men wrestling with the mechanism of the gate, and the relentless, ever present trickling of the water.

"You're married, aren't you," said Angelica after several minutes, and Georgina nodded. "Got any children?"

"Two," she replied and went on to tell the girl about Jake and Sarah.

"You must be worried about them." Georgina swallowed as the realization of just how much she missed them hit her again.

"I think more about how they'll get on without me than anything else," she confessed. "They're both still so little."

"Hey, come on," said Angelica softly, "you're going to get back to them. We'll all be out of here soon. Don't you worry."

Georgina sat up straight and drew a deep breath.

"I know," she said, "I know. It's hard, that's all. Tell me about yourself." The girl laughed.

"You wouldn't think it to look at me now, but up

there," she pointed a finger at the roof, "up there I'm a model. I do photographic work for magazines and T.V. commercials." Georgina laughed back. Despite what Angelica said about her appearance, it was easy to believe that she was indeed a model, and a highly successful one at that. The wet clothes that clung to her body revealed a figure that would be the envy of most other women and her face had a vibrancy about it that was attractive even in her present bedraggled state.

"I was on my way back from an early session," she explained. She laughed again, "And you know what's so stupid?" Georgina shook her head.

"I was modeling bikinis, swimwear. It was for a fashion house catalogue. I never thought I'd be swimming myself on my way home."

The sound of footsteps made them turn round. The two men were approaching from the direction of the tunnel mouth. They had evidently abandoned their work on the flood gate.

"No good?" asked Georgina when they came near. Rees shook his head and took a seat beside her. His face was weary and dispirited. "No bloody good at all," he said morosely, "the hoist is completely broken. I thought we might be able to rig up something but it can't be done."

The four of them sat in silence. At length Angelica asked, "So what do we do now? If we can't shut the flood gate, what do we do about the water that's coming in?"

Rees did not reply at once. He wiped his face with the sleeve of his jacket and got up and went to the edge of the platform. The water had reached a point less than two inches below the edge. During the last hour it had risen by almost three feet. At that rate they had only another two hours at the most before the water would be above their heads. It was possible that they might be able to stay afloat for a while by swimming, but in the cold and dark he doubted if they would survive for more than a few minutes.

"We've got to give ourselves more time." He turned back to the others and faced them squarely. "The way things are at present we won't have more than a few hours left to us. Now I think it is very probable that even now a rescue attempt is being made to try and bring us out of here. But it will take time. Mr. Russell and I have been trying to block off the end of the tunnel to stop more water coming in. Well, we haven't been very successful. So now we are going to try a different approach."

"What's that?" the stockbroker asked, his face registering surprise.

"You see the gate at the other end of the platform, the one that leads to Waterloo?" Rees played his torch in that direction. "Well, if we could open that, mind you, I'm not saying that we will be able to, they weigh ten tons each those gates. But if we could open it the water in the station now would run down into the tunnel under the river. That would give us several more hours."

"Why don't we go into the tunnel ourselves and shut the gate behind us?" Russell asked. "Surely then we would be safe from the water until rescuers could find us?" The engineer shook his head.

"No, we can't do that you see because the gate has to be operated from this side, we couldn't close it behind us. We shall be lucky to get it open as it is."

Angelica and the stockbroker had succeeded, after much effort, in lighting one of Russell's cigarettes which had been in his gold case and had therefore got less damp than Angelica's. Georgina watched them both reveling in the pleasure of the smoke. Rees gave them a moment or two before calling them back to work.

"If one of you ladies could hold the torch for us while we turn the wheels, it would be a big help," he said.

They all walked slowly down to the end of the platform. In the dim light of the single torch the flood gate appeared massive and immovable. A heavy block of steel twice the height of a man. The two men climbed down into the water and examined it more closely.

"Usually this door is closed by remote control from Leicester Square," Rees told them. "It takes less than a minute. I don't know whether the strength of two of us will be enough to wind it back manually, but we shall just have to try."

"We shall have to do more than that," remarked Russell. "Look there," and he pointed to the edge of the platform. Near where Georgina was standing the water had risen level with the top and had begun to spread across the surface. Even as they looked further streams appeared, joining up with the others to form a swiftly growing pool.

"It's rising faster than I thought." Rees seized hold of one of the winding handles and began to turn it, and on the other side of the steel door Russell did the same.

"It's no good," he gasped a short while later after they had been straining and heaving for several minutes. "It's too heavy, we can't shift it." He stepped back exhausted and leaned against the wall. Sweat was running down his face.

"Aye, I'm afraid you're right." Rees mopped his face. "These pulleys were meant to be operated by two men a side. You and I will never do it by ourselves."

"Do you think it would make any difference if we both came down and helped?" suggested Georgina.

"I doubt it," grunted the Welshman wearily, "but we'll try it. Give us a minute to get our breath back."

Georgina clambered down into the water gingerly. The cold was worse than she had remembered, the filth and muck floating in it repelled her. With difficulty she crossed over the submerged track, her skirt dragging at her feet, and gripped the heavy wheel.

"Right now," called Rees when they were all in position, "all together. Heave!"

Together they heaved at the wheels with every ounce of strength they could summon. Georgina felt the muscles in her arms and shoulders cracking with the strain. They had balanced the torch on a ledge in the wall, but it had swung away from them so they were working almost blind. In front of her Georgina could see Rees' face contorted with effort as he shifted his grip, catching one of her fingers between his hand and the metal, and the pain nearly made her cry out. They seemed to go on and on and she was all but fainting when Rees suddenly relaxed his hold.

"It's no use," he said, "we're not going to move it. We might as well get back up out of the water."

Exhausted and depressed they floundered over to the platform and climbed up. They seemed to have achieved nothing except to drench their clothes once more. A thin layer of water now covered most of the platform, swallowing up the surface around them. All of them realized that they now had very little hope left of getting out and Angelica began to cry again.

"We'll go and sit on top of the door at the other end," Rees said when they were all out of the water, "that should keep us dry for a bit anyway."

The largest item of the pile of equipment that comprised the parts for the diaphragm to close the tunnel leading to the Strand, was the main part of the door unit which stood over six feet high and was thick enough to provide a reasonable perch to sit on. They had turned the torch off to save the batteries and they sat without speaking in the dark feeling utterly defeated. Georgina thought of Derek and the children, she imagined him trying to tell them that she was dead. Would they stay in London she wondered or move away, and how would Derek cope with a job and two small children? Tears began to run down her face at the thought. Beside her Angelica and Russell tried to console her but nobody was feeling cheerful. The water had completely covered the platform, leaving only the tops of the benches exposed. Slowly and ominously it crept upward, faint ripples could be seen at the tunnel mouth where the flow poured in relentlessly. There seemed to be no hope left for them.

*   *   *

The river had triumphed all along its length. From Newham and Greenwich in the east to Richmond and Hounslow in the west, almost seventy square miles lay under water. A million and a half people had been directly affected with flood water surrounding their homes and flats. Another two million were without electricity as a result of the loss of the power stations and damage to the distribution network, and most of these were also suffering the consequences of the failure of the drainage system. With the outfalls to the east lost, and many pumping stations under water, the effluents that accumulated during a normal day threatened to become a health hazard to the whole city. Virtually the entire telephone network had been put out of action and a high proportion of gas production and storage capacity had been destroyed.

Between Kingston and the sea there was no method of crossing the Thames except by boat. Waterloo, Charing Cross, Victoria, Blackfriars and Fenchurch Street main line stations had been closed because of the surge, and the lines running into Liverpool Street from East Anglia had been cut at Stratford by flood water spreading up the Lea valley. The M4 motorway had also been blocked when Fulham and Hammersmith were inundated as far as Shepherd's Bush. Moreover the explosion at Bankside and damage to other generating stations had deprived the southern region railway of a large proportion of its power, thus leaving one of the most densely populated regions of the country without its most vital transport.

Final estimates showed that up to half a million people found themselves caught on the wrong side of the river with no means of reaching their homes. A colossal number of private cars, buses, coaches and commercial vehicles had been lost, but even those fortunate enough to possess a car found it all but impossible to drive anywhere near the flood zones. Quite apart from the sealing off of whole areas by police and army cordons, and the ban on private transport using the clearway routes, the surge had caused drains to back up and overflow in areas considerably removed from the main flood district. Drivers found their way blocked time and time again as they drove round desperately seeking a road that would lead them clear. Enormous traffic jams built up in some areas, paralyzing whole sections of otherwise unaffected parts of the capital, and greatly obstructing the movement of official convoys.

It was later estimated that approximately seventy-three thousand people died as a direct result of the first inrush of water, including those killed in the two major incidents: the trapping of the train load of passengers in the Underground and the firestorm in Battersea. Over and above this, more than a hundred and fifty thousand people suffered serious injuries during the first two hours of the emergency. These ranged from the appalling wounds received by the men caught in the Bankside explosion to simple fractures and cuts sustained by people falling down or being struck by floating debris. Without aid, or the means to reach somewhere where they could be cared for and treated, a further thirty thousand of these were to die during the night and following day.

At two o'clock in the afternoon at a window in the south front of the fifth floor of Bevan Tower, Eileen stood with tears streaming silently down her face. Her gaze was transfixed by the scene below her, a scene so horrific as to be beyond comprehension. Against a background of belching smoke shot with sparks and leaping tongues of flame the final nightmare of the city's destruction was unfolding before her eyes.

In the water below, hundreds of men, women, children, old age pensioners and babies were struggling for their lives. Caught between fire and flood the inhabitants of the streets near by had been driven from their homes by the advancing flames, and forced to try and swim to safety. Six entire streets were ablaze near the towers and the conflagration was spreading fast; the crackle of the flames and the sound of collapsing roofs and walls was clearly audible inside, and the wind swirled a cloud of incandescent fragments past the glass.

Between the flats and the fire ran the main road, and on the near side the tower was surrounded by a car park and the wide open space of a children's play area. All this was now completely submerged, and so deep was the flooding that not even the tops of the trees or the high wire fence round the playground showed above the water. Since Eileen had come up to this floor nearly an hour ago looking for her daughter, who was playing happily on the floor with the other children, she had lost count of the number of people she had watched trying to swim away from the fire and reach the flats across this wide belt of deep water. There seemed to be no end to them. Desperately splashing groups of figures, clutching on to anything that floated, frantic to escape the greedy flames behind. One or two, she saw, had managed to construct homemade boats or rafts, but these instantly attracted hordes of clinging swimmers, whose weight soon capsized or swamped them.

There was nothing that could be done to help. There were no boats in the vicinity and no sign of help from the rescue services. At first, people in the flats had tried throwing pieces of wooden furniture down in the hope that some might be able to use them, but always they drifted off in the wrong direction. The coldness of the water, the currents that flowed between the buildings, the unseen obstacles beneath the surface, but above all the shock of the bewildering disaster that had suddenly befallen them, took a terrible toll of the fleeing crowd. Again and again the pathetic groups split up, became separated and disappeared as their members slipped exhausted beneath the muddy water. Eileen saw anguished men trying to support their wives and children in a hopeless battle against the flood, and mothers holding their babies in their arms as they drowned. The old lasted no time at all.

"Why doesn't somebody help them? There must be something they can do?" Eileen heard a voice speaking as though a long way away. After a moment she realized it was her own. With an effort she pulled herself together, collected Marlene and went out into the corridor. Away from the dreadful sight her head began to clear. Mopping her eyes with a handkerchief she set off down the stairs still feeling badly shaken. The damp stench of the flood water rose to meet her as she descended and she lit herself a cigarette to mask the smell.

On the next floor they came face to face with four dripping and shivering men wearing blankets who had managed to reach the tower windows of the block and been pulled inside. All four were obviously badly shocked by their ordeal, staring dazedly about them as their rescuers led them off to be cared for in an upstairs flat. One, a boy in his teens, had cut himself badly on the forearm, and blood was seeping through his sleeve and dripping unheeded on to the floor. Eileen hurried on past, holding Marlene tightly by the hand.

The landing and corridor of the second floor were full of people milling about and talking at the tops of their voices. A few more blanket clad survivors stood in a dejected huddle at the foot of the stairs while two women argued with the caretaker over where they should go. A knot of men by the window at the far end of the passage were trying to drag something through. There was a chorus of encouraging shouts, and with a high-pitched yelp, a large black mongrel dog slithered through, to be greeted warmly on all sides.

"Oh, poor thing, isn't 'e wet." Eileen recognized the voice of the woman who had offered to listen for the kettle, and went up to her.

"I'm sorry I was so long upstairs," she apologized. "Did Mr. Pole get his bottle?"

"The bottle!" the woman exclaimed guiltily, "I forgot all about it when this started. I ain't heard it whistle, though."

"My God! It'll have boiled dry by now." Letting go Marlene's hand, Eileen pushed through the mass of people to her own flat and opened the door.

Inside the flat was full of gas, but its odor was masked by the smell of filthy water, mud and damp clothes from the corridor outside and Eileen was totally unaware of it. She was at the kitchen door when she took another deep drag at her cigarette.

The explosion killed Eileen instantly, blowing out the entire flat and hurling her body into the waters below. A violent tremor ran through the building and the floor of the flat above, deprived of support from the wall sections, collapsed downwards, crushing to death two women who had been in the sitting room. In the second floor corridor nine people were killed instantly by the searing blast which ripped through the interior wall and brought heavy slabs of concrete crashing down upon them. On this floor and the one above there were nearly a score of others who received serious injuries as a result of this blast, and who lay moaning among the wreckage.

Their agonies, however, were to be pitifully short. Barely seconds after the explosion, flames licking the wreckage ignited the gas trapped between the flood level and the ceiling of the first floor. Ever since the morning the pocket of explosive vapor had built up, spreading from room to room along the water line, until it filled all the remaining space and a layer of gas stretched right across the block.

The wounded were just beginning to pick themselves up when the detonation of this gas resulted in a series of shattering explosions which literally cut the building in two. Reflected upwards by the water, the blast tore through the reinforced concrete sections that surrounded it with devastating force. Near the center of the explosion the huge slabs were pulverized into fragments of rubble, entire walls were broken and flung outward, floors split and collapsed into the center of the block, carrying with them the bodies of their occupants.

In a neighboring block a quarter of a mile away, watchers heard the deep boom of the explosion and saw a cloud of smoke and debris bellow out suddenly around the lower floors, amidst which larger fragments could be seen raining outwards. The great tower seemed to sway and shiver from the violence of the shock, and even before the echo of the explosion had died away it began to tilt sharply to one side.

The sides immediately above the area of the blast buckled suddenly, as walls and floors lost the cohesive tension which had bound them together, disintegrated and crumbled apart. Another tremendous blast ripped through the block as more gas ignited within the lift shaft. A crack appeared running down one face, which widened quickly, gaping open to reveal the interior as a huge portion slipped and fell away, crashing into the water in a fountain of spray. Tiny doll-like figures were visible for a moment tumbling through the air, with bits of furniture and bedding, as the contents spilled out.

The tower leaned over at a much greater angle, more cracks appeared, splitting the facade, more floors buckled, the whole building was breaking up. Then slowly, unbelievably, with a roar that shook the ground and rocked buildings a mile away, the vast structure fell, thundering into the surrounding water like an avalanche. Clouds of spray and smoke shot up, great waves, reaching higher than the roofs of nearby houses, surged outward; among them there bounced and rolled lumps of concrete weighing tons, spreading a wide circle of ruin and devastation. The topmost part of the block fell, by some terrible mischance, upon the end of a street which was already partially ablaze, transforming it into a furious inferno of destruction in which the occupants of the flats perished beside those of the houses.

For the others in the tower, there was equally little chance of survival. Burnt and mutilated by savage explosions, crushed by falling masonry, those who were not instantly killed perished swiftly in the water that raged about the debris, or drowned as they lay trapped among the ruins of their own homes.

When the spray cleared, the horrified onlookers could see only an area in which scattered heaps of unrecognizable wreckage were all that remained. Where Bevan Tower had stood, only a few blackened edges of concrete projected above the water. Round about, the broken fragments of the great building lay half submerged by the flood. Every one of its inhabitants, together with more than a hundred others caught up in the calamity of its fall, was dead.

* * *

The President was driven up to London after lunching with the Queen and other members of the Royal family at Windsor, to see for himself the results of the catastrophe which had struck the capital. He was taken to the underground headquarters beneath High Holborn, where he met the Prime Minister again and was given a briefing on the situation and the problems that might arise as a consequence of the flood.

Shortly after three forty-five the two heads of state, in company with senior officials and followed by a party of journalists who had discovered the whereabouts of the government, climbed aboard high-axled military trucks and headed off in the direction of the Strand. Their destination was Somerset House, which was still approachable by this means and from whose terrace it was possible to view the river and gain an idea of the magnitude of the disaster.

For several minutes the two leaders stared out across the water at the drowned streets where familiar landmarks rose grotesquely out of an immense lake. To the southwest, quantities of dark smoke boiled upwards into the sky from the firestorm in Wandsworth, and despite the gale force winds, formed a gigantic pall above the city. Immediately before them the embankment was deeply sunk beneath the river and ships moored there now appeared to be lying anchored in midstream. Everywhere a picture of utter desolation met their eyes. The newsmen clustered round with their cameras and microphones to record the scene for posterity.

At the Kingsway flood room, which they visited next, they listened to the latest information coming in from the emergency services and the borough control rooms and heard Alan Carswell explain the steps that were being taken to meet the crisis. Finally they returned to the underground headquarters beneath its massive gray office block designed to absorb the initial blast of a nuclear bomb and shield the vital installations beneath.

When they reemerged some time later the waiting journalists clamored for a statement and the President addressed them briefly before stepping into the limousine which waited to take him back to Heathrow Airport.

"What I have seen today," he said, "has been an unbelievable and horrifying tragedy. That it should have happened to one of the world's greatest cities makes it all the more terrible. I am returning to Washington at once, where I shall straight away be going before Congress and asking them to vote whatever is required in money and resources to rebuild London and help her brave people.

"In the meantime I have already instructed that all available supplies of helicopters, inflatable boats, amphibious vehicles, pumps, portable generators, and any other item which we possess and which may be required by the British government, be airlifted here at once, even if this means reducing the combat effectiveness of military units. Whatever we in America can do at this time shall be done."

*   *   *

At Bankside the local police had finally succeeded in bringing in a doctor by boat from Guy's Hospital to attend to the injured. Already they were too late to save the life of one man who had died shortly after the failure of the first attempt to get help. With great care three of the injured were placed in the boat and sent back to the hospital, while the doctor remained behind to treat the others.

"I don't know how much they will be able to do there," he told Alan Watts when the boat had gone. "Guy's has got very little power and two of those chaps need extensive surgery pretty quickly if they are to pull through. They are running a kind of shuttle service out to hospitals beyond the flooding so your friends may be put straight on to that, but I'm afraid it's very slow."

Alan left him treating the less severe cases and went to gather in the remainder of his men. The police had told him that they intended to evacuate the station as soon as the sick had been taken away. It would be a relief to get out. His own home in Lambeth must have caught the flooding; he wondered if he could persuade the police to take him up and rescue his family. He was thankful that he had been able to telephone his wife before the overtopping began and tell her what to do, but even so he was worried about her.

*   *   *

Alan Carswell had ordered that Kingsway central be kept constantly informed about the position of the rescue party in the tubes. When the observers at Leicester Square became worried by the rapid increase in the amount of water coming down the tunnels he had immediately arranged for additional pumps to be sent to the station. The decision did not pass without criticism.

"We shall have to use one of the machines that were being sent to reduce the level at Westminster Hospital," a fire brigade officer told him.

"Can't you take one from somewhere else?"

"No, sir," the man replied without hesitation. "We just haven't got any more available in that area. Most of our pumps have been taken up to Hammersmith."

"You'll have to use the one that's going to the hospital then," Carswell replied. "The lives of ten people depend on being able to keep the water down for the next hour."

"Yes, sir, I suppose you're right," said the officer uneasily. "It's just that Westminster's a maternity hospital. They've a lot of babies in incubators and things like that, and they've been badly hit."

"As soon as we possibly can, we'll let them have all the pumps they need," Carswell promised him, "but in the meantime I'm not going to abandon Derek and the people with him when they are counting on us."

Despite intensive efforts with the new machines, however, the levels in Leicester Square and Strand stations continued to rise ominously fast.

"It's looking bad," the line supervisor told him a quarter of an hour later. "We have tried to cut the flow every way we can. We've got pumps in at four different stations now, but the water's coming up faster than we can cope."

"How far has the rescue party got?" Alan asked.

"According to their last report they have managed to swim through the submerged section between Charing

Cross and Strand and now are only a short way from
where we think the surviving passengers may be. In-
cidentally, they have found the man who tried to get
out with the guard. He was dead. But they say the
water is getting deeper all the time. We are afraid that
by the time they start back the tunnel will be completely flooded."

"They have breathing apparatus, though. Surely they
can use that."

"Yes," agreed the supervisor, "but if they have to
swim it will take them too long to get back. Their air
will give out before they complete the journey. They
must be able to make at least half of it without using
their tanks. To be honest," he said, "I don't think they
could swim for more than a short stretch of the tunnel
completely under water, particularly the women. It will
be pitch black and freezing cold, and there are a lot of
cables and wires to get caught up in. It's a hell of a long
way to go in those conditions."

Carswell replaced the receiver despondently. The
truth of the supervisor's words was inescapable. The
chances faced by Derek and the rescue team had been
slim when they started out, now they were nonexistent.
Flood water was pouring into the tubes from hundreds
of different points, through station entrances, down ventilation shafts and cable conduits, and along open por-
tions of track. The attempt to reach Georgina and the
remaining survivors had been a race against time, and
it looked as though that time had run out.

*   *   *

Derek forced his way wearily down the flooded tunnel.
Behind him, he could hear Paul puffing with exertion
as he labored through the water. They were wading up
to their chests and the extra depth was slowing them
up alarmingly. For the last ten minutes of the journey
he had been expecting to see a light ahead and hear

the voices of Georgina and the other passengers. Yet still there was no sign of life in the tunnel in front.

As it was the station came upon them almost without warning, taking both of them and the passengers completely by surprise. Rees had switched on the torch to check the water level and the light had outshone the beams from the rescuers' torches until they were at the very mouth of the tunnel.

Derek stepped out into the station to find himself staring up at Georgina sitting perched on the flood gate with her legs drawn up underneath her. With a cry she leapt down on to the platform below and struggled toward him. He grasped her to him and hugged her with all his strength.

"Darling! Darling!" she sobbed with tears of relief. "How did you get here? and why? and . . ." she broke off to bury her face in his shoulder.

"I've come to get you out of here," he told her, stroking her hair. "We've brought breathing sets and masks, and we're going to take you all back up the tunnel."

The other members of the team had climbed on to the platform and were greeting the passengers. Pat had already began radioing the news back.

"I reckon you didn't arrive any too soon," Rees commented as he fastened the breathing set Pat had given him on to his back and adjusted the mouthpiece. "What's the depth like in the main tunnel back there?"

"It's deep," Pat told him, "right up to the roof in places. What are our chances of being able to open that gate, d'you think." He pointed to the flood gate at the far end.

"It would lower the water level all right if we could do it," agreed Rees. "We tried to open it ourselves about half an hour ago but we couldn't move it and I think now maybe it's too deep. You have to stand on the tracks to get at the handles."

They left the others helping the three passengers into

the equipment they had brought and went down to take a look. Even walking on the platform had become difficult and the benches were completely submerged.

"Did you see where the water is coming in from?" asked Rees. "It started rising here all at once about an hour ago."

"There's a heavy flow at Strand," Pat replied, "but apparently it's coming in all round now. If we can't get this gate open we're going to have a hard time on the way back."

When they reached the gate Pat found it was just as Rees had said. The handles were so far beneath the surface that he had to wear his mask in order to get down to them.

"I'm afraid you're right," he gasped when at length they had given up. "It's impossible to get any leverage under the water. I'll get the other men down though, maybe if we all try together we can shift it."

At Pat's call the rest of the party hurried down the platform and together they tried to wind back the heavy gate. But the water made it impossible for them to bring their full strength to bear on the handles and they floundered about hopelessly, their hands slipping in the blackness.

"We will just have to try and get back up the tunnel as it is," Pat said eventually when they had finally abandoned their efforts. "We may still be able to get through." The others looked at him anxiously. Georgina and the passengers felt the relief that had come with the arrival of the rescuers ebbing away.

"Could we get through at Strand do you think?" suggested Bruno. "We should be able to manage the tunnel as far as there." Pat looked uncertain.

"It might be O.K. if the flow in the passages to the surface isn't too strong," he said doubtfully, "but in any case the deepest flooding lies between here and Strand. After that it gets easier."

Derek listened to them argue. He was inclined to

agree with Bruno that their best route might be through Strand, but if the level became much deeper it was unlikely that they would be able to find the stairs that led upwards. He pictured them fumbling in the inky water, searching blindly for the doorways beneath the surface. None of them had been in the station for years and anyway it had been extensively rebuilt while it had been closed. For the first time he realized that they had very little hope of getting out alive. He squeezed Georgina's shoulder comfortingly.

"Listen," he said to the others, "we can't stand here. Our best bet is to walk as far as the next station and then decide whether to go on or try and make it to the surface."

The words were hardly out of his mouth when there came an ominous creaking and cracking sound from the shuttered doorways to the escalators.

"What the hell was that?" exclaimed Paul. "It sounded like the roof was about to come in."

"It's the new passage through to the escalator shaft," Rees answered. "It was made after the shutters were put in so we had to rig up a temporary barrier. The water must have lifted some of the timber supports we used to wedge it with."

"We'd better get out of here fast," Pat began wading up the platform. "If that door fails we've had it."

There came another series of creaks from the door and a snapping sound as though a piece of timber had broken. In the arched platform the noise rang unnaturally loud, echoing back off the walls. Derek felt Georgina tighten her arms about him. Hastily they set off after Pat praying that the barrier would hold. When they drew near he saw that a section of the steel sheeting had bent outward before the enormous pressure behind. A massive baulk of wood floated up as they drew abreast, evidently dislodged by the rising water. He pushed on towards the far tunnel, dragging Georgina with him. The sounds from the door seemed to have stopped, with any luck he thought the weight of water on this side would take some of the strain off the barricade.

They had passed the last of the doorways and were nearly at the end of the platform once more when the makeshift barrier shattered with a crash like the explosion of an enormous cannon. Great fragments of metal were hurled against the walls and roof with terrific violence, and water from the drowned station above foamed through the gap as though a dam had burst.

Numbed with shock, the first instinct of each of them was to struggle frantically through the flood that now swirled about their chests in a desperate attempt to reach the northern tunnel entrance. Waves stirred up by the inrushing torrent slapped against their faces setting them choking and coughing. Looking at the fast rising level Derek realized that any hopes they might have once had of escaping up the tunnel the way they had come were doomed to failure.

"Back this way!" he shouted to Pat and the others in front of him. "We'll have to go up through these stairs. We'll never make it down the tunnel."

"Are you crazy?" Paul screamed at him as he fought his way back against the flow to the nearest of the four doorways. "If you open that shutter you'll drown us all!"

"We shall drown anyway if we stay down here. Our only chance is to get out through the station here. If we open the doors we'll be able to swim up when the water coming in equalizes the pressure." Seizing the chains that controlled the mechanism Derek began working the pulley. The door groaned and squealed as the steel shutter slid protesting upwards. At the sound Paul flung himself on the engineer's back and dragged him away.

"You fool, you're going to finish us if you touch that!" Derek struggled to throw him off and they wrestled furiously.

"Can't you see there's no way out except this. The water will be up to the roof before we've gone a hundred yards."

"Leave him Paul! He's right," Pat shouted, forcing a path towards them. "This is the quickest route to the surface. We've got to take it." Paul looked unconvinced but he relaxed his hold on Derek, allowing him to resume his efforts with the pulley.

Slowly the heavy shutters grated upwards releasing a second flow of pent up liquid into the already half-drowned station. The pressure on the steel was so great that it took the combined efforts of both Derek and Pat tugging on the chains to wind it back up against the roof, while the force of the current through the gate threatened to sweep them from their feet.

"Jesus, we'll never get up the stairs against that." Bruno eyed aghast the mill race streaming outwards, his voice almost lost in the roar of the water.

"It'll ease off when the level rises higher," Derek shouted back. "Get your masks on, the rest of you. We haven't long." He helped Georgina fit her mask and mouthpiece properly. She looked pale and frightened. Taking a length of rope he fastened it about her waist, then joined it to one of the straps on the harness of his breathing set. Out of the corner of his eye he saw the station engineer, Rees, doing the same with Angelica.

"I had better lead," the Welshman called to him. "I know this station better than the rest of you. You will find the escalator straight in front of you; it climbs for thirty feet, then you'll come out into a big chamber where all the passages meet. We have to cross that and climb another escalator up to the surface. I'll hammer on the door when I start."

It sounded simple but Derek pictured in his mind the confusion and bewilderment they would experience as they blundered through the blind passenger concourse, seeking the way up, all the time fighting the currents that tried to drag them downwards. Trapped in the stairs and passageways would be the drowned bodies of more than three hundred people who had been caught in the flood when the embankment wall burst. There was every likelihood that the majority of the survivors would be joining them; as they became disoriented in the darkness and lost their way while their air gave out.

Pat was sending a final message through to Leicester Square. With a crackle of static the reply came over the air.

"We are sending everything we've got down to meet you. The entrance facing the river is closed up but you can still get out the other side. We will also watch the District Line track in case any of you come up in the open section."

"O.K." Pat replied. "The level here is rising fast, it will be over our heads within three or four minutes. I estimate we shall have to wait as long again before the flow slackens enough to allow us to get through."

"Understood. All pumping operations are being suspended to avoid drawing water back up the tunnels. Charing Cross report that they will attempt to run lights from an emergency generator to illuminate the entrance to the station."

"Thanks," Pat said, "that may be a lot of help."

"Good luck," the operator signed off, "we'll see you on the surface."

The worst part of their ordeal consisted of waiting by the door while the water rose around them. Georgina held tightly on to Derek's hand; the unfamiliar apparatus she breathed through seemed strange and unreliable and the thought of having to swim underwater in it terrified her. Dribbles of water began to form inside her mask as the level covered her face shutting out the light. She caught a last glimpse of the outline of Derek's head, then she was in utter darkness clutching on to Derek to stop herself from floating upwards.

Instantly she found herself transferred from the

world of sight to a world of noise and feeling. The sound of the water rushing through the doorway was vastly magnified as though she was in the middle of a waterfall. In the background she could hear odd thumps and bangs from pieces of debris being whirled against the walls by the turbulence. Her own breathing sounded alarmingly loud in her ears. She squeezed Derek's hand and felt a reassuring pressure in answer.

About her she could feel the pull of the current swirling with undiminished vigor. There was a slight tug at her back. They were standing close together in a bunch, holding on to each other so as to ensure that no one would be left behind when the others went through the door.

They seemed to wait for ages before the flow from above eased enough for them to be able to move against it. Three dull clangs sounded from near at hand and she recognized the signal they had agreed on. She was finding increasing difficulty in keeping her balance in the water, her natural buoyancy causing her to sway forwards and left off the platform. Judging by the movements she could detect from the others behind her they were experiencing similar problems.

Derek's hand gave a jerk, he was starting to move forward. Bumping and swaying she followed, using her free arm to propel herself through the water. Her ears had begun to ache and she swallowed hard to clear them; the pressure in the tunnel had increased sharply. Her hand encountered a solid object ahead. At first she thought it was the wall, then she felt the edge of a metal sill and realized it was the inside of the door. Derek was ahead of her, tugging her after him through the narrow entrance and into the stairwell beyond.

Fighting to keep a hold on her sanity, Georgina forced herself to try and remember the layout of the station. The steps of the escalator should be only a few steps past the door and the ascent was steep. Into her mind flashed a vivid recollection of the panic-stricken descent from the concourse above that she had made not long ago. She tried not to think of the corpses that must be lying unseen in the darkness close at hand.

They moved forward very slowly, hampered by their reluctance to let go of each other and lose contact. Georgina felt her husband lead her hand down to the harness belt on his waist and she gripped it tightly, freeing him to press ahead with both arms. With a jerk she found they were going upwards, presumably Derek had reached the first steps of the escalator. The motion broke the hold on her own back of the person behind, allowing her to start floating ceilingwards again but reaching out she felt the side rail of the escalator and began to use this to draw herself up towards the passage above.

The stair shaft seemed larger than she remembered, but in the total obscurity it was impossible to judge distance or time, even her own position in the water seemed uncertain so that she could not be sure whether she was floating horizontally or at an angle. Strange sounds came at her out of the darkness, reverberating in her ears, frightening and confusing her with their distorted tones. The pressure had eased somewhat though and she swallowed again. Her ears cleared, but the strange booming and clanking noises remained.

Their ascent stopped, Georgina could sense Derek hesitating, trying to work out his position. She knew that he used the tubes only occasionally and wondered if he knew which direction to take. The stairway to the surface lay ahead of them across the hall, although to their rear was another escalator that usually brought passengers down from the level of the street.

Derek swam out into the middle of the passageway. Movement was more difficult here with nothing to cling on to. Their bodies floated off the floor, compelling them to swim properly trusting to the rope to keep them close to each other. The sensation of moving through the black water like this was more disorientating then ever. She sensed herself surrounded on all sides by an immense void in which her sole link with the outside world was the rope tugging at her waist. Near what she guessed must be the middle of the hall her foot kicked against something soft and heavy, and which she knew instantly was the drifting corpse of a drowned passenger.

With a convulsive jerk she snatched her leg back and thrashed desperately away, her senses reeling with horror, till the rope tightened and she was brought up short. Then very slowly she felt Derek pulling her back towards him. He must have realized what had happened for he found her hand again in the dark and began leading her on again.

They collided with no more bodies, though every nerve in Georgina's body was straining for the slightest brush with any object in the water and she felt sick and faint with the horror of it. At last, in front of them they discovered a wall and began feeling their way carefully along it, searching for the entrance to the escalator. It seemed to go on for ever in an unbroken line; Georgina felt Derek hesitate again and stop, and at once a terrifying conviction that they had gone wrong filled her brain. Visions of the two of them blundering about in endless water-filled passages among crowds of swaying corpses rose before her. She felt an overpowering desire to scream and swim frantically away in the opposite direction, in any direction but the one they had taken.

Before she could move, however, Derek had started off once more. He took a couple of steps, paused and then seemed to be drawing her backwards into the middle of the concourse. Following him she bumped heavily into a large, solid object at knee height with a surface that was somehow familiar. Derek's hand gave a strong pull, lifting her over the obstruction and then they were climbing for a second time. She recognized the smooth arm of the escalator rail beside her providing a firm hand-hold with which to haul herself up towards the top.

Georgina's relief at reaching a recognizable part of the station at last instead of the awful confusion that she had known till then was overwhelming. With renewed hope she followed the path of the stairs upwards. Once again her ears registered a drop in the pressure making her swallow hard to unblock them. As she did so she became conscious of a marked increase in the noise about her, the source of which appeared to be from up ahead. Then straining through the darkness her eyes detected a faint but unmistakable glow of light.

With a splash, her hand burst suddenly to the surface into what appeared, after the appalling darkness under water and the hours spent in the tunnels below, to be a brilliantly lit scene. Men with powerful lamps were standing in the flooded station, stretching out their hands to draw them to safety, with shouts of encouragement. Someone was hammering loudly on a pipe close at hand and she realized that must have been the cause of the noise she had heard on the way up. People were crowding round, supporting her arms and helping her round the submerged ticket barriers and guard rails. She was still wading up to her shoulders, but even so, between the surface of the water and the top of the doorway to the outside, she could catch a glimpse of daylight.

A moment later she was through the entrance into the open air and flinging her arms round Derek, laughing and crying with happiness and relief.

*   *   *

It was four-thirty and the light had nearly faded from the sky when Derek, bathed and wearing a borrowed suit of clothes, returned briefly to Kingsway. His arrival was the signal for an outburst of cheers and congratulations on all sides.

"It was an amazing feat. God only knows how you did it!" Alan Carswell greeted him. "None of us here thought you'd make it back alive."

"We didn't all," Derek told him curtly. The fulsome reception embarrassed and annoyed him. Paul Frean had failed to get through to the surface with the rest of them. Somehow he had become separated from them and lost his way in the maze of drowned passages beneath the ground, unable to find his way back before the air in his cylinder was exhausted.

"One piece of good news," Carswell said after a moment's pause, "is that the tide seems to be ebbing at last. Bracknell say the depression is moving away towards the continent and filling as it goes. The winds have dropped already and we've been able to send a helicopter up to make a preliminary survey of the damage. You ought to go and get some rest now, you've done enough."

"I shall do soon. I just wanted to check that we're ready to start work on the breaches as soon as the river retreats." The two discussed the position until, just as Derek was about to take his leave, the Minister appeared from the conference room.

"Allow me to add my congratulations to those of the rest of the staff," he beamed unctuously, "it was a splendid achievement, quite splendid." Derek felt his anger rising again. "I gather we can begin the task of cleaning up very soon," the Minister continued, speaking to the room at large, "and at this point I should like to put on record my admiration for the way everyone has behaved. You have all performed your duties magnificently in an extremely difficult situation and I know that the citizens of London, of this great city of ours, will be grateful for the preparation you made and the way in which you carried them out. Don't you agree, Mr. Thompson?"

"The citizens grateful!" Derek exclaimed savagely. "Why should they be grateful? What the hell have we done for them, except allow a catastrophic flood to strike with almost no warning, devastating the heart of the city, half-paralyzing the country and by the time it's over accounting for the deaths of over a hundred thousand of them, and all the time we've just sat and watched it happen. Preparations!" Derek snorted contemptuously. "What preparations? We haven't made a single one worth the name. If they have any sense, they'll crucify the lot of us."

The Minister's face turned white.

"I don't see what else we could have done," he replied in a strangled voice.

Derek snarled back at him. "We could have told them how real the danger was," he said, "instead of pretending that everything was under control with nothing to worry about. We could have involved them in practice alerts instead of holding our own private exercises by ourselves, so that they knew what to expect if a flood came. We could have set up a proper warning system instead of relying on a few air raid sirens from the war which nobody could hear. We could have had more boats and pumps ready, and high-axled trucks. We could have protected our hospitals, our power stations, our gasworks and sewage farms and our Underground system. There were a thousand things we should have done, but above all, before anything else," he shouted at the room, "we could have finished building that goddamned flood barrier."

Not a single person spoke a word. Derek picked up his coat and walked out into the cold night.

ABOUT THE AUTHOR

A descendant of Sir Arthur Conan Doyle (and a great-great-great-nephew of Richard Doyle the *Punch* illustrator), RICHARD DOYLE was born in the Channel Islands in 1948 and spent the first twenty years of his life in Ethiopia, the Middle East and North Africa. After leaving school at the age of fifteen, he educated himself for the next two years before going to Oxford University where he took a degree in law. Between 1970 and 1974 he worked on the stock exchange doing investment analysis before deciding to try to earn his living as a writer. His interests include literature, history, philosophy, comparative religion, mathematics and traveling. A nomadic existence has led Doyle, for the moment, to Rockport, Massachusetts, where he is working on his third novel.

The following pages
contain an exciting
Special Preview of a
major new novel, as
gripping as **Airport,** as
glamorous as **Murder On
the Orient Express**

IMPERIAL 109

by Richard Doyle

1

By radio: 1310 hrs LOCAL TIME. FRIDAY 10 MARCH 1939. KISUMU, UGANDA TO ALL AIRPORTS: SOUTH AFRICA – ENGLAND – NEW YORK MAIL PLANE, IMPERIAL AIRWAYS FLIGHT 109 REGISTRATION G-ADHO CATERINA LEFT HERE FOR MALAKAL – KHARTOUM – CAIRO. ETA MALAKAL 1700 hrs. END.

Five thousand feet below the flying boat, the marshes of the Sud stretched out in every direction. From the borders of Uganda, the swamplands run for more than four hundred miles through equatorial Sudan, covering an area greater than England, where the broad Nile all but loses itself in a maze of sluggish channels and creeks. It is a region of neither dry land nor open water but of limitless green papyrus reeds, water hyacinth, stagnant pools, quicksand, and river mud. The fierce equatorial heat, the humidity, and the ever-present risk of disease carried by the millions of swarming insects have combined with the other natural hazards to make the Sud one of the last unexplored areas of Africa.

A heavy storm had lain over much of the region, but now the dense clouds rolled away in the direction of Ethiopia, and the flying boat cruised on in brilliant sunshine. With their gleaming white paint, raking prows, and high wings sprouting from the crests of their hulls, the S30C Empire-class boats of Britain's Imperial Airways were some of the most beautiful aircraft ever to fly, carrying passengers in a style and luxury unmatched since the passing of the great air ships of Germany a decade earlier, and never to be seen again. Spanning the immense distances separating the British Dominions around the earth, the flying boats set standards taken from the leisured days of the previous century, emulating the style of travel found on the voyages of the great ocean liners, as if in defiance of the new order that would soon sweep away the last trace of the Imperial past.

In the captain's seat on *Caterina*'s flight deck sat Desmond O'Neill. Lean, wiry, an inch under six feet in height, he had the dark hair, blue eyes, easy charm, and quick temper common among his Irish ancestors. He glanced out at the scene below. The Sud never failed to impress him. Considering, he reflected wryly, that he had probably flown over the area at least fifty times since taking command of *Caterina* two years ago, he should have grown used to the sight by now. The section between Mombasa and Cairo, twenty-five hundred miles of swamp, scrub, and plain desert, was the worst part of the five-day, Durban-to-England trip. Monotonous landscapes, the long hours in flight were broken only by refueling stops at dirty, fly-blown river stations in sweltering heat. For passengers and crew alike, it was a relief when they finally reached the delta.

The flying boat lurched slightly in an air pocket, and there was a momentary surge of power from the engine as the Sperry autopilot corrected the loss of altitude. Desmond's eyes flicked over the instruments on the control panels. On the main fuel gauge the fat white needle pointed to 205 gallons, and Desmond knew at once it was fractionally too low. He leaned forward and tapped the dial with his fingernail, a habit left over from the early days of his flying career, but *Caterina*'s sophisticated equipment was a far cry from that of its forebears, and the needle remained obstinately on the mark.

"You know what that means?" he asked with a sigh. Beside him in the first officer's seat Kenneth Frazer shifted uneasily.

"What's that skipper?" Frazer asked in apparent surprise.

"You know damn well," Desmond snapped angrily. "We've got a fuel leak, and there's only one place it could be coming from—that port wing tank. Did you check it out as I told you?"

Frazer's face flushed. He was a tall, well-built young man with pale features and carefully smoothed fair hair, more concerned with his appearance and prestige, it seemed to Desmond, than with attending to the essential details of flying passenger aircraft. "I followed your orders exactly," Frazer answered stiffly. "The engineers stripped off the wing panels, and we examined the tank carefully. As I told you, we found only one small leak, which was sealed. The tank had hardly been touched. . ."

Desmond's eyes narrowed as he made quick mental calculations. Their present hop was a long one—720 miles from Kisumu, on the shores of Lake Victoria, to Malakal at the northern end of the Sud marshes—and to save weight the flying boat was carrying fuel for only 800 miles.

"Ralph," he called out to the wireless operator at the rear of the flight deck, "can you give me a fix on our exact position? I want to check our fuel reserves."

"Aye, aye, skipper," the reply came back above the background noise in the cockpit. Younger than the two pilots, still in his late twenties, Ralph Kendrick had a lazy good humor that seemingly no amount of frustration could upset. He too had been with the *Caterina* since her commissioning two years ago in 1937.

Ralph unclipped the small hatch in the cabin roof. Wind whistled shrilly through the opening. Beside him, fixed to the bulkhead on a swivel mounting, was a loop aerial for the Marconi direction finder. Ralph locked it in position. By rotating the aerial on different frequencies, it was possible to take accurate bearings on the series of radio beacons located at stations along the route. These could then be plotted on the chart to give an accurate fix on the aircraft's position.

"We're 218 miles due south of Malakal," he reported when he completed his calculations, "and 110 miles south-southeast of the emergency landing station at Shambe."

Desmond figured the answer briefly. There was still enough fuel for them to reach Malakal—provided the rate of leakage remained steady. He looked out the window at the wing on his left. There was no sign of fuel spilling out, but that in itself was no guide. *Caterina's* thousand-horsepower Bristol Pegasus XII radial engines were gulping fuel at the rate of two gallons a minute.

"We'll monitor the gauges over the next thirty minutes," Desmond decided, glancing at the control panel. "If the situation gets any worse during that time, we'll have to divert to Shambe."

Ralph Kendrick chuckled. "The passengers will love that," he said. "An unscheduled stop with plenty of time for sightseeing in the swamps."

"Damn the passengers!" Ken Frazer snorted angrily. "London will go crazy if they hear their precious cargo is stuck out here."

There was silence. Frazer had touched on a sensitive subject. *Caterina*'s cargo was no ordinary freight load. She carried more than a ton and a half of gold from the South African mines—two million dollars worth at the internationally agreed price of thirty-five dollars an ounce. . .

There could no longer be any doubt about the leak. Even before the half hour was up, it was clear that they were losing fuel at a rate of more than two hundred gallons per hour. To reach Malakal, still 140 miles away, was out of the question.

"If the loss gets any worse we will have enough problem reaching the emergency landing area, let alone Malakal," Desmond said. "Ralph, give me a course for the station at Shambe. Tell them we're coming in low on fuel, and request emergency services to stand by. Assuming they have any, that is," he added sourly.

"OK, skipper, I have the course for you," the radio operator replied at once. "Steer 310 degrees north. The station is approximately forty-five miles distant. We should reach it in twenty minutes at our current speed. . ."

Satisfied that he was on the correct bearing, Desmond eased back the throttle levers slightly, allowing *Caterina*'s speed to fall back to 110 knots to conserve the remaining fuel. *Caterina* was capable of cruising at a maximum of 165 knots with a minimum stalling speed of 73 knots.

"Shambe reports landing area clear and all services on standby," Kendrick said.

"Fine," Desmond replied. "I'm taking us down to two thousand feet, so we'll have a better chance of spotting the station." He pushed the control yoke forward as he spoke, putting the aircraft into a shallow descent. "OK, Ken," he said when they had leveled off at the new altitude, "take over and keep her on this bearing, will you? I'm going to have a word with Sandy and let the passengers know about the change in schedule."

Sandy Everett was the flying boat's purser, an enthusiastic, likable nineteen year old who had joined *Caterina*'s crew six months earlier on leaving school. He had an office in the mailroom immediately behind the flight deck, and he was responsible for the needs of the passengers.

The purser's true title was that of mail clerk, although he was always referred to as the purser, the term being borrowed from the ocean liners whose luxury and elegance the flying boat sought to equal. Mail had been the real reason behind Imperial Airways' bold decision four years ago to order twenty-eight of the flying boats straight off the drawing board as well as fourteen Armstrong Whitworth AW27 land planes. Under the Empire Air Mail Scheme set up that year, it had been agreed that all first-class mail would be carried by air throughout the British Empire at current surface rates. Imperial won the contract and with it a substantial government subsidy. The aim was to foster the spirit of unity among the empire's members, and from the start, it proved enormously successful. . .

With the exception of the cargo hold in the tail and a small space in the nose used for storing ropes and other mooring gear, the whole of the flying boat's lower deck was given over to the use of the passengers. There were four separate cabins designed to accommodate varying numbers of people according to demand. All could be converted into comfortable sleeping compartments in the event of a night flight, although nights were normally spent at first-class hotels, and whenever these were available the aircraft stopped for a while for lunch as well. The immense profitability of the mail loads meant that the passengers traveled in far greater luxury than would otherwise be possible. *Caterina* was eighty-eight feet long, and four double-decker buses could have been fitted into her hull, yet on this trip she carried only eleven passengers.

The double soundproofing on the passenger level reduced the sound of the engines to no more than a hum. The floor was thickly carpeted, and the effect was more like the first-class interior of an ocean liner than an airplane. . .

The galley door beside him opened with a click, and Sandy Everett emerged into the passage. "Andy and I are just getting the passengers' tea ready," he said, smiling. Andy Draper was the steward. "Shall I bring some upstairs for you?"

Desmond shook his head. "You'd better leave that for now, Sandy," he said. "We're losing a lot of fuel from that tank we holed at Mombassa, and I doubt if we will be able to reach Malakal. I'm going to take us down for an emergency stop at Shambe. We'll be landing in about a quarter of an hour. . ."

"Right, sir," Sandy said. "I'll just tell Andy, and then I'll go and inform the passengers that we'll be landing in fifteen minutes."

"I'll do the rear cabins myself," Desmond told him. "Most of the passengers will be there. You can tell the ones in the smoking saloon, and then make sure that they actually get back to their seats before we start to descend."

"OK, skipper, I'll see to it." Sandy nodded earnestly, and Desmond had to restrain an impulse to smile.

"One last thing," Desmond said before turning back to the gangway. "Don't mention that we are low on fuel. Just let them think it's a routine stop to inspect the repairs we had done earlier. I don't want them getting worried. . ."

"Let me tell you, my lad," he said. "I know all about Shambe—and it's worse than anywhere. For a start, we don't normally let passengers ashore there if we can help it, in case they catch yellow fever. The mosquitoes bite deep enough to draw blood; it's hot as a Turkish bath, and it stinks of mud."

"So we keep the passengers on board while the engineer looks at the tank?" asked Sandy. "They won't like that."

"Can't—not while they're working on a fuel tank," Andy replied, bending to stow a teapot. "It's the fire risk." Andy was an expert on all airline regulations. "Which means," he continued, "that you and I will have to go ashore and make sure they don't do anything stupid."

"OK," Sandy said. "I'll go tell them the good news."

"One more thing." Andy called him back. "We will have trouble with the female passengers when we land. The natives here don't wear clothes. Not unless you count a string of beads around their waists—and they only wear them if they're married. When I was here before, a general's wife fainted getting into the launch. She fell in the river. Stupid cow said it was the heat."

The promenade cabin, immediately aft of the wings, was the flying boat's greatest attraction and understandably popular among the passengers. The largest of the four cabins, it contained seating for eight as well as a wide area running the full length of the port side that was left free for passengers to stroll about and admire the view through the panoramic windows in the hull at standing height. . .

Laura was bored. She had been bored ever since she had entered the cabin, and she was bitterly regretting that she had been so foolish as to leave the smoking saloon. Standing beside her was a young lieutenant in British Royal Navy uniform. Fresh-faced, popeyed, and, for all his youth, unbearably pompous, Ian Thorne had striven manfully to impress her from the moment they had joined the aircraft at Durban. His opening remark—"I say you're American, aren't you? I can tell, you know, by the accent"—had earned him a look that would have dropped a more sensitive man where he stood. But he had plagued her with constant attention and a never-ending flow of inane conversation. He was either incredibly thick-skinned, she thought wearily, or simply too stupid to notice how offhanded she was being. Unfortunately, there was seldom any way of avoiding him during the flight.

"It's such a pity, Mrs. Hartman," he was saying, "my having to leave the airplane at Alexandria while you go on to New York. It's so nice talking to you." He had a sudden thought. "I say, we stop for a day in Cairo first. Perhaps I could show you the sights. I've been there before, you know."

"Thank you, but so have I," Laura replied dryly. "And in any case I shall have a lot of work to do when we get there."

Thorne looked crestfallen, but before he could reply, they were joined by another passenger. Dr. Van Smit was a small wiry man of about fifty, dressed in a neatly cut brown suit. He was very sunburned about the face and hands and had clever, sharp features. He described himself as a consultant geologist, although he appeared to earn his living primarily from card playing and gambling. Both his name and his pronounced accent proclaimed him to be a South African.

"I understand you have been visiting my country, Mrs. Hartman," he said politely. "Did you enjoy yourself there?"

"Yes, very much, but I'm afraid I only saw a little of it," Laura confessed. "I was there a week, and I had to spend most of that time in Durban. I'm secretary to Mr. Curtis," she explained.

"That would be the Mr. Curtis who is chairman of the Klerksdorp Mining Company? I have heard a great deal about him. I gather he is traveling with us, is that not so?" the doctor inquired.

"He's taken the after cabin," Laura told him. "He likes to be able to work while he is traveling. . ."

"My husband used to work for Mr. Curtis in South Africa," she said, somewhat irritated. "He was a mining engineer, and when he was killed in an accident last year, Mr. Curtis offered me a job as his personal secretary. He said he needed someone who understood a bit about the business. It was very generous of him."

The flat tone of her voice was enough to tell the two men that the subject of her husband was still painful. For a short while they gazed out the windows in silence. It was Ian Thorne who spoke first.

"Are you interested in mining, Dr. Van Smit?" he

asked as a frown passed over the South African's features.

Before Van Smit could reply, Desmond O'Neill stepped through the cabin doorway and came over to them. "I'm sorry to spoil your viewing," he said, "but I'm afraid you will all have to return to your seats. We are going to make an extra stop, and the aircraft will be landing on the river at Shambe in a quarter of an hour."

"Shambe," the doctor echoed. "Shambe. That is a most unusual place to stop. Is there something wrong?"

Desmond hastily reassured him. "We just want to take the opportunity to check the repairs that were made yesterday," he said. "We won't be delayed very long."

"Well, I'm glad," Laura peered out of the window. "It looks green and cool down there, and Khartoum will be so hot. It will be nice to rest here for a while."

"It may appear pleasant enough from this height, Mrs. Hartman," Dr. Van Smit replied grimly, "but you are looking at one of the most terrible regions in all Africa: the marshes of the Sud. Fifty thousand square miles of fever- and mosquito-ridden swamp. Captain O'Neill must indeed be concerned to be bringing us down in such a place."

Desmond look at him sharply. Van Smit had a knack of making disconcerting remarks. "I think you exaggerate a little, doctor," he said, keeping his tone deliberately casual. "Certainly Shambe presents no problems to us. The company has maintained a rest house and servicing facilities there for many years." Van Smit gave an enigmatic smile. . .

The after cabin was the most luxurious accommodation on board, and since it was the farthest from the engines, it was also the quietest. On this flight, it had been booked as a private stateroom, and its sole occupant was Stewart Curtis.

To Desmond's surprise, the news of the unscheduled landing appeared to irritate Curtis immensely.

"This is a confounded nuisance," Curtis snapped, laying down his papers. "Any delay will be extremely inconvenient for me. I have most important business to attend to. Surely this inspection could be carried out at Malakal?" He was heavily built, with a square, thick-jowled face, somewhere in his fifties, dressed in a Savile Row suit cut from tropical weight cloth. A British multi-millionaire with holdings in mining, steel, and armaments who had started as an office boy and made his first big killing by selling off war surplus material in the twenties, he survived the depression to become a leading industrialist and a key figure in the new South African mining market.

"It's damned inefficiency," Curtis snorted. "None of you people would last ten minutes working for me. We were delayed at Mombasa so that damage caused by your crew's carelessness could be put right. I see we shall have this excuse brought out the whole way to New York."

Desmond responded, tight-lipped. "I am sure this will be the last delay."

"It better be, captain," the financier retorted, "because if it isn't, I shall be making complaints to London that will have you back on the ground loading luggage." Indicating that the interview was terminated, he returned to his papers.

"Mr. Curtis," Desmond said quietly, restraining his anger, "I don't know what your understanding of modern aircraft is, but I can only assume it to be extremely limited. Any extra stops or delays will be motivated by consideration for the safety of this craft and its passengers. If I decide that such delays are required, then I will make them, regardless of what you or anyone else may say or do about it." Curtis gazed at him with astonishment. "Furthermore," Desmond continued, "if you are ever again as rude as you just have been, either to me personally or to anyone else on board, I'll put you off at the next stop and leave you there."

It had been a long time since anyone had dared speak to Stewart Curtis in such a manner, and the shock left him speechless. Seeing the rage and surprise evident on Curtis's face, Desmond judged it prudent to withdraw. . .

Back on the flight deck, Desmond saw at once from Ken Frazer's face that there had been no change for the better. Resuming his seat hurriedly, he ran his eyes over the instruments. Their safety margin was dropping.

"I've cut our speed to 105 knots," Frazer told him, "but it doesn't seem to have made any difference."

Desmond did some rapid figuring. The tanks were draining at an increasing rate, and on the main fuel gauge the needle had swung past the red danger mark. The gauges were notoriously inaccurate at very low readings, and it was possible that the position was not as serious as the gauge indicated; on the other hand, the engines could run dry at any second.

In heading directly for Shambe, their course had taken them away from the main river, which had bent sharply to the east for several miles; the aircraft was now flying over an area where the water was thickly clogged with reeds and mud. A ditching here would almost certainly result in the total wrecking of the aircraft.

"How long before we reach the open river again?" Desmond asked, taking the controls. *Caterina* was still flying sweetly, her four engines in synchronization with each other and no trace of the falterings that would signal the presence of air in the fuel leads. Once that began, they would have only a minute or two in which to select a place to ditch.

"We'll be over the river in approximately twelve minutes," Ken shouted to him, "just before we hit Shambe."

That was little help. There would be no prospect of making a safe landing before they reached the station, and it was too late to turn and head directly for one of the main channels. Twelve minutes. If the fuel gauge was reading correctly, they had barely sufficient reserves to reach the river.

"I'm going down to five hundred feet," said Desmond to the others. "Send a message to Shambe that our fuel situation is now critical."

Down below, ignorant of the danger they were facing, the passengers peered excitedly from the windows at the startled flocks of birds that rose on every side, scattering swiftly as the great plane winged low over the marshes.

Imperial Flight 109's unexpected landing in Shambe is just the first in a succession of tension-filled events in store for the passengers and crew. In addition to characters introduced in this excerpt, you will meet other fascinating people; including: two German refugees fleeing from Nazi terror; a disguised Nazi officer in pursuit of the pair; a mysterious Italian nobleman and his beautiful wife; an Arab fanatic on a mission of revenge.

The outcome of this journey on the eve of the outbreak of World War II, involves scandal and politics, passion, terror and great destruction—ending in a shattering climax over New York.

The complete Bantam Book will be available June 7th, on sale wherever paperbacks are sold.

RELAX!
SIT DOWN
and Catch Up On Your Reading!

☐	11877	**HOLOCAUST** by Gerald Green	$2.25
☐	11260	**THE CHANCELOR MANUSCRIPT** by Robert Ludlum	$2.25
☐	10077	**TRINITY** by Leon Uris	$2.75
☐	2300	**THE MONEYCHANGERS** by Arthur Hailey	$1.95
☐	12550	**THE MEDITERRANEAN CAPER** by Clive Cussler	$2.25
☐	2500	**THE EAGLE HAS LANDED** by Jack Higgins	$1.95
☐	2600	**RAGTIME** by E. L. Doctorow	$2.25
☐	10888	**RAISE THE TITANIC!** by Clive Cussler	$2.25
☐	11966	**THE ODESSA FILE** by Frederick Forsyth	$2.25
☐	11770	**ONCE IS NOT ENOUGH** by Jacqueline Susann	$2.25
☐	11708	**JAWS 2** by Hank Searls	$2.25
☐	12490	**TINKER, TAILOR, SOLDIER, SPY** by John Le Carre	$2.50
☐	11929	**THE DOGS OF WAR** by Frederick Forsyth	$2.25
☐	10526	**INDIAN ALLEN** by Elizabeth B. Coker	$1.95
☐	12489	**THE HARRAD EXPERIMENT** by Robert Rimmer	$2.25
☐	10422	**THE DEEP** by Peter Benchley	$2.25
☐	10500	**DOLORES** by Jacqueline Susann	$1.95
☐	11601	**THE LOVE MACHINE** by Jacqueline Susan	$2.25
☐	10600	**BURR** by Gore Vidal	$2.25
☐	10857	**THE DAY OF THE JACKAL** by Frederick Forsyth	$1.95
☐	11952	**ORAGONARD** by Rupert Gilchrist	$1.95
☐	2491	**ASPEN** by Burt Hirschfeld	$1.95
☐	11330	**THE BEGGARS ARE COMING** by Mary Loos	$1.95

Buy them at your local bookstore or use this handy coupon for ordering:

WHAT IF . . .

Fires, floods, air disasters, political intrigue. Events that could happen . . . and do in these exciting best-sellers. Guaranteed to keep you on the edge of your seat.

DON'T MISS
THESE CURRENT
Bantam Bestsellers

Bantam Book Catalog

Here's your up-to-the-minute listing of over 1,400 titles by your favorite authors.

This illustrated, large format catalog gives a description of each title. For your convenience, it is divided into categories in fiction and non-fiction—gothics, science fiction, westerns, mysteries, cookbooks, mysticism and occult, biographies, history, family living, health, psychology, art.

So don't delay—take advantage of this special opportunity to increase your reading pleasure.

Just send us your name and address and 50¢ (to help defray postage and handling costs).